DANCE
OF A
BURNING
SEA

DANCE
OF A
BURNING
SEA

The Mousai Series

E.J. MELLOW

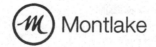 Montlake

Published by Montlake, Seattle
www.apub.com

Amazon, the Amazon logo, and Montlake are trademarks of Amazon.com, Inc., or its affiliates.

ISBN-13: 9781542026086
ISBN-10: 1542026083

Cover illustration and design by Micaela Alcaino

Printed in the United States of America

For Phoenix,
my fire-born sister,
whose flame dances
to its own rhythm

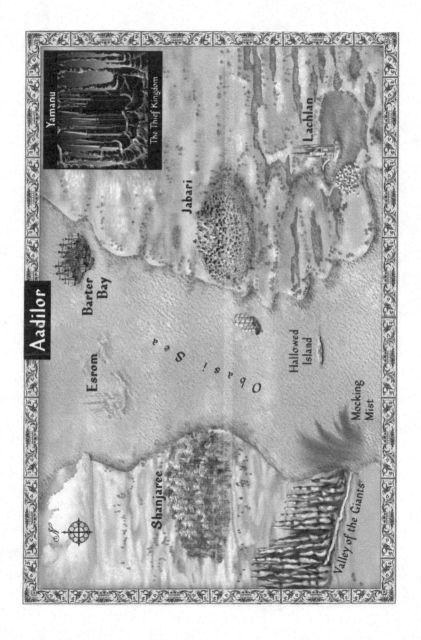

She was second born out of fire and rose,
Gifted with beautiful twisting and twirling,
But careful, my darlings, when reaching too closely,
For you'll be cursed with more than a yearning

If you dance with the daughter of flame
If you dance with the daughter of flame

She may flicker like honey and sunshine,
She may be as light as the day,
But easy, my dearest, for a sharp tip be hiding
in her softly curving sway

If you dance with the daughter of flame
If you dance with the daughter of flame

So look lively, my sweet, my innocent pet,
If you get caught in one of her turns;
Her touch may start soft, start silky, start soothing,
But it will always end in a burn

When you dance with the daughter of flame
When you dance with the daughter of flame

—A verse from Achak's Mousai song

PROLOGUE

A pirate stood watching a man die.

It was not an unusual occurrence given such a profession as his, yet this time he had nothing to do with the matter.

One might wonder what sort of macabre court invited guests to watch someone he tortured. The answer was quite simple: the Thief Kingdom's. The crowd surrounding the pirate pushed closer, their ornate disguises poking into his worn leather coat, hungry for a better glimpse of the madness taking place in the center of the room. The smell of overperfumed bodies, sweat, and desperation crept under his mask, invading his nose. And not for the first time this evening, he was reminded of where he stood: in the most ruthless and debasing kingdom in all of Aadilor, whose lenient laws invited large purses and larger fools, trading secrets and heavy coin for nights of folly and sin.

The pirate had attended tonight not only out of curiosity but also for his own ambition. He had fought hard to build a new life after abandoning the old. And while his current existence mirrored little of what he'd left behind, that was rather the point. Now his decisions were entirely his own, no longer weighed down by history or expectations.

At least these were the things he told himself.

While he had not set out to become a pirate, he certainly didn't see reason in fighting the delinquent those in his past thought him to be.

After all, he had not been born a man to act in half measures.

And so he had commandeered a ship and recruited a crew to serve him. Now this, he thought: an opportunity to be the first pirate captain in the Thief King's court.

That constant ambitious hunger clawed like a greedy beast in his chest, for he knew he would do everything in his power to secure a seat at court. Even if a small part of him regretted entering the opulent black palace.

His attention slid away from the cloaked and covered figures around him and back to the performance.

The pirate had seen many die, but never in so beautiful a way as this.

In the center of the onyx hall performed three women: singer, dancer, and violinist.

Their liquid-hot song and intoxicating rhythm expanded from them in a rainbow of colors, their threads of power hitting unceasingly against a prisoner chained in the middle, a whipping of notes punishing skin, but instead of screams of pain, the man moaned his pleasure.

Here were goddesses incarnate, brought from the Fade to lure the living to the dead, for their powers spoke of old magic. A time when the gods had not been lost, when Aadilor had been washed in their gifts.

Their costumes were lavish, spools of inky hues, beads braided into silks that dripped into feathers and embroidered lace. Ornate horned masks covered the trio's identities. And though their performance was not directed at him, the pirate was still washed with a cold dew of desperation, felt the strong pull of their magic.

Gripping.

Teasing.

Tempting.

Devouring.

It was a weaving of powers, meant to bewitch the mind and imprison the body. A spell of madness, it was, and the captive in the center its puppet.

The prisoner howled in agonizing ecstasy, one hand reaching for the dancer as she skimmed teasingly near. His chains clanked against their restraints, keeping him out of reach, and he flopped to the black marble floor in a fit of anguish, wriggling and clawing at his face. His nails dragged through rivulets of blood dripping from his nose and ears, mixing with the puddle of urine beneath him.

And the pirate watched.

Never had he witnessed such vicious beauty, but he was learning quickly that in this world, the most dazzling things were fatal.

And these three truly sparkled.

Any with the Sight could see their all-consuming power, for only those with magic could detect the magic in others.

If the pirate were to use his gifts, his would shine green.

The executioners swam in an intoxicating mix of colors, ever expanding from the center of the room where they performed.

"The Mousai," a woman had whispered upon him first entering court.

The King's deadly muses.

Deadly indeed, thought the pirate.

His skin beaded with sweat behind his silver mask as his mind spun under the consuming melody echoing in the hall. The dancer pulsed her hips to the beat, sending bursts of her fire-tinged magic into the air, a hand clapping awake a dream. His body shivered in longing.

The singer's voice split into three, four, five—a soaring soprano of golden threads from her lips that followed the violet chords gliding from the violin.

The pirate had never wanted more. But wanted what exactly, he could not say. He only felt need. Desire. Desperation. And beneath it all, hollow sorrow. A painful emptiness, for he could never have what his soul yearned for.

Their power.

Ouuurs, his magic cooed, reaching out. *We want them to be ours.*

Yield, he commanded silently, tugging back. *I am your master, not they.*

Tightening his hands into fists, the pirate tried to keep his wits about him. He could hear the moans of the giftless court members beside him, held by chains as if prisoners themselves. He wondered why any normal mortal would have stayed. With blood so easily manipulated, certainly they'd known what would come? But this was the allure of the Thief Kingdom's court, he supposed. To be close to such power, to experience such deadly euphoria, and live. A tale to boast of later. *Listen to what I have been clever enough to survive.*

He peered around the crowd, every face disguised, wondering who else were potential court candidates. Which one of them would gain access to the palace, be invited to the most decadent debauchery and all the secrets and connections that came with it? He knew to be asked here of all nights, to witness what was no doubt a mere sliver of the king's power, was a test. Everything in this world was a test.

He had already lost once.

Now, he would win.

A lick of heat ran down his body, drawing his attention to the dancer as she twisted past, the teasing scent of honeysuckle drifting in her wake.

There was not a sliver of her skin or lock of hair exposed. Her face was hidden behind beadwork and silks, even her legs to her toes covered, but she moved as if nude, as if looking upon her voluptuous curves was a lewd experience. Yet her identity remained utterly obscured.

As did her companions'.

Such care to remain hidden while being seen.

As everyone practices here, thought the pirate. Well, except the prisoner.

His mask had been ripped from him as he was dragged into the center of the room. The final debasement of his sentence. He had cried out then, covering his wrinkled features with his hands, shielding his graying hair from eyes. Even with an impending death sentence, it appeared no one wanted their sins of the Thief Kingdom to follow them, not even to the Fade.

The tempo picked up, the violinist running bow over strings at a dizzying speed. The singer's voice soared ever higher, shaking the chandeliers as the dancer twisted again and again and again around the prisoner.

Their powers spun, sending gusts of wind through the hall.

Kneeling, the captive threw his head back as he strained against his chains toward the ceiling. Their magic swarmed high. He let out a final scream, a plea to the Mousai, as their spell, laced purple, honey gold, and crimson, pumped into his body, streaming endlessly until, finally, his ragged form swallowed it whole. He glowed like a star as the pop, pop, pop of his bones breaking echoed in the hall.

The light pulsing beneath his skin extinguished at the final snap of his spine.

The prisoner crumbled to the ground.

Lifeless.

His soul sent to the Fade.

A terrifying beat of quiet settled over the hall, an echoing loss of the Mousai's magic, now gone.

A whimper from one of the giftless.

And then—

The chamber erupted in cheers.

The Mousai bowed with regal grace, as though they hadn't just melted a man from the inside out. In fact, the pirate sensed the energy in the room holding a tinged afterglow of lust.

Even he found himself panting.

At the realization, his intentions sharpened, the fog muddling his mind lifting.

He was not a man prone to wild proclivities. To have nearly forgotten himself sent a wave of uneasiness through him.

Doors at the far end of the hall swung open, and the crowd surged through them, into the postperformance party. But the pirate remained motionless, his gaze on the forgotten body of the prisoner. He studied features that held hints of highborn society before faceless guards came to carry the corpse away.

It was known that the prisoner had been a court member. His rank, in the end, seemed to have done little to save him. It appeared the Thief King only accepted thieves who stole for him, not from him.

A good thing in the end, for this meant a seat had opened up tonight.

But was this the world the pirate truly wanted to be a part of?

Yes, his magic purred.

Yes, he agreed.

The question was how to acquire the necessary power to move more freely in it.

The pirate roamed between the various masks surrounding him, taking in their painted skin and shrouded fashions. The burden of keeping one's identity hidden here was a chink in one's armor. There were many secrets locked tight in this palace, in this kingdom, vices not fit for gentle ears and respectable society. But with secrets came the opportunity for leverage. And leverage was what the pirate was determined to gather, for the path to priceless treasure came in many forms.

A reflection caught his eye, the swaying of the dancer's hips twinkling her onyx beadwork as she wove through the guests. He took in her ample silhouette, her fiery mist of magic radiating with her movements. Like an approaching snake, a plan began to slide into place.

As if sensing a predator, the dancer turned, horned headdress standing tall in the crowd. And though her features were covered, the pirate knew the moment her eyes met his, for a river of hot current smacked into him.

But then she was moving away, disappearing into the shadowed court.

He started toward her, and as he did, his nerves buzzed in anticipation of what he'd do next.

Yesss, his magic cooed in delight at his daring thoughts, *we are not cowards like they.*

No, he agreed, *we are not.*

With a sure hand, the pirate removed his mask.

The warmth of the room hugged his already-warm skin. He took a deep breath in, the scent of freedom running sweetly along his taste buds. Those he passed stared with shocked whispers as they took in his features, the first of their potential kind to reveal themselves.

He dutifully ignored them.

His identity would not be his weakness here. Not like all these others who clung to their disguises and false securities.

Let them know me, he thought.

Let my sins follow.

He had already been called a monster. Why not live up to the name?

After all, monsters were needed to make heroes.

And Alōs Ezra would become the kind of monster who made heroes of all.

A considerable time later,
years, in fact,
when wounds are old scars

CHAPTER ONE

*W*hen throwing knives across a crowded tavern in the Thief Kingdom, you were one of two things: an excellent marksman with everything to gain, or a poor marksman with nothing to lose.

Whether you were the former or the latter, you were most certainly a fool.

Niya Bassette happened to admire foolishness.

So it was without great surprise that she let loose a blade straight into the throng of unsuspecting patrons at the exact moment her two sisters did. They whizzed, end over end—one a hair's length from clipping an ear, another sliding between the fingers of a hand in motion, a third nipping off the glowing end of a cigar—all to stick with a wet thwack into an apple a bartender had been eating on the opposite side of the room.

Had been, of course, being the key words, given his meal now found itself pinned to a column beside him.

"My knife struck first!" exclaimed Niya, her heartbeat giving an extra thrilled thump as she twirled to face her two sisters. "Pay up."

"I fear your eyesight is going, dear," said Larkyra, adjusting her pearl disguise. "It is my blade that is in the middle."

"Yes," agreed Arabessa, "but it's clearly my dagger which is deepest pierced, which means—"

"Nothing," finished Niya, a bubbling of annoyance stirring. "Which means absolutely nothing."

"Given you are now in my debt for two more silver," said Arabessa, her brass mask shining in the tavern's torchlight, "I understand your resistance to agree, but—"

"WHO DARES THROW BLADES AT ME?" bellowed the bartender from behind the bar, interrupting what Niya had expected to be a long-winded standoff.

The tavern drowned in a thick silence; every disguised face in the building swiveled toward the commotion.

"Theys did!" a man in a long-nosed mask shrieked from the opposite side of the room, pointing an accusing finger toward Niya and her sisters. "Theys threw thems at me earlier and put a hole right through me's hat."

"Better your hat than your head," grumbled Niya, eyes narrowed at the informing weasel.

The barman slowly turned their way as the crowd parted like a rip in a stocking.

"Sticks," muttered Niya.

"You," growled the man.

For being so large, he jumped over the wide bar with surprising nimbleness. Niya's eyes traveled up as he straightened to his full height. His figure was that of an overstuffed sausage, his arm muscles had forced the sleeves of his tunic to be cut away so they could swing freely, and his leather mask was one with his tough, wrinkled skin.

"I was really hoping we wouldn't have to fight our way out of this bar tonight from way back here," sighed Larkyra.

"Doors are merely one way to leave a room," pointed out Arabessa as she glanced up through the rafters above.

Niya followed her gaze, finding a skylight letting in the glowworm starry night of the Thief Kingdom's caved ceiling. "One way indeed," she agreed with a smile.

"Which of you three wants to be sent to the Fade first?" growled the approaching barman, his heavy footsteps shaking the floorboards.

"Just so we're clear," said Arabessa as they backed up in unison, "we were not throwing at *you* but at your apple."

"Yes, if you were the target," added Niya, "you'd most certainly be in the Fade long before us."

"Not helping," muttered Larkyra as the man gave a roar, charging forward.

"Time for that exit." Arabessa took a running leap onto a nearby table, her navy suit gleaming like fresh blood in the candlelight. Those seated scampered back before she jumped and swung herself from a beam up into the rafters.

"But our knives," protested Niya, glancing past the stampeding man to the glint of her blade still impaled in the bar. "I just stole that one."

"And you'll steal many more," said Larkyra, picking up her skirts and, with all the grace of the duchess she now was, copying Arabessa's retreat.

The crowd gave a hoot of approval, seeing a flash of her white-legged bloomers.

"Look out!" called Arabessa from above.

Niya didn't need to see the fist to sense it swinging toward her. And it wasn't the usual sort of sensing, either, like the touch of a shadow to a shoulder. No, this was an ability that came with Niya's particular kind of magic. For though the Mousai were off duty tonight, her and her sisters' magic never were. While Arabessa was the musician and Larkyra the singer, Niya—she was the dancer. And with her gift came the ability to do a score of beautiful and awful things. In this particular moment, it allowed Niya to tap into the energy an arm gave off right before it swung, the heat of skin nearing. Motion was her study, her obsession, and precisely what had her dropping into a roll, just missing the impact that surely would have broken her jaw, as she slid under a table. Booted feet were all around her, as well as the smell of beer-soaked wood and damp sawdust, as she scurried along the ground through the crowd, thankful for her loose-fitted pants that allowed her better movement.

Reemerging a few tables away, she found herself beside the man with the long-nosed mask from earlier.

"Well, hello there." She smiled, serpentine.

The rodent jumped, readying to flee, but Niya, always quicker, snagged his collar. As she kept one eye on the bartender, who was busy searching the packed tavern for her, she pulled the man against a wall, determined to teach him a lesson in manners. "I'm going to let you live . . . tonight," she whispered. The scent of hay and dirt filled her nostrils—a farmer. "But it would be good to remember the old kingdom's rhyme. Do you know the one of which I speak?"

The man quickly shook his head, eyes widening as he looked past her, to the large form Niya could now sense moving their way. She had been found.

But she still had time for this.

"Those who point and shout," began Niya, "tattle and tale: in the Fade they'll sail, but not before their tongues be snatched out." The man squeaked a whimper as she grinned wider. "So keep silent and pray to the lost gods we never cross paths again." Niya shoved the small man away, then dropped a sand's grain before the bartender's fist could collide with her head. He punched through the wood-slatted wall, the surface splintering with a loud crack.

"Sir, I'm sure we can work this out without becoming violent," said Niya, spinning into the center of the room, patrons moving to give them a wide berth.

"*You* are the ones who threw knives at *me*!"

"Again, to clarify, it was at your apple."

A growl shook from the bartender's throat as he snapped off a nearby toppled chair leg, the jagged end no doubt a stake to spit her on. Guests hooted their excitement, free entertainment always a welcome sight, and out of the corner of her eye, Niya saw money exchange palms, bets made on who would be left standing. Her fingers itched to get in on the odds.

But before she could, Niya felt a new form moving quickly toward them.

"No one but I can stab my brother!" yelled a large masked woman, her voice a deep rumble as she rushed Niya.

Stepping sideways, Niya scrunched up her face as the brother, choosing that moment to attack, rammed into his sister. The tavern shook with a boom as they collided.

"It's good to see siblings so close," said Niya.

The giants shoved one another, snapping, as each fought to get to her first, the crowd's encouragement for a fight growing ever louder.

The vibrations in the room spun across Niya's skin like a caress, her magic purring in delight at the charge of energy. *Yes*, it crooned, *more*. Niya could have soaked it all in, moved her body in a way that would paralyze most in the room merely by their watching. But with gritted teeth she restrained the urge to let loose her powers, reminding herself again that the Mousai were off duty tonight.

This evening they were not to be the Maniacal Muses of the Thief King, as some called them here. Sent to trance those who dared disobey their master into the dungeons or, worse, bring them to wait for their fate by the foot of his throne. No, tonight they were meant to be no one—or more accurately, anyone. Indistinguishably distinguished in their random collection of fine-sewn costumes. And while the Thief Kingdom was no stranger to magic, it would be unwise to play all of one's cards so openly. An individual's gifts were like a calling card, an identifiable trait, especially for someone as strong as she. If any here witnessed a performance by the dancer of the Mousai, there was a chance they'd find similarities with Niya's gifts.

So instead, Niya reeled in her magic, which always burned to be set free.

"Playtime's over," called Arabessa from her perch on a ceiling beam, where she and Larkyra still waited by the skylight.

"Blasphemy," shouted Niya as she wove through the pressing crowd. Vaulting over the bar, she dropped into the center. "Playtime has no end." Gingerly she plucked the gold-dipped hilt of her throwing knife from the wooden column—a small piece of apple clinging to the tip.

"Please don't tell us you've kept us waiting for *that*," groaned Larkyra, skipping to a closer beam above.

"I won!" Niya displayed her blade. "And you both know it! I owe you nothing."

"By the lost gods," called Larkyra over the raucous cheers erupting as the twin giants detangled themselves enough to come closer to Niya. "I'll easily give you four silver so long as you get your arse up here."

"Love." Arabessa balanced beside Larkyra. "Never reward a rat with food when it's already made a mess of your kitchen."

"Rats are resourceful, hardy creatures!" shouted Niya. "And besides, I'd hardly call this a mess—"

The bar exploded, bottles and glasses flying every which way as the giants barreled through the middle. Niya twirled between spraying splinters of wood and bent away from the grasping graze of fingers as she went tumbling back into the tables and chairs. Her back smarted against a corner, but she pushed through the pain, forcing herself to keep moving. She rolled until she was behind a tipped-over stool. Curling into a ball, she felt the warm splashes of liquid soak into her silk shirt as shards of glass impaled the slab of wood she hid behind with a thunk, thunk, thunk.

A breath of quiet fell over the hall. Droplets of spilled spirits hitting the ground before—

Madness.

As if the destruction were the invitation the despicable patrons had been waiting for, a brawl erupted. To Niya's right, a stocky woman in a parrot mask slammed her chair over a group she had been sitting with. Their playing cards flew up in paper fireworks.

A slim creature covered in chain mail flung their body into the wrestling crowd.

Niya sighed. She was officially the least interesting thing in the room.

How boring, she thought.

Though she might be a fool in wanting to change that, she was no idiot. A Bassette knew when their welcome was up.

Catching the eyes of Larkyra, then Arabessa, and giving a nod, she watched her sisters skip their way across beams, back to the sky-light, nimble as the thieves they were, and swing themselves up and out through the narrow opening.

"No!" the barman bellowed at their retreat. He and his sister punched a nearby column, as if they'd gladly have the entire ceiling cave in if that meant they'd get their hands on one of them.

Niya took their moment of distraction to slide to the front of the tavern and slip out of the curtained exit.

The fresh caved night splashed across her skin as she was met with a small crowd gathered along the lantern-lit street. Curious gazes hid behind disguises, whispering to one another as they angled this way and that for a better view, wondering what delight or fright might be inside the Fork's Tongue tavern, especially one that was causing the sign outside to swing so enthusiastically. They got their answer when a body was thrown through a window into the street.

Letting out a laugh, Niya hurried down a nearby alley, making her final escape. She breathed in the cool air of the Thief Kingdom, glancing through her eye mask to the glowworm-covered ceiling far above. The illuminated creatures twinkled in an array of greens and blues while giant connecting stalactites and stalagmites towered across the city, more pepperings of lights from dwellings carved into their sides. The city's dark beauty never ceased to astonish Niya, and she let out a contented sigh, keeping to the shadows before turning onto Luck Lane. It was easily accomplished, given that the Betting District held extra-thick lengths of darkness. It concealed the games that didn't fit inside the gambling halls, the kind that were too messy to clean. The cockfights, iron-knuckle brawls, deplorable dares—all for a slip of silver.

Small fires flickered down alleys, illuminating hunched forms gathered close as the smell of iron and sweat filled the air. As she walked on, she caught sight of a crowd watching two creatures shoveling plates of rocks into their mouths. Drool and snot dripped from their half-obscured masks as the competitors forced more in. The spectators hooted in excitement as a game master quickly made slashes on a board behind them, counting stones. Niya squeezed by the group, passing Macabris, one of the more expensive and exclusive clubs. The pristine black marble facade stood out among the surrounding humble establishments. A bright crystal chandelier hung high in the doorway, shining on four mammoth disguised bodyguards stationed by the door.

"You are full of lies," laughed a lady in a cat mask to her companions, who stood waiting in line outside the club. "No one has seen the *Crying Queen* in months."

Niya stilled beside them, ears prickling at hearing mention of the notorious pirate ship.

"I swear on the lost gods," answered a form wrapped entirely in velvet. "I am friends with the port master in Jabari, and she told me a few of the crew docked there just last week."

"So the *Crying Queen* is in the Jabari harbor?"

"I never said that. Merely some of the crew."

"Without the ship, how do they know these pirates belong to it?"

The question was met with silence, but Niya remained where she was, heart beating quick as she bent down as though to tie her boot's laces.

"Exactly," continued the woman. "You don't. These sort all look alike. Salt dried and suntanned darker than a belt's hide."

"Plus," added another, "Alōs Ezra might have iron balls, but he's not a fool who would send his crew out in the open after all this time in hiding. If *you* had learned this, the Thief King surely would have days prior. And the only news we'd be hearing tonight would be regarding his public disembowelment at court."

"Well," harrumphed the velvet companion, "whatever the truth, one thing's for certain—Lord Ezra can't hide forever."

"No," agreed a fourth. "And let's hope he does not. That face is meant to be seen."

"Seen under my skirts," added the woman.

The group's snickers were drowned out as they were ushered into the club, the warm light and crowded bodies within disappearing with the closing of the doors.

Niya remained crouched at the edge of the busy sidewalk, hardly feeling the knees and swinging arms knocking into her shoulders. It was as if her entire body had been doused in cold water. The mention of the pirate captain, even after all this time, still had her reacting.

Like a struck match, annoyed flames erupted in Niya's veins, and she stood.

No, she thought, moving through the thick sea of citizens once more. She was only reacting because he and his crew had been on the run for the past several months. Hiding like cowards from the death sentence on their heads. If they couldn't take their possible punishment, they never should have stolen *phorria* from the Thief Kingdom. The potent magical drug was too dangerous uncontrolled, which was why it was only allowed here, in the hidden city that held in chaos. The Thief

King kept a very watchful eye over its use and trade within the dens of his kingdom.

Which of course made Alōs getting away with leaking it for so long that much more impressive. From the moment Alōs had won his seat at court, Niya had watched his quick rise to a high-ranking member. He was a viciously ambitious man, more slippery than an eel, but even so, Niya often wondered why he had broken such a treasonous law. Like the group had mentioned, Alōs Ezra was no fool. He would not have risked all that he had worked hard to gain without a good reason. Niya hated that she cared to know what his reason was.

She hated that she thought of him at all.

She hated . . . well, him.

Which is why I must put him out of my mind, she thought decidedly.

After all, the pirates of the *Crying Queen* could not be in Jabari.

"It would be impossible," she muttered, skirting a corner. The Thief King had eyes in every port in Aadilor, especially Jabari—the city outside this kingdom where Niya and her own sisters lived.

"It's only a rumor," continued Niya as she stepped through an open archway and into a quiet courtyard. Tall brick buildings surrounded her, black shutters closing up every window. "And the lost gods know we've gotten plenty of rumors over the months."

"Rumors of what?" asked Larkyra as she dropped down from a neighboring roof and landed in a crouch.

"Rumors of you losing your edge," said Niya, not wanting to mention anything about Alōs to her sisters, especially unfounded rumors. Whenever the pirate was brought up in their circle, it only had Niya replaying that summer four years prior, which ultimately had led to a very stupid, dreadful, and horrible night. A night that even Larkyra and Arabessa did not know of. And if Niya had her way, never would. She had hid all notice of her heartache and guilt from her family, turning it over and over until it remolded into a desire for revenge.

"I fear it is your edges that have become soft," corrected Larkyra while dusting off her skirts. "What with you leaving the tavern without making even one patron bleed."

"The night's still young; how about I remedy that with you?"

Larkyra shot her a sharp grin, her pearl eye mask twinkling in the lantern light. "I fear that would only prove my point further when you fail to do so."

Niya's annoyance sparked, her hand going to the blade at her hip, until—

"Ladies, please," interrupted Arabessa as she dangled from the ledge of a second-floor balcony. "We wouldn't want to ruin such a wonderful night with me carrying both your lifeless bodies home, now would we?" She landed delicately on the first floor's thin railing before hopping to the ground, a graceful cat.

"Yes, wonderful night indeed," declared Larkyra. "Leave it to you, dear sisters, to show me a grand night out before I leave for my honeymoon."

"Of course," said Niya. "Such special treatment is not merely handed out to anyone."

"Especially not by you," mused Larkyra ruefully.

"I do wish you would have listened to more of my suggestions for tonight's events, though," said Arabessa to Niya.

"Yes, but the last time I did that," explained Niya, "I distinctly remember two carriages exploding."

"But were we under attack then too?"

Larkyra nodded. "We were."

"Oh, well, I must have forgotten that part."

"The sickness of your old age," said Niya.

"And the fatigue of mine." Larkyra stifled a yawn.

"You're younger than both of us."

"Which doesn't change that I'll be a monster if I don't get some sleep before Darius and I leave tomorrow."

While most had honeymoons directly following their weddings, Larkyra and her now husband, Darius Mekenna, the newly anointed duke of Lachlan, had been too busy rebuilding and revitalizing his once-cursed homeland to celebrate. Now, with his people and territory beginning to thrive once more, he and Larkyra were set to go on a holiday to one of their southern estates.

It was only natural they took Larkyra out for a hen night before she left. Still, Niya hadn't thought it would end *this* early.

"We'll all go," said Arabessa.

"No," protested Niya. "Let's have another drink. Macabris is just around the corner."

"I wish we could, but—"

"But nothing. You're not even in your cups, little bird! We have both failed miserably if you're not stumbling home tonight."

"Darling, I *cannot* be sporting a headache and nausea in the morning. Darius's and my carriage ride is long, and it will grow even longer if I'm forcing us to stop every few turns to empty my stomach."

"When did you become so boring?" grumbled Niya.

"You mean responsible?"

"Same thing."

"You know," said Arabessa, "you and I have to be up early as well, for Father has invited the Lox family to breakfast."

"By the Obasi Sea," groaned Niya. "Talk about boring. And whatever happened to luncheons? Breakfast is entirely too early to receive guests. What will the neighbors think?"

"I'm sure Father would rather they gossip about our odd hours of entertainment than our . . . other oddities."

"You mean like how odd looking his eldest daughter is?" challenged Niya.

"More like how his second child can't sit still for more than a single grain fall in public."

"It is not my fault Father's guests are always so dull. I have to move around in fear of falling asleep from boredom."

"While listening to your gripes is always riveting," said Larkyra, fishing a portal token from the pocket of her skirts, "I suggest you save a few for conversation tomorrow."

With the tip of her blade, Larkyra pricked her finger, letting a drop of crimson hit the center of the gold coin. Bringing it close to her lips, she whispered a secret—one that Niya, despite her best efforts, always failed to hear. The token flashed as Larkyra flicked it into the air. Before it fell to the cobblestones, a glowing doorway shot up from its center, revealing another city's dark alley stretching out on the other side.

There were a handful of ways to get to and from the Thief Kingdom, but surely the simplest was with a portal token. The problem lay in acquiring the right one, for portal tokens were sparse, with only the most powerful able to create them. Luckily, the Mousai had a direct connection to a creature capable of making the coins with a snap of their fingers. Of course, Niya knew, convincing them to do the snapping was the hard part.

Without another word, Larkyra hiked up her skirts and slipped through the portal's door, quickly followed by Arabessa.

Niya paused at the glowing entrance, a heaviness weighing on her chest. Nights like these, with them all out together free to play, were growing sparse now with Larkyra settled down with Darius. If she had known their evening was to end so soon, she would have . . . well, Niya didn't know what she would have done differently. Except perhaps teased Larkyra more.

"You coming?" asked her youngest sister, standing close to Arabessa on the other side of the portal door.

Shaking off her nostalgia, Niya stepped through, immediately becoming enveloped in the new city's dry heat. While the Thief Kingdom smelled of wet dirt, fires, and incense, here fresh jasmine floated through the air. And beyond their narrow alley, the sun was rising.

Niya breathed in the city of her birth: Jabari. The jewel of Aadilor, it was called, for it housed the most diverse trade in the southern lands. Its richly built buildings on the northern peak gathered like a shining diamond toward the sun.

Behind Niya, the way back to the Thief Kingdom snapped shut as Larkyra returned the portal token to her pocket.

In its absence, the alley somehow now felt . . . less.

"Ready, sisters?" asked Arabessa, prompting them to remove their masks.

Niya waved a hand over her face, a mist of her orange magic seeping from her palm. *Release,* she silently instructed. There was a tingling of her disguise unsticking before it dropped into her fingers.

Niya rubbed her eyes. Her masks always felt more natural in place than off.

Yet here, in Jabari, their disguises were of a different nature.

In Jabari they were the daughters of Dolion Bassette, the Count of Raveet of the second house. An esteemed family who, to any casual observer, held no gifts or connection to a deplorable city cloaked deep inside a mountain. And for good reason. While this city held many splendors, magic was not one of them. Here citizens eyed such powers with distrust, ostracizing those with magic from the community. Niya could not blame them. Aadilor's history was fraught with the gifted taking advantage of the giftless. Best if each kind stuck to their own lands.

But secrets needed places to hide, and for creatures as powerful as Niya and her sisters were, it was best to hide in plain sight.

Tucking her mask into the reticule looped around her waist, Niya followed her sisters out of the alley.

The wide streets of Jabari's upper ring were quiet, aristocrats having no need to wake before sunrise. The sisters turned onto a street lined with large marble homes, their wrought iron gates holding back pristine green lawns where morning lilies and roses readied to bloom.

Despite the peaceful hour, Niya couldn't shake a cool touch along her neck as they turned a corner. A sensation detectable through her gifts. She glanced over her shoulder but saw only empty road.

She waited to feel the energy again, a sign that someone might be mirroring their steps, but none came.

It was probably a rat, she thought as she hurried to catch up with her sisters, the moment quickly forgotten.

What Niya did not take into account, however, as she entered the gate to her own home, was that sometimes the magic tingling of being followed was instead the basic human instinct of being watched.

CHAPTER TWO

*H*ot tea splashed across Niya's hand as she filled her cup until it overflowed, arousing her from the belief she had just entered the Fade from boredom.

"Really, my flame, the Loxes were not as dull as all that," her father, Dolion Bassette, said from his usual spot on their veranda, where he lounged like a lion beneath the soft morning sun, his white cheeks growing rosy.

"You're right, they were far worse," grumbled Niya. If it hadn't been for their lighter prepared breakfast, she was convinced the Loxes' visit would have yawned into lunch.

"The younger daughter, Miss Priscilla, was not so awful," said Zimri as he leaned into his chair.

"You would say such a thing," replied Arabessa. "She all but spoon-fed you your food, the poor lovesick child."

"I cannot help how my charms affect those around me."

"Is that what you call them? Charms? I always thought they were better described as annoyances."

Zimri cut Arabessa a look, staving off whatever retort he wished to speak.

Smart move, thought Niya, for Arabessa could be quite the verbal viper, especially when she and Zimri sparred. Niya had her own theories as to why, not that she'd ever share them out loud. She valued her life, after all.

Zimri turned from Arabessa and sipped his tea, gazing out at the city's red-tiled roofs stretching beyond their balcony. His thick black hair shone under the gentle rays, his purple morning coat vibrant against his black skin and the white flora decorating their veranda. Niya took a moment to study his wide shoulders and strong physique. It felt like only yesterday that their father had brought Zimri home, a skinny and quiet teary-eyed boy. Dolion had been good friends with Zimri's parents, and upon their tragic death at sea, as Zimri had no other close relatives, their father had taken the lad under his wing and raised him as his own. The Bassette girls knew what it was like to lose a parent and had quickly shepherded the youth into their close circle. It was only natural he'd begun to shadow their father in his duties, growing into the role of the count's right-hand man with utter seriousness. *Sometimes to an annoying degree,* thought Niya dryly. She already had an older sibling. She surely didn't need two.

If only they all could have stayed the carefree children they had once been, running loose in Jabari and beneath the Thief Kingdom's palace. For Zimri was one of the few who knew the secrets the Bassettes guarded behind spelled walls and within hidden cities.

Niya smiled to herself, quietly reminiscing about the earlier days when it had been all too easy to convince Zimri to sneak off with them, despite the reprimand they might receive if found out. A time before she and her sisters had been forced into other responsibilities regarding their gifts, and Zimri into his duties to help their father. And now this, more change. Niya glanced to the empty chair across from her, where Larkyra usually sat.

"How quiet our mornings now are with Lark gone," mused Dolion.

A sharp twinge entered Niya's chest at her father's words, which were so close to her own thoughts. "She's not *gone*, Father. Her room is just as it always is, ready for her to return."

"You mean *visit*," clarified Arabessa. "She does not live here anymore."

"I know that." Niya frowned. "But it's not as though she's in the Fade with Mother. She still lives."

Silence filled the veranda along with a blow of guilt as Niya realized what she had said. "Sorry, Father, I didn't mean—"

"It's fine, my flame." He waved his hand. "I know what you meant. Of course Lark is still with us. It's merely an adjustment, not seeing all three of you girls together like always."

"Darius and Lark could have moved in here, you know," Niya pointed out.

Arabessa snorted into her cup. "Are you mad? Yes, I'm sure every duke who has a large kingdom and multiple castles would *much* rather abandon his homeland and tenants to take his brand-new bride to move in with his in-laws."

"Well," Niya said, tipping up her chin, "when you say it like that—"

"You realize how silly you sound?"

Niya's magic stirred, hot, along with her temper. "I was only saying—"

"All right, you two," said Dolion placatingly. "And to think I just admitted how quiet it now was."

"Even with only one of them," began Zimri, "it's *never* quiet."

Dolion laughed. "Too true."

Niya shared a similar scowl toward both men as her sister.

"At least now, with the three of you no longer under one roof," continued her father, "should I dare hope that there will be less scheming afoot within our halls?"

"You raised us as thieves and mercenaries," explained Niya. "Scheming is inevitably afoot."

Dolion's russet brows rose, his long hair like a mane as it fed into his thick beard. "I would not reduce the role this family takes on for the people of Aadilor to such common titles as those."

"Yes, yes," appeased Niya. "We are noble thieves then, executioners with the highest of morals."

"Indeed. When born with such gifts as you and your sisters are—"

"We must do what we can for those who are born without." Niya finished her father's constant rhetoric.

"Precisely." He nodded, satisfied.

Niya sighed. At times she found her father's stringent attitude toward their moral responsibilities tiring. Though she understood why he held so tightly to doing good in this world. Why he sent Niya and her sisters on missions to steal from the few wicked wealthy to give back to the many lacking innocents. He was making up for the sins that swam in a darker throne room, offsetting the orders and expectations placed on his children when they were disguised as the Mousai. For while Dolion was a count and doting father, he was also the creature who inspired cautionary tales. He was the Thief King. And for that he seemed to be forever atoning. But Niya understood that the Thief Kingdom existed to contain what would otherwise live chaotically throughout Aadilor. Her father played his parts because he needed to, and he raised his children to understand theirs.

Niya watched her father stroke his slowly graying beard, peering out to the city.

What burdens must weigh heaviest on him? wondered Niya, having a sudden urge to hug the man.

She was about to do just that, until she was seized with a sneeze. And then another.

"Oh no." Niya stood, searching the veranda.

"What's wrong?" asked her father.

"Where is he?" growled Niya, holding a hand to her nose.

"Where's who, dear?"

"Cook's darn cat." Niya glanced under her father's chair. "Aha—*achoo!*" The orange beast was curled peacefully behind his feet. "Get out of here," demanded Niya. "Oh, no you don't. Don't you dare rub your fur all over my new skirts, you—ouch!"

A hiss filled the air before a blur of orange streaked from under the table into the house.

"That vermin scratched me!" shouted Niya. "You know I'm allergic to cats, Father. Why did you allow Cook to keep that thing?"

"He was hurt and needed a home."

"And now I am hurt and need it to leave."

"He has left," said Arabessa.

"You know what I mean! Either I stay or it leaves."

"That's only one choice," Zimri pointed out.

"Precisely."

"You really must calm yourself," said Arabessa. "You're making quite a fuss over nothing."

Calm myself!

Niya crossed her arms, her magic jumping beneath her skin with her prickling irritation. "When you're as allergic as I am," she declared, "it is not nothing. So no, I will not *calm down*."

"No surprise there," muttered Arabessa.

"Excuse me?"

"Nothing."

"It didn't sound like nothing."

"Then you can add 'hard of hearing' to your ailments."

"You all bore me." Niya snatched up her shawl from her chair.

"My flame," said her father, "your sister is obviously trying to rile you up."

"And it worked."

"As it usually does." Arabessa sipped her tea.

"What does *that* mean?" snapped Niya.

"How do I put this delicately?" mused Arabessa. "You have an anger problem."

"I do not!"

Neither her father nor Zimri nor Arabessa responded; they merely allowed the echo of her raised voice to bounce around their veranda.

"Okay," she ground out. "Maybe I do, but what of it?"

"You know," began her father, "your mother was also known to run hot on occasion."

Niya blinked, the rising fight in her momentarily collapsing at the mention of her mother. Her father was not one to talk much of Johanna, even more than a decade after losing her following the birth of Larkyra.

"She did?" asked Niya.

"Mmm." Dolion nodded. "In fact, it's why she often wore this brooch." His large fingers absently stroked the accessory adorning his jacket. It was a simple design of a compass, the gold worn as though it had been rubbed similarly for many years. Niya had seen her father wear the brooch before, but she had never given it much thought.

It was her mother's? A pang of hungry longing entered Niya's chest then, as it did anytime she learned another piece of the puzzle that was her mother.

"She said when she touched it," continued her father, "it helped ground her. Helped give her pause when she felt lost in her emotions or thoughts. 'It allows me to find my way,' she would say." He smiled softly. "It was also a good tell for when she was growing angry with me. I knew when to back off if her fingers gripped this."

"Perhaps you could find a similar talisman, Niya?" suggested Arabessa. "It would have to be larger than a mere pin, however. Maybe a thick bracelet? Or three?" She grinned. "Mother may have had a temper, but I doubt it rivaled the volcano you house within."

Niya's gaze snapped to Arabessa's, her powers once again wriggling hot in her veins.

"Well," said Zimri to Dolion, "there went that nice moment."

"You cannot say I didn't try." Her father shrugged.

"You know," began Niya, "Larkyra never complained of my temper."

31

"Not to your face," quipped Arabessa.

Niya's hands grew warm as her magic surged to her palms. *Burn,* it whispered.

Arabessa must have noticed Niya's sudden shaking control, for she lifted a manicured brow as if to say, *See, volcano.*

Niya bit back a growl.

"Fine," she said, forcing a lightness into her tone. "As it appears we are handing out observations of others, then, my *dear* Ara, here is some sisterly advice: if you like someone"—Niya pointedly glanced between her and Zimri—"try not to insult them."

Arabessa's eyes widened and her cheeks reddened as Niya turned from the group.

She strode quickly through the high-ceilinged halls, to the lower levels of their home, thoughts fuming.

How dare Arabessa, she thought. *I may have certain . . . quirks, but so does she!* Plus, perfection was not something they'd been raised to admire. Scars, struggles, and flaws made one interesting. Niya was how she had always been, and *now* it was an issue? "No," she grumbled, "I will not change, not for anyone." There was too much of that happening these days anyway.

And as her father had pointed out, her mother had held passion too. If anything, she was proud to share a trait with a woman who had been so well respected as Johanna Bassette.

If she could live with such fire, so can I.

Taking a deep breath in, Niya's coiled muscles eased slightly as she found her way down to the kitchens and caught sight of a familiar form by the back door.

"Charlotte," called Niya, hurrying over to her childhood lady's maid as she was clasping on a cloak. "If you are going out, I'd like to join you. I'm in need of fresh air."

The stout woman eyed her uneasily. "I'm not going for a stroll, my lady, but to the market."

"Perfect. I love the market."

"Then you agree to carry a basket?"

"Of course."

"That will grow heavy as the day goes on?"

"I'm strong."

"Which you'll eventually have to lug back from the Trading District. *Uphill.*"

"By the lost gods," exclaimed Niya. "Am I considered both hot-headed *and* lazy?"

Charlotte dutifully remained mute, which ultimately served as Niya's answer.

"This entire household is tiring!" Niya swung on a thin cloak that hung by the door before snatching up an extra basket. "So I lose my temper on occasion. That hardly makes me a monster."

"Uh . . . of course not, my lady." Charlotte worked her old legs to keep pace with Niya as they exited the shaded servants' entrance to the back gate.

"Have I not shown I also have redeeming parts to my character?" asked Niya. "I can be warm and calming and kind and charming and—"

"Humble," added Charlotte.

"Yes, exactly!" agreed Niya. "If any of us were to be criticized for our demeanor, it most certainly should be Ara. I mean, look at the way she organizes the items on her vanity. She uses a measuring stick, Charlotte, a *measuring stick.*"

"Yes," said Charlotte. "Who do you think fetched it for her?"

"*Pfft*, precisely. I'd rather take a hot head over an uptight arse."

"My child." Charlotte placed a gentle hand on Niya's arm, causing her to slow. "I do not know what has gotten you into such a tizzy—"

"I am not in a tizzy," huffed Niya.

Charlotte's gray brows lifted.

"Fine, I'm tizzying, but you would be, too, if your character was so hunted down by Arabessa as mine was this morning."

Her lady's maid watched her closely as they walked. She had raised the three Bassette girls since infancy and was more of a grandmother than a maid. And like all their staff, she knew the secrets they kept, for the Bassettes in turn kept theirs, their house becoming a sanctuary of sorts for the few gifted in Jabari. "Usually you enjoy sparring with your sisters," said Charlotte.

"I always enjoy it."

"You don't seem to be enjoying yourself now."

Niya thought on that. "No, I suppose I am not."

"Why not?"

"I . . . don't know. I guess, lately . . . it's just not the same . . ."

"Without Lady Larkyra?"

"I'm being silly," said Niya, grasping her basket tighter. When had she become so sentimental?

"You girls are many things," explained Charlotte, "and yes, silly is most assuredly one, but showing your loyalty and love for one another should not be included in that. It's okay to miss your sister."

Niya felt a twinge of discomfort at being read so easily. But Charlotte was right, of course. She *did* miss Larkyra. Not that she would ever tell her sister. By the Obasi Sea, Niya would never hear the end of it!

Still . . . Larkyra was the youngest, recently turned nineteen. How was she married and moved out of the house already?

"If you ask me," continued Charlotte, "you all have grown much too quick. But it's to be expected, I suppose. You three are not like most."

"Thank the lost gods for that," said Niya. "Being like most is boring."

Charlotte chuckled as they entered the Trading District, where the marble mansions from the higher ring of Jabari were replaced with brick merchant buildings, the street growing thicker with citizens scurrying to acquire goods. Shouts of prices rang over their heads from various street venders, the smells of smoked fish and roasted nuts mixing in the air.

"So our little bird may have flown the nest," said Charlotte as she stopped to pick through a stall of mushrooms. "But so will all of you in time. After all, you *are* one and twenty and Arabessa three and twenty."

"Charlotte." Niya raised her brows in mock horror. "Don't you know it's rude to discuss one's age?"

"You mention mine daily."

"Nonsense. No one knows how truly ancient you are."

"The point I am trying to make," continued her lady's maid, eyes beady as she paid the vendor and they walked on, "is that I have watched you Bassettes adapt to many things, only growing stronger. Though home might appear different now, none of your duties are. You will always have your responsibilities to keep you together. Plus, you have me and the rest of the staff. Most of us are too old to go very far."

Niya smiled at the wrinkled woman, a bit of her melancholy lifting. "You're right."

"Always am," tutted Charlotte.

Letting out a laugh, Niya continued to follow Charlotte around the market, the ache in her chest easing as she replayed the old woman's words. She and her sisters *would* always have their duties to bring them together. In Jabari, but especially in the Thief Kingdom.

The Mousai, after all, were inseparable.

As the morning slipped into afternoon, Niya and Charlotte split up to fetch the final items on the list. And after leaving the seamstress, Niya decided to treat herself to a rice square, which she sat to eat in the Maker's Courtyard. It was her favorite spot in the Trading District, where she slipped onto a shaded bench facing a large fountain that glistened refreshingly under the heat.

Salty-sweet flavors flowed over her taste buds as she bit into her snack, a grin on her lips as she watched children escape the grasp of nannies and mothers to splash in the cool water. *Today is finally starting to turn around,* she thought contently, taking another bite.

The sound of more excited hollers brought Niya's attention to a winding alley to her left. The path appeared empty, but hoots echoed toward her again, and she didn't need to see it to know exactly what elicited such a mix of reverie and disappointment. A bet.

With her mood lifting further, Niya stood. *How delightful would it be if I won back what I spent on this rice square,* she thought gleefully as she finished it off in two more bites. Her magic twirled, just as excited, in her veins, for any promise of gambling meant a promise of movement, energy for her gifts to nibble on just as she had nibbled on her snack.

Following the noise down the winding path, she eventually found a group of children hunched over a game by the wall. Two of the older kids traded rolling a pair of eight-sided dice, eliciting more loud shouts. *Match-a-roll,* she thought, a popular game she had played often as a young girl. Niya grinned as they rolled again with more hollers of encouragement.

None had taken notice of her at their backs until she said, "I bet you two silver that you cannot roll that same number within two tries."

Six sets of eyes blinked up at her.

"No, do not go," said Niya hurriedly as the children scurried to escape. "I swear I'm good on my bet." She pulled forth two silver from her skirt's pockets. The kids stopped, eyes widening. These street mice probably had never seen such coin so close. "It can be yours if you are willing to play."

"We got nothing equal to show for it, missus," an older girl said.

"Hmm, I see. Well, I'll take whatever you might have in your pockets that you are willing to lose."

"Who says we be losin'?"

"Who indeed." Niya quirked a brow, amused. "Is it a bet, then?"

The two older children exchanged looks.

"Go on, Alba." Another kid nudged the girl. "You and your brother would be stuffed like pigs if you got hold of dem pretty full moons."

"All I have is this, missus." Alba's brother produced a tiny pouch from his pocket, spilling out a single seed scoopling.

Niya smiled at the small golden ball, ancient etchings over its surface. She had not seen one of these in a turn. When kissed by a flame, seed scooplings would burrow through any surface. She and her sisters had played with them as children, much to their housekeeper's horror, given she would later have to stop up all the holes made around their Jabari home.

"A fair trade, I would think," declared Niya. "Can you be our game master?" She turned toward the smallest of the bunch.

The boy enthusiastically nodded, no doubt never having been given such a role before.

"Very good. We are now trusting you with our bets." She passed the boy her silver, and Alba's brother handed over his pouch with the seed scoopling.

As the brother and sister each took up a die, the whole raggedy group leaned in, licking their lips in anticipation, eyes wide with excitement.

Niya was well acquainted with the emotions spinning in these children. For her, a gamble was a success from the start. That racing of her heart, the sweet smell of exhilaration as clusters of people watched the flip of a card, the turn of dice, the final energy of motion before lives could change forever with a mere grain's fall. She and her magic sighed at the prospect of it all.

The first roll resulted in huffs of disappointment from the children as the dice totaled thirteen rather than the betted sixteen.

"We'll get it on the next one, Alba, I'm sure of it." Her brother gathered the dice and handed her one.

But before they could throw again, a current of movement flowed toward Niya from the other end of the alley, where another road cut through.

Niya stilled the children's hands, glancing down their narrow, empty street.

"Hey! What are you—?"

"Shhh," Niya hushed the girl, tilting her head as the heavy hum of energy hit along her neck once more. "Are you lot expecting company?"

"What?"

"Are more of your friends meant to join you?" She moved to stand in front of the children.

"No," said Alba, glancing around Niya's cloak.

Niya's gaze narrowed as she concentrated on the sensations of footsteps and swinging limbs she now felt flooding their surroundings. The thickness of bodies walking toward them, the energy a group gave off when breathing together, the shifting on feet. It was heavier than that of youth. Weighted. Adult. And then it fell still.

Niya's pulse quickened.

"You may as well show yourselves," she called out, her voice echoing down the lane.

Everything remained empty, quiet.

She tried again. "Only cowards and thieves have reason to hide."

The only motion was the children gathering closer around her.

"Missus, I don't think there's anyone—"

The small boy's words were cut off as three forms turned into their street. All had black cloths wrapped around their noses and mouths, obscuring their identities, and their garb was odd for a summer in Jabari, thick and layered, made for durability rather than show. But what really caught Niya's attention were the blades in each of their hands and others displayed around their waists.

"Thieves, then," declared Niya, her stance shifting along with her magic, a promise of a scuffle charged in the air. "Children, I think it's time you run along."

"But what of our game?" asked Alba.

"It seems you have won by my forfeit." Niya didn't take her eyes from the figures as they slowly stalked closer. *This shall be fun,* she thought.

"That's not fair to you—"

"As I'm sure you are well aware, life is not fair. Now please, make haste and leave."

A tug on her cloak. "Come with us."

"I would much rather ensure this trio does not follow us first. Now go." She pushed at the closest child. "And be sure to spend those full moons recklessly. Youth is meant to be spoiled."

She felt the children's hesitation, but then they turned and ran. Alba was the last to go, and she pressed something into Niya's palm.

"A fair trade, I would think," the young girl said, echoing Niya's earlier words.

Niya met Alba's world-wise gaze. An expression too old on one so young.

"We'll call for help." And with that, Alba sped down the other end of the alley, leaving her holding the pouch containing the seed scooping. Despite herself, Niya smiled.

"Now." She turned back to her guests, pocketing the item. "What is it that I can help you with?"

Sure, they might *look* all brass and brawn, filled with hard punches, but three thieves Niya could handle. Three were—

Four additional figures, similarly masked, appeared behind the group from the connecting street.

Okay, thought Niya, *seven makes it interesting.*

Her magic stirred, impatient, but she ignored it. This was not a time to show her gifts. Sliding a hand inside her cloak, she curled her fingers around one of the two daggers tucked away at the back of her skirts. She might be dressed as a lady, but she'd been raised to always be prepared for a fight. The problem lay in what exactly the thieves wanted.

"The most precious thing I have is a child's toy," said Niya. "So think wisely if that is worth getting bloody for."

The group paused but offered no reply.

"I see it is up to me to make conversation, then. How about I introduce you to a friend of mine." Her grip tightened around her knife's hilt in the same moment a thief launched a sack into the air, another quickly sending an arrow soaring. Niya twirled back as the two collided above her head. Green smoke exploding from the bag.

"You poxes," she laughed. "You missed—"

But then she smelled it.

The sweet scent of *gaffaw* bark—a sleeping vapor—and a lot of it, filled her lungs.

It didn't matter how powerful one was, how well versed in magic or decorated in fighting—*gaffaw* bark, once deeply inhaled, got the best of all. Which was why it was illegal in most of Aadilor.

"Sticks," cursed Niya, right as her knees gave out and she hit the ground. Hot stone smacked against her cheek. The edge of her basket, filled with items for home, now forgotten by her side. As the green smoke dissipated and her vision blurred, boots stepped before her. All of them were dirty. Covered in scuffs and marks, the leather peeling back from soles. *And is that a toe peeking out?* Niya felt a slip of annoyance that a group that took such poor care of their footwear could best her, and so quickly. But then her annoyance faded to nothing as her eyes rolled back and she tumbled into darkness.

CHAPTER THREE

Niya woke to a gentle rocking. The screech of gulls soaring high above and the rhythmic splashes of oars cutting through waves. Her head throbbed as the residual effects of the *gaffaw* bark lingered, and she swallowed against the dryness of her throat.

Lying on her side, Niya found her hands were bound at the wrists behind her back, in what she could only assume was the belly of a rowboat. Her view was obscured by a moldy sack smelling of fish, but she caught tiny pinpricks of daylight shining through the stitching of the bag. Her shoulders ached from her unnatural positioning, and her legs felt sticky and heavy beneath her skirts, as if the material were still drying after being soaked by water. A warm breeze filtered across her neck, stirring the silk sleeve of her dress. The cloak she had been wearing appeared to be no longer with her.

At least I'm still clothed, she thought.

Her magic slowly stirred awake in her belly as she grew more conscious.

Burn, it hissed groggily, and then, *Killlll,* it demanded, hot and impatient as it woke fully.

Yes, yes, thought Niya placatingly. *In due time.* First she had to figure out where, by the lost gods, she was—and why and thanks to whom.

Then she could burn and kill and laugh in the face of whoever would be so idiotic as to kidnap a creature like her.

She had not recognized any of the thieves. Their clothes weren't identifiable as any Jabari gang she was aware of. Yet their actions had surely been organized by someone. Her capture had been quick, precise, using a substance that left little room for error. But who would want to steal her away? If their intentions had been to rob, they would have merely taken all her possessions and slit her throat or left her to wake long after they'd gone. Was it possible they recognized her as the daughter of the Count of Raveet? Was this to be a kidnapping for ransom?

How boring, thought Niya.

Refocusing on her surroundings, she decided she was definitely surrounded by water, salt water, if the birds and smell were any indication. Which meant she was most likely floating on the Obasi Sea. Given it was the only sea in all of Aadilor.

But the question remained: How far from shore were they? And which shore? And how far from Jabari? Or any recognizable place?

Okay, so there were a few more answers Niya needed.

The first, she decided, was how many occupied their boat. The seven thieves who had started all this?

Closing her eyes, Niya forced herself to relax, first her muscles, then her mind. She let the rocking of the boat seep into her skin, let the water hitting up against the sides caress her magic, which responded to motion. Her powers flowed, warm and pleased at finally being used, tingling through her entire body as she expanded her senses further, feeling the energy a hand gave off as it wiped sweat from a brow, the strong rowing of arms. She cataloged the inhales and exhales. Four souls sat around her. Two by her head, two by her feet.

Four . . . I can take four.

Subtly pulling against her bound wrists, she tested the ropes' strength. They were tight, but her fingers were free enough to do damage.

Quietly now, instructed Niya to her magic as she fluttered her fingers. There were slithers of liquid heat in her veins as a small flame awakened at her fingertip. Niya forced her breathing steady, her senses prickled to those around her. She had to do this fast, before they smelled the burning of the rope or saw that she indeed held fire. After all, one's advantage lay in surprise.

The boat thunked against another object, shifting Niya to roll onto her back. Her flame was snuffed out, her ropes remaining too tight to break.

Sticks, she silently cursed.

Niya felt her companions stir. The heavy footfalls of boots against the boat's wooden floor, the sound of rope being cinched, and the muttering of voices.

Her pulse continued to thump loud in her ears as rough arms lifted her.

"Oy, she's a heavy one," a man grunted by her head.

"Did you think she'd get lighter on the way over?" came a woman's reply as she grabbed her ankles.

Niya's annoyance prickled hot.

"Then let me lighten your load," Niya ground out as she slammed her slippered heel into the girl's face. There was a satisfying crunch of a nose breaking. The woman cursed as she fell back, dropping Niya's legs.

All that diligent kidnapping, and the fools didn't take care to tie her feet together.

With her senses buzzing, Niya backward headbutted the man still gripping her shoulders, her skull smarting with the contact.

There was a splash of water, the man falling in, as Niya landed in the belly of the boat. Rolling to her feet, she breathed hard as she found her balance, concentrating on the rest of the surrounding waves of movement. The dirty sack covering her head was insufferable!

A ripple of energy from a hand reaching for her caused Niya to spin around before slamming her shoulder into the culprit's side. A yip of surprise followed by another splash. Niya backed up, tripping on items by her feet, before steadying once more in the swaying boat. Her arms groaned at remaining bound behind her, the sun streaming in dizzyingly through the small holes in her head covering. Sensing another presence pushing up from in front—Niya kicked out.

But this time, strong hands grabbed her ankle, blocking.

"You'll be paying for that, girl," hissed the woman whose nose she had smashed. She twisted Niya's leg, sending her spinning.

Niya was suspended in air for what felt like a full sand fall before the slap of cold water enveloped her.

Her mind screamed in disorientation as the sting of salt water filled her nostrils and throat. She thrashed in panic, her eyes blinking open, but the sack was still over her head, not allowing her to see which way was up.

Tucking in her legs as tightly as she could, she managed to slip her hands in front, her shoulder sockets burning.

By the Obasi Sea, let me live through this.

Just then, there was a strong tug to her dress's bodice, part of the material ripping as she was hauled backward. Four pairs of hands dragged her over the side of the boat, the hard wooden edge digging and scratching into her hip.

Niya coughed and wheezed against the material of the bag, drenched and stuck over her face.

"Take this blasted thing off me!" She wriggled and fought against the unforgiving grip of her captors.

"A spicy one, she is," grunted a man as they held her down.

Niya's energy felt frayed, a damp mess spread too thin at the commotion. She desperately tried to rein it in, pull in the pieces that groped for clarity. At least enough to cast some sort of spell. *Anything* to blast these bastards off her. But there were limbs and hands and weight pinning her from every angle. "I will kill you all!" she screamed before a rough hand slammed over her mouth.

She bit it, *hard*, through the sack, and her teeth punctured skin.

A howl of pain before another hand smacked her skull against the bottom of the boat.

Her vision blurred.

Grunts of her attackers holding her down filled her ears as Niya desperately took in a lungful of air.

She couldn't breathe. Couldn't move.

The cloth over her head stuck wet against her lips with each panicked breath.

Don't let them suffocate me! she screamed imperiously to her gifts. Her magic responded like an eruption, for though Niya could not move, those around her could, and her powers greedily pulled in the energy they gave off, sucking in every drop to then burst from her palms.

"What the—"

"She's on fire!"

The thieves sprang back, their grasps loosening.

"Quick!" screamed another. "Put this bitch down!"

Niya's binds snapped as the flames ate through the rope, her arms free.

"You're all dead!" she roared, reaching for the cinched cloth covering her face. She felt weak, exhausted by the extreme use of her magic, but her fury kept her moving.

She barely caught a sliver of a sunset sky before a large blanket was thrown on top of her. Weighted hands pressed the sticky, wet material against her, and there was a sizzling of steam as her fire was doused. Niya sucked in air, readying to scream her frustration, but then all too quickly something sweet burned her nostrils on the inhale.

By the lost gods, not again!

The cloying flavor of *gaffaw* bark was everywhere.

And then it was nowhere as Niya collapsed once again into black.

With a gasp, Niya sat up and then groaned. Her head felt split open. She was free of her binds and blindfold, but her body ached as if it were one giant bruise, and though her clothes were now dry, they felt clingy against her skin. She lay on a soft brown animal hide, and a lantern flickered on top of a wooden crate in front of her, sending warm shadows through the small compartment.

Moving gingerly, Niya took in wood-slatted walls; a single door to her right, no doubt locked; and no windows to be seen. The air felt stuffy but had a rather pleasant aroma, like a perfumed hothouse in Jabari.

By the stars and sea, please let me still be close to Jabari.

This day, if it was even still the same day, had returned to being horrible.

Niya needed to get up and look around, find a way out, but she was exhausted. Thirsty and yet, unfairly, needed to relieve herself. Her escape could wait a few grain falls.

Rubbing her wrists, the skin raw and angry where the rope had dug in, she took in the state of herself. Her fine green day dress was stained and torn, and she lifted her right foot, wiggling her exposed toes. *Just great.* She was missing a slipper. And they were her favorite pair. Niya pushed away a clump of her red hair, which lay loose and matted down her back. She was an absolute mess. And this, more than being attacked, drugged, and dragged to the lost gods knew where, really upset her.

She was never a mess.

"I fear my crew was rather rough in bringing you here." A deep voice floated from behind her. "But what do you expect when you put up such a fight in coming?"

Niya's skin ran as hot as the lantern flame before her, her heart kicking into a faster rhythm.

No, she thought. *Please, nonononono.*

Glancing over her shoulder, her entire body a tense coil, Niya found glowing turquoise eyes peering out of a black-shrouded form. His face was all sharp angles in the dim light: brown skin, full lips, and inky hair that was tied back at the base of his neck. It was a face that could tempt many and had, much to their deep regret, and one he never covered up when entering the Thief Kingdom. Not all had the courage for such open bravado. Even the Mousai, some of the most feared creatures in the kingdom, made sure to be masked, for their true hair color never to escape a headdress, for the shade of their skin to be hidden. No one but their closest brethren were allowed to know of their more respectable lives in Jabari. And even those trusted few were bound silent by a spell, on pain of losing their tongues in consequence.

This man, however, wanted his face known, wanted to be remembered for his sins. He had told her so, years ago, which should have been her first warning.

But Niya was never good with warnings.

Alōs Ezra, the infamous pirate lord, sat tucked into a corner, his shoulders so wide they hid his chair's back. Niya forced her attention away from the deep V of his tunic, which displayed his strong, smooth chest. Her mind was a cruel beast as it brought forth memories of her fingers grazing that very skin. Quickly, she blinked the visions away, jaw clenching.

In contrast to her stiffness, the pirate was an image of repose, his hands casually interlocked over his stomach, a jeweled pinkie ring sparkling in the lantern's light. Niya's gaze roamed all the way down to his crossed ankles, covered in sea-weathered boots, and that was where her attention remained—on the soles of his shoes.

For it was the only type of soul this man had.

Alōs was no friend of hers or anyone's.

Her magic wrestled against her skin to be freed, to do what it always wanted to do when this man was near. *Buuuuuuurrrm*, it screamed. *Kiiiiiiiiiiill.*

The history that hung between them was the one secret Niya had kept from her family. It was her burden, the one she had been carrying for the past four years.

"There's a heavy purse attached to your whereabouts," said Niya, ignoring the demands of her gifts along with the protesting groan of her sore legs as she stood, ensuring her back was no longer to him. The pirate's relaxed stance didn't fool her. The most lethal of snakes often played dead.

"I would hope so." Alōs leaned forward, resting his elbows on his knees. "I'm a priceless commodity."

"One that wishes their death, it would seem. There were rumors of your crew docking in Jabari. But I couldn't believe the *Crying Queen* would be so sloppy after hiding like cowards for all these months."

"Cowards run," clarified Alōs. "Others hide so they can plan."

Niya laughed, cold and hard. "No amount of planning will save your neck, pirate. What the Thief King wants, the Thief King gets, and he seeks to make a trophy out of your head."

"I'm afraid it would not keep well, detached from my body."

"All the more reason to cut it off. I'm sure I am not the only one who would enjoy watching your looks wither and decay."

"Are you calling me handsome?"

"I'm calling you a fool. I knew you to be smug, but not naive. *No one* is above the law in the Thief Kingdom. What were you thinking, stealing *phorria* from it?"

"If I didn't know better, I would think that was concern in your voice."

Niya ground her teeth as the pirate's ice-shard energy enveloped her, his strong magic, tinged green, curling from his body with his smile.

"What?" Alōs cocked a brow. "No snarky reply? How you disappoint me."

"Not a first, I imagine."

"Nor a last, I can bet."

"What am I doing here?"

"I have kidnapped you."

Niya scoffed. "Have you now?"

"Would you like me to tie you back up so it appears more authentic?" His eyes shone, predatory.

"I'd like to see you try."

"Just as I adore seeing you struggle."

Niya narrowed her gaze, one hand sliding to her back, to her knives, but her fingers grasped air.

"No proper kidnapper would let you keep those," explained Alōs.

"You'd be smart in returning them."

"I'd argue that would make me rather stupid."

"Stupid*er*," clarified Niya.

Alōs grinned. "I've missed your spark."

"You know nothing of my sparks."

"Oh, but we both know that I do. Just as I knew where to tell my crew to watch for a curvy redhead in Jabari. I must say, the Bassettes' estate is quite lovely."

Niya's vision dripped crimson as her blood boiled. Guilt and outrage mixed potently with her magic. It was one thing to threaten her but another entirely to threaten her family.

While Niya might not have had her knives, she had other tools that could do far worse damage.

Yes, her magic crooned, satisfied. *Let us free.*

When she fluttered her fingers at her sides, flames erupted on each of her fingertips. There was no point concealing her gifts from this man.

"Ah, ah, ah," he tutted. "We're on a ship. With cannon powder. You set fire freely ablaze in here, and the whole place will go up."

"So?"

"So I know you're strong, pet, but how long can you tread water in the middle of the rough sea? That is, if you survive the blast—and the sharks."

"I'll be sure to save enough wood so I can float." She pushed her flames to burn brighter.

Alōs sat back, seeming not at all concerned by her threat.

"I'll ask one last time, Alōs: Why am I here?"

"We both know why."

"Remind me, then."

A beat of silence as his stare bored into hers. The flames along her fingers fluttered their anticipation. *Burn,* her powers whispered, *burn,* as the room grew suffocating with Alōs's unwavering attention. His energy always seemed to churn, pulse, reach, a weed looking for more ground.

"All right," he began. "Masked or not, we both know I'll always recognize you, Niya Bassette." His eyes roamed her disheveled body. "Sister to Larkyra and Arabessa Bassette, daughter of Johanna and Dolion Bassette, Count of Raveet, of the second house of Jabari . . ." Niya's blood ran cold and colder still as Alōs flicked out icy-green threads of his magic, ticking off each name and smothering her flames with a hiss, until he stopped on the most important one. "Dancer of the Mousai."

Niya watched a smile twist its way across Alōs's lips. This was the nightmare she had dreaded since that cursed night so very long ago, when she'd been nothing more than a foolish young girl tricked into believing something stupid—that she had found love. Here sat the one person in all of Aadilor who knew every one of her identities and wasn't spellbound to keep them secret.

"And as I promised that night," continued Alōs, his voice chilling the air, "I've come to collect."

CHAPTER FOUR

*A*lōs had always found pleasure in watching a fearsome creature become cornered, especially if he was the one forcing them back.

He had worked hard to obtain this winning card and had waited patiently to play it. Leverage was the most valuable currency in their world, and he'd known the moment he'd first seen the fire dancer perform that acquiring the identities of the most-feared creatures in the Thief Kingdom was not something to trade in without an invaluable return on investment.

It had been a risky endeavor, sacrificing a part of himself he knew he could never regain. But what things worth having were easily caught? Four years Alōs had held on to this information, watching Niya squirm in rage, knowing he held her fate in his hands. But now was the time. He needed something, badly. And luckily for this woman, she happened to have the key that would free him to get it. Removing the bounty on his head was merely the necessary first step.

"You bastard," spat Niya, shoving the blazing heat from her palms.

Alōs pulled up his own magic, which sat like dewdrops on his skin, forcing up a shield. His veins buzzed as if ice swam within. Their gifts slammed together, his cool, hers hot. The two powers sizzled, water and fire creating steam, canceling each other out.

A heavy silence hung over the room, the wetness in the air still lingering, and he pulled what liquid he could grasp into his veins once more.

He watched as Niya began to lightly sway her hips.

Oh, no you don't, he thought.

Alōs knew this woman, had studied her kind of magic, and understood that, while she was strong, only movement held her power. Just as proximity to water held his.

Swiftly, he stood, kicking a sandbag that rested on a box beside him. It thudded to the ground, and the fur rug directly below Niya snapped up, capturing her like a fish in a net and cutting off the beginnings of her spell. He would have truly been stupid if he hadn't ordered this room rigged before placing her inside. The hunter's trap now hung from a rafter's beam, the perfect snare for Niya and all her graceful movements.

She thrashed and screamed, the tightly cinched bag swaying.

"There'll be no more of that," said Alōs, circling her.

"I'm going to kill you," came Niya's muffled growl.

"You have every right to try." He poked the bag. "But I wouldn't."

She let out another snarl, the trap still wriggling.

Alōs grinned.

"Whatever you have planned," Niya ground out, "it won't work."

"And why is that?"

"Because even if I don't get the chance to kill you, my sisters will."

"It's quite humorous hearing threats from you when you're tied up so nicely."

The smell of something burning floated past Alōs's nose, and he glanced up; the rope cinching the bag closed was on fire. *Clever girl,* he thought.

The tie snapped and the rug fell open, depositing Niya with a thunk. She rolled out of the fur and sprang to her feet, a small flame flickering on her pointer finger.

"I only need a little to do a lot." She smiled and launched herself forward.

Alōs spun away, but the room was so small it merely put him in striking distance on the other side. In a blur of motion, she kicked him in the stomach, and he staggered with a grunt. She continued to move dizzyingly as the tiny cabin began to heat with her gathering magic.

An orange blast shot out of her core. Alōs threw up his hands, forcing out his gifts through his palms, a cool current of green that deflected her hit.

She twirled left, away from the ricocheting spell. It crashed into the far wall, singeing its surface.

Annoyance bloomed in Alōs's chest at seeing his ship harmed. His focus sharpened.

While Niya might have been one step faster, his advantage lay in his size combined with the confined space. It was only a matter of crowding his prey.

She knocked against stacked crates as she dipped and wove from his attempts to grab her, but despite her evasion, he kept sliding forward, knocking away spell after spell, forcing her into a corner. Within a grain's fall, he had her against a wall, forcing her arms by her sides, her legs tightly pinned between his thighs.

"You shan't be placing any spells on me this night," he growled in her ear, breathing in the familiar scent of honeysuckle after a rain through her salty sweat.

"We both know I can do many things to remove myself from your grip." Her blue eyes blazed as they met his.

"Yes, but because I value my ship, I'd prefer it not to come to that."

"Something you should have thought about before *kidnapping me* and bringing me aboard."

"Valid point, but still. Can we stop all this nonsense? Really, fire dancer, how much longer will you try to kill me?"

"Forever," spat Niya, struggling against his hold once more.

He pressed harder into her, holding her as tightly against the wall as he could until she gasped for air. "It would be a fool's errand," he began. "For if I am found dead on this ship by your hand, there are those around Aadilor that will be sent instructions of where to find what I hold in my mind."

Niya went still.

"You are finally starting to understand?"

"Let me go." Her quick breaths were hot against his neck.

"You will behave?"

"For now."

It was as much as he could hope from her.

He released his grip, and Niya quickly withdrew to the other side of the room.

Alōs stomped out the small flame still eating away at the rope attached to the fur.

"What is your plan, then?" she asked.

He straightened his jacket. "I am holding the Mousai's identities ransom for a pardon from the Thief King."

When Niya made no reply, Alōs found her unfocused gaze staring into the corner of the room, a frown on her lips. He knew this was her nightmare realized, for him to finally use this knowledge for his own gain, for her sisters to possibly find out what she had given away to a monster like him.

If he were anyone else, he might have felt bad for the fire dancer. But Alōs had stopped feeling many years ago. He had sacrificed enough from caring. He was still sacrificing. He had no more decency to give.

And he was glad.

Such emotion made one weak, and he had made sure to rid himself of as much fragility as he could.

"But why do you need me to make such a bargain?" asked Niya after a beat, eyes resuming their hard edge. "Surely you could have made your trade without all this extra work of bringing me here."

"It's to make a point," he clarified. "We both know the Thief King does not respond well to threats—"

"He pulls the bowels from any who make them."

"Let alone ones from those he already has a bounty on," continued Alōs. "I knew I had to hold one of his precious pets prisoner for him to sit up and listen. Plus, with you aboard, it stops him from merely blowing up my ship to be rid of me."

"You will not get what you want," declared Niya.

"We'll have to wait and see, won't we? That is, if your dear sisters ever come to rescue you. After all, the Mousai must save one of their own."

"They'll find me." Niya tipped her chin up, and Alōs studied her in the low lantern light. Her red hair was wilder than before, covering half her face as the green neckline of her dress slunk down one shoulder. It threatened to expose parts of her body many creatures would pay dearly to see, his crew especially. Her skirts were ripped and frayed, and her one bare foot was smudged with dirt. Yet even so disheveled, she remained poised, her gaze holding nothing but confident contempt.

"Perhaps," said Alōs.

"They *will*."

"If you're so sure, shall we place a wager?"

Niya's eyes sparked, and he held back a grin. *That's right,* he thought, *a pretty gamble just for you.* Her identity wasn't the only secret he knew. He'd watched, more than once in the Thief Kingdom, as she succumbed to her vice of playing fate's hand.

"A wager?" she repeated.

He nodded.

"About my sisters coming for me?"

"How about the time it takes for *anyone* to come for you?"

"Anyone?"

"Anyone."

Niya sucked in her bottom lip in thought.

"Have a number in mind?" asked Alōs. "Feel free to make it high, for who knows how long it will take for you to be missed, let alone found."

"Three days."

Fool, he thought.

"Three? Are you sure? You do not know how far we might be from Jabari or the Thief Kingdom. And do not forget the *Crying Queen* has evaded detection this long. We both know how your impulsive decisions can land you in all sorts of jams."

Niya's lips thinned. "Three."

"Very well." Alōs pulled a small pin from the lapel of his coat. He pricked his palm, allowing a bit of blood to pool in the center. He gathered the buzz of his gifts, letting it float forward in his veins, a cold whisper. As he set his intentions, he pushed out a thread of his magic from his cut. "And what do you wager?"

Niya eyed the green glow of his spell circling his hand, apprehension clear in her features. "Must it be a binding bet?"

"Against a slippery creature like you? Always."

This way I can also keep a closer eye on you, thought Alōs darkly. Binding bets ensured payments were met by allowing the winner to be able to locate the debtor. And neither could kill the other while bound, lest their own life be sent to the Fade as well. Any extra security against the wrath of this lethal creature, Alōs would take.

Niya remained still, no doubt mulling over the same details, wondering if they put her at an advantage or disadvantage.

"But if you're having doubts about your sisters . . ." Alōs began to withdraw his offered palm.

"No." Niya stepped forward.

Alōs's pulse quickened as he suppressed a grin. *That's right,* he silently cooed to her. *You've taken plenty of reckless chances thus far; why stop now?*

Niya reached for the pin, but Alōs shook his head. "As you pointed out earlier, you can do a lot with a little."

She frowned but stuck out her hand nonetheless. He slashed quickly, keeping the cut small. Niya didn't flinch as crimson began to seep out. She moved her fingers, her orange magic swirling forward to mimic the circle of his.

"If *anyone*"—she locked eyes with him—"comes for me in, or before, three days' time, you will allow us to leave peacefully, sign your silence about the Mousai's true identities, *and* destroy wherever you have the knowledge hidden in Aadilor."

"That is a hefty payment." Alōs cocked a brow.

"It's to be thorough. I'm not the only slippery creature in this room."

Alōs weighed his options for a moment. "All right," he agreed. "I'll allow you to leave peacefully, will sign my silence and destroy any knowledge of your identities hidden around Aadilor. *But* if no one comes for you by the first light of the fourth day, you will serve a year as crew to the *Crying Queen*."

"What?" Niya pulled her hand away. "That's insanity."

"Knowing the Mousai's identities is practically priceless and the fastest way to remove my bounty," said Alōs. "I would be a fool to bet for anything less."

"But you don't like me. Why would you want me here?"

"I don't like most of my crew, but that doesn't stop me from enjoying ordering them around. In fact, it makes it all the better."

"I don't know how to sail."

"I don't need a sailor."

Niya's brows knitted together. "I will *not* be the entertainment."

Despite himself, a deep chuckle rumbled from Alōs's throat. "Why worry, fire dancer? If you're so sure you'll win, think of all you'll regain. My wager should hardly be a threat."

"A year . . . ," she repeated, more to herself.

"Time's already falling." Alōs nodded to their hands. "Make the bet or don't, but we both know your secrets are not safe with me."

She took in a steadying breath and glanced down at their blood-covered hands, where their magic pulsed in reds and greens in anticipation along their skin and reflected in Niya's eyes, which seemed to hold a thousand thoughts.

And then . . .

"Vexturi," said Niya, shoving her hand into his. *My oath.*

Alōs's dark heart gave a thrilled thump.

"Vexturi," he echoed, binding the spell.

Their individual magical gifts burned bright before intertwining, spinning where they gripped one another. Alōs's palm felt slippery against hers but stuck as a heat licked between their grasps while the circle shrank, absorbing into their skin with a snap.

Niya pulled her hand away first as the outline of a thin black band appeared around her wrist. An identical one now marked Alōs's—a binding bet to be determined.

It is done, he thought.

And Alōs was extremely pleased.

CHAPTER FIVE

Niya wanted to scream.

Or cry.

Or both.

By the lost gods, what have I done?

Alōs had exited swiftly after their binding bet had been secured, leaving Niya remaining numbly behind, thoughts racing.

Had she made a horrible mistake? Could she actually win and, after all this time, finally have her and her sisters' identities safe? *Why did I only say three days?*

"I'm here to get you cleaned up and show you around." A woman's voice brought Niya back to the small compartment, to where a figure now stood in the shadows by the open door. Her head was shaved save for a line in the middle, and her black skin gleamed warmly in the low light.

She peered at Niya with indifference.

"I don't care to be shown around," said Niya, turning from the woman.

"And cleaned up? Captain doesn't like any on his ship to look like they've been dragged aboard from the bottom of the sea."

Niya arched a brow as she settled a steely gaze back on her unwanted companion. "But that is precisely what has been done to me."

"Doesn't mean you have to remain lookin' like it."

"Go away," said Niya, her mood souring further.

When no reply came, she found the woman had done just that.

But there, on a crate by the open door, a pile of clothes had been left.

Niya adjusted the collar of her new tunic. The white top was snug but far cleaner than her soiled dress. The brown trousers fit her eerily well, and while the boots were too big, given she wasn't wearing any socks, she supposed they were better than remaining barefoot.

She peered at the small pouch in her hand, brushing a thumb over where she could feel the bump of the seed scoopling inside. It was astonishing this had survived her journey here, hidden inside the pocket of her ruined skirts. More astonishing yet was how that day in Jabari now felt like a lifetime ago. But this little trinket had made it, a strange anchor home that placed a reassuring hope in Niya's chest.

Pocketing the item within her new trousers, Niya studied the discarded rags by her feet. Her once-beautiful gown, hand-sewn by Jabari's top seamstress, reduced to shreds. She sighed, a tiredness gripping her. In fact, in the aftermath of all her rage, Niya felt rather run down. She was exhausted and, despite her now somewhat-clean clothes, desperately wanted a bath.

And after, she wanted to change into one of her soft silk robes. And Charlotte to hum a reassuring melody as she brushed her hair into soft waves. And she wanted food. By the lost gods, she wanted *heaps* of food. Niya wanted eclairs from Milezi, Jabari's best pastry maker, and two-day-soaked brisket from Palmex de V piled onto freshly baked honey rolls.

But she wasn't going to get any of those things.

At least, not anytime soon.

Weariness gripped Niya once more as she rubbed at the marking of her binding bet. The dim lantern light flickered across the black lines wrapping her pale wrist.

As the days progressed, the band would slowly fill in, counting down the days left for her sisters to show. If they did not . . . well, Niya could not think of that.

They will find me. They will. And then this whole mess will be over.

Suddenly desperate for fresh air, Niya swung open the door. She was only slightly surprised it hadn't been locked, not that a lock could stop her, but she supposed Alōs found no need to try to cage her when their binding bet was a shackle enough. For her win to count, she had to remain aboard the ship.

As she stepped into the hall, Niya was met with the woman she had felt waiting on the other side for some time now. "If you insist on remaining outside my room," she began, "I guess you might as well give me this grand tour you speak of."

The woman cut her a dry grin, displaying checkered gold-capped teeth before she led the way down the tight corridor. As they walked, Niya took in her guide more properly. She was tall, with sinewy muscles along her exposed arms, where a ring of five welted burns sat like ornamentation on each bicep. A long dagger was strapped to her thigh, and with her shaved head and more than a dozen gold loops piercing the rim of her right ear, she had the look of those who hailed from Shanjaree in the far west of Aadilor.

While Shanjaree was known to have pockets of magic, Niya could sense no gifts stirring in this woman. There was no metallic sting to the air or trail of colored smoke one could pick up with the Sight.

Climbing upstairs, they entered into the light of early morning.

Niya squinted against the harshness of it, though she greedily breathed in the salty air that pushed refreshingly across her skin, whipping her already-disheveled hair around her shoulders.

"Welcome to the *Crying Queen*," said her guide.

As her eyes adjusted to the bright day, she was able to take in the massive gleaming ship stretching out before them. Black-and-gold detailing edged banisters, railings, and masts, above which puffed white sails like giant clouds.

Men and women scurried like rodents this way and that, climbing to reach crow's nests, tie ropes, and adjust sails.

Niya had been aboard the *Crying Queen* before but had never given it much attention. Her mind had been focused on a different task then, a journey she had been on with her sisters.

At the thought of Larkyra and Arabessa, a bloom of pain and longing expanded in her chest.

What were they doing now? Had they even noticed she was gone? Were they scared she might be dead?

Niya rubbed at her sternum, as if that could rid her of the horrid feeling of guilt.

"This is the foredeck," said the woman as they walked. "Gun deck is a floor below us. Stern of the ship is behind us, and forecastle deck and bow is at the front."

Niya barely listened, instead studying the crew, who seemed to crawl out of every crack to study her. They were made up of every age, licking blistered lips as she passed, forty pairs of hungry eyes gleaming, no doubt seeing her as she had been presented—their meal ticket to their freedom from the Thief King. Pillaging and commandeering vessels were not the only ways pirates made a silver. Blackmail was a familiar pastime for rodents such as these. And while Niya was used to being ogled, usually enjoyed it, today she desperately wanted to be invisible, overlooked, and safely alone with her thoughts and feelings.

But she couldn't let these pirates know that. Here she had no flexibility to be vulnerable. So Niya smiled a sharp smile to each and every person they passed, flames erupting to her fingertips as she gave a few a little wave.

Their gazes clung to her displayed gifts, some stepping back, others returning her bravado with their own cruel grins, colorful curls of their magic seeping from their forms.

Interesting, thought Niya.

"What are you mutts standing around for?" barked her guide to the gathering group. "It's not as if we have never had a prisoner on board. Back to work!"

Hearing how the woman spoke each syllable with purpose and clarity, Niya's attention swung back to her, reassessing. *More curiosities,* thought Niya. While her guide might have had the look of a pirate, Niya knew then she had not been born into squalor.

"But she holds the gifts," said a small girl, clear fascination in her tone.

"And? So do our captain and Saffi and Mika and half of Aadilor. Ain't nothing special about this one, Bree; now back to the ropes with you."

In a blink the girl scampered up a mast, no ladder or rope needed, before she was a small dot standing in a crow's nest.

"Best not to flash those gifts of yours so openly," said the woman to Niya. "There are still a few here that are looking to get revenge for the burns you gave them earlier."

"How serendipitous, for I'm still looking to get revenge on those who dragged me here."

Her guide tipped her head back and laughed, drawing Niya's eyes to her bruised nose and the matching discoloration under her eyes.

"The handiwork of your foot," explained the woman as she caught her gaze. "So no revenge needed with me."

Niya set her shoulders. "I do not think your injury is at all equal to what I have suffered being brought here."

"We've all got sob stories, and I can guarantee those aboard have worse ones than yours, so don't be looking for any sympathetic ears here."

Niya's annoyance prickled along with her magic. "You know nothing of me or my life."

E. J. Mellow

"No," agreed the woman. "But I don't need to. If what the captain says is true and you're worth so much as to help us get our bounty dropped with the Thief King, you're more than expensive—you're connected. Or at least your family is," she added, assessing. "And most of our prisoners, like you, have lived cushy."

"I can guarantee you," began Niya coolly, "none of your prisoners have *ever* been like me."

"I suppose none of them have been as troublesome to get on board, but you all end up hog-tied and captured in the end."

Niya's temper flared, her magic spinning around in her gut to show this woman just how *troublesome* she could be. But she gritted her teeth against the urge. Suspicions were apparently already overflowing on this ship regarding her connections. No use in fanning the flames.

"Thank you for your lovely tour," said Niya through clenched teeth. "But I am no longer in the mood for company."

The woman quirked an amused grin. "Then you better change your mood quickly, for you're on a pirate ship, girl, and there's always unwanted company around."

Do not singe off that insufferable smile, Niya told herself. *Do not show her what happens to unwanted company when unwanted company sticks around. Do not. Do not. Do not.*

Niya strode from the woman, stopping at the bow, where she grasped the railing.

The ship cut through the waves far below, churning sea-foam to splash up against her skin, cooling her temper.

"By the Obasi Sea," growled Niya as she felt the woman approach. "You truly cannot take a hint!"

"Before I leave," said her guide, ignoring her outburst, "Captain wanted me to let you know that if you're hungry, some of the crew are always eating in the main galley."

"Then it's a good thing I am not," lied Niya.

The pirate eyed her for a long moment. "I'm Kintra, by the way." She extended a hand.

Niya did not shake it.

Kintra displayed her checkered grin again. "He's right. You are stubborn."

"*He* knows nothing of me."

"He knows enough to give you this." Kintra pulled a lumpy biscuit from her pocket and a capped pouch from around her neck. She placed both on the small ledge under the railing by Niya. "He'll not have you starve," explained Kintra. "Said there's no value in the dead."

Niya's gaze narrowed. "How thoughtful."

"He's a chivalrous prince like that." Kintra winked. "Enjoy."

Niya resisted throwing the biscuit over the railing as Kintra strode away.

No value in the dead.

Niya scoffed. *Well, that shows how little he knows of the Fade.* There were plenty of treasures to be found in the land of the dead, priceless knowledge to be collected. One only needed to be willing to give up a year of their life for a visit. Like she was apparently willing to do for her secret to be safe.

Niya scrubbed a hand over her face, shoulders drooping.

There was that annoying ache in her throat again that threatened tears, but just like before, she forced it away. The last thing she needed was to start blubbering.

As she stared into the distant horizon, empty of land or vessel or any living soul, Niya's thoughts tumbled.

She had been quietly trying for years to escape the tangled mess she had put her and her family into. The irony wasn't lost on her that the very man who'd placed her in this predicament was now offering her a way out.

Running her thumb over the band on her wrist, she replayed the possible consequences of her actions, which had haunted her daily.

If their Bassette identities were linked to the Mousai, everything their father had built in Jabari would be ruined. The Bassettes' position of power in the city would be lost. And worse—they'd be exiled, hunted, and not only by Jabari's citizens for lying about having magic but by any they had ever threatened, maimed, or hurt in the Thief Kingdom as the Mousai.

That left a long list of potential threats.

They could find refuge in the Thief Kingdom, of course, abandon their Jabari lives and permanently take up their position as the Thief King's deadly servants. But what would that mean for Larkyra and her husband, Darius? Newly married, with his lands just returned to him. The duke would be forced to abandon them or Larkyra. And Arabessa . . . her issues were of an entirely different nature.

No! Niya dug her nails into the railing. *It will never come to that.*

Killing Alōs was the only solution Niya had found, but he was a cunning and powerful pirate, used to surviving all manner of dances with death. Over the years, she had paid three assassins, and each of their heads had been delivered to her in gift boxes left in her dressing room within the palace.

"Bastard," grumbled Niya.

Alōs's life had proved harder to snatch away than others, which Niya resolved was a good thing in the end, if his warning of having their secret hidden in other places in Aadilor was true. Plus, now he had the binding bet to protect him from her lethal blow.

The only reprieve lay in the fact that Alōs had no knowledge of her father's true connection to the Thief King. *By the stars and sea, let him never learn of that!* Alōs would have a whole other deck of playing cards then.

Niya shivered, her gaze fixing back on the open sea.

They seemed completely alone, lost, and forgotten where they sailed. Time moved strangely here, Niya realized, on the endless water, where only the sun above might tell how far they'd gone.

What would a year feel like here? wondered Niya. A year serving under Alōs Ezra. Having to obey every one of his commands.

Her magic hissed at her thoughts. *Nevvvvvver.*

Never, agreed Niya.

These might have been the highest stakes she had ever bet against, but for her family she would risk anything. And her sisters *would* find her, and all this would soon be over. The risk would be a reward in the end.

As the sun slipped higher in the sky, the heat beating against her skin, her stomach gave a pleading growl. Niya stared at the disfigured biscuit beside her. She *really* didn't want to touch it, didn't want to take any more this ship offered. Any more *he* offered.

Tricks, thought Niya.

Everything in this world, *his* world, held tricks.

But after another sand fall of standing under the harsh sun, Niya's throat growing more and more parched, she took up the animal-hide pouch with a curse and gulped heartily.

The water was warm as it ran down her throat, but it was water, and Niya was at least thankful for that. She knew ale and whiskey were a ship's main drink. Fresh water was hard to come by in this line of work and even harder to keep clean.

Niya grabbed the biscuit next, and though she loathed every small bite, her hunger pangs waned, and she ate it to the last crumb.

It wouldn't do to be famished when my sisters come, she reasoned.

Today, thought Niya, turning her gaze to the thin line where sky kissed sea. *They will come today. Today. Today. Today.*

But the lost gods appeared to have a different plan. For the only thing that appeared when the sun traded places with the moon was Niya's growing fear that perhaps, once again, she had made a horrible mistake.

CHAPTER SIX

*A*lōs would never go as far as to say he was happy, but for the first time in many months, he felt at ease. Standing before the large latticed glass windows that filled the back wall of his captain's quarters, he idly played with the ring on his pinkie. Though the red stone that sat inside was small, he could feel the pulse of tucked-away magic it held. Just as he could sense his powers prickling in contentment along his skin at being surrounded by open water. He could think better at sea, hearing the waves, tasting the salty air with each intake of breath. Water was a gift. Water was his home.

"You have history with this girl," said Kintra from behind, where he knew she sat, ankle propped up on knee, half-drunk glass of whiskey in hand.

"I have history with many people in Aadilor," said Alōs, turning from the orange glow cast by the setting sun to refill his own drink.

"Yes, but this seems . . . personal."

Alōs raised a brow in Kintra's direction. "I would think any kidnapping and ransom seemed personal. It would be rather odd to snatch up a creature I had no idea about."

"You elude my meaning for a reason."

"If I elude anything, let it be the death sentence on my head." Alōs slid into his chair behind his large wooden desk.

"On *our* heads," clarified Kintra, who remained slouched in the seat across from him.

Alōs waved an unconcerned hand as he sipped his whiskey, the burn a comfort down his throat. "It is me the king will want on a spike if this does not go as planned."

"And will it not go as planned?"

Alōs met Kintra's attentive brown eyes, a smile curling on his lips. "It will go above and beyond planned."

This Alōs knew with his entire being, for he only made a move when he knew the calculated risk of the outcome, and betting against his precious secret of the Mousai was more than calculated—it was a sure win.

It wasn't magic that had kept his ship hidden, for he knew magic was a fingerprint to any skilled tracker, especially one with as much power as the Thief King. No, this was something greater, made from Aadilor's own splendor.

They were sailing in the Obasi Strait. A length of sea where the east and west currents crashed together, creating a blind spot for all location spells, portal doors, or other kinds of magic trying to penetrate in. It was rough to sail into, but once in the seam it was an easy ride, almost luxurious, for not even storms visited this stretch of air and water. No one knew the exact cause of the phenomenon, but any good pirate knew of the strait. It was the only real sanctuary for deplorable people like him and his crew. If you passed another vessel, you let them be, even if it held your greatest adversary. Honor wasn't merely a law among the honorable. Though few, there did exist rules even the deadliest of pirates would not break. The sanctum of the Obasi Strait was one of them.

It was with this assurance that Alōs had lured Niya into his binding bet, for not even those who held all of Aadilor's knowledge would be able to find them here within three days. It would be like searching for a particular grain in a sandglass.

"It's a good thing I'm on your side"—Kintra shook her head with an amused grin—"for on anyone else, I'd find such cockiness a real pain in my arse."

"Which would be surprising, for cocks are usually never allowed anywhere near you, let alone your arse."

Kintra flipped him a crude gesture, which Alōs returned with a raised glass before taking another sip.

He usually *never* allowed his crew to act so boldly with him, but he and Kintra shared a different sort of relationship, a longer history than any on board. Even longer than his and Niya's. Though Kintra was smart enough never to act so brazenly in front of his pirates. Behind closed doors, however, she was the closest thing Alōs had to a friend. That was, if he were the sort of soul who needed such companionship. Which he was not.

"I still do not know why you want her to become a crew member," said Kintra. "I may not have the lost gods' gifts, but even I know she's powerful. Dangerously so."

"Precisely. Think how much quicker we can get what we need with someone like her at our disposal."

"Alōs." Kintra cut him a dry look. "A secured binding bet will not make her a compliant lamb."

"No, but it will make her forced to serve this ship."

Kintra seemed unconvinced. "I do not trust her."

"As none aboard should."

"She hasn't acted like the others we have kidnapped for ransom."

"And how does she act?"

"Calmer."

"And this is a bad thing?" challenged Alōs.

"It's . . . unnerving."

Alōs laughed. "Well, well, the formidable Kintra admits to being unnerved by a woman half her size."

"She stands by the bow all day," said Kintra, ignoring his jab. "Just stands there, looking at the horizon."

Alōs did know this. He had watched her there this very morning.

Niya's red hair had whipped about her shoulders as she'd leaned against the railing, peering out at the second day's light.

Alōs had imagined the emotions tumbling through her mind then: anger, disappointment, confusion, despair. That precious pride of hers slipping away like her hope to be free, only herself to blame.

He did not feel bad for putting her in such a predicament. Everyone had choices and was responsible for their outcomes. Alōs knew that better than most.

His gaze landed on the ornate silver sandglass on his desk. It was beautifully crafted, with delicately carved leaves winding up each column, but he drew no pleasure from it. He had detested the object the very day it had been given to him. The grains always seemed to fall much too fast.

But it reflected his choices. Choices he would overcome no matter the cost.

No one survived in this world by remaining pure of heart. There was a reason the worst of the worst sat on thrones, controlled cities and men—because they were the ones willing to do what others could not stomach. Niya herself was no pure soul. He knew the fire dancer did what needed to be done to keep her position within the Thief Kingdom. Alōs had watched her and her sisters, the terrifying Mousai, commit their fair share of sins, and all in the name of their king.

So while Niya might hold spite for what Alōs had done to her those four years ago and was having her pay for now, it was a hard-taught lesson she would have learned eventually. If it hadn't been he who betrayed her, it would certainly have been another. And another after that.

In this world you had to be deadlier than the deadliest one in the room.

So just like then, when Alōs had seen an opportunity to take more from Niya, he had. Why let go of a rare beast when you had just acquired her? Someone as powerful as Niya was a useful asset. Especially when he wasn't nearly done finding all he sought.

Alōs felt over the red stone in his pinkie ring, a growing habit these days. *Yes,* he silently mused, *having her talents in my arsenal would certainly speed things along.* It *had* to.

His eyes narrowed on the silver sandglass once more.

Time was no longer a luxury.

"I'm not sure how the crew will take to her becoming one of us. Usually there's a vote."

Kintra's words brought his mind back to where they sat in his quarters, the setting sun behind him painting the room in an orange tint.

"Once *our* bounties are dropped," began Alōs, glancing toward her, "and the crew are welcomed back into the Thief Kingdom to return to their debauchery and folly, they should not care who sails aboard our ship for a year."

"Fair point," admitted Kintra.

"I'm nothing if not fair."

"I'm sure those you've sent to the Fade would beg to differ."

"Yes, I'm sure they would, given most begged quite a lot in their final moments."

"Cowards," scoffed Kintra before finishing her drink with a swig. Placing her empty glass on his desk, she stood. "Since all will go as planned, as you have assured, then tomorrow night we still sail out of the strait?"

"We still sail out of the strait," confirmed Alōs. "And when the fourth light hits, be sure to bring our guest below deck. I have a feeling she'll attempt to try better luck overboard."

"Are you sure she's worth all this trouble?"

"She's the only way the Thief King might pardon us."

Kintra watched him for a moment. "Who *is* this girl, Alōs?"

"Someone worth the trouble," answered Alōs. "Now go; I have many important things to ponder."

She gave him a mocking salute. "Aye, Captain."

As Kintra strode from his quarters, Alōs turned to watch the setting sun slip below the water, ignoring the deafening hiss of grains falling behind him as he twisted his ring, around and around. The magic inside the stone stirred, awakening his own gifts. *Hoooome,* it purred.

Alōs ignored this too.

This ship was his home. Nowhere else.

Steepling his fingers, Alōs replayed Kintra's last question.

Are you sure she's worth all this trouble?

Yes, thought Alōs. Niya was proving to be worth more than he had originally bargained for. He dared to think what more he could gain with her so near.

Soon the light in his cabin dimmed to night, and a tingling sensation circled his wrist, but Alōs didn't need to look down to know that the mark of his binding bet, in the end, would remain an outlined band—a debt to be collected.

Alōs grinned, feeling the future in his dark heart.

Victory was on the horizon.

CHAPTER SEVEN

*H*is smile is deliciously sinful, *thought Niya as the man approached. But perhaps it was so because no mask covered his handsome face. Here, an act of bold recklessness. Both traits Niya enjoyed to a dangerous extent.*

His power touched her next, a cool caress of green expanding from his body. And just like his physique, his gifts were strong, born from a long lineage, Niya knew, for her own gifts were the same.

Arabessa and Larkyra sat on either side of her in their costumed splendor, resting amid the debauchery taking place after one of their performances in the palace. Disguised court members crowded the shadowed room. Bodies were pressed up against one another as spirits were poured into mouths, dripping down hints of exposed skin before being licked clean. Hands roamed inside garments as a steady tempo of music made by a quartet of musicians in one corner twisted about the sweat- and incense-filled air. The evening had started like all the others, and Niya had assumed it would end similarly—a rather monotonous bore.

But the presence of this man, with his glowing turquoise eyes, which remained on her rather than on either of her slender sisters, and his exposed features, cut of beauty and dark allure: it awoke a swirling sensation in her gut. An anticipation. A much-needed excitement.

"Good evening," said the man, his voice a deep rumble as he stopped before them.

Niya said nothing, only watched him curiously from behind her head-dress, as she knew both her sisters did. The Mousai were meant to be seen as a fearful tool in the Thief Kingdom, pretty creatures with a lethal touch. To retain their mystery, they had to remain just that, mysterious.

"My name is Alōs Ezra," said he, black coat swirling with his flourished bow. "The lord and captain of the Crying Queen."

Ah, thought Niya, a pirate. She had heard whisperings about this Crying Queen, the ruthlessness of her growing crew, but she did not know a captain such as he claimed her.

Niya's magic swam awake, warm and bubbling, feeling her interest pique.

"I must compliment you on your performance," continued Lord Ezra. "It was quite extraordinary. If a touch dramatic."

To this Niya grinned behind her disguise. Normally those who approached them only pandered and preened. "One might say that by definition most performances," began Niya, unable to help herself, "are meant to touch on the theatrical."

"Well volleyed," said Lord Ezra, his eyes seeming to burn brighter at hearing her reply. "If ever we were to play chess, remind me to cheat, for I fear that may be the only way to win against you."

"Who said I would not be cheating as well?"

"Who indeed?" The pirate grinned, a flash of white against his brown skin.

Niya wanted to say more, play more with this tempting man, but a jab from Arabessa's gifts stopped her.

Careful, her sister's magic seemed to say.

Niya prickled but obediently remained mute.

Lord Ezra seemed to read the shift, for he bowed again, but not before meeting her gaze one last time. "I look forward to our games," he said. "Especially the cheating kind."

Not until the pirate strode away from them, disappearing into the cloaked crowd, did Niya realize he had only addressed her the entire time, never once glancing at either of her sisters.

A new smile curled onto her lips. Games, *she thought.* Niya was very fond of games.

The room in the palace shifted and changed as splotches of new visions appeared before Niya. They came and went as though she were looking up at the dancing surface of a dark sea, moonlight reflecting down, fragmented.

Niya now slipped into a shadowed corner, unseen by her sisters amid the tangling crowd of creatures in the palace, knowing he'd be waiting, his energy calling to her. Turquoise eyes glowed as he stepped forward from the darkness. Her heart beat quickly as he tenderly grazed a finger down her costumed form. The scent of sea clinging to his clothes invaded her headdress, the scent of midnight orchids in the crook of his neck, pulling her closer. His ever-present power, a refreshing tingling enveloping her heat, shielding them during all those soirees in the kingdom. The deep coo of his compliments and clever replies each night, his desperation for her as his burning gaze bored into her disguise.

"I love you, fire dancer," he rumbled while running a finger along her covered neck, down, down, daringly close to her breasts.

Niya's magic erupted in her chest at hearing his words, her body, for the first time, not knowing what to do, how to react. She breathed heavily, her skin aching in a way she had never known. "Alōs," she whispered.

"Yes," he purred. "That is my name, but what is yours? Let me know you, fire dancer. Or is that what I am to forever call you?"

He only needed a first name, a tiny glimpse of skin to go with her tempting curves, the color of her hair so he could hold the shade close to his heart. He had shown himself so freely to her, after all, his sinner's smiles, his unwavering attention. It was for her, *only for her; could she not do the same?*

"Alōs," she could only respond in agony. "Alōs."

"Alōs." Niya bolted upright, a cold sweat blanketing her as his name disappeared on her lips. She blinked to pure black.

Heart racing, she snapped her fingers, bringing alive a tiny flame to burst from her palm.

The windowless cabin stretched out before her. Niya was still aboard the *Crying Queen*.

The lantern beside her cot must have snuffed out while she slept. When she threw her flame inside, the wick lit with a hiss, bringing more light to her room, before Niya collapsed back into her hammock, gripping her hands into fists.

Her body felt hot and frigid at once. Her magic swam inside her veins in confusion along with her thoughts. Was she upset? Angry? Pleased? Happy? Experiencing pleasure or pain?

By the lost gods. She dared not close her eyes again.

It appeared even in sleep she would be haunted. Memories she had believed she had pushed desperately from her mind roared to life like some resurrected beast.

It's Alōs's magic, thought Niya grumpily. *Being around it for so long has set loose the visions.*

Visions of when she might have been clever but had ultimately been naive. Though a part of her of course had known of Alōs's danger then, felt it in each of his words, temptation was sweet for a reason: it masked the bitterness of poison underneath. Camouflaged the destruction lurking below the surface, waiting to take hold once you gave in. And after months of courtship, give in Niya finally did. A moment of ecstasy for a lifetime of regret. A young girl's fantasy: that she was the one exception to a monster's loveless heart.

As it turned out, her life was to be not a love story but a cautionary tale.

Look here, children; here is a story of how not to be.

Niya grunted, pushing away her self-deprecating ghosts as she stood.

"Today I will leave all this behind," Niya said to the empty room, straightening her shoulders. Today was the third day. The final day. *But all is well,* thought Niya as she pushed away that ever-creeping fear. *Today my sisters will come, and I will never have to think of that man and that stupid night again. Today I will be set free.*

Niya felt trapped. For this morning, more than any of the others, the pirate lord's cool energy was a consistent needling along her back.

She might have been standing the farthest she could from him, gripping the railing along the bow of the ship while he stood at the other end, beside the *Crying Queen*'s wheel, but she knew his gaze was upon her.

She always knew.

The flutter of her magic seemed to pick up speed, her heat responding to his touch of cold.

In fact, she felt him everywhere she walked. His presence was spread across every board on this ship, a slip of icy-green haze that whispered, *Mine. All of this is mine. Including you.*

Niya hated it. Just as she now hated the sea.

The open fresh air: too windy.

The peaceful waters: monotonous.

The constant sun against her skin: a recipe for sweat, wrinkles, and sunburn.

Her magic buzzed impatiently in her veins as she stared at the ever-empty horizon. She half believed she could will a portal door into existence, one that would reveal a ship with two figures in black robes and gold masks sailing toward her.

But her hope felt fleeting, a fish believing it was the hunter to the dangling worm. Not the hunted. Not the caught.

"I must know," came a deep voice from behind her. "Do you feel standing in the blazing sun all day will have them find you sooner?"

Niya had sensed Alōs drawing nearer, but she had hoped it was to speak with one of his nearby pirates.

She took in a calming breath before meeting his turquoise gaze as he stopped beside her. His dark hair was loose around his shoulders, his angular features made softer in the morning light. "Why, Alōs, that is so kind of you to be concerned at all with how I feel."

A lilt of an amused grin. "It is my duty to care for all my pirates."

"I am *not* one of your pirates."

"Not yet."

Niya clenched her teeth together, anger flaring as she turned back to the endless sea before them. *Just ignore him,* she thought. *If I ignore him, he'll go away.*

"Speaking of becoming one of my crew, you know you cannot continue to sleep in that private cabin after today," explained Alōs from where he annoyingly remained beside her. "You'll be bunking with the rest of the pirates below deck."

"After today I will be back home with my sisters."

Alōs tsked. "All these years, and you still have not learned that optimism is a fool's step forward. It will always have you falling into a ditch."

"Well, I'm glad we can at least both agree that this ship is a real pit."

"This ship," said Alōs, a rare edge entering his tone, "is the fastest and most sought-after vessel in all of Aadilor."

Niya blinked up at him, a stir of elation that she had found a weakness in the mountain of stone. "Are you sure? I had heard that the *Wild Widow* was the fastest in Aadilor. It certainly is bigger."

"Which is precisely what makes it *slower,*" countered Alōs. "The *Wild Widow* could never keep up with the *Queen.*"

"Care to wager?"

Alōs met her gaze before his eyes traveled to her crooked grin. "Gladly," he began. "But it won't get you out of the bind you've once again tied yourself in."

Niya's smile dropped.

"I see the reality of your predicament has returned," he continued. "Good. Now, do not torture yourself further, fire dancer, by standing here getting burned. I invite you to take a reprieve. We can sit in my nicely shaded quarters and discuss what your role will be here. I'll even pour us a bit of whiskey as a peace offering."

Niya was astonished she had not tried to throw him overboard already.

"So long as I remain on this ship," said Niya, hating how her voice shook with her rage, "there will be *nothing* peaceful between us, pirate."

Alōs studied her a long moment. His smooth features remaining a placid lake. "Very well," he said at last, "but know it is you who has set the tone of your new beginning here, not I. And be warned, no matter how difficult you may think you can be, I promise, you have no idea how difficult having me as your captain can become."

With that, Alōs strode from her, his movements those of a graceful king returning to his throne beside the wheel.

Niya growled in frustration as she spun around to grip the banister.

Kill him, her magic replied to her fury. *Burn him to nothing but bone.*

I wish, she thought, glaring down at her binding bet. Once this blasted thing was off her wrist, by the stars and sea, she would certainly try.

How dare he act as though the results of their bet were already cemented.

The pompous arse!

He's only trying to get into my head, she reasoned, attempting to calm herself.

But sticks, where were her sisters?

This was its own form of torture, standing still. Waiting.

Niya was not used to waiting.

She took matters into her own hands, but what could she do presently?

Niya tensed as an idea gripped her. Spinning her hands, she sent a burst of her magic into the air. And then another. Forming orange clouds of smoke to float higher and higher.

Signals.

Any with the Sight *had* to see them, even at a far distance.

Why hadn't she thought of this before?

For the rest of the day, she remained exactly where she was, sending her colorful magic into the azure sky. She desperately pushed past the ache in her body as her magic became exhausted, depleted.

Rest, it whimpered. *Rest.*

But she couldn't. Her time was almost up.

But in the end her gifts decided for her, when she was only able to produce the smallest wiggle of steam from her fingers.

Niya slumped against the banister, breathing heavily, wanting to lie down, to sleep. By some miracle she didn't. She kept staring at the empty horizon. Hoping, wishing, that anyone had seen her magic. Hoping and wishing even when Kintra came to give her bread and water; it remained untouched and became sullied in the heat and salt air. She remained as still as the horizon in front of her as the sun began to set, throwing out a dark blanket of stars.

Niya stared and waited, strangling her growing panic. She became unmoving, unfeeling. She could almost believe herself becoming a statue, the kind that lived on in myth.

The girl stood so long unblinking that she did not notice when the wood of the ship grew up, over, and around her, claiming her soul. If you look carefully, my child, at every passing vessel, you might see a woman carved into the bow, forlorn in her frozen scream. For that is indeed the Crying Queen.

As if the lost gods had heard her fears, eventually a sliver of light cut across the dark water, a slowly ascending knife dragging across her heart as the sun rose.

Nononononononono.

Niya's final plea thrashed wildly in her mind, raked down her skin. She stood on the deck, captured in her disbelief, her nails cutting into the banister, her breaths all used up.

Her left wrist began to tingle, but she would not look down, would *not* watch the black band of her binding bet inking its last stretch and filling in completely. Her debt, her chains. *A year,* it whispered. *A year.*

Niya stared into the center of the sun as though she could force it back beneath the surface.

It did not yield.

The sun rose, proud and defiant, above the Obasi Sea. Niya's free will swallowed up by light as her eyes began to throb and water.

Tears of pain.

The first light of the fourth day awoke bright, new, and calm—an utter nightmare.

Chapter Eight

Niya remembered little of how she'd come to be blindfolded, hog-tied, and then bound and secured some more in a holding cell that sat deep in the belly of the *Crying Queen*.

There had been a lot of screaming.

She remembered that.

As well as quite a bit of blood, none her own, of course, dirtying her face and clothes further.

As soon as the fourth day had broken fully, Niya had lost all reason.

She had to get off this blasted boat!

Present binding bets be damned.

As she stared down into the churning sea cutting against the bow, she barely batted an eye at the prospect of the Fade taking her if she did not survive the dive toward her escape. Alōs could find her in the land of the dead to serve her sentence. Sanity was a thing of the past now.

Unfortunately, her plans were quickly foiled. Before she could get a foot up on the banister, she felt them approach, ten of the strongest crew.

"Come to take in the view with me?" she asked the group, inching closer to the ledge.

"We have instructions to take ye below," said a hulking man, eyes narrowed beneath his stringy hair, which was pasted over his brow, as he calculated her stance.

"Thank you," said Niya, gripping the railing. "But I prefer it up here."

"It ain't a request," explained a woman, gray braids hanging to her waist. Niya sensed she was one of the few crew members who held the gifts.

Niya's own magic jumped alive then, ready to fight.

"Captain's orders," another added.

Niya's scowl deepened.

It did not sit well that Alōs had predicted her next move.

Nevertheless, she did not wait long to act.

Niya turned and jumped onto the ledge, kicking away the outstretched arms she felt reaching for her, but there were too many limbs compared to her two feet. With a tug to her pants, the crew pulled her back to the deck, grasping tightly every inch of her body.

"If you value your lives, you will let me go," she growled, twisting and thrashing as best she could. Her skin began to heat with her magic, intent to *burn burn burn.*

"That's exactly why we won't," grunted the gray-haired woman, calloused hands only gripping tighter as a hard surface expanded from her palm, shielding her from Niya's growing heat. Blue mist stretched out.

Magic, thought Niya.

"Cap'n's bite is far worse than yers," said the oily man from earlier, bending close to her ear.

"I can assure you," said Niya, teeth gritted, "it is not." With a headbutt to the man's temple and a bite to the shoulder of the woman, Niya bent low before popping up to blast off the rest of the pirates' grasps. Spinning, she swiped up two pirates' blades from their hips, caring little as she slashed through skin, her breaths coming like cannon blasts in her desperation to escape.

Niya twisted and twirled, bent and skipped over limbs lunging toward her. She was nearly able to scramble back toward the ship's rail when their numbers doubled. The pirates slid down from ropes and masts and poured out from below deck. *By the lost gods,* she thought, *are there any left to sail the ship?*

Niya had begun to pull forward her magic once more, too ready to char them all to cinders, but the next thing she remembered through her white rage was an anvil of weight knocking her to the deck. Bodies, dozens of them, piled above her as she wriggled and screamed. Crew members yelled as well, calling for more aid as she pulled in energy from their movement, a dizzying sensation as she transferred it into her gift, using it to singe them off. Their clothes caught her magic, eliciting flames before buckets of salt water and sand were thrown on top of them. The sizzle of steam. She coughed and wheezed as a cool presence was suddenly above her.

Alōs's blue gaze was bone chilling but unmoved as he watched her growl and curse like the beast she was as his crew pinned her to the deck.

"Ensure she cannot move a pinkie," his deep voice had rumbled as he'd thrown more ropes to one of his pirates. Alōs's was the last face she had seen before a blindfold had covered her eyes and she'd been dragged away.

Niya growled from where she currently lay on the damp floor of her holding cell.

She felt like an animal, and not in a good way.

Her sight was taken by her blindfold, every stitch of her bound tight by rope and chain. Arms and legs bent painfully back behind her and bound together. Even her fingers were meticulously pinched into place.

Her awareness felt frazzled, the grace of her movements stolen.

"I'm going to kill you all!" she screamed, her voice hoarse, throat aching.

She was only met with the creaks and rocking of the boat.

With a groan, she managed to roll from her belly to her side.

How has this happened? How have I ended up here?

You have an anger problem. Arabessa's words, which seemed so long ago now, slithered over Niya's memory mockingly.

By the lost gods, how Niya hated when Arabessa was right.

Perhaps if she had not reacted so impulsively on deck, she'd be back in her small compartment, able to think more clearly to search for a way out.

Instead she had dug herself into a deeper hole, and now she was growing more and more resigned that she might never crawl out.

Her sisters had not come.

They had not come, and Alōs still held their identities in the palm of his hand, as well as her servitude for a year.

Niya had ruined everything.

She was a horrible sister.

A traitorous daughter.

She deserved every bit of pain she now suffered.

Tears finally ran hot down her cheeks.

Niya despised crying—she thought it a useless expense of energy—but she was no longer in control of herself.

With her arms beginning to tingle, the first sign they were falling asleep, she felt herself giving in to her fate, her fight leaving.

No, hissed her magic, twisting uncomfortably in her gut at sensing her resignation. *We are most powerful. We are most deadly. We will have our revenge. We will!*

"How?" she whispered, almost whimpered.

In tiiiiiime, her gifts cooed. *When they least expect it.*

"Yes," muttered Niya, encouragement brewing. "Yes."

Her magic was right. She was one of the Mousai.

I have melted flesh from bone, she thought. *I have stripped smiles from the most ruthless.*

"You will know my wrath!" screamed Niya into the compartment, her last push of energy, before she began to laugh.

It was an unhinged sound, even to her own ears, but she could not stop.

With her cheek pressed into the dirty floor, her limbs twisted and numb, she laughed and laughed and laughed.

Because though her sisters hadn't come, they would.

Despite her current captivity, it would take more than this to break Niya and, more importantly, Niya's faith in her sisters.

They *would* come.

And once reunited, they'd send more than a few new souls to the Fade.

CHAPTER NINE

Niya awoke to the sound of boots shuffling into her cell. Rough hands lifted her by her arms and hauled her up two flights of stairs. The air grew fresher with each of their strides, before she was deposited with an *oof* onto a hard floor.

"Cut her legs loose, but keep her arms and hands chained down," came Alōs's deep command.

"You sure, Cap'n?" asked a gruff voice. "She's a crazy sort of bird, she is. Better to stuff or eat her lot than keep 'em as pets."

Niya spat on the boots she sensed in front of her.

"OY!"

Niya's face whipped back with the hit, the side of her mouth burning as the taste of blood blossomed along her tongue. Alōs barked an order for his man to stand down. "Her spit is the cleanest thing on you, Burlz. Now do as I say."

With a muttered grumble, Niya's wrists were tugged and bolted down behind her, to an anchor on the floor, before her legs were freed. She held in a cry as blood rushed painfully back into them and she was forced to kneel. Still blindfolded, all Niya could concentrate on was the agony lacing through her body, her muscles having been twisted awkwardly for too long.

Water was roughly poured into her mouth, and she gulped and spluttered greedily, the liquid warm as it ran down the front of her shirt.

With a tug, her blindfold was pulled away, and Niya squinted at her new surroundings.

She was in the captain's quarters. Moonlight streamed in through a large paned window at her back. Standing candelabras lit the dim space, sending flickers of warmth along the bookshelves. Kintra and the man whom she now assumed was Burlz, the oily oaf whom she had fought with on deck, stood by one of the two closed doors in the room.

Niya knelt beside a large mahogany desk, Alōs peering down at her like some dark wildcat from his chair. "Two of my men are covered in stitches," he began. "Three others are still in the infirmary with severe burns from your tantrum yesterday."

"Is that all?" Niya attempted to sound bored.

"You will pay for your actions." Alōs's gaze was steady. "And I fear the sentencing will be decided by my crew."

Niya glanced to Burlz, taking in his grin and the way his black eyes promised pain.

Try me, she wanted to snarl in return. His slap would not go unpunished.

"I vote they throw me overboard," suggested Niya. "Anything to get me off this bloody ship."

"It is too bad you feel that way," replied Alōs coolly. "For that will make your next year here rather uncomfortable."

"I will return whatever discomfort I suffer tenfold," ground out Niya, pulling against her binds, the shackles straining against her wrist.

"You should really work on not always putting up a fight," said Alōs, leaning into his chair. "Your life would be much more enjoyable if you did. Take mine, for example. I get most of what I want with barely lifting a finger."

"Then you won't miss them when I cut them from your hand."

Alōs arched one dark brow. "Despite appearances, they'll be happy to see you're much the same."

"Who?"

"The Mousai, of course." Alōs grinned. "They've arrived."

Niya blinked, confused for a moment.

And then—

A *BOOM* shook the room, sending books tumbling from their shelves and the candelabras swaying. Niya steadied herself on her knees as a high-pitched note pulsed through the floorboards from above—more heavy objects hit the deck overhead.

By the Obasi Sea. Her magic erupted through her with her burst of adrenaline. *My sisters, they are here!*

Niya smiled, wide and sharp. "None of your crew will survive their wrath."

"Kintra," Alōs said to his quartermaster. "Let our guests know where we keep what they seek before there's no longer a ship for them to search."

Kintra quickly exited through the door she guarded.

"Burlz," commanded Alōs. "I'm sure you'd like to do the honors."

The large man held vengeance in his eyes as he removed a piece of cloth from his trouser pocket, stepping toward Niya.

"I'm sorry to have to do this," Alōs explained, gaze holding no empathy, "but I can't have you interrupting our negotiations."

Niya tried shifting away from Burlz, but chained to a floor, she didn't get far. The pirate tightly cinched the cloth into a gag between her lips, making her wince. "Just a preview of what I'll be doing to ya later, sweetheart," whispered Burlz, his oniony breath causing her eyes to water. With his threat, Niya's magic wrestled along her skin, and she snapped forward with a muffled growl.

Burlz smiled as he retreated to the wall.

You'll be the first sent to the Fade, thought Niya.

There were more shouts from above, a smashing of barrels, before all fell silent.

Only the hissing of grains through a silver sandglass on Alōs's desk could be heard.

Niya's gaze swung to the closed door.

Her heart was beating like stampeding beasts, and she attempted to settle herself, to calm the chaos of the past few days that kept her magic a tumbled mess in her veins. She needed her focus. She needed it so she could find the movements that belonged to *them*. Her sisters were here. Her sisters were *finally* here. And she homed in on that thought, that security.

Closing her eyes, Niya breathed deeply, settling the buzz vibrating through her. She could feel through walls better that way, sense what was beyond. Even as weak as she was, she managed a light search, pulling energy from the movement on deck to stretch out her magic. It crawled out from her skin like mist, rolled along the floor, and slipped under the door, hitting up against every object that moved and swayed—a net holding boxes, the heavy shuffling of feet—until . . .

There, the familiar spice of energy, the delicate movements of limbs, swishing robes. Energy she *knew*.

"Fascinating," she heard Alōs say beside her, but she ignored him, ignored that he could see the orange and red trails of her magic flowing from her, searching his ship. Ignored whatever sort of power that might give him through understanding more of her abilities.

All Niya cared about were the footsteps getting closer, and then . . .

Niya's eyes flew open as the door did. Kintra walked in, followed by figures wearing black hooded robes and expressionless gold masks. Two tall, one short. They swept into the middle of the room like smoke, taking up the entire space. Their magic was charged, pulsing, ancient, and catastrophic in that it was a grain's fall away from being set loose. It hummed its rage.

Let us show you how we greet our enemies.

91

Niya had never seen the Mousai from this vantage point, given that she was usually in the shorter imposter's place, but she delighted in how terrifying they seemed. Niya met the gazes of the two taller Mousai—Larkyra and Arabessa, her sisters.

Something in her chest lurched. How good it was to see them. How devastated she was for when they would find out what she had done.

As she watched her sisters' eyes roam her extremely disheveled form, a darker intensity of their magic expanded around them like storm clouds rolling in.

The door to their chamber slammed shut, bolt locking with a click. The candelabras' lights dimmed, shadows stretching unnaturally.

Oh yes, thought Niya. Her sisters were *furious.*

Good, hissed her magic.

Yes, agreed Niya. *Here lies my revenge.*

Alōs remained seated, hands folded over his chest in repose, as the Mousai swung their attention back to him.

"There was already a bounty on your head, Lord Ezra," spoke the middle Mousai, whom Niya knew by her voice was Arabessa. "But kidnapping a favorite court guest of the Thief King does not bode well for any mercy he may have granted."

"Mercy?" Alōs's brows rose. "Is the king getting soft in his old age?"

A shriek flew from the other Mousai—Larkyra—and with a single note, she sent a standing candelabra crashing through a windowpane behind the pirate.

Alōs pushed back a lock of dark hair that had been blown into his face. "If you didn't like the decor, I could have had those removed a different way."

"Our orders are clear, pirate," boomed Arabessa. "Retrieve this lady and bring you to the Thief King. If you don't wish to come, we kill you here. Those are your options."

"That is clear." Alōs steepled his fingers as he leaned farther back. "But before you do either, could you answer me this? Was it easy to replace her so fast?" He peered directly at the shorter Mousai.

It was a nonsense question to any but those who *knew*, which made it perfect. Here was Alōs Ezra, the reptile who need not grow hands, for he got what he wanted without lifting a finger. A snake.

The Mousai remained silent, but Niya could feel the energy shift, the new tension in her two sisters' shoulders. This was the moment when her foolishness cursed her family. *I'm so sorry!* she wanted to yell. *I'm so sorry!* All she managed was a moan through her gag.

Larkyra's gaze momentarily flashed to her, questions lingering.

"I see I may have granted myself a third option?" queried Alōs. "Shall we have a private conversation?"

The door behind the Mousai unlocked and swung open—their answer.

Alōs glanced a silent command to Kintra and Burlz: *Leave.*

Dutifully they turned and strode from the room, closing the door again behind them.

Taking a sip from a goblet on his desk, Alōs waved a hand, sending a cool green veil of his magic to settle along the walls, coating the new hole in his window. "Now we may speak in confidence."

"And what secrets do you wish to share that will have us spare your life?" the disguised Larkyra asked.

"My secrets are in fact *your* secrets. But a trade can make me forget them."

"Speak plainly, Lord Ezra."

"In so many words, I find it fascinating that there are three of you standing before me, when one of the Mousai kneels by my feet." He gestured toward Niya beside his desk.

Her entire world cracked open. Unable to bring herself to look at her sisters, she concentrated on a spot on the floor. *Coward,* she thought, hating what might come next. *What will they do? What will they say?*

The silence was thick as Niya's heart continued to break, over and over and over, waiting.

"That's right." Alōs finally spoke again. "Your beloved Niya exposed who the Mousai truly are, and I must say, it's my great pleasure to finally officially meet the Bassettes."

Betrayal betrayal betrayal. The word rang harsh in Niya's ears as she felt the knife-sharp gazes of her sisters.

She winced where she knelt, still unable to look up despite how their magic smacked against her with their shock.

How? Why?

Both questions Niya had tormented herself with for years. How could she have allowed herself to be lured, seduced, her own powers used against her? For what? To feel wanted, that extra spark of reckless excitement?

Pathetic.

There was a flurry of movement as the shortest Mousai threw off their robe and removed their mask. Their form grew a great deal taller than any in the room. A man stood before them, wrapped in purple silk pants and an intricate pearl-studded choker that fanned out over his bare chest. His black skin shone like a moonless night against his thick beard, his violet eyes gleaming.

Achak—one of the most ancient beings this side of the Fade—was here. They were a creature whose history was woven into that of the Thief Kingdom. And just like Alōs, they never donned a disguise while there.

When everything feared you, there was nothing to fear.

"How clever you have proved yourself, Alōs," said Achak, his voice starting deep before lilting into a higher register. In the next breath his figure rippled, arms and shoulders shrinking to become those of a woman. For Achak was in fact a brother and sister, two souls wrestling back and forth for space in one body. They shape-shifted from one to the other whenever one desired to speak, often dizzying present company. No one knew their exact origin, but thankfully they had been a friend and teacher to the Mousai since they'd first come into their gifts. Thankfully, because to be a foe of Achak meant one rarely lived long enough to attempt becoming friends. Achak was powerful, erratic, and, above all, the guardian to the entrance of the Fade.

"Clever." The sister echoed her brother's words, adjusting a silver band wrapping her forearm. "But still rather predictable."

"Well," began Alōs, "no one can be as unpredictable as you, my dear Achak. I'm glad to see the Thief King let you out of your floating cage."

Achak grinned, white teeth flashing, and quickly changed back into her brother. "Child, don't you know goading only works on the weak minded? Now tell us your demands so we can all be on our way. It smells of feces in here."

"That's probably her." Alōs pointed to Niya.

Niya stared death toward the pirate, fury heating her heart.

"This is ridiculous," said Larkyra, removing her mask next and pushing down her hood to reveal her delicate features. "The only demands are that we'll be taking our sister before or after taking your life. You choose."

Relief washed through Niya. Larkyra had called her *sister*, not *dead-to-me sister* or *wretched creature* or *spineless mole*.

Could it be that they would forgive her this treachery?

"Nice to finally see your beautiful face, Larkyra. And may I extend my congratulations on your recent nuptials." Alōs played idly with the ring on his pinkie, still exuding control. "As for killing me, Niya had similar plans, but as Achak probably already knows and you ladies should learn, I have contingencies to all plans."

"Very well." Arabessa was the final one to remove her disguise. Her inky-black hair was twisted into a high bun, her angular beauty another severe mask as she stared down the pirate. "Tell us why we should still be listening to you."

"If you kill me, the secret I know of the Bassettes' connection with the Mousai is hidden around Aadilor waiting to be revealed. But I can destroy all knowledge for a trade."

"You bluff." Arabessa eyed the man.

"I could be. The question is, Can you live with the risk of finding out?"

Risks, bets, wagers. All of Niya's vices playing out before her eyes, and her family had to pay the price.

If we get out of here, she thought, *I swear by the lost gods I'll never bet on anything again.*

"What is your bargain, then?" asked Arabessa.

"I'll sign over my silence, ensuring destruction of the memory stones that hold all I know of the Mousai, and will release your sister with no fight, if the Thief King removes his charges from me and my crew."

"No!" groaned Niya against her gag, wrestling with the shackles pinning her arms back. "It's a trick!" Alōs might destroy the memory stones and remove her chains, but she'd still be obligated to serve him for a year. Such a trade would not remove their binding bet. Her sisters had to understand this! They had to figure out another way to ensure her true freedom.

"That is a heavy trade," said Arabessa, ignoring Niya's struggles. "A favor to us from the Thief King as well as a pardon to you."

"I have faith that he will see the importance of one to allow the other."

"It seems your faith might be misplaced. The king does not take threats lightly, nor does he bend to any other's will. You might find all four of us outcasts in the end or, more likely, new residents of the Fade."

"Perhaps, but I'm willing to roll that die."

"Do you really value your life so little?" challenged Arabessa.

"Quite the opposite. I merely have more to gain than lose at the moment."

"Are you sure that's true, *Lord* Ezra?" asked Achak, seeming to say a great deal more than what was spoken.

Niya took note of how Alōs's gaze narrowed.

"Do we have a deal or not?" he asked.

The room hung suspended, a free fall from a high cliff, as her sisters both turned, looking at Niya. The weight of their stares slammed a new dagger into her heart. Larkyra was frowning, pain rimming her eyes, obviously wishing to do a thousand things. Arabessa, however, remained poised as ever; nothing in her features revealed how she truly felt seeing her younger sister tied and mangled on the floor. Niya didn't know whose expression was worse.

"Achak," said Arabessa, attention remaining locked on Niya, "do you have a Secret Sealer?"

"Always travel with one." Achak pulled out a small, intricately carved silver cylinder from their trouser pocket.

"But what of the pardon?" asked Larkyra.

"As it turns out, the king gave me one of those before we left."

A room of surprised eyes turned to Achak; even Alōs's dark brows lifted.

"Children, need I remind you he's the Thief King, of the *Thief Kingdom*?" explained Achak. "If he can't predict the mind of swindlers and crooks, who can?" With a snap of their fingers, a small glowing amber cube appeared, hovering above the palm of Achak's hand—a king's pardon.

Niya watched Alōs's hungry gaze devour the object. Something so small that meant so much.

"So we have a trade?" asked Larkyra.

"It appears we do," said Alōs, grinning.

Wait! No! Niya thrashed further. She pulled and pulled and pulled against her chains, the wood floorboards creaking under the force. Her sisters only needed to glance at the mark around her wrist; then they would know, but there was a reason Alōs had bound her arms so tightly behind her back. *The bastard!*

"By the lost gods." Larkyra moved toward Niya's struggles. "This is insufferable."

Alōs quickly stepped from behind his desk, blocking her way. "She will be all yours once it's official."

Larkyra's eyes narrowed, assessing the imposing pirate.

By the lost gods, if only Niya had more energy so she could gather enough power to burn through the metal shackling her. Currently she could do no more than warm them up. She was so blasted tired. She needed sleep, food, and a dozen baths.

"Fine," said Larkyra impatiently. "Let's make this official, then. Niya handed over to us, along with your silence on our identities, all knowledge hidden destroyed, in return for you and your crew's pardon in the Thief Kingdom."

"And no killing this night," added Alōs.

"And no killing by or of either party this night," agreed Arabessa from behind them.

"*Vexturi.*" Alōs smiled, a snake's smile, as he extended a hand.

"*Vexturi,*" said Larkyra, shaking it.

"*Vexturi,*" echoed Arabessa, stepping forward to do the same.

NO! Niya let out a last muffled scream. *Noooooooo!*

She slumped, defeated, as she watched her sisters shake the pirate's hand.

The rest of the trade went quickly. Achak captured a prick of blood from Alōs's finger with the Secret Sealer, binding him silent regarding their secret lest he find himself without a tongue, before dropping the pardon in his palm. The glowing golden cube spun warmth along Alōs's brown skin as he held it up, eyes gleaming with triumph. Niya felt queasy. Next Alōs gave her sisters a list of where his memory stones were hidden to be destroyed, signing the parchment with a truth oath.

It was done.

Just like that.

As Alōs approached her to remove her gag and binds, he and Niya locked eyes.

His turquoise depths held no hint of his feelings; only apathy swam in his dark heart.

In Niya's, only hate.

"I will have my revenge," she hissed once her muzzle was removed.

"Not for a while," he replied, tone even.

Niya's magic hit against her veins—*we hate we hate we hate*—but then her sisters were pulling her to them, and her mind was on an entirely different matter.

"I'm so sorry," she heard herself say, her voice a raw mess, her heart and body a pool of pain. She was eternally sorry, for forcing them to make such a trade, for revealing their secrets, for her smell, for everything. "I'm so sorry," she repeated again and again.

Larkyra shushed her, holding her tight. "All will be well. All *is* well."

"No, you don't under—"

"We can discuss this mess once we're off the ship," assured Larkyra, gently placing one of their robes around her shoulders.

The small act of kindness destroyed Niya further, especially when Alōs spoke from behind them.

"I'm afraid your sister will be staying."

"Excuse me?" Larkyra turned, brows raised.

"Niya may no longer be my prisoner, but she won't be leaving."

"What are you playing at, Lord Ezra?" Arabessa stepped closer to Niya.

Alōs's cool gaze found Niya's once more. "Shall you tell them or shall I?"

She wanted to tell *him* a thousand things, all sharp and bloody and painful, but her throat had seized in her panic at the prospect of disappointing her sisters further. *How have I messed this up so thoroughly?*

"Tell us what?" asked Arabessa. "What is going on?"

Alōs pulled up his coat sleeve, revealing his wrist and the black-outlined band that sat against his brown skin, empty, a debt waiting to be repaid.

Her sisters glanced at the mark with confusion, and then . . .

"No." Arabessa turned to Niya, voice a whisper. "No."

Niya closed her eyes, forcing back the tears that sat hot and ready.

"Tell us this isn't—" Arabessa snapped her mouth closed as Niya lifted her arm, displaying her chafed red wrist and the black mark of her binding bet—filled, a debt waiting to be paid.

"Niya," breathed Arabessa. "What have you done now?"

CHAPTER TEN

"What do you mean, you're leaving without me?" Niya watched in horror as Arabessa pulled up her black hood, instructing Larkyra to do the same. "Didn't you hear what I said?"

Niya had just finished explaining the reason for her binding bet, trying her best to ignore the penetrating eyes of the pirate lord, who stood watching by his desk. She refused to see Alōs's smug expression. Hadn't he done enough? Hadn't he won enough? Niya wished she could remove the blade at his hip and ram it clean through his chest. If she wouldn't die in the process, of course.

Argh! This is maddening!

"We all heard what you said," explained Arabessa. "Which is why we're leaving."

"*With* me," Niya clarified, staying her sister's hand as she went to put on her mask. "Listen, Ara, I know you are mad—okay, furious," she quickly corrected, seeing her sister's incensed gaze harden. "I mean, by the souls in the Fade, *I'm* furious at me. But please, don't you see? I was trying to put a final stop to all this. I was trying to fix it."

"Yes, and you appear to walk on quicksand," she replied curtly. "Always getting more entrenched in the mess you're trying to escape. A binding bet? How could you, Niya?"

"If you had found me *sooner*"—Niya's voice shook with her sudden anger, her desperation—"I wouldn't be in this mess at all!"

Arabessa's brows nearly rose to her hairline. "I fail to see how *any* of this is our fault. Did we not just secure our identities after *you* revealed them?"

"You're right; I'm sorry." Niya's cheeks burned. "I didn't mean that. I am grateful. *Of course* I am. It's just that . . . I didn't know what to do. You must understand, since that night . . . the things I have done to try to fix this on my own. I never meant . . . that is . . . it wasn't supposed to happen this way."

"Niya," said Larkyra gently. "How *did* it happen? How did he learn who we are? If he tortured you for the information, we'll find our venge—"

"I did not lay a finger on her." Alōs's cool voice slipped through their conversation. "Not a painful one, anyway. She willingly showed herself to me—isn't that right, my fire dancer?"

"I am not *your* anything," Niya spat.

"Perhaps we should all take a seat and a deep breath," suggested Achak, waving their hand to produce chairs.

Arabessa ignored them as she turned toward Niya with a frown. "What is he talking about?"

"Yes," Larkyra agreed. "What happened, Niya?"

Alone.

She stood alone.

"I was young," began Niya.

"This will definitely be a long one," muttered Achak as they settled into a chair.

No one else moved.

"And stupid," continued Niya, wanting more than anything *not* to discuss this with Alōs in the room. "But the mistake hasn't and *won't* be made again. The details are not important."

"*Young?*" Arabessa turned to the pirate. "How long have you known our secret, Lord Ezra?"

"Did I not just say the details don't matter?" Niya cut in.

"They matter very much," countered Arabessa. "You put all of our lives at risk."

"Please," Niya pleaded, her magic swirling chaotically with her desperation. "Let us go home. I can explain it all after a bath, or twelve, and then you can decide my punishment."

"Dear," said Larkyra gently. "We all know it is the king who will decide that."

"Yes." Arabessa fixed her gaze on Niya. "He shall. In the meantime, it seems our sister has stumbled into her own punishment. She will remain here to pay out her debt to Lord Ezra."

"I shall not!"

"You have no choice. Do you not understand how a binding bet works? Your every move is traceable. It's to ensure you won't skip out on payment. The bet's winner can locate the loser wherever, whenever."

"Yes, of course I know this, but—"

"And no magic can break it." Arabessa charged on. "Not even creatures as powerful as Achak. Hence why it's called a *binding* bet."

Niya floundered, a new panic seizing her. "That can't be true."

"Afraid so, my child," said Achak, now in the brother's form, where he reclined in their chair, eyes sympathetic. "As hard as it is to hear, your sister speaks true. About the binding bet and you remaining here. The Thief King will never allow you back into the kingdom as part of the Mousai with such a chain. Wherever you go in Aadilor, Alōs can know. Any secret place you hold dear in Jabari can and will be tracked. You're a walking liability until your debt is paid."

Niya clenched her jaw. "But . . . but I *can't* stay here for a year!" said Niya, imploring her sisters, Achak, *anyone*.

"Do you have any broken bones?" asked Arabessa.

"Uh, no."

"Have you caught some sickness or disease you'd presently need a healer for?"

"I don't think so . . ."

"Are you scared for your life aboard this ship?"

Niya considered this. "Not exactly, but I—"

"Then I see no reason why you would need to first leave."

"How about a *bath*," Niya bit out.

"Yes." Larkyra wrinkled her nose. "She does rather need one of those."

"Unnecessary," interjected Alōs from where he had been watching the entire exchange, leaning against the edge of his desk, boredom in his features. "We may be scoundrels, but we can, at the very least, appear respectable. Now that you're a part of my crew, you'll most certainly be getting a washing. I am sorry to say those clothes we've already provided you were your only pair. But their current soiled state is your own doing, of course."

"Argh!" Niya charged him, her magic bubbling to the surface along with her rage, but Arabessa snagged her arm, pulling her back.

"Stop this," she demanded. "Have you learned nothing from your hot-tempered outbursts? You cannot always act on your every whim and feeling. Maybe then you will stop finding yourself in these situations."

"Sound advice that I myself have tried explaining to her," said Alōs, examining his nails.

Niya bit down her scathing reply, her body shaking with fury. *He will suffer. He wiiiiiilll,* promised her gifts. But then Niya met her older sister's eyes and took in the disappointment that hung there. Her anger left her in a whoosh.

Despite her best efforts, Niya's lip began to quiver, her eyes filling with tears.

Arabessa's hold softened then, and she tugged Niya and Larkyra toward the other side of the room. Away from the pirate.

"Listen." Arabessa spoke calmly but sternly, a mother to delinquent children. "We do not know how the Thief King will respond to being forced to make such a trade for us. You will be punished, no doubt. He may add a longer sentence for you or something worse—"

"Nothing could be worse than that." Niya quickly wiped at her eyes.

"We *also* do not know what discipline Father will decide for you," Arabessa continued. "What you revealed, Niya . . ."

"I know." Niya balled her hands into fists. "By the lost gods, *I know.*"

Empathy finally entered Arabessa's eyes. "Yes, it seems you do. So know this as well: We will ensure the current debt you must pay out to the pirate will be considered as part of your punishment. We will do our best to plead for whatever leniency can be offered, given the circumstances."

For the first time since being dragged aboard, Niya felt a small slip of hope. Arabessa *did* still love her. Despite her outward anger, she cared, Larkyra cared, and that alone steadied Niya's heart and mind. Yet still, Niya didn't know how to respond to such kindness. A part of her felt forever unworthy of any sympathy her sisters might bestow on her, given what she had done. Her voice cracked with her emotion as she said, "Thank you."

"Now tell us." Arabessa laid a hand on her shoulder. "How long ago was the night that started all this?"

"Four years."

"Four—!"

Arabessa held up a hand, cutting off Larkyra. "All right." Arabessa spoke slowly, appearing to measure this new information. "And our masks, they are spelled to remain on unless we wish otherwise, so how did he . . . ?"

Niya's reddening cheeks and silence seemed answer enough.

"I see," said Arabessa. "Your dislike for the man makes sense now."

"I *hate* him."

"Understandably so, though it does not change your circumstances. Four years of this secret, Niya." She shook her head. "I wish you would have told us."

"I wanted to, but I was scared and ashamed and . . ."

"Brokenhearted?" murmured Larkyra.

"*No,*" she answered emphatically, almost too much so. "I couldn't bear your disappointment. Nor the king's or Father's wrath. I was an idiot."

"Yes."

Niya winced, her sister's words like a knife in her heart. But she did not contradict her. How could she?

"There is one last thing we must know," said Arabessa. "And please, understand no anger or disappointment will come from us. That night . . . did he do anything to you that was untoward?"

"What do you mean?"

"Did he force things upon you? For if he touched you wrongly in any way, we will leave this ship in splinters, binding bet be damned."

"He did not," she assured.

Arabessa nodded, a tightness loosening along her jaw.

Niya's own shoulders slumped, the reality of what was about to take place hitting her hard. She was to remain here a year. *A year.* A ringing filled her ears as she took this in, took in the reasoning of her family. She had no choice but to stay.

Niya was going to be sick.

"How will I survive this?" she asked, desperation in her tone.

"You'll survive it as we must all things," said Arabessa. "One sunrise at a time."

"If we're quite done here," interjected Alōs, pushing up to his full height and rounding his desk. "After your lovely entrance, I have a ship that needs to be righted and a new crew member that needs training.

Such sentimental conversations can be saved for when your sister is returned."

Niya glared at the pirate. He responded with an equally chilling stare. Gone were the cunning grin and playful charm of a host entertaining guests. Returned was the master of this ship, a man who had gotten exactly what he wanted. Alōs had no more time to play.

"We will ensure our letters find you," said Larkyra, squeezing Niya's hands. "And whenever you're at port, please send word. We will find ways to see one another."

Niya hardly heard her words as her skin chilled. "A year," she whispered, unbelieving.

"Knowing you"—Arabessa pressed a strong hand to her shoulder—"you'll be running this despicable lot in no time."

Niya nodded, not knowing how to say this goodbye. Not wanting to. "Tell Father . . . tell him . . ."

"We will," assured Arabessa. "He will know. And please." She moved closer, lowering her voice. "Do keep your guard high here. This lot may blend in easily within the Thief Kingdom, but pirates have very different sets of rules at sea. And this captain . . ."

"What about him?"

"I sense he needs something important, something only being able to sail more freely with his bounty dropped could get him."

Arabessa's words sparked alive a small pulse of hope in Niya's chest.

I sense he needs something important.

Niya's mind suddenly filled with new schemes.

"Yes." She nodded. "Yes, you're right."

She might have been chained to this ship, but she could keep a watchful eye on the pirate captain while here. No one was without their secrets, and Alōs was bound to let one slip if she paid attention. Just as she was now bearing the consequences, knowing the *right* secret of another could allow many advantages in this world. Perhaps knowing the right one of Alōs's could help Niya acquire her freedom before the year was up.

"Just be careful," said Larkyra. "We won't know as quickly if you're in need of us saving you again when you're out sailing in the middle of the Obasi Sea."

Niya met her younger sister's concerned eyes, the weight of what she and Arabessa had recently done for her hitting once more. "I am sorry," she said. "I really am. And . . . thank you. Thank you for coming and . . . and . . ."

"Yes, well." Arabessa interrupted her spluttering. "There will be many moments in our future where you can make it up to us."

"Many, *many* moments," added Larkyra, with her own hint of a smile.

"Be brave." Arabessa took Niya into an embrace.

"But not too brave," concluded Larkyra as she joined in.

The hug was quick, but Niya was grateful for every grain fall.

For when would they do it again?

"Shall we, my darlings?" asked Achak, their chair disappearing as they stood.

Niya's sisters stepped back, leaving a painful void in her chest.

Pulling up her black hood, Arabessa turned to address Alōs, her features returning to their cool mask. "Fair warning, pirate—if *anything* happens to our sister while she's in your care, you will have us to answer to. And you have my word, no matter what tricks you use to hide, we *will* find you, and your death will be neither quick nor painless."

"Then I shall die as I have lived."

Arabessa held his steady gaze, seeming to assess Alōs's words.

Niya wondered about them as well, but then Arabessa and Larkyra were putting on their masks, and the final moment was here.

"I'm sure we will see you sooner than later," said Achak as they approached Niya. "We have been in need of a holiday for some time."

Niya merely nodded, her heartbeat sounding outside her body as she watched the group exit as they'd entered.

Larkyra was the one to stop at the door, holding Niya's gaze behind her gold mask, one last look of courage, before she, too, slipped out of the captain's cabin and into the shadows.

It was truly done.

Their family's secret was safe.

And Niya's sentence had begun.

How is this possible?

Niya didn't know how to feel. How to think. What now to do.

She remained still, staring at the empty doorframe, where her whole world had recently left her behind.

A cold slip of energy along her neck brought her back to the room, reminding her who else was still in it.

Alōs was now sitting at his desk. He did not look at her as he scribbled notes into a ledger. He appeared too large a form to be able to make such delicate markings, his hands too strong for his thin quill, his body too soulless to be made up of flesh and bone.

She loathed every inch of him.

"Kintra will show you to your responsibilities," he said, not lifting his eyes. "You may leave now."

Niya blinked, ice curling around her spine. "That's it? That's all you have to say after . . . everything? After you've gotten all you've wanted?"

Alōs stopped writing, his gaze slowly meeting hers. "Welcome aboard the *Crying Queen*, pirate."

CHAPTER ELEVEN

Niya decided there was no limit to Alōs's evil.

Under the hot sun of a new day, the endless sea a backdrop all around her, she found herself standing before the gray-haired woman she had fought earlier—one of the few Niya had so far learned held a portion of the lost gods' gifts. Burlz was also present, the greasy oaf who had slapped and gagged her within Alōs's quarters.

Burlz drank in the sight of her, his promise of pain still glimmering as he licked his dry lips.

"Niya, this is Saffi, our master gunner," explained Kintra, gesturing to the muscular woman, who assessed Niya with narrowed brown eyes. She could feel the pulse of her metallic magic. "And this is her crew." Six pirates, Burlz included, stood around Saffi. "You'll be eighth in her artillery team."

No one said anything as Niya studied the group just as they studied her. Distrust swam in the salty air.

"Right, then," continued Kintra. "I'll leave you all to it."

"Wait," said Niya, stopping Kintra's retreat. "What of this bath Alōs—"

"*Captain* Ezra," corrected Kintra, voice stern. "He is Captain or Captain Ezra to you, girl."

Niya prickled at the chastening but nonetheless replied, "Yes, of course. And this bath that the *captain* said I could get? When can I expect it?"

Laughter filled the deck beside her.

"Yes, please let us know when all our baths will be ready," guffawed a skinny man, his pale skin splotchy with sores, only four teeth visible with his wide grin.

"I'd like mine drawn with rose petals," added a round woman, slapping a hand to Burlz's back on a chuckle.

Niya pinched her brows together, annoyance flaring. "I see I have said something that amuses you all. But I take my hygiene seriously, which it is more than apparent that you do not."

Her comment sobered a few.

Good, thought Niya.

Kintra merely shook her head. "You'll find your *bath* in one of the barrels you can lower into the sea along the main deck," she explained. "Or you can wait for the next time we are in port and find your washing in town."

"Or ya can strip right here, and I'll wash ya real good," said Burlz, eyes leering at her chest.

Niya's magic hummed hot with her growing irritation. "How kind of you, Burlz," she said, mock sweetness dripping, "but seeing as you smell worse than a cow's underside lying in the heat, I fear you'd only make anyone you go near reek just the same."

The large man's grin flattened just as the two pirates on either side of him took a step away.

"All right, you rodents," said Saffi, gray braids swinging as she turned to her team, "enough group bonding. I've got it from here, Kintra. Thanks for the extra hands. I only hope she doesn't end up being extra weight."

"So do I," muttered Kintra, giving one last appraising gaze to Niya before she strode away.

Niya clamped her jaw together to keep from letting loose another scathing remark. *I am here for a year,* she reminded herself soberly. *I do not need friends among these pirates, but it would be easier if they were allies.* As Niya had found out the hard way, a ship full of forty or so enemies was one too many for her to take on alone.

"All right, Niya," said Saffi, "you'll pair up with Therza today. She's the most patient of us so can show a green calf such as youself how we work. But know now, I run a tight team, especially with how we protect this ship and disarm others. The *Crying Queen* has a reputation to uphold, and I ain't gonna have anyone change that."

"Yes, ma'am," said Niya, which earned her a contented nod from Saffi before she turned to shoo the rest of her men and women to continue in their duties.

Niya was left to find a round woman who must have been Therza smiling up at her. Niya herself was not tall, but Therza seemed to almost be the same shape and size as the cannonballs stacked beside them. Her black skin gleamed with sweat under the hot sun, but she wore a lopsided grin as though the heat didn't bother her in the least, as well as a glassy gaze that perhaps spoke of too many days breathing in cannon powder.

Unlike Saffi, this woman held no gifts. In fact, Niya was the only other in their artillery group who did.

"All right, Red," said Therza, "let me show you how to become one of us."

"Red?" wondered Niya as she followed the woman to a nearby cannon.

"I ain't never seen hair as pretty and bright as yours before," explained Therza. "Like fresh blood," she mused almost longingly.

Niya decided then that Therza would be best as an ally.

With efficiency, the woman explained how the *Crying Queen* was gunned by eight cannons, four on either side. Any more would slow them down. "Plus, we use these children as a last resort." She patted the heavy black metal. "Ships sunk to the bottom of the Obasi Sea are useless to raid. Better to sail close and quick so as to crawl on board for an attack. But that don't mean we don't take care of our kids, now does it?" she added before explaining how they needed to swab and clean the cannons every morning and night, lest they rust in the salt air.

While Niya didn't know the difference between a jib and a spinnaker, she knew a thing or two about defending and fighting, so it was with a fascinated eye that she found herself learning the rest of her responsibilities, which included the task of loading and aiming cannons.

Everything happened quickly after that. Therza took her around to introduce her to more crew members than she'd be able to remember, gave fast tutorials about the rest of the ship, and divided duties.

No one yet asked of Niya's background or why they had a new pirate among them. They seemed to know better than to question their captain's orders and, Niya surmised, had pasts of their own they'd rather not resurface anytime soon.

And despite the crew's surly appearances and hard gazes, Burlz and his skinny sidekick, whom Niya had learned was called Prik, were the only ones to really give her a hard go of it as the days progressed. She caught them on more than one occasion dirtying the iron shafts she had recently cleaned with muck and sand. But Niya kept steady, despite the duo's daily attempts to incite her.

As Niya scrubbed her assigned cannons clean once more, sweat dripping down her neck under the endless daily blaze of the sun, Arabessa's words flowed strongly around her. *You cannot always act on your every whim and feeling. Maybe then you will stop finding yourself in these situations.* Even her father's comment about her mother helped steady her. *You know, your mother was also known to run hot on occasion.* If Johanna had found ways to calm her emotions, so could Niya. This time, she truly decided to listen to the advice of her family. After all, the long game of revenge was something Niya was practiced in, and for what she wished to do to Burlz and his puppet, Prik, she would need a better reason than a bit of delinquent antics from the men to grant it.

As the sun and moon practiced their endless chase of morning and night, the open waters remaining empty of land or ship, Niya's muscles began to hurt in places she had not thought possible. Even her scalp ached, but it was a soreness that meant her body was moving, her magic pumping strongly through her veins. She'd take that any day over being forced still. Even the pranks the artillery team played on her, oiling the cannonballs so they would slip through her fingers, spoke of them beginning to warm to her.

"There's always a bit of hazing when guppies come aboard," Therza had said, slapping Niya good-naturedly on the back after she'd retrieved her dropped ball. Niya had gritted her teeth and smiled through the cackles, continuing her tasks. Though she was currently still the butt of their jokes, she was at least a part of them. Niya knew from growing up around scoundrels and thieves that they acted like wolves in a pack. To be ignored by her team would be a far worse fate.

Before she knew it, a week had passed.

As Niya stood from her task of wiping down the cannonballs to stretch her back, a sobering realization hit her: she hadn't thought of her family or the curse of her binding bet in quite some time.

Frowning, Niya looked out to the open water from where she stood at port side. The sea shimmered a deep blue as the sun reflected like white diamonds off small waves, today's constant breeze the sweetest poultice against her sweating skin.

It appeared being busy had kept her mind from dropping into melancholy regarding her fate, regarding where exactly she was, on Alōs's ship, as part of his crew . . . for a year.

"Good job, Red," said Saffi as she strode past, assessing the gleaming stack of cannons before Niya. Therza's nickname seemed to have spread, and Niya hated that it was growing on her as well. It made her feel . . . a part of something.

But I'm already a part of something, she silently argued as she snatched up her rag, resuming shining the already-shined balls. *My family, the Mousai. I don't need anyone else, especially not anyone on this ship.*

For to enjoy any part of her daily life on the *Crying Queen* or with these pirates felt like becoming a traitor to her pride, to all she had worked and suffered in her attempts at getting out from Alōs's grip.

With a tired sigh, Niya put her thoughts toward her home once more. She wondered what her sisters were up to right now. Were they together in Jabari or frolicking in the Thief Kingdom?

With a sudden suffocating grip, there it was again, the wave of sorrow at her current fate, followed by a painful bout of jealousy.

Damn it, she silently cursed. *This is exactly why I must stay busy.*

Sulking was useless.

There was enough on board to occupy her mind, and more than enough to complain about.

To start, the food here was disastrous. With no place to keep things cold or frozen on a ship, everything was dried, salted, smoked, or pickled. Every meal was a pruned, shriveled mess. Niya knew there were chickens aboard, for she could hear and smell them in the galley, but it seemed eggs were saved for the precious captain. The cook, Mika, merely laughed when Niya suggested slaughtering a few birds for the crew.

"We've been at sea for almost a fortnight, Red," Mika said while waving around his knife. "So unless we raid a ship carrying crates of these feathered rats, the ones left aboard wouldn't satisfy half a pirate here."

Niya would later learn that this pear-shaped, gap-toothed man was also the *Crying Queen*'s surgeon.

She prayed to the lost gods she would not find herself in serious need of his aid.

Niya's other major complaint had to do with her new sleeping arrangements. No longer in her private compartment, she had been shown to the crew's quarters two floors below deck. This was when she wondered if being a prisoner was perhaps a better status. Hammocks were stacked three tall and too many rows deep. Niya was forced to be sandwiched between men and women, subjected to their snoring, flatulence, and other distasteful sounds and smells. She couldn't even bring herself to think long on the toilets. Basically, holes cut at the water level at the bow of the ship, allowing waves crashing in to be the only form of cleaning the vents. The smells alone were suffocating.

At least her two bunkmates seemed decent. Above her slept Bree, the tiny girl with wide eyes and a short blonde crop whom she had met the first days aboard the *Crying Queen*.

Bree was just as curious and animated as then, and so small that when she lay in her hammock, she barely created a dent in the sheet. Her size was a benefit, Bree had explained, for she was a sheet trimmer.

"It's my job to help get the ship back up to speed after tacking and keeping the spinnaker flying during jibes."

Niya had merely nodded up at the girl from her hammock, having not a clue what Bree had uttered.

"Which means she's gotta be a little monkey and be quick in climbing all over the place," Niya's lower bunkmate, Green Pea, had popped his head out to explain. Though he was nothing like the vegetable, Niya had learned Green Pea had gotten his name because he had been the newest addition to the crew before Niya had come aboard. "As green and pea brained as a newborn," Therza had explained. He was part of the pit crew and had told Niya her first night sleeping above him many of his duties, though Niya had stopped listening as soon as he'd mentioned dropping the spinnaker.

Now, as she lay in her swaying hammock below deck, Niya's body exhausted from her recent day's work, Green Pea's small, mewling snores floated up from under her.

"He falls asleep as soon as he lies down," said Bree, from where she was peering down at Niya from the edge of her hammock.

"Whereas you turn over to prattle questions at me as soon as I do," countered Niya, closing her eyes. *If I close my eyes, perhaps this time she'll get the hint and just go to bed.*

"I know you can play with fire," said Bree, "but is that all your magic can do?"

Niya opened one eye to stare up at the girl. "If I tell you all I can do, you'll have nightmares for the rest of your days. Now go to sleep before it's too late."

"Truly?" breathed Bree. "Can you do as much as the captain?"

This had Niya snapping both eyes open. "I guess you'd have to tell me what the captain can do for me to agree or not."

"Oh, he can do practically *anything.*"

I doubt that, thought Niya sardonically.

"Name one," she goaded. She already knew Alōs's magic was strong, but to learn anything new about the pirate captain was too good a chance to give up. *Secrets. Everyone has secrets.*

Perhaps this could be the advantage Niya needed, *something* to finally be able to best the soulless bastard.

Niya watched Bree glance around the compartment before leaning closer to Niya and whispering, "He can walk on water."

Niya raised her brows, unable to hide her genuine shock. "Walk on water?"

Bree nodded.

"I don't believe it," said Niya, settling back into her hammock.

"Well, I didn't believe someone could hold fire in their hand and not get burned until I saw you do it," explained Bree.

Niya frowned. Not enjoying that Bree had a point.

But still . . . *walk on water?*

"How?" asked Niya.

Bree shrugged above her. "Water seems to feed his gifts, so I guess why wouldn't he be able to control it enough to walk on?"

Realizations slammed hard into Niya then. *Water seems to feed his gifts.*

By the Obasi Sea, *of course*!

How had Niya not put this together before? His magic was always so cold, wet, especially as it came out to block her heat whenever she tried to hit him with a spell.

Alōs was also said to have come from Esrom, the hidden underwater kingdom; it would make sense his gifts would be connected to something that surrounded his people's land. *Interesting,* thought Niya. Did all the gifted from Esrom power their magic the same way? What would happen if he were in a dry landscape? Would he become weaker in his magic, as Niya did when she could not move?

Niya's mind reeled at what this could mean.

Leverage, her magic cooed.

Yes, she agreed, a genuine smile creeping across her lips.

So happy was she with this new information that Niya slipped into a peaceful sleep for the first time since stepping onto the *Crying Queen*, momentarily forgetting she was surrounded by deadly pirates. Especially two who were watching and waiting in the dark.

CHAPTER TWELVE

Wake up! hissed her magic into the depths of her mind, just as the creaking of floorboards interrupted Niya's dreams of a dark kingdom hidden inside a cave, the splendor of costumes and familiar laughter.

Niya snapped her eyes open as a large shadow passed overhead, a subtle wind from an arm rising.

Niya caught it on the downfall. She struggled to hold a jagged dagger a few hairs above her chest. Burlz grunted and ripped the knife out of her grip before swinging down again.

Niya twirled out of her hammock, falling past Green Pea's, before hitting the ground in a crouch.

On her way to stand, she kicked out the legs of a second attacker who was standing nearby.

He fell against the floor with a grunt, and Niya instantly recognized the reedy figure—Prik.

The two pirates had approached her from either side of her bunk as she slept.

The scrawny worm was scrambling to his feet just as Burlz squeezed through the break in the hammocks to lunge toward her.

She twirled away, her magic swirling at the ready in her gut, but she pushed it down. *Not yet,* she thought, backing down the alley that was made from the rows and rows of sleeping pirates in their bunks. Niya wanted to feel the satisfaction of punishing Burlz and Prik with her bare hands.

"I said I'd be gettin' you back for disrespectin' me," sneered Burlz as he stalked toward her, his gaze glassy from drink but no less burning with his loathing. "Might as well not make me chase ye, deary. It only gets me goin' more."

"Then that makes two of us," said Niya, ducking to enter a new row. "Playing with my food always makes it taste sweeter."

Pirates beside them began to stir and wake. Bree's small head peeked above her hammock behind Burlz's shoulder, eyes wide. In the next breath she had crawled from her bed and scurried up the far stairs leading on deck.

So much for bunkmate loyalties, thought Niya as none of the other crew moved to intervene. In fact, most told Niya and her assailants to shut up and let them sleep.

Burlz ducked into the same row as her. "You seem the type of gutter trash that needs nightly remindin' of their place."

"And you seem the type of swine whose prick is so small they need to hurt others to feel big," countered Niya. "Or perhaps you have no prick at all, which is why you need this one to feel like you do."

Sensing his sidekick approaching from behind, Niya threw back an elbow.

"Oof," grunted Prik as he doubled over, dropping a wire rope he had been angling to wrap around her throat.

Niya punched him in the face, blood splattering from his lips as one of his four teeth was flung free.

"You bitch!" he spat, dropping to his knees and searching for his tooth as though he could put it back.

Niya ignored the man on the ground as she ran straight toward the charging Burlz. Using a beam for leverage, she kicked off it, spinning and knocking away the dagger in his hands. She swung against a hammock, a crew member growling in protest at being jostled from sleep, before she threw herself up and onto Burlz's shoulders, wrapping her legs around his neck and locking her ankles together.

She squeezed.

Burlz growled and clawed at her legs for release.

She didn't give him a sliver.

Yes, purred her magic, *harder.* It vibrated in her veins. Her hands heated with her gifts, and she pressed them against Burlz's face.

He howled, the smell of his burning flesh filling Niya's nostrils, and she grinned.

Burlz smacked them up against another beam, over and over, but Niya just grunted through the pain. Nearby lanterns flared along with her magic, which she pushed to feed into her muscles and reinforce her strength to tighten her legs, tighter, tighter, until—

Crack.

Niya jumped from her perch as Burlz toppled to the floor, dead. Neck broken.

The crew's quarters were drenched in silence as Niya took in deep breaths, her magic crackling around her, hungry for more movement, for her to dance. Those with the Sight would have been able to see the red haze pulsing from her skin. She looked from Burlz's lifeless body to Prik, still bent over at the far end of the row.

Niya picked up the dagger that she had kicked to the floor. "All right, lover boy," she crooned, stepping over Burlz and toward Prik. "You're next."

"You'll stand down now, girl," Kintra's voice commanded from the stairs behind Niya.

Turning, she found the quartermaster's dark gaze, a small Bree by her side. Kintra glanced over the scene, from Burlz's body and the sniveling Prik to the pirates who watched on from their hammocks, before her hard eyes landed back on Niya. "You're to come with me," she said. "The captain wishes to see you."

CHAPTER THIRTEEN

Niya would be the first to admit that murder was often a tedious business.

And despite the lore surrounding him, the Thief King was a lenient master, considering the heathens he allowed to make up the majority of his kingdom. To lose favor with him meant you had done something very terrible indeed.

Niya would always remember the first life she and her sisters had been ordered to send to the Fade. She'd been fourteen, young, but old enough to respect the power she had been given at birth.

Despite it being winter in most of Aadilor, Niya was warm within the Thief Kingdom, tucked into her bed beneath the palace. Her sheets were silky against her skin as she stretched, letting out a yawn. Her night had ended only moments ago, but it had been a night like many others here. She and her sisters had been entertaining the court members for the past year, their performances consisting of spinning a roomful of guests into slobbering animals. Yet Niya could always feel the potential for more as she danced, tempting whispers within her magic. More desperation from the crowd, more twisting of pain into desire. The potential to make puppets of the giftless and hypnotize the less powerful. It called to Niya, just beyond the surface of her skin, buried in the center of her flames—hot, consuming, greedy. Take, it crooned to her. Consume.

Niya turned over, eyes resting on the dancing flame of the candle beside her bed. She had felt all these emotions earlier tonight. But Arabessa was always there, with her guiding notes and perfectly played instruments keeping Niya from walking forward into that dark, Larkyra from twisting her voice sharp. Arabessa, their conductor, who kept the Bassette sisters contained.

A knocking at her door brought Niya's thoughts back to her chambers.

Who could that be?

It was absurdly late. Or rather way too early, a time when not even the thieves and gamblers kept court. But the knocking sounded again before a servant entered, one who'd been born without sight.

"The king orders an audience with the fire dancer," they explained.

"Right this moment?" grumbled Niya, sitting up.

"Immediately. Your companions are to meet you in the hall in a quarter sand fall."

Niya knew they meant her sisters, though none here knew that they were related, only that they performed together.

In a rush Niya found herself cloaked and disguised in her gold mask, entering the throne room with Larkyra and Arabessa.

None of them knew why the king had sent for them, but even if they had, Niya would still be gripped with a crackling of nerves as she was now.

Their master sat within his swirl of black smoke at the far end of his throne room, only his suppressive power seen and felt.

Before him knelt a woman, her long gray hair covering her bowed head. A shattered mask lay in pieces beside her, while her arms were bound behind her.

"We have a traitor in our midst." The Thief King's deep voice filled the cavernous chamber, and the smoke covering him vibrated with each of his words.

Niya's skin chilled in anticipation, feeling her king's anger in the air, flowing in the lava lining their narrow walkway. He was not their father in these moments. No, Dolion Bassette was merely a shadow in their presence, possessed by whatever ancient power kept the Thief King ruling, filled with memories and knowledge and secrets from a time when the lost gods had not been lost but had roamed Aadilor in their glory.

Niya stood silent beside her sisters, waiting by the foot of his throne.

"It appears this creature desires that our kingdom be split open, that all of Aadilor know how to get in. Isn't that right, Valexa?"

The woman's head snapped back. Her pale complexion was folded and wrinkled, gaps of missing teeth showed in her snarl, and yet her eyes held youth, clarity, in their glowing yellow depths.

She is a senseer, *thought Niya, feeling the thick magic stirring in the woman. One with gifts that could not reach out, only inward, as they listened to the minds around them, reading thoughts.*

Niya instantly shuttered her mind, just like Achak had taught her and her sisters.

Yet the woman must have sensed her effort, for her gaze fell to Niya, then Larkyra and Arabessa, taking in their black cloaks and gold masks. A twisted grin inched up her face.

"These three," she croaked. "These three are special to y—" She sucked in a sharp breath as the king's power squeezed, a silver leash flowing from his clouded form and wrapping around hers. She coughed as he let go, a wheeze mixed with a laugh. "You cannot hide behind your smoke forever," she forced out. "The sins of this kingdom will be known. Your sins and your sinners. Such a place must be found. Destroyed!"

A purist. How boring.

"No." Valexa turned her attention to Niya, hearing her thoughts, and Niya silently scolded herself for letting her guard down. "I once was like you, a cretin of gluttony and glory and vice. It will serve you for a time, child, but know this: it will destroy you in the end. Masks, they are. Nothing but thin veils. This place is a disguise for evil to roam free, to let damnation out without guilt following lost souls home."

"And without such a place, where do you think these 'sinners,' as you call them, would go?" the Thief King rumbled. "How would they curb their vice? Let out their carnality? The Thief Kingdom exists to relieve Aadilor of what would otherwise plague its lands. To accept what is deemed unacceptable. We welcome chaos to allow calm."

Niya had heard these words before, in lessons from their father. For the world to remain at peace, it needed a place that could safely hide desires otherwise condemned by society. The world needed a sanctuary for pleasure and folly and sin. Which was why the Thief Kingdom was not marked on maps of Aadilor: to maintain a semblance of control over who came and went, to allow their king to collect the secrets of every soul who entered his domain, to keep the havoc in.

"But you know this," the king mused. "You needed this kingdom once, Valexa. Very badly."

"And I have paid for that need ever since," she spat.

"A price you agreed to. Do not place blame on others for decisions you have made. You have lived long enough to know such ways are tiresome."

"Too long," she mumbled.

"A burden you will no longer shoulder after this night."

Niya looked to her king, as did Valexa, but the black-and-silver cloud around him remained impenetrable.

"Silencing me will not stop others. I have spoken of the evil here, of the tyrant who rules within the caved city. Others feel as I, and when they find this place, Aadilor will—"

Valexa's words were cut off. The king's magic tightened around her once more, her complexion turning purple from the blockage of airflow.

"My devoted subjects," the king's voice boomed, acknowledging Niya and her sisters. "I called you here tonight to extend an invitation at my court. You perform for my subjects, but now I ask you to perform for me. Will you help keep this kingdom safe from those who wish it otherwise?"

Niya's heart picked up speed, her magic gleeful with the dark promises that spun in the air. She had been waiting for this moment.

Niya and her sisters answered as one. "We will, my king."

"Will you obey my commands loyally and without question?"

"We will, my king."

"The tasks ahead will not be easy. Most will fear you, some will hate you, but all will respect you. Are you willing to become such creatures?"

Niya could feel the thrum of energy from her sisters, from each of their gifts, their quick hesitation, before, "We are, my king."

"Then I name you my Mousai, members of the Thief Kingdom's guardians," he declared. "And to prove your faith to me and our people, you will send the guilty before us to the Fade."

"You are . . . all . . . monsters," Valexa gasped through the king's grip, her eyes full of determined fire, it seemed, until the very end.

"Perhaps," the king replied, "but even the sun casts shadows."

A sand fall later, Niya and her sisters stood in the dark hall of the court, dressed in one of their many opulent disguises, fully covered from head to toe to fingertip in costume. Despite the hour, the hall was now packed with court members. Word seemed to have spread fast regarding the Mousai and their intended performance. A buzz of excitement filled the high-ceilinged black onyx hall. Desire to watch punishment and pain.

Achak stood in the center of the hall. Valexa knelt at their feet.

"Our king has found a traitor in our midst," the brother said, hushing the crowd. "It appears there are those who do not condone the conduct of this kingdom. There are those who wish it to fall at the mercy of the ignorant and fearful."

Boos and shouts of displeasure echoed against the cool, inky walls.

"Here kneels such a member. They have been linked to the many explosions that have taken lives and destroyed irreplaceable parts of our kingdom."

The yelling grew louder. Niya's magic spun impatiently inside her veins at the mass of movement and energy to feed off. She did not yet know how to feel about sending Valexa to the Fade, but she soaked in the anger in the room, solidifying her resolve that the bent, broken woman before them deserved her end.

"Our dear magic performers, the king's Mousai, have agreed to demonstrate what we do to those who dare defy our master, who dare to cast judgment on those who have done them no harm. Who are different from them." Achak lifted their voice higher. *"Our dear Mousai will give us a performance none have yet seen. They will give us a performance that will send this soul to the Fade."*

The following roar was deafening, the spiked hall reverberating with animalistic glee. Niya felt heady with their excitement. Yes, *purred her gift.* Yesssss.

Yet still, Niya felt a slip of uncertainty. What will it be like to dance without constraint?

"Follow my lead," Arabessa whispered beside Niya, her form unmoving as she held tight the neck of her cello. Larkyra stood on her other side. None but they would be able to tell she was speaking. *"Do not doubt the right of this wrong, sisters. Our king guides us true."*

The floating chandeliers dimmed, save for one right above where the Mousai stood and Valexa knelt. Achak slipped away into shadows to stand with the others.

Niya met the gazes of each of her sisters through their masks, seeing the resolve in Arabessa's eyes, the trepidation in Larkyra's. She understood why Larkyra would be nervous.

While this would be Arabessa's and Niya's first kill, Larkyra had suffered endless hardship with taming her gifted voice since birth. An upset wail from her had unintentionally harmed many. Niya and Arabessa certainly had the scars, as well as a buried cat, as proof. Larkyra had only recently learned to master her voice's immense destructive power, which made Niya wonder why she would be asked so soon to let it out again. But while Niya could question her father, she could not doubt her king. His reasoning for things ran deeper than their Jabari lives or even this caved kingdom.

For a moment Niya and her sisters did not move but held each other's stares. We are one, *the energy around them seemed to say.* We are forever bound by what happens next.

With a collective deep breath in, they began their performance.

A melodic note from Arabessa's cello had Niya twisting softly to the tune. Her eldest sister sat to her right, her arm and fingers fluidly moving to bring forth a song that spun its way into Niya's bones. It was a haunting tune, deep and drugging. It started simple, but Arabessa soon used her powers to double and then triple the notes, layering one on top of another.

Niya's hips swayed before she turned her body over completely to the swirling tempo. She felt her skin warm, as if it glowed from the fire in her blood, and perhaps it did, but Niya's thoughts had turned inward, to the whispering of her powers.

Bewitch them, spin them, draw them in. Their souls are weak for you to win.

Niya closed her eyes under her disguise, allowing her limbs to move as desired. Larkyra's voice joined in, elevating the vibrations in the room to edge insanity.

Though she had heard it many times, Larkyra's singing still devastated Niya. So beautifully inhuman were the notes flowing from her mouth that they made one instantly desperate, hungry. As if the listener knew such sound had left with the gods and this moment would be fleeting.

Arabessa's song picked up speed, as did Larkyra's. Sweat ran along Niya's brow as she wove between their magic, bending and twirling through the purple and golden threads, adding her own red to dazzle in the air. She spun in circles around their prisoner, sensing the senseer's desire and agony as she strained against the shackles that kept her bolted to the ground. Valexa was trying to fight against their spell, but she was old, and her capture had weakened her. As though Niya had plunged a sharp knife into skin, she sensed her powers take hold of the senseer. But instead of screaming, the old woman moaned, surrendering to their sweet torture, swaying with the tempo they set.

Larkyra concentrated their efforts by molding her voice into words.

Welcome to your final summons,
The will of our righteous king;
No one slips here uninvited,
For only terror and agony we bring

Bend forward and break the traitors,
A promise to darken all dreams;
Here is your final undoing,
Our pleasure to let out your screams

Niya was now merely a reaction to Larkyra's song and Arabessa's sounds. In the distance she could hear a scream, like steam from a kettle, but it was lost in her dark euphoria. Her magic had turned dangerous, hotter and pointed, a slice from a sharpened blade. The sensation was frightening in that it felt so good.

But Niya's worry was weak, for faith in her eldest sister was stronger. Arabessa would keep them true, guide them back. Arabessa would make sure they fulfilled the purpose of their performance.

And Arabessa did.

She conducted them, pushing and pulling her bow against strings.

It is time, *her melody said.* It is now.

Niya danced her thread of magic to ball up into the center of the room with her sisters'. The air turned vibrant with their mixed spells. A star shining deadly bright.

Burn, *her magic cooed.* Feed on flesh and bone. Take her heartbeat for your own.

Yes, *she thought,* yes.

Niya's mind filled with the crescendo, melody and notes soaring high, high, high, until it all came crashing down on the woman, a glittering, deadly wave. Her head tilted back in a scream. Their spell funneled into her open mouth, the star swallowed up with a snap of her jaw.

Thud.

The body dropped.

The room was drowned in dark quiet.

A single chandelier shining light on what remained.

Valexa lay motionless on the black marble floor. Her shackles broken, her eyes and mouth frozen open in her last pleading wail as blood trickled from her nose and eyes.

Niya breathed heavily in the stillness that settled over her mind, deaf to the roars of hedonistic delight rising from the court around her. All she could do was stare at the body by her feet.

Dead.

She had killed someone.

They had killed someone.

She was terrified.

She was excited.

She was . . . she was . . .

A tingling along her neck made her aware of his presence. She tilted her head up to an empty balcony covered in shadows. Though she could not see him, she knew he was there, blending into the jagged edges of his palace, watching.

Their king.

He spoke not a word, but she felt what he did not say—pride.

That was the night his precious Mousai were born.

CHAPTER FOURTEEN

Niya tried and failed to ignore the cold stare of Alōs as he sat behind his desk. A full moon framed him from behind as his ice-shard energy filled the room, setting a crackling of frost to stretch along the windows at his back.

When Niya breathed, it came out in cloudy puffs.

She had seen Alōs plenty of times in the past days, but it was always on deck, in the open air. She had almost forgotten the suffocation of standing near him in a confined room.

Burlz's corpse lay on the ground between them, a large rhino put down.

Despite Alōs's obvious rage, Niya did not feel a slip of guilt at seeing the dead man.

Better to let everyone on this ship know what happened when you tried to hurt her.

I hurt back.

Kintra pushed into the room, handling Prik by the collar, before dumping him beside Niya. The man sniffed, head bowed as he cradled his recently knocked-out tooth. Alōs did not spare Prik a glance as Kintra placed a curled wire rope on his desk before standing sentry beside him, arms folded over her chest.

Alōs's smooth voice finally broke the silence. "Only a few weeks aboard my ship, fire dancer, and you're already making enemies."

Niya lifted a brow. "I had an enemy aboard this ship before I stepped on deck."

"Indeed," he mused, leaning back in his chair. "Yet it appears you wish to make more."

She narrowed her gaze, frustrated at how easily he could incite her. "I have done nothing but what has been asked of me since becoming part of your crew. If that causes bad blood, then I suggest you rethink how things are run here."

Alōs tsked, glancing toward Kintra. "Killing a crew member, as well as insulting her captain? How shall she be punished?"

"Some time spent in the box might suffice," suggested Kintra, eyes remaining pinned on Niya.

"Hmm, that does sound appealing."

"As *I* recall it"—Niya's hands tightened into fists at her sides—"I was sleeping in my hammock when this lot tried to stick me with a dagger. If killing was afoot this night, it was not planned by me."

"What say you, Prik?" Alōs finally turned his attention to the reed of a man next to Niya.

"Lies, Cap'n," he said, eyes wide as he pointed toward her. "She's a shifty creature, she is."

"Interesting," said Alōs. "Yet there are other witnesses to Niya's story, saying you and Burlz were seen approaching her cot as she slept. So either they lie to me or you do."

"No, I'd never, Cap'n," he pleaded, shaking his head. "Sure, Burlz might have meant her harm, but I was just walkin' through. Off for a bit of winks."

"I see." Alōs studied the man as he played with his pinkie ring. Niya had begun to notice he did that a lot. She also thought it odd he was wearing jewelry at all when he never had in the past, at least none she had accounted for before. "And the Pixie Tail?" The pirate gestured to the wire whip on his desk.

Prik's energy fluttered nervously beside Niya. "We all have some protection on us, Cap'n," he explained. "And a good thing too. She was coming at me with a knife!"

"After you tried to wrap that Pixie Tail around my neck," Niya accused. "Not that you managed. How's that tooth of yours, Prik?"

The scrawny pirate turned red. "You bitch!"

"That is enough," commanded Alōs. "I have heard all I need to in regards to tonight's events. What I'd really like to discuss, Prik, is how you came into owning this device." Alōs slid a finger along the sleek silver wire.

"Yes, well, that . . ." Prik gripped the tooth in his palm tighter. "That I can explain."

"Please do, for I remember it being a part of the bounty of the Cax Island raid. But how odd, since that bounty has yet to be divided."

The room became very still as Alōs's blue gaze pierced Prik's.

"Is this your way of saying you're of a rank to pick your prize first?" asked Alōs.

"No, Cap'n. Never! I just—"

"Have you decided we are all now allowed into the treasury to pocket whatever we wish, whenever we wish it?"

"No, no! I—"

Without standing from his chair, Alōs flung out the whip so fast Niya hardly felt the energy Alōs gave off picking it up.

She watched as the wire encircled Prik's neck with razor sharpness before the pirate lord tugged hard, sending ribbons of blood to gush from the thin man's throat as he was decapitated. Warmth splattered along Niya's cheek. Prik's head hit the wooden floor with a sickening thunk and rolled, eyes bulging, before the sight was covered up by his body falling on top.

In the next breath, Kintra threw down a large blanket that had been resting by her feet, Prik's pooling blood from his severed neck turning it a deeper shade as it became soaked through. The quartermaster quickly and dutifully gathered up all the parts of the thin pirate into the cloth and, with a grunt, swung the sack over one shoulder.

"Captain hates a mess," Kintra explained to Niya, then shuffled past and through the door, but not before calling back, "I'll grab Burlz next, Captain."

With a buzz in her ears, Niya returned her attention to Alōs, who had remained seated behind his desk this entire time.

She did not need to look down to know Burlz's body, which remained in the center of the floor, would be covered in the blood of his friend.

Niya had experienced Alōs's cruelty firsthand, but not his lethalness—until this moment. Rumors abounded, of course, but such things were hardly reliable sources. And if it weren't for Niya's own years of experience with torture within the Thief Kingdom, what she had just witnessed would have reduced her to a blubbering mess.

As it was, she stood firmer in the face of such a threat.

"I may employ thieves," said Alōs, his voice even as he cleaned off the Pixie Tail with a handkerchief, "but I shall not tolerate stealing aboard the *Crying Queen.*"

"Noted," said Niya.

Alōs looked up from his task, penetrating gaze meeting hers. "Do you understand why?" he asked, placing the whip down.

Niya shook her head, eyeing his every move, every breath. The way his angular features shone predatory in the candlelight.

He is just as feral as me, she thought. *Unpredictable.*

"It is not that it would be stealing from me," he explained, "but stealing from the crew. From the men and women that have done equally hard work aboard this ship. If I allowed thieves to roam here, there would be no order, no common goal. Just chaos. A ship cannot sail long in chaos."

How odd that these words echoed her father's. Though the reason the Thief Kingdom existed was to keep chaos in.

"But you are pirates," said Niya. "Are you not meant to create and thrive in chaos?"

Alōs folded his arms over his broad chest as he leaned back in his chair, eyes assessing her. "Perhaps in time you'll come to learn we are more than that."

She gave him a dry look. "Says the man who just decapitated someone beside me."

"To the woman who just killed a man below deck."

"He started it." Niya crossed her arms.

"Someone always does."

They held each other's stare, a beast and a monster.

And for the first time in many years, Niya was reminded of how similar they were.

It left a bad taste in her mouth.

"You'll be taking over Burlz's duties until his role is replaced."

Alōs's words gave her a jolt. "What? That's not fair. He's the one—"

"It is not up for discussion." He cut her off. "This is the law aboard the *Crying Queen*, and as one of her pirates, you must abide by it."

Niya pressed her lips shut, her nostrils flaring. She was not used to taking orders from any but her king, her father, and perhaps, begrudgingly at times, Arabessa. It took all her strength not to try out that Pixie Tail for herself.

Alōs seemed to understand her struggle, for a dark grin edged his full lips. "You've got a bit of blood here." He pointed to his own cheek. "And here."

"It's not the first time," she quipped, not moving to remove it.

Alōs's gaze sparked, amused. "No, I don't suppose it is." Bending toward one of the drawers behind his desk, he pulled something free.

"Seeing as you managed to kill without them, I see no reason why you shouldn't have them back."

Niya snatched her holstered blades from the air as he threw them her way.

She felt over the worn leather sheaths, running fingers along the detailed carved handles of her knives, before looking back up at the pirate, pulse quickening.

More tricks?

"You have always known I do not need a blade to be lethal," she said.

"Do you wish for me to remain their master, then?"

Niya gripped her blades tight. "No."

"Then I believe a thank-you is usually the proper response to such a gift."

"It is not a gift when they were always mine." She narrowed her eyes, distrust still clawing in her chest.

What is he up to, giving these back to me?

"You and I both know that in thievery, ownership is fleeting."

She held back her reply, not wanting to give Alōs any more ammunition to test that theory. Her blades were back in her possession, and that was all that mattered. As she strapped them around her hips, a calmness settled over Niya at feeling their familiar weight. *Hello, old friends.*

"Get what rest you can," said Alōs, the moonlight behind him outlining his large form in his chair. "In addition to acquiring Burlz's responsibilities, I will need you when we dock at our next port tomorrow."

She didn't like the sound of that. "Need me for what?"

"It'll be explained tomorrow."

"When we dock where again?"

"A place we all can have a bit of fun," he replied with a dismissive wave of his hand. "Now go; these antics tonight have set me back in my work."

Despite being shooed away like a bothersome child, Niya did not argue. She was all too happy to leave the pirate lord's suffocating confines. Wherever they were going tomorrow, she'd find out then. Tonight, she had done quite enough, learned quite enough. She desperately wanted to get back to her hammock and sleep.

Though there was one stop she desired to make first.

After traveling through the tight dark hall that snaked from the captain's quarters to stairs leading on deck, Niya breathed easier as she stepped into the cool night air.

The stars were bright pricks of light as they spanned the endless black sky, the sound of waves hitting up along the ship loud in contrast to the quiet deck.

The calm sea must have only required a thin crew this evening. She was thankful for the restful energy floating around her; it allowed her gifts to settle from the earlier scuffle with Burlz and Prik.

Speaking of, Niya glanced over the ship, hoping she wasn't too late. As she found Kintra's familiar silhouette at the far starboard railing, relief washed over her. The quartermaster was talking to Boman, the *Crying Queen*'s main navigator, who was a burly, gray-bearded old man who seemed to prefer responding in grunts rather than in words.

At their feet rested a stuffed sack.

Prik, thought Niya with a smile. She started toward them. Despite how the slimy pirate had completely and utterly repulsed her, she couldn't help but notice his rather darling leather vest. A vest that she believed worked much better with her outfit than with his. Now with Prik dead, he had little use for such an item. And as Niya had learned early and practiced too often, bloodstains could be cleaned.

CHAPTER FIFTEEN

Alōs glanced up at the tangled mess that was Barter Bay. Which, in fact, wasn't actually a bay but what it would look like if every sailing vessel on the Obasi Sea had come crashing together to make a floating city. Massive clusters of ships, knotted and roped together, some stacked five stories high, rose proudly from the water. Crisscrossing hanging footbridges decorated the skies, helping civilians get from one destination to another. Boats were hoisted up by winches to the sides of halls. Others sat beneath oared awnings, creating vendor stations that lined the river avenues. Trinkets from all over Aadilor dangled off fishing line, while shop owners shouted competing prices at the boats that clogged the snaking waterways, carrying visitors. Others turned to call out to those who walked along the boarded sidewalks above.

It was a massive anthill of movement, and though thousands of anchors held it to the seafloor, Barter Bay still had the tendency to drift, making its location a hunt every time. But Alōs knew these waters better than most and could predict the currents well enough to find the city in one go.

As they squeezed by other vessels traveling in the tight waterway, hungry seagulls squawked overhead, mixing with the soft lapping of waves against his rowboat. Alōs sat on the back bench, Kintra beside him, along with Saffi and Boman—his helmsman—rowing. Niya sat at the bow, the afternoon light painting her red hair a warmer amber as she took in their surroundings. By the way she studied the intricately stacked ships, peered into every vendor's stall, and asked Boman and Saffi more than a dozen questions, he could gather this was her first visit.

"You'll draw us a pickpocket looking so doe eyed," grumbled Boman in response to another one of Niya's queries, his gray hair tangling in the sea breeze. "Haven't you seen a city before?"

"Certainly," replied Niya as she stared up at a woman who leaned out of a port window they rowed past, breasts bursting from her low neckline, enticing customers inside, "but that doesn't stop my wonderment when visiting new ones or old."

"Well, at least put on a scowl along with that wonder whatchamacallit," grunted Boman. "We're pirates from the *Crying Queen*, for the Obasi Sea's sake. We can't be seen looking so green."

"I think Niya can handle herself just fine," said Saffi. "Or did you not hear about Burlz?"

Alōs had told his master gunner that she had lost two of her artillery team last night. But not surprisingly, Saffi had taken it in stride. She had seen and lived through worse, after all. She would certainly live through this. It also helped to hear that Niya would be working double duty until they could find replacements. While Prik's execution would go unquestioned by his crew, seeing as he'd stolen from the lot of them, it was not Niya's place to take Burlz's life. Sure, he'd attacked her first, but the appropriate punishment for such action was saved for the captain and crew to vote on.

She would have to learn their ways and accept them if she wanted such a night not to be repeated by others.

"I could have taken that squid," Boman snorted. "All hot air and thin skin, he were."

Alōs bit back a grin listening to the old man. Boman had perfected the art of a displeased mutter. A quality Alōs found rather charming. It was almost an added bonus that he also happened to be the best navigator on the southern seas. He had been the first and only one Alōs trusted to sail his beloved *Queen*.

"I'd have paid to see that," laughed Saffi.

"Then show me your coin, girl, for if that corpse still be on board, I'll happily prance with his shadow."

"Save your energy for tonight's task, old man," Alōs said to Boman as they came to dock at their stop. "Afterward we can talk of you dancing with the dead."

"Aye, Cap'n," said Boman, tying up their boat before they each stepped onto the wooden walkway.

The sun had dipped beneath the jagged stacked buildings, casting a pink hue to the small sliver of sky visible in the tightly built city. Lanterns were being lit, twinkling honey gold along port windows and guiding their way up the planked path.

"Saffi and Boman." Alōs turned to them. "Make your way to Fate's Fall to secure what we need. We'll meet you there later tonight."

"Aye, Cap'n." His pirates departed down a side street, disappearing into Barter Bay's labyrinth.

Alōs led the way down another busy street, Niya and Kintra following in silence as they walked a thin alley. The planked floor wobbled up and down with each of his steps as it sat above the flowing sea beneath. After ascending a spiral staircase at the end, Alōs stepped onto the second street level. This area was even more crowded, the sea air mixed with the heavy scent of bodies. It was the Trinkets and Trades District, a place where citizens from all over the world came to pawn items, make deals both legal and illegal, and trade in materials and knowledge. Barter Bay was a city where things were brought so they could be left, ties to the original owners wiped away, all for a promise of sailing away with fatter pockets and a clearer conscience.

Alōs had been one of these patrons once, which was why he had to be smart with how he was to get what he needed tonight. The item he hunted was from a trade many, many years ago, and he'd meant it never to be traced back to him. He hoped the information he had procured was true and the trader was still in residence here, but more importantly, he hoped that her nightly vices had not changed.

"Where are we going?" Niya appeared at his side and kept pace with him as she eyed a group of Pilgrims, men and women dressed in red robes, loitering along a wall. They chanted the teachings of the lost gods, or what they believed them to be, while blowing the ash of burned prophecies from their palms. A large cloud struck a passing woman, and without pause, she turned and punched the nearest Pilgrim in the face.

The echoing yells of the fight faded as Alōs walked on.

"Well?" Niya prompted.

He glanced her way. Niya's hair was halfway pinned up this evening, the rest a wave of red down to her waist. A waist that Alōs noticed with dark amusement was now tightly cinched with Prik's old vest, her white shirt underneath cleaned. It appeared she'd even polished her dagger hilts at her hips.

She must have been excited to finally get off the boat, he thought, be around other people, as most of his crew was after such a long sail.

"We're going to a shop," he said.

"What kind of shop?"

"One that sells items."

"Come off it, Alō—I mean, Captain," she corrected sourly. "If you need my help, you'll *need* to tell me why."

Rounding a corner, they squeezed onto a footbridge that dangled over open water.

"As you just pointed out, I'm indeed your captain. I don't need to tell you anything but my orders."

"Your predictable responses grow tiresome," she said just as she was forced to press closer to him as a cluster of citizens walking the other way passed. He could smell her honeysuckle fragrance, and he was none too pleased about it.

As soon as they crossed to the other side, he stepped away. "Then I suggest you cease trying to converse with me," he countered.

Niya frowned before her gaze snagged on a few people who stared at them as they walked by. "You must come here often."

"Why do you say that?"

"People seem to know to give you a wide berth. Like him." She pointed to a round man in an ostentatious purple paisley suit who hid behind a bodyguard, his bug eyes peeking out from the larger man's side. "And them." She gestured to a group of men and women who shrank away as soon as his attention landed on them.

"They merely know who not to cross," said Alōs as they entered the garment district, where brightly painted sails hung from masts rising high above the stacked ships.

"Mmm," was Niya's only reply.

"We're here." Alōs stopped in front of a storefront that was made from a bow. A welcoming yellow light streamed from the port windows. He gestured for Kintra and Niya to walk inside and stepped in behind them.

The air was warmer as he entered, thick with lilac incense. Every inch of the small shop was covered in drapery, fine silks, exotic tops, and hardly there bottoms.

"I agree you're in need of a wardrobe change," said Niya, fingering a fur hat on display. "But nothing here quite screams *lunatic pirate captain*."

"That's because all those items are in the back."

A woman in a blue feathered dress stepped from behind a rack of clothes. A jeweled monocle sat over one of her eyes, highlighting their mismatching blue and green. Her blonde hair was pulled up with an assortment of pins that sparkled in the lantern light, and a woven orange wrap was draped around her shoulders. She gave off the impression that she made a game of dressing in the dark.

"Regina." Alōs bent to kiss the woman's round cheek. "Looking fresh as always."

"If I had known to expect a visit from you, my wicked prince of the sea, I'd have worn my best frock."

"All your frocks are the best."

"What an incorrigible charmer you are." She swatted him playfully. "But yes, this isn't called Regina's Regalia, the Finest Finds on the Southeast Seas, for nothing. Now what can I do you for, my lord?"

"We're here for her." He nodded to Niya, who was watching his and Regina's exchange with curiosity.

"Me?"

"You'll need an outfit for tonight," he explained. "I've brought Kintra to help get you sorted while I make a few other stops."

"An outfit for what?"

"You'll be dancing."

"Oh, I don't think so." She plunked a fist on her hip.

"I'll need it to be . . . persuasive." He turned back to Regina. "She'll be performing at Fate's Fall."

The shop owner gave him a secretive grin. "My specialty. Do not worry, my lord." She eyed Niya's form. "I have just the thing."

"And I have just the thing to cut it up." Niya's hand slipped to her daggers.

"Kintra will make sure she behaves," Alōs assured. "And will settle our payment."

Before Niya could protest further, he turned and strode out of the shop, rejoining the crowds in the streets. He could have stayed to argue with her, but he preferred to have Kintra and Regina do it in his stead. He had enough to get in line for tonight—he didn't need the added headache of extinguishing a fire dancer. And if he was perfectly honest, he did not think he was up to the task. Not again.

Alōs's pinkie felt uncomfortably empty as he watched the small man in front of him examine his ring under a magnifying glass. The jeweler's back room sat quiet, as Alōs had asked for private service as soon as he had entered. Two large oil lamps burned on either side of the man's desk, casting an orange glow onto his delicate hands as he turned the ring this way and that. The red jewel in the center glowed like fresh blood.

"How extraordinary," said the jeweler. "I have only ever seen a stone like this . . ." Round eyes, made rounder by his spectacles, peered up at Alōs. "We have met before, haven't we?" he asked.

"It's best for you if you remain uncertain," said Alōs.

The jeweler's throat bobbed. But he nodded, understanding.

"How long will it take to remove the stone from the ring?" asked Alōs.

"You can come back in—"

"I will stay here until it is done."

"Yes, of course," he corrected himself. "But you might be waiting for some time."

Alōs placed a bag of coin on the table between them, the top loose to reveal a gleam of silver.

The jeweler licked his lips. "It will be ready in a half sand fall."

"Perfect." Standing, Alōs retrieved the pouch. "When it's done," he explained. "And I cannot stress enough that not even a grain can be chipped from this stone. It must remain exactly as when it was fitted inside the ring."

"Yes," said the man. "I remember from when we originally split it from the other—"

"Thank you," Alōs said, cutting him off. "I appreciate your care in this matter."

"Of course. Exactness is needed when it comes to precious items such as this."

Yes, thought Alōs, *especially when they are more precious than your life. Or mine.*

Striding to the corner of the room, he leaned against the wall, watching the man work. He did not care if his presence made the jeweler nervous; he would need to deal with it and adjust. Alōs would not let that ring, or more specifically that stone, out of his sight. It had cost him dearly to reacquire, a trade in *phorria* that had left him hunted by the Thief King.

He only hoped obtaining the other piece would not be filled with similar consequences.

Which was why he was glad to have Niya's talents this evening.

It had been many years since he had seen the woman whom he had sold these pieces to. It would only draw further suspicion for him to show up asking after them now. She'd no doubt wonder why he wanted them back after he had so quickly asked her to rid him of the stones.

Alōs needed his next moves to be discreet, untraceable, unquestioned.

Better to have another gain this information. Someone who had the power to spin minds into putty. A woman who had lured him in with her dance.

Tonight, Alōs would make her lure another.

CHAPTER SIXTEEN

Alōs sat playing a hand of Cutthroat in one of the opulent lounges within Fate's Fall. His attention drifted over the other tables, filled with patrons in some of their finer clothes, pretty purchased pets perched on laps. This establishment's eclectic and exotic entertainment alone brought in visitors to Barter Bay just as much as trades. It reeked of money and desperation and took up two entire ships, their hulls fused together, at the north end of the city.

Save for Macabris in the Thief Kingdom, Fate's Fall might be the next best place to go for a high-stakes gamble, to indulge in illegal dining, or to fulfill fantasies.

Alōs caught sight of Saffi and Boman tucked in a far corner, taking turns at Fat Chance, a dice game where the odds were almost always against you, but the winnings were large. Saffi howled in excitement, gray braids swinging as she slapped Boman on the back.

They had secured all they needed for tonight—the private room, Niya's place among the dancers—and so far the information they were going off was holding up. If the night continued to go well, Alōs would let the rest of his crew out for a bit of fun before they set sail again.

Pirates needed buffoonery as much as they needed blood.

Alōs turned to find Kintra's tall form weaving through the tables toward him.

"She's ready," she said as she came to his side. His quartermaster had put on a finer black tunic tonight, the gold rings in her ears shining in the low light.

He glanced back at the cards in his hand. "Well?" he asked his opponent, a thin man in a pin-striped robe who sat in front of him. "Cutthroat or fold?"

The man had been stalling his answer for the better part of a quarter sand fall, and Alōs's patience was more than used up.

"You must call it now, sir," the dealer urged him as well.

His opponent swallowed. "C-cutthroat," he said, displaying his cards: three swords and three boulders.

Alōs laid down his two vipers and four daggers.

The man turned pale.

"You know the rules, sir." The dealer cleared the cards from the table. "Empty the entirety of your pockets and billfold."

"But it's all that I have!"

The dealer sighed, bored. "It's called Cutthroat, sir. That's rather the point. Now, do I need to call management over?"

"No." The man slouched. "It's just, how will I be able to pay my way back to my boat?"

"Perhaps you can swim," suggested Alōs as he stood. "I'll collect my winnings upon my leaving."

"Of course, Lord Ezra." The dealer bowed.

Alōs loomed over his still-seated opponent. "And be warned, sir. If you keep even *one* silver from me, I'll know, and I'll be more than pleased to show you the real reason it's called Cutthroat."

The man's eyes bulged, and Alōs shot him a smirk before turning to leave.

"How did it go?" he asked his quartermaster as they descended the rugged stairs to the lower floor.

"It was not easy," admitted Kintra. "She put up quite a fight after you left, once she learned of her actual task. She's got a temper, that one. But we left in one piece, and I paid Regina a bit extra to keep her in our good graces."

"Thank you."

The pair walked past a second saloon that stretched the breadth of the ship, the lavish chandeliers lighting the red couches and tables filled with more merriment and patrons. Alōs nodded to a few he knew and winked at others he knew better, though he didn't have the time to stop and chat. Perhaps later, after he got what he'd come here to find. But even then, while his crew could rest, he knew he could not. Despite the leisurely aura he often gave off, Alōs hadn't rested in a very long while.

Not since he'd been given the sandglass that sat on the desk in his quarters, the trickling hiss of falling grains reminding him of the potential loss of the only thing he had ever truly cared for in his life. Alōs had sacrificed everything for him, for them, only for his actions to return to haunt him.

Could he never have peace?

There was too much at stake now, too much to fix, and Alōs's mind was in a constant state of whirring, of fast actions to get quicker results. Which was always how mistakes were made, like the mishap with the *phorria* from the Thief Kingdom. But there had been no other choice. Which appeared to be his forever curse: anything done for good, he could only fulfill with great evil.

Why try to be virtuous, then?

It was a question Alōs had stopped asking himself long ago.

If the lost gods were determined to make him a villain, then a villain he would be.

As they came to a lushly decorated corridor lined with private entertainment suites, Alōs turned to Kintra. "Does she look the part?" He knew he didn't need to ask such a thing, but the question fell from his lips anyway.

"See for yourself." Kintra gestured to where the dancers' dressing rooms sat at the end of the hall. "She'll be the one in green."

Alōs strode past the guard at the entrance, acknowledgments given, and pushed aside a curtain to enter an overperfumed, chittering room. Glass mirrors leaned above stretches of tables where men and women painted their faces with extravagant imaginings. Some were designed like wild beasts or tear-stricken kittens, others like voluptuous beauties and wrinkled hags. Their bodies were adorned with an assortment of tantalizing fashions, from a sequin-covered bodysuit to sheer frocks to complete nudity. Alōs's gaze skipped over it all as he walked the rows, ignoring the whistles and catcalls as he passed.

"Tell me what number you'll be in tonight, darling." A man dressed in little else but silk stockings smiled, leaning against his friend. "I'll be sure to give you the lounge special."

"Another time, perhaps," said Alōs as he kept walking.

Reaching the very end, he was about to turn down another row when he spotted her, for how could he not.

Niya was surrounded by a horde of other dancers, all preening. Some touched her green silk robe or complimented her mane of red hair, sections swept up to create an intricate braided crown, while others threw their heads back in laughter from something she'd said. Niya was at center stage, as if back in the Mousai's dressing rooms beneath the Thief King's palace after a performance. She would have been masked there, hair tucked away, face shrouded, but her energy was much the same. Alōs had often watched her then, merely one of many others invited to the Mousai's connected rooms for a postparty, where finer spirits and debauchery were always promised. Niya was glowing now as she'd glowed then, resplendent, though she carried a hint of danger. A heady mixture that burned any who drew too near.

Except him.

Because for Alōs, the threat of the fire dancer ran deeper than attraction or power. Niya represented the temptation to be reckless, to react without thinking, to act on basic instinct and desires. And these were luxuries Alōs could never afford. Even when his actions appeared negligent, they were in fact the result of carefully calculated decisions. Years of rebuilding a life he could control after suffering an old one that had controlled him.

This was why Alōs had made sure to never get singed by Niya's tantalizing fire. He had done so by extinguishing it.

As Niya noticed his approach in her looking glass, her smile dropped, the red haze of her energy pulling inward. At the evident change in her mood, her admirers glanced up at him. With a quiet word from her, they dipped away, though a few curious gazes still lingered.

"Regina and Kintra did well," he said, stopping behind Niya and meeting her gaze in the mirror.

Niya's eyes thinned. "I know better than those two about creating an outfit to dance. I could have put something together with my eyes closed."

"Did you create this?"

"Practically."

"Then you did well."

She seemed unsure what to do with his compliment. "I also remember saying that I would not be the entertainment. Yet here I am." Niya gestured to her costume. "Now explain."

"I only ask for tricks you're well accustomed to performing. Just think of tonight like any other night you go scheming for your king."

"Except you are not my king."

Alōs smiled sharply. "I am for the next year."

Niya laughed at that, the sound sending a cloud of magic flowing off her. Alōs stood utterly still as the warmth washed over him. "Sure," she said, mirth still twinkling in her eyes as she picked up a jar of powder and began to dab her nose. "Whatever you men need to tell yourselves to help you sleep at night. Now, who is this Cebba Dagrün? Kintra says she's who I'm to perform privately for?"

Alōs slid onto a stool beside her. "She is the most notorious trader in Barter Bay," he began quietly. "She can flip any item, hide any trail, and pay the highest price. Once she sees something she wants, she will obtain it, even if the item was not intended to be sold."

"She sounds lovely."

"She's ruthless."

"Even better."

"Yes." Alōs regarded Niya's profile, her smooth skin made tan from her days working in the sun. "She's entertaining company if you're not in her debt."

Niya's brows lifted. "And you are?"

"Not exactly. But I need something from her."

"Then why not go ask her for it yourself?"

"Because I do not want her to know that I'm looking for it. And before you riddle me with more questions"—Alōs raised a palm, cutting off Niya's next words—"it is not your place to doubt your captain's orders: only to obey."

"You are enjoying this binding bet entirely too much," Niya replied dryly as she leaned forward to put down her powder. The movement caused her robe to reveal a sliver of her emerald-corseted chest beneath. Despite himself, Alōs glanced down.

It was a mistake.

Alōs had seen many beauties in his lifetime. Had bedded most of them. But here stood the definition of a temptress.

Images of his body pressing against Niya's flashed before him, warm skin on skin. The tangle of red hair through his fingers.

Memories of their past.

Alōs gripped the hilt of his sword, disturbed by visions that had not swum forward in many years. Shaking them off, he refocused on where he sat and on Niya's last words. "Is it a sin to enjoy what little entertainment this terrible life gives us?" he asked.

"When it's at my expense, yes," replied Niya. "It is a sin punishable by death, actually."

"Then I look forward to my trial once your debt is paid. For now, listen and obey."

Something passed over Niya's green gaze but was gone before he could identify it. "Aye, aye, Captain." She gave him a mocking salute. "Now, what exactly is it you want me to do?"

"Cebba is a regular patron here. Comes for private entertainment the last day of every week. You are to trance her with your dance. She needs to be made pliable to give up information."

"Does she carry the lost gods' gifts?"

He shook his head. "Her ruthlessness lies in other areas. You will be able to spell her easily."

"I'm not sure if I should be flattered at your confidence or appalled at your willingness to put me in harm's way."

"And here I thought you were always the harm in anyone's way."

"Such flattery tonight." Niya's eyes grew calculating. "You must really want whatever it is you seek."

You have no idea, thought Alōs as he retrieved a piece of paper from his pocket. "These are the words I need spoken to her, the question I need her to answer."

"'Where did your biggest red stone go?'" Niya read the note before looking back up at him. "A pirate hunting treasure? How cliché."

"Yes, we are quite the boring lot."

She glanced at the note again. "It's quite vague, you know. Are you sure this will get you the right answer?"

"It will." Alōs snatched the slip of paper from her fingers and slowly fed it to a nearby candle on her dressing table. The flame jumped higher, hungrily devouring the note to ash. "I'll leave how to go about getting it up to you. You may take your time if you'd like, but I have a feeling your dance will be over rather quickly."

"Why's that?"

"Because, my fire dancer"—Alōs gave her a lazy grin as he stood— "Cebba Dagrün has a terrible weakness for redheads."

Leaving Niya to finish getting ready, Alōs found his way into one of the many hidden alcoves at the backs of the private entertainment rooms. Management used these spaces to keep an eye on their employees, or for a pretty price, a voyeur could occupy one of them for a few sand falls. Tonight, Alōs was to be that voyeur.

Peeking through the tiny hole in the wall, Alōs took in the dim circular room beyond. It was lined with low plush couches draped in black velvet. Small glass lanterns hung from the ceiling and set a warm glow to the opulent red patterned wallpaper.

The door opened, and a waiter ushered in a tall woman with braided dark hair pulled to one side. She wore tight black trousers, a gleaming sword at either hip, and a richly woven purple traveling coat over a white, tucked-in tunic. Alōs's magic stirred in his veins along with his anticipation as he studied the two parallel scars that ran from her hairline to either side of her chin. They were red and angry against her pale skin, newly made. He was not surprised. Cebba's line of work, *their* line of work, placed all sorts of undesired opponents in their path.

Cebba took the bottle of spirits from the chilled bucket the waiter brought in and poured two glasses. She settled into the center couch, propping her booted foot over her other knee, before tipping her head back and emptying one of the glasses. Music from the upstairs bar poured into the room through the ceiling vents, stirring a heady, muffled rhythm.

Alōs stood waiting.

He and Cebba were not friends, but they were not enemies either. They had an understanding. Each was in the trade of acquiring and disposing of valuables and favors. Still, what he'd said to Niya was true: Cebba must not know what he sought. It was dangerous for any in their line of work to know what another desired—it often made others desire it too. The price tag would only go up from want, rather than need, and reacquiring this item was no game he would risk playing. The only one of his crew who knew what they were truly after was Kintra, and her loyalty to him ran deep.

The door opened again, and Niya entered. A black shawl was pinned into her red hair, obscuring the bottom half of her face, and her long green silk robe was cinched at her waist, covering what hid beneath. Her petite feet were bare.

Alōs took in a steadying breath as he watched Cebba's appraising eyes run over Niya, a disquieted sensation stirring in his gut. The trader knocked back her second glass.

Niya flowed over to the bottle of spirits and in a fluid movement had another flute refilled in Cebba's hands.

Cebba grinned, a lioness pleased.

Words were exchanged, too low for Alōs to hear, but in the next breath, Niya stood in the center of the room and began to sway. Her hips moved the sheer material of her wrap, exposing one smooth, pale leg. Her arms ran over her curves, sensual, grabbing bits of the material as she explored her hills and valleys. Though Alōs was not in the room, he could practically feel the magic flooding from Niya's core as her red haze of magic began to fill the space. He had been in her presence enough times when she danced to know the effects, had felt the liquid heat of her power caress his skin, working to make him pliable to her will. If his own magic didn't sit like dewdrops of iced armor around his body, he would be putty in her hands, like all who didn't possess the lost gods' gifts. Like Cebba. The poor bastard.

The trader's eyes were already beginning to glaze over.

Niya moved faster to the beat echoing through the walls, and in the next breath her robe fell in a puddle at her feet.

A hiss filled Alōs's ears, and he realized with an uncomfortable twist that it was his own breath.

Niya exposed a body full of softness and curves, of exploring lengths and voluptuous hills. All of it was artfully disguised to tease. The emerald green of her corset pushed her full breasts to near bursting, and her laced stockings contrasted deliciously with her exposed arms, thighs, and shoulders. Waves of her scarlet mane spun and glimmered with each of her twirls and sways, a flame flickering in the breeze.

While Alōs had seen Niya dance many times, it was never while revealing so much . . . skin. And though they had slept together, him touching her completely bare, stroking his hands over her smooth dips and valleys, seeing her like this affected him. Whenever she danced, it affected him. Even with his magic barrier, her moves awoke prickles of heat inside his chest.

Alōs suddenly felt too hot in his clothes; the alcove where he stood was too small. His breaths were coming out fast and uneven. Here was her danger, her temptation for all to let loose their control, give in to their desire. But the trick, he knew, lay in the after. He had *never* let it, *her*, affect him after.

Picking up her silk wrap, Niya spun it in the air, her magic catching it and splitting it into two, three, four strands, the room becoming a tangle of material, movement, and desire.

Alōs's heart thudded as Niya drew closer to Cebba, who sat stunned on the couch, a bit of drool slipping from her lips. Niya was a viper entrancing its master, winding its tail around and around until it gave a snap, a bite.

She rubbed her corseted chest along Cebba's, curled her hips forward and back as her robe draped over them in a moving wave. Niya drew close to Cebba's ear, parted the shawl covering her mouth, and licked.

Cebba collapsed into a boneless mass under her.

Niya pulled away. A pleased gleam danced in her eyes as she turned to stare exactly where Alōs was spying from.

Their eyes locked, and she winked.

Alōs snapped back from the peephole, an unwanted flutter in his chest. Glancing down, he saw his hands were balled into fists. He shook them out.

None of that, he ordered silently.

He quickly pushed whatever was wriggling for freedom in his chest back below the surface, smothering it until he no longer felt movement. He filled his mind with visions of pain and suffering, thought of all the people he had sent to the Fade, some deserving, most not. He thought of those he had left hurt and broken, disappointed, the woman in the next room included. He thought of every horrible, despicable thing to ice over his thawing veins. He refroze it all. Made his body once more into a tundra, for nothing could live in ice. Not even regret.

When he felt like himself again, in control again, Alōs pushed back his shoulders and strode from the viewing room. Those he passed in the narrow hall moved out of his way as he left the entertainment suites. He entered back into the lower lounge and headed straight for an empty booth at the back, where only dim lighting shone.

Kintra slid into the seat opposite him, passing him a glass of whiskey.

He took it back in one swallow.

Kintra raised her brows. "Something go wrong?"

"It's all going perfectly." He signaled a passing waiter for a refill.

"Then why do you look like you'd like to slit someone's throat?"

"Because I'd always like to do that."

His quartermaster eyed him skeptically but remained quiet. She was smart enough to know when to push and when to keep silent. Which Alōs was thankful for. He was in no mood for explanations.

Especially when there was nothing to explain.

His sour mood was due to how long they'd been at sea. His energy was spun too tight. And the lost gods knew he hadn't had any sort of release in a very, *very* long while. Despite all he still had to plan, ensure, Alōs decided he needed to visit a pleasure house, tonight. It had been some time since he had called upon Eldana and Alcin. He hadn't seen either of them the last time he'd docked in Barter Bay. He would fix that. They always knew how to relax him, and he enjoyed pleasuring them to the point where they felt more like the client than he did.

Yes, he thought, *that will set my thoughts right.*

Alōs had just finished his second whiskey when Niya plunked down beside him, dressed again in her regular clothes, daggers strapped to her hips. The only things that spoke of her time performing were the red flush of her cheeks and her mischievous grin as her gaze met his.

Alōs frowned, wishing she had sat beside Kintra instead. The warmth of her magic slid over him, and he tensed before pushing out his own gifts to sit along his skin, cool armor.

"Well?" Alōs asked.

She raised a delicate brow at his curt tone. "I'm fine, thanks," she said. "No one murdered me or took advantage." She poured herself a drink from the bottle that rested on their table. "But I guess you would have seen that, wouldn't you?" Her grin grew before she took a sip from her glass.

Alōs waited, unamused.

Niya rolled her eyes before nodding questioningly toward Kintra across from them. "Shouldn't she leave first?"

"She's good," explained Alōs.

"Interesting," she mused, reassessing the quartermaster.

"What did you find out, Niya?" Alōs urged once more, his patience more than used up this night.

"What you seek is in the Valley of Giants."

"By the Fade," hissed Alōs as he drew his brows together. "Are you sure?"

The valley was a month at sea away, at least. And that was only the first annoyance of this destination.

"Yes, considering that was practically the only thing Cebba was able to mumble over and over by the time I was done with her."

"Well, sticks." Kintra folded her arms over her chest.

"Is that not good?" asked Niya.

157

"It's fine," ground out Alōs, his mind tumbling with exactly what this information meant. Mainly that his visit with Eldana and Alcin would have to be postponed. *Damn the lost gods.* He had too much now to figure out if they were to set sail tomorrow.

"Fine?" Kintra snorted, giving Alōs a knowing look.

"What?" Niya glanced between them. "What is it?"

"Let's just say"—Kintra waved over a waiter for another bottle—"the crew will not be pleased."

CHAPTER SEVENTEEN

Niya should not have had that last drink. But who was she to say no when one of her crewmates offered to buy her one, or three? Cradling her chin in her hand, Niya leaned on the table in front of her, her body warm and her head buzzing as the bar around her appeared to sway.

Of course, that could have been because the low-lit tavern she had followed the *Crying Queen*'s pirates to floated on the fringes of Barter Bay.

"And then she jumped onto his shoulders and snapped his neck with her legs," said Green Pea beside Niya as he slapped her on the back, causing her to slip from her perch on her hand. She righted herself before her face hit the table. "With her legs!" he repeated.

The pirates around her laughed, spilling some of their drinks in the process.

Niya smiled along with them. *These pirates are fun,* she thought groggily.

It appeared Burlz had not been the most popular among them.

And while Niya still did not regret one bit of her actions that night, she'd be lying if she said she were not relieved that most of the crew seemed almost grateful that she had done what most of them had wanted to do for some time now.

"Tell the part again of when she accused him of not having a prick," said Boman across from her. "That's my favorite part."

"All right, you lowlifes," said Saffi as she leaned against a nearby wooden column. "I think we've stomped over Burlz's watery grave enough. Let's move on to different entertainment, shall we?"

"I've got dice," said Felix, a reedy kid whom Niya had probably heard speak three times since coming aboard the *Queen*.

"Oh, then let's play Roll, Punch, Spit!" suggested Bree, snapping up the die from Felix's palm.

While Niya loved a good dice game, she needed some air. Pushing up from the table, she squeezed her way out of the group and onto the wraparound deck.

She took a deep breath in as she gripped the cool railing. The fresh air sobered her slightly, her magic not feeling as sluggish in her veins. An expanse of visiting ships stretched out before her in the dark waters; yellow lanterns glowed along their distant decks where they sat anchored for the night, a blanket of stars salting the sky overhead.

She liked Barter Bay.

It reminded her a lot of the Thief Kingdom. The hodgepodge of citizens, the array of vice and trade. Even while dancing tonight, though she hadn't enjoyed the fact it had been ordered by Alōs, Niya had reveled in slipping back into a performance. Her magic had sighed, content, as Niya moved and flexed her powers, which had quite honestly felt trapped inside her the past week.

Cebba had been too easy a target in the end, for Niya had barely begun when the tradeswoman was nearly too far gone from her spell to pry information from.

Where did your biggest red stone go?

Niya's pulse quickened as she replayed the question, just as when she'd first read it on the slip of paper Alōs had handed to her. Here was one of his secrets she was determined to learn.

I sense he needs something important, something only being able to sail more freely with his bounty dropped could get him.

Arabessa's last words to her floated forward.

Yes, thought Niya, anticipation building. It was growing obvious that what he sought was very important indeed. But important for what? Or perhaps the better question was, For whom?

She had taken note that Alōs no longer wore his pinkie ring when he had met her at Fate's Falls.

Was this connected? Or merely a coincidence?

Niya was desperate to find out.

Leverage, her magic purred within her.

Yes, leverage was what she was after. Leverage helped everyone, and Niya would gladly take any help if it could get her out of her binding bet faster. How, exactly, she could not yet say, but when the moment presented itself, she was sure she'd know.

"Tired of our company tonight?" asked Saffi as she came to stand beside Niya along the covered deck.

The master gunner's brown skin was warm under the swaying lanterns hanging above them, her gray braids shifting forward as she leaned on the railing.

"Needed a bit of air," explained Niya.

Saffi nodded. "Yes, that lot can really stink up a room."

Niya smiled before a thought sobered her. "I am sorry to have caused you to lose some of your team," she said.

Niya believed Burlz had deserved his death, of course, but she was not without feeling for how this might affect Saffi's ability to protect the ship. The master gunner was an exacting boss, but she was also fair, and Niya found herself admiring the woman.

"It's a bit of an annoyance, but a long time coming, I suppose."

"What do you mean?"

She glanced over at Niya. "Prik and Burlz were as much of a liability as they were assets. Those sorts of pirates never last long on any ship."

Saffi's response prickled uncomfortably along Niya's skin. Perhaps because she believed the same could be said of her. She had not exactly been the most . . . cooperative in all her duties the past weeks.

She blamed Alōs, of course. When it came to that man, she couldn't help but fight. It was a reflex too hardened in her muscles to change. Alōs meant danger; Alōs meant nothing could be trusted.

"They were rather awful," Niya agreed with Saffi.

"They were right swine," said Saffi before taking a sip from her mug. "And in my opinion, the way I've seen Burlz treat women, he deserved more than his neck being snapped. So I don't blame you for putting him down. And don't even get me started on Prik. *Fool*," she spat. "Thinking he could touch the Cax Island bounty before the rest of us. I would have cut off his head myself if the captain hadn't."

Niya raised her brows. She knew the crew was ruthless, but she had never heard the master gunner speak so mercilessly about any on board. The way she had acted around Burlz and Prik certainly hadn't given away her loathing for them.

Saffi caught Niya's surprised expression. "I've shocked you, have I?" She grinned. "We all don't get along like we might seem, Red," she explained. "But it's not my place to make trouble aboard the ship. I'm here to do my job like the rest of us."

"But surely if more of you had issues with Burlz and Prik, you could've said something to the captain."

Saffi shrugged. "The captain had enough to worry about."

Niya's ears perked up at that. "What do you mean?"

"You know, with the bounties on all our heads from the Thief King."

Ah, yes, that, she thought, slightly disappointed that Saffi hadn't revealed something else. Something Niya didn't yet know about Alōs.

Secrets.

Leverage.

"Did you know what you were all doing in stealing *phorria*? What it would mean once you got caught?"

Saffi leveled a calculating gaze on her. "Do you mean, Did we know the risk we all took?"

Niya nodded.

"Yes," said Saffi.

"And yet you still went along with Alōs's orders to steal the drug from the Thief Kingdom, though you all could have been killed by the king?"

"The *captain*," Saffi said, correcting Niya's slipup, "always puts such big decisions to a vote."

"A vote?"

"Aye, he may be our captain, but he needs us as much as we need him. Boats don't sail well with crew that ain't inclined to sail them."

Niya let this information settle. She was surprised that such a symbiotic relationship existed between Alōs and his pirates. She always viewed him as an unyielding captain, at least with how much he enjoyed bossing everyone around. Could he truly care for what his pirates wanted?

Niya glanced down to the rippling water, not enjoying the tingling of jealousy that rose with the idea of Alōs allowing his crew to be a part of making such important decisions. For she could not help thinking of her father, the Thief King, and how his commands were exactly that, commands, never to be questioned. And Arabessa, chastening her whenever she had an outburst, despite often being the one to incite them. In contrast, the pirates hardly blinked if Niya awoke in a foul mood or cut them with words if they annoyed her. In fact, this lot merely gave it right back, her attitude blending in seamlessly with their own. At these thoughts, a prickle of unease wriggled in Niya's gut. Though she was chained to the *Crying Queen*, could there be more freedom here than at home?

Guilt instantly gripped her.

Traitor, her magic hissed. *Disloyal.*

No, she thought. *No. I didn't mean it! My family is my everything.* They had done and would do anything for her. Just as she would for them.

Shaking off her sudden nonsense emotions, Niya glanced back at Saffi. "So what did you all gain from risking such a treasonous act against the Thief King?"

"'Treasonous act'?" Saffi repeated before laughing. "By the lost gods, you really must have high-ranking connections in the kingdom to speak so loyally."

Niya did not respond, merely shifted as warning bells went off in her head. She had to be more careful with her words. Otherwise she might allude to exactly how connected and *loyal* she was.

"But what we gained," Saffi continued, her eyes glazing over as she looked out to the dark waters, a fond memory arising, "was more coin than any of us had ever seen for doing such little work. We didn't even have to kill anyone for it."

Niya snorted. "You chanced your lives for some silver?"

"It wasn't just 'some silver,' Red." Saffi's narrowed gaze swung to her. "It was enough money for us to be sitting pretty for the rest of the year. Which we now are. Yeah, sure, we got caught in the end, but our captain got us out of that mess. He always does. Which is why we trust his decisions, no matter how dangerous. We'd sail any course he sets, for he's never led us astray yet."

Yeah, he got out of that mess because of me, thought Niya sourly.

Despite Saffi's words, she didn't believe for one grain fall that Alōs had risked all he had gained in the Thief Kingdom merely for some silver. No matter the amount.

Niya rubbed at the mark of her binding bet on her wrist, the black band feeling heavy on her skin.

Riches might have been the story he'd painted for his crew, but she knew Alōs well enough to understand his goals were bigger than monetary gain. They always had been. Power, status, information to blackmail with. These were the things he hunted.

But she kept quiet regarding her suspicions of the pirate captain.

It was clear her doubts would not be shared with her current companion. Plus, it was best to not let on that, besides Burlz and Prik, there might be another traitorous crew member in their midst, despite temptations of freedom she might enjoy aboard their ship.

Niya was determined to find out what secrets Alōs kept hidden, what treasure he truly hunted, and why. And when she did, she would not hesitate to use every last piece of that leverage against him so she could truly be set free.

CHAPTER EIGHTEEN

Alōs leaned over his desk in his quarters, studying his maps of Aadilor's far west lands. After returning to the anchored *Crying Queen* outside Barter Bay, he had given the rest of his crew leave for the night. His ship now sat quiet in the early hours of dawn, a light pink stretching into his windows. He knew most would not be returning until late afternoon, Niya included. She had been more than pleased to go exploring with Saffi and the rest of his pirates.

Alōs had yet to tell his crew where they were next to sail.

Pirates took bad news better after a night of mischief. But to be safe, Alōs had divided up the bounty from Cax Island for when they returned. He might be a ruthless leader, but he was also a fair one. He knew when to put honey in his pirates' pots. People followed their leaders easier when they believed they were treated equally among their own. It was strenuous work, being the *Crying Queen*'s captain. A constant balancing act between assuaging other people's egos and exerting his strength to keep the ornerier pirates in line. Alōs was good at it, however. Being a leader. But perhaps it was merely in his blood.

Twisting his compass over previously marked lines, he outlined a few new routes they could sail to the Valley of Giants. He would double-check each with his helmsman, Boman, but he knew only one would get them there the fastest.

As he studied the jagged coastline of the west lands, he stared at the River Pelt, which led to their destination. It was wide enough that they could sail a large distance in, but getting there would be the tricky part. The air was drier in the west, the sun hotter, promising treacherous storms through the cooler waters as they mixed with the heat. Cold clashing with hot always caused tension.

Then there was the Mocking Mist.

This, more than the length they had to sail or the rough sea, was what his crew would not be pleased about. Few could handle what the mist had to say if they didn't take precautions.

His mind drifted back to last night, when Niya had repeated all the information that had flowed through Cebba's pliable lips.

She had let slip that someone from the Valley of Giants had come to the trader, seeking a stone worthy of the royal family's daughter—the next in line to be queen. They had left with the most valuable gem Cebba had, the bloodred one, making her pockets grossly fat for years.

Alōs could imagine; it was this original trade to Cebba that had afforded him his ship and the first of his crew.

Though it was not much information, it was all he needed for this next leg.

In spite of Niya's recent performance provoking unwanted, heated memories, Alōs had been right; she was a valuable asset.

And she was his for a year.

A rap at his door brought Alōs back to his quarters. A cool sea breeze filtered through an open windowpane at his back. "Enter."

Kintra stepped in, face grave. "You have a visitor."

A figure floated in behind her, their magic a metallic pulse funneling into his chamber. Cold, but soothing. Familiar. They wore a hooded robe of rich blue that hid their face, with an intricate silver pattern sewn along the edges.

Alōs straightened, his focus sharpening. "You may leave us."

The room hung in silence as Kintra walked out, the door shutting with an audible click.

"I thought we agreed you were never to come here."

"We did," said a man as he pushed back his hood. "But when I saw it empty, I could not resist."

The visitor's hair was as white as the moon, his skin brown like Alōs's, and he had similar glowing turquoise eyes. A silver tattoo started at the tip of his nose and expanded up and over each of his brows. It was the marking of the High Surbs from Esrom, the hidden underwater kingdom. Alōs's homeland.

He watched the man's gaze fall to the silver sandglass on his desk.

Alōs's chest tightened with unease. "What are you doing here, Ixō?" he asked.

"It is your parents."

"I have no parents."

"You soon may not."

Alōs went very still as he forced down a sharp pang of panic. He was ice. Stone. He did not feel. "Tell me."

"Your mother became sick after the last moon letting. She passed last night."

Alōs remained silent. Numb.

"As you know, it is common with our kind that are bonded with such love," Ixō went on to explain, "that one cannot live long without the—"

"I remember the teachings you High Surbs spouted. I do not need another lesson."

"Yes, well." Ixō's chin tipped up. "We fear your father is quick to follow."

"And?"

Ixō appeared momentarily appalled. "Your father bade me to find you. He wants, *needs*, you to come home, to see him."

My father. Home. The armor around Alōs's heart thickened, his magic swirling through his veins to protect him. "It is no longer my home," he said. "Hasn't been in a very long time. You and I both ensured that."

"Esrom will always be your home. It is forever in your blood, despite your banishment."

"It is precisely my banishment that keeps it thus. My place is now on this ship and wherever the sea takes me."

"Please, Alōs." Ixō stepped closer. "If not for your parents, then for your brother. Come for Ariōn."

Ariōn. The center of Alōs's heart, which he locked up tightest, shivered. He leaned forward, digging his knuckles into his desk. "All I've ever done is for him. Where I am now is because of him."

"And he knows this," Ixō assured. "Your parents do . . . *did* as well. Why do you think no guards have disturbed you whenever you've made anchor in Esrom? Despite how fleeting your stay or how well you try to hide, they have always known when the *Queen* sails in."

This knowledge did little to help ease Alōs's growing frustration.

"Because I never step onto Esrom's shores, and I never let the citizens know that I am there. I keep my ship in the sanctuary waters as law decrees for unapproved visitors. Are you saying I will have sanction to step onto the islands if I do return?"

Ixō's eyes lowered. "No."

Alōs laughed, humorlessly. "So my brother and my dying father are meant to come aboard this ship? Crawling with pirates? I think not."

"I will organize your safe passage to them. You know there are ways in that will not be watched. The private beaches to the west have not been used since you've left. Please, Alōs, do you not wish to see your parents one last time?"

His magic jumped along with his rage. "I have already made peace regarding my final meetings with Tallōs and Cordelia. Why should I ruin that with a memory of one dead and one ill?"

"To comfort Ariōn," pleaded Ixō. "You know he grows weaker when he's distressed."

Alōs closed his eyes, the fight leaving him, as it always did when it came to his brother.

Finally, he met Ixō's gaze. He didn't need to speak his answer for the surb to know he would come.

The *Crying Queen* rang with the shouts and scuffles of his crew preparing to set sail. Getting to Esrom was not like getting to most places. They wouldn't glide along the ocean waves but rather under them. In an air-pocket tunnel where no sails would be needed for their journey.

Alōs stood at the wheel beside Boman and watched the fluid coordination between the cockpit and foredeck, his crew boss yelling commands. This was the part he always reveled in, the commotion before setting off to a new destination. Even scoundrels could be choreographed.

Saffi paced the main deck below him, yelling instructions to her team, who worked with grunts and groans to secure the cannons. Alōs's gaze locked onto Niya as she pulled ropes tighter, the heat glinting off her hair, painting it a bright orange.

Even now, Niya's body flowed in a smooth rhythm to her orders, not a step tripped or movement wasted. She had proved to be a quick study in her duties. But this did not surprise Alōs, for he had understood early that she was a clever and adaptable creature. Like him.

"The anchor's up, Captain," Emanté, his boatswain, said as he approached. His white skin was always in a different state of sunburn, yet never once did he complain. The young man seemed to enjoy any time spent under the sun, as his currently bare chest proved.

"Then prepare all to hold on," instructed Alōs.

"I've got a good grip on her, Cap'n." Boman nodded to his sturdy grasp on the wheel.

His pirates knew what to do when told they were going to Esrom.

Kintra ascended the stairs from the main deck to come to Alōs's side. Holding a bowl, she extended him a clean knife. Alōs picked up the blade and rolled up his sleeve, displaying a few old cuts on his forearm. He sliced a new one open.

Kintra held the bowl beneath his arm and caught every crimson drop before handing him gauze and a bandage.

Wrapping his forearm, Alōs met Niya's curious gaze from where she stood below. Her attention fell to his bandage.

A flicker of displeasure settled over Alōs. What he was about to show her not many had seen. But it could not be avoided.

Placing his back to her, he rolled down his sleeve as Kintra carried the bowl to each corner of the ship, using a rag to mark sections of the banisters with his blood.

Only those from Esrom could locate the hidden realm and open the passageway that led to the underwater city. Alōs's blood acted as the tether that could always return him to his place of birth. It was said to have been a gift from the lost gods to Aerélōs and Danōt, the first people of his homeland, before the city had sunk to the seafloor. A way for their children to always find their way home. Alōs's mother used to retell the story to him and his brother as she tucked them in at night.

His mother.

His mother was dead.

Walking to the stern, Alōs grasped the banister and stared out at the calm sea. Barter Bay had now shrunk to a mere smudge on the horizon behind them.

Ixō had left immediately after his visit, jumping into the waters, his ancient surb magic creating an air pocket around himself as he descended into the depths, finding his way back.

Alōs could do the same, but getting his ship and crew there safely was an entirely different matter. And he could not leave them topside. He didn't know how long this trip would take. Plus, there were advantages in sailing to Esrom, one being that when you left, you could get to farther parts of Aadilor quicker than if you sailed above.

Anything to get him closer to the Valley of Giants, he'd take.

Inhaling a deep breath, Alōs began to push his magic into the wood. His muscles strained as he pushed out his gifts, the icy magic crawling through his veins and out of his skin. Like sparks and crackles of light, his gifts swam through the banister's density, stretching the entire length. *Mine,* his magic hissed, *all of this is mine,* until it hit the markings of his blood at each corner of his ship, connecting like a click of a lock. Any with the Sight could see the ship now ringing and pulsing with his magic, glowing brighter as he forced out as much of the lost gods' gifts as he could, until the air grew cold, frosted. His breaths came out in icy puffs.

He held his beloved, his *Crying Queen,* in a hug.

And then, when he felt all was secure, Alōs spoke the words that would get them to Esrom.

"Dōs estudé." My home.

The waves below his ship roared as they crashed away, a tear ripping open across the sea, sending the *Queen* swaying. Fish flopped to the surface, chunks of foam flew, and salt water sprayed across Alōs's face. His body felt torn in two as he fought for control, his magic wanting to sever him as it stretched from his skin, pulled at his bones, but he held steady.

It wasn't until he felt as though he might topple overboard, until his nerve endings sizzled their exhaustion, that a wide chasm opened beneath them and the *Crying Queen* fell through.

CHAPTER NINETEEN

A cool mist peppered Alōs's skin, wind whipping back his hair, as they traveled through a hollowed-out waterway. It was called the Stream, the passage beneath the waves that could be created to sail to Esrom.

Sea life did not penetrate inside the tunnel of air but could be seen swimming outside its current. The Stream took them down, deeper into the waters, and as the sunlight dimmed, glowing jellyfish and other illuminating marine life lined its liquid sides, urging them forward. The *Crying Queen* skimmed along the bottom of the Stream's floor as it soared at a dizzying speed.

No matter where you sailed from in Aadilor, the journey to Esrom through this passage always took exactly a full sand fall. Which made this path one of the easier to travel, despite being underwater and requiring magic and blood.

But Alōs was not scared of blood.

Their journey had barely begun when Alōs saw the blue glow at the end, heard the roar of the waterfall that was the final entrance to the hidden city. It cataloged all who entered and exited, and as the *Crying Queen* passed through, the ship was awash with shimmering dust, a punctured layer of magic, as they left the Stream and swam into new waters.

The true splendor of Esrom took up Alōs's vision.

A sparkling kingdom at night stretched out, the star-filled sky camouflaging any hint that they were indeed deep down at the bottom of the Obasi Sea. Warm, fragrant air filled Alōs's lungs on a deep inhale. *Home,* his magic purred.

Alōs's nerves danced with a fighting mix of relief and dread.

In the midst of the calm waters, three large islands stood proudly in the distance, while smaller isles floated above in misty clouds. Woven bridges connected them like silk spiderwebs, and glowing waterfalls crested their shores, pooling into the sea below. Thin fishing boats slid by lazily, their lanterns spots of warmth in the dark. But what drew all visitors' eyes was the palace that stretched up gracefully from the center island, soaring above the dense foliage that covered the land. The architecture was a spectacle of shimmering starlight that looked as though it were made up of diamonds, and thin silver turrets sprouted from every rooftop, allowing floral blue ivy to climb and wind over their expanses. It was a castle that inspired bedtime stories and the promise of better times. Here floated the islands of Esrom, a sanctuary for all of Aadilor.

Banished or not, Alōs could not help the twinge of pride he felt whenever he looked upon it.

Anchoring the *Crying Queen* in a hidden inlet along the southern side of the main island, Alōs steadied his resolve as he went to instruct his crew to stay aboard.

None had dared disobey the order since Tomas. Tomas, whose skull was now a bookend in Alōs's chambers.

Striding along the main deck, he passed Niya, ignoring her penetrating gaze on him. She no doubt wondered why they were here. But as she must learn, like the rest of his pirates had, no one questioned the captain when it came to Esrom.

Alōs stopped beside Kintra where she waited for him by the portside banister. "I do not know how long this will take," he admitted, a squeezing discomfort hugging his chest at what he was about to do.

What he had been guilted into doing. "But I will be back as soon as I can."

"We'll be here, Captain," said Kintra, her features filled with understanding. "Take whatever time you need."

He had confided in her regarding Ixō's visit, but still, he did not enjoy any grain of pity. He was Captain Alōs Ezra, the most merciless pirate in Aadilor. Pity was not for the likes of him and his cold heart.

"Make sure she behaves," he said, not needing to explain who "she" was. "Tie her back up if need be."

"I can hear you, you know?" said Niya from behind them.

They both ignored her.

"Aye, Captain." Kintra nodded.

Alōs faced the distant beach on the main island, where gentle waves hit the shore in a rhythmic crash. He took a deep breath in, tasting the sweet air. His gifts had replenished quickly once he'd entered his homeland; his muscles felt stronger, his mind sharper. The sea was everywhere, and his body vibrated with the sensation.

With a final resolve and a prickling of ice armor running over his skin, Alōs grasped the banister and swung himself over the rail, dropping down. He stopped right above the water, his magic flowing out of him like a waterfall, pushing against the gentle waves beneath his feet. Alōs hovered in midair.

Forward, he thought, which was all it took for him to float away from his ship and toward his old home.

He approached a small, secluded beach; his boots crunched against the sand as he stepped onto land.

Alōs paused, staring at the dark awaiting jungle that spilled out along the perimeter. He had not been on these shores in a very long time.

But he had taken on more frightening things than this, so with sure footing he continued forward.

The fresh scent of night and moss greeted him as he entered the forest. The air cooled as the buzz of bramble beetles and light hoppers filled the night's silence. Twilight blooms glowed purple and blue, painting the trunks of trees in an array of colors, lighting his way. Not that Alōs needed light. He knew these woods intimately, and no amount of time away would have had him forgetting the paths he had taken many times as a boy.

Alōs soon stepped from the wild tangle of trees onto a dirt road. A large ivy-covered wall stood between him and the capital city on the other side. Alōs stared at the stone. As a child, he had climbed those vines before falling and skinning his knees. But he had not cried. Alōs would learn later the amount of pain required for him to shed tears.

Turning left, Alōs remained in the shadows on the fringe of the road, ignoring the spots of light cast by the lanterns along the wall to his right. He took note of how their normally orange flames had been switched to ones that glowed silver.

Esrom was in mourning.

Yet despite knowing why, Alōs kept his emotions placid.

He'd already had his time to mourn the dead many years prior.

No one met him as he made his way down the path, and eventually he stopped in front of a wooden door that he knew hid behind dangling vines. Parting them, Alōs gave two, then three knocks.

The door swung open with a rusty creak, revealing Ixō on the other side. The High Surb held a torch that threw flickering light across his metallic brow tattoo. His glowing turquoise eyes were filled with pain beneath his hood.

"They're gone," said Ixō in greeting. "Tallōs left us by the time I returned. Your parents are now together again in the Fade."

The words settled atop Alōs's skin like hot ash from a pyre.

They're gone.

He dared not speak.

Ixō waited, no doubt hoping Alōs would reveal grief, some sliver of emotion.

He did not.

With a frown, Ixō turned and led them down into a cool tunnel, one that eventually changed to limestone and then marble walls.

Panic shot through Alōs as the fragrance of jasmine reached him and the familiar soft trickling of meditation pools echoed down the passageway like a warning. They were about to enter the palace.

Ixō pushed aside hanging vines, revealing a courtyard.

Glowing ponds filled the circular space with light. Moonlight lilies bloomed with purple buds on the water's surface as firebugs floated through the space like pollen.

The courtyard sat empty, quiet, as Ixō took hurried steps to cross through.

Alōs drank in the spiral columns lining their walk, up to the vaulted stained glass ceilings, a majestic scene of a blue sky. Silver adorned every edge, every curl of a candelabra, every crack in the intricate tiled floor.

Familiar. It was all too familiar.

Alōs shouldn't be here. He should never have come.

Especially as he felt his gifts buzzing across his skin with contentment, crooning and sighing with longing recognition of the magic that stirred heavy in these halls, the power that flowed from the High Surb who led the way.

Stop that, he commanded silently to his gifts, ignoring how they hissed when he hardened them to ice in his veins. He could not afford nostalgia.

Ixō stopped at a corner, making sure they were still alone, before turning down a smaller hall, a less opulent one meant for servants to pass through. Their path twisted, had them climbing stairs before they were blocked by a wall. Or what seemed like one. Ixō placed his torch in the awaiting holder mounted nearby, and with a quiet click, a hidden door slid open.

"Ready?" Ixō hesitated at the threshold.

Alōs stared at the low candlelight streaming in from the room beyond, his feet feeling chained down.

Ready?

No, he thought before striding past the surb.

Immediately he was hit with a heady dose of incense and the heat of a roomful of candles ablaze. In the center of the chamber stood a magnificently carved bed whose canopy depicted a twinkling night sky. As Alōs walked around it, he did not look at the bodies beneath the sheets; instead his attention remained on the young man who stood at the foot of the bed.

He was dressed immaculately in seafoam green, the material, which was detailed with white thread, draping his thin body in an intricate wrapping of loose pants and long tunic. His smooth brown skin shone with youth, but what set him apart was the addition of silver skin running over his hands and up his wrists like frayed gloves. The same metallic discoloration ran down from his dark hairline and over his forehead, as if he had been turned upside down at birth and dipped in a pool of liquid metal. It was a marking of a sickness stopped, of death frozen.

Candlelight glinted off the man's sharp alabaster crown as he turned his head. Milky-white eyes landed on Alōs, the bit of blue they'd once held now a faded dream behind a thick veil. Though the young man was blind, Alōs knew he had other senses to help him see.

"Brother," whispered Ariōn.

The word rang in Alōs's ears, the sound a mix of exhaustion and relief.

Brother.

Alōs had not heard it spoken by this young man's lips in a very long time.

Without thought, he walked forward, pulling his younger brother into an embrace. "Ariōn."

It had been three years since they last were together, and many more since Alōs had been in this bedchamber, in this palace. But as he held Ariōn, breathing in his familiar scent of mint and sea air, it felt like no time had passed at all.

"They are gone," said Ariōn, his voice still sounding so young. "It is just you and I now." He stepped back but did not let go of Alōs.

This was when Alōs noticed the falling of sands. His brother had grown since he'd last seen him, now almost equaling Alōs in height. His shoulders were wider, too, but his hands were still boyishly soft, his chin void of stubble.

"They asked for you," continued Ariōn. "Each before they went to the Fade. Mother and Father, they asked for their sons."

Their sons.

The words sent shards of ice falling from around his frozen heart. Alōs held in a wince of pain. *Dangerous.* It was always dangerous to come here, and not just because he wasn't allowed. Alōs couldn't play the caring older brother *and* remain the ruthless pirate. One would always win out over the other, and he could not let emotions in, not when it had taken him so long to force them out. He could not hurt if he did not feel, did not need to mourn if nothing was lost. And to give up this land, this peace and beauty, his family—and to survive beyond it—Alōs had to leave behind everything that went with it. Himself included. He was no longer a brother. No longer "their son." He was not Alōs Karēk, firstborn to the crown, but Alōs Ezra, the infamous pirate lord.

"Their son was with them," said Alōs. "*You* were here." He stepped from Ariōn's grip and was met with a frown.

"But we *both* should have been."

"Do not lessen your final moments with them on my account. It happened as it was meant to, or have you learned nothing from your High Surbs' sermons?"

Ariōn glanced toward Ixō, who had remained quiet in the shadows.

A shared concerned expression marred each of their faces.

But Alōs's attention turned from them as he finally gave in to the pull that had hooked into him since he'd stepped into this room. He looked at the two bodies lying motionless in their bed.

Their hands were clasped together above the sheets. Eyes closed. Their dark, aged skin was a shade paler, grayer, stiff. Their white hair was combed neatly beneath their silver-dipped coral crowns.

These lifeless bodies had once been Alōs's source of eternal happiness; now they were the source of his deepest guilt.

The king and queen of Esrom.

Alōs stared at Tallōs and Cordelia Karēk and waited.

But the bitter irony of manifesting a cold heart, of fortifying it so thoroughly against emotion, was that it worked. For as Alōs gazed upon his dead parents, he felt nothing.

CHAPTER TWENTY

Niya knew she was going to follow Alōs as soon as he left the ship. He might be her captain, but he was *not* her king, no matter what he thought.

Leaning against the railing, Niya stared at the main island's distant shore, at the silver-spun palace, which erupted through the thick green vegetation like gemstones through dirt.

Alōs walked on water, she thought with unease. Bree had been right.

What else was he capable of?

Despite their past intimacy, it was growing apparent they had been as good as strangers then.

Niya shifted with discomfort at the thought. It appeared the pirate captain had many tricks up his sleeve that she had yet to learn.

And learn she certainly would.

While the crew seemed entirely too uninterested in why their captain had gone ashore alone, she was crawling with curiosity.

What did Alōs need in Esrom so badly that he'd diverted them from their journey to the Valley of Giants? Did it have to do with this red stone he sought? But most importantly, why did he hide within his own homeland?

He had docked them deep within this shadowed cove. Out of sight.

Niya's curiosity was not merely overflowing. It was drowning her.

Alōs is afraid of something in Esrom, thought Niya. *Why else would he go to such pains to remain a ghost in his own home?*

Whatever the reason, she needed to find out what it was immediately.

Leverage, her magic cooed.

Leverage, she agreed, tapping her foot impatiently.

If played right, whatever was here could be the key to shortening her binding bet.

A desperation gripped hold of Niya. She had to get off this boat.

Turning around, she glanced over the deck.

Saffi was leaning against a cannon on the starboard side, talking with Therza. Green Pea and Bree were sitting together up on the ropes of the mainmast, feet dangling in the cool night air. Emanté sat in a nook by the stairs leading up to the quarterdeck, head back and eyes closed. Kintra and Boman were most likely below deck or in the galley with Mika, while the rest of the pirates were in similar repose, relaxed, lazy, taking advantage of their captain's absence. For who knew how long he'd be gone.

It took hardly a grain's fall of thought for Niya to conclude what she needed to do next: spell a ship full of pirates to sleep.

Niya had already learned that brute force was a familiar adversary for this crew. One she had yet to win against them. Stealth was needed here, magic as subtle as the evening's breeze.

After they'd spent a night of debauchery in Barter Bay and then immediately been ordered to set sail, it was only natural they take advantage of their captain's absence with a nap. A *very* long nap.

Niya stalked closer to Saffi. Those with magic she would need to take care of first. As soon as those with the Sight saw her haze of powers, they'd know something was up.

Taking up a rag found at a nearby cannon, Niya settled herself behind the master gunner. With each wipe and shift of her body, she let her magic slip from her, keeping it low and to the ground.

Sleep, it whispered in her veins, crawling to slink up Saffi's legs. Niya sensed a tug of resistance, the thick layering of the master gunner's gifts growing aware of an intruder. Saffi shifted to glance behind her, a furrow on her brow, but Niya was more gifted than she, and like a lioness pouncing, she forced her magic to lunge forward, smacking Saffi right in the head, a cloud of red. The master gunner blinked, dazed, before a loud yawn overtook her and she fell into Therza's arms.

"By the stars—" Wide, confused eyes landed on Niya as the short woman tried to hold on to Saffi's much larger form. But then Niya gave a flick of her wrist, and Therza, too, was covered in a hazy mist of Niya's magic.

Both women fell to the deck, asleep.

Niya smiled, continuing to pour out her slumbering spell as she swayed around the deck.

Close your eyes, she fed into her movements, a lulling whisper. *Rest until I return.* She twirled around Felix and a few more of his cockpit team. They each sank to the ground, snores sounding. Feeling emboldened, Niya let her spell grow stronger as the pirates began to nod off, one by one. Until the entire *Crying Queen* was covered in her magic, any soul within range falling drowsy before lying down for a long nap. Bree and Green Pea dangled above, heads bowed over rope, unconscious.

Coming to a stop, Niya stood on the quarterdeck by the wheel, taking in her work. Across the ship, men and women leaned on one another, heads bowed, eyes shut; others sprawled along the deck, curled around coils of rope or bent along the banisters of crow's nests, asleep. The gentle sway of the ship a mother's rocking, the movement feeding further into Niya's gifts.

"If only you were here to see this, Ara," said Niya, hands on hips as pride filled her. "No longer could you say I am too reactionary, for this one I thought through."

Yes, she imagined her sister answering. *And look what that got you—exactly what you desired.*

"Sticks," said Niya sourly. Arabessa's advice had been right, again. "She's always right," she continued to grumble as she descended below deck, pushing her spell to meet any pirate in her way, before she went to find Kintra.

The quartermaster was in the captain's quarters with Boman, looking over maps laid out on Alōs's desk. Kintra glanced up at the squeak of a floorboard and frowned, finding Niya in the doorway. "What do you—"

Niya threw up her hand, cutting off Kintra's question and sending the potent magic she had gathered on deck to hit the quartermaster square in the face. She and Boman collapsed, one on top of the other on the desk. Tiny mewls of sleep filled the room.

With a giddy grin, Niya danced her way back up top, singing a favorite lullaby of Larkyra's.

Slip quiet into your tangle of dreams
Let your eyes grow ever so heavy
Sleep is waiting to taste new schemes
You could not create in your daily medley

Sleep soundly, sleep deep, sleep away
Until awakes a new day.

Close your mind and I shall close mine
It is time we block out our worries
Now is our chance, my dearest, my darling,
to make all our other stories

Sleep soundly, sleep deep, sleep away
Until awakes a new day.

Once on deck, Niya turned her back on the slumbering ship, intent on finding where Alōs had gone.

It was awkward work lowering one of the boats strung to the side and rowing to shore by herself, but she managed. As Niya did most things. She had grown stronger in her time on the *Crying Queen*, her body molding different muscles than it had under any of her previous training, the skin along her hands and feet calloused from rougher work than throwing knives and kicks.

As she neared the shore, waves pushed Niya the rest of the way onto the beach. She jumped out, pulled her boat farther up along the sand, and tied it to a large piece of driftwood. Niya wiped at the sweat on her forehead with the back of her hand, scanning the perimeter of the dark jungle. The air was thicker here than it had been on the ship. It held a pleasantly warm breeze that pushed through her white shirt. It was also quiet, peaceful with the lapping of waves behind her. There were no shouts or sounds of people or even a hint there might be a city, let alone a palace, beyond the jungle that stretched before her. Which was a good thing. Niya didn't need the extra burden of being stopped before she had even begun.

The section of jungle that she had seen Alōs enter sat empty, but that was not a problem.

Niya's magic allowed her another trick. While she could sense movements, she could also pick up trails of old ones, especially if they belonged to those who held the gifts, so long as they'd been recently made. And Alōs's energy of movement she had memorized early on. It oozed from him like perfume: cool, buzzing, and powerful. It was eerily similar to her sisters'.

Honing her powers, Niya sent out a gentle mist of her magic to detect another's. Like dust being blown over liquid, Alōs's trail appeared. It was faint but there, hovering in the air. A light-green energy that led into the thick foliage.

With pulse quickening, Niya followed.

The crashing of the shore faded behind her and was replaced with sounds of wildlife as she wove between closely growing moss-covered trees and ducked under bright, glowing flowers. Twinkling bugs filled the night air, and she watched a spider with bright-silver legs climb along a leaf. She drank it all in, this new wild kingdom, the place where Alōs had been born. Part of her wanted to remain in the woods, look upon every new thing, but with a shake of her head, she kept on task.

Alōs's trail was beginning to fizzle out, and she would not squander this opportunity.

Reaching the jungle's end, Niya stepped onto a dirt path that appeared to line the side of a large wall, where hints of a town rested on the other side. She squinted into the night, waiting for anyone to pass.

None did.

In fact, she could feel no movement anywhere.

It was as if all kept to their homes this night. Warm glows emanated from the other side, and though she was desperate to climb over and see how the people of Esrom lived, that was not where Alōs had gone.

Turning left, Niya followed where the faint line of his magic still floated in the night along the edge of the path.

After barely a quarter sand fall, Niya stopped, the trail gone cold.

"Sticks," she muttered, spinning in a circle.

It was as if he'd just disappeared.

Confused, she ran a hand through the vines in front of her and, with a jump of excitement, felt a strange groove in the stone. She pulled the vines away to reveal a door.

"Sneaky pirate." She grinned.

It was clearly locked, but locked doors rarely stopped a Bassette. With a fluttering of her fingers, the handle clicked open, uncovering a dark stretch of tunnel.

Stepping through, Niya touched the cool, wet stone on either side of her, feeling her way forward in the black abyss. Her soft tread echoed dully along the dirt floor, mixing with her breaths. She walked like this for some time until a hazy glow at the end of the path appeared.

Her magic tingled along her skin as she hurried forward, her heart picking up its pace as she stepped into an enchanted courtyard filled with glowing pools. A floral fragrance danced around her invitingly, and she stood entranced.

What beautiful place is this?

Niya tipped her head up, drinking in the sparkling turrets stretching high above her.

By the stars and sea, she was in the palace.

Niya drew her brows together.

Why would Alōs come to the palace?

Before she could wonder further, she felt the energy of people approaching and darted behind a thick bush.

A group of servants in white passed through the courtyard. They held baskets of linens and trays filled with candles. Not a one spoke as they entered and then exited into a covered walkway at the other end.

On silent feet, Niya slunk in the other direction, following what little bits of Alōs's trail she could still detect.

She found herself walking through an opulent hall, where an intricate tiled mosaic decorated each of her steps and a beautiful depiction of a sun-filled sky made up the stained glass ceiling. The sparkling of silver was everywhere, and Niya's chest hummed in pleasure at the beauty.

But as she continued, Niya began to notice two things:

One, Alōs's trail of magic seemed tangled up with another's; and two, the palace was extremely empty. Besides the servants from earlier, she had yet to find a single guard or court member.

Niya's mind spun with what this could all mean. Where was everyone? And who was Alōs meeting in the palace? And why?

The energy in the air also felt off. It was oddly heavy and sober for how beautifully this kingdom glowed. Had something happened?

Niya's pace quickened as her curiosity burned stronger.

Turning a corner, she peered down a dark, thin corridor where it appeared Alōs had gone. But she was growing uncertain, as the magic in this place muddied up her Sight. Everything seemed to shimmer and sparkle with the lost gods' gifts. The art, the fabric draping the walls, even the insects that floated by.

She glanced behind her, to the quiet palace hall, wondering if she should backtrack. *No,* she thought, *I've made it this far; if anything I might pick up his trail at the end.* Turning back, she stared down her new path. No candles lit the way, but Niya had grown up in a palace of her own and knew when she'd found a servant's hallway. Slipping into the shadows, she felt her way forward, walking for what felt like forever before coming to a dead end.

A single torch sat in a sconce, lighting up the marble wall and revealing a tiny crack in its surface.

Niya pressed a hand to it and smiled when it gave easily.

She cautiously stepped through, finding herself behind a thick drape of fabric. She remained there when she sensed a group in the room beyond.

A voice filled the chamber.

Alōs's voice.

Niya stopped breathing.

"I can't stay much longer," he said.

"I'm glad you came at all, brother," said another man.

Brother?

Niya's heartbeat thumped erratically as she chanced a peek through an opening in the drapery.

She was in a bedroom, and a massive, beautiful one at that.

A large bed took up the majority of the space, and a canopy mimicking the night sky floated above. Hundreds of candles lit the space, throwing warm light across the opulent woven rugs and furnishings. Three figures stood at the end of the bed.

Alōs loomed large in his black leather coat, brown skin exposed at the base of his neck before giving way to his white tunic and black vest. His sword handle peeked out at his hip. Niya drank in his strong presence, which dominated that of his two other companions.

A man in blue robes stood across from him. And despite his long, braided white hair, he looked young, perhaps Niya's age. An ornate silver tattoo glimmered across his smooth forehead. It was a marking Niya had never seen before.

The third man appeared the most delicate, almost frail in comparison to Alōs. He was by far the youngest. His hair was as dark as night, dramatized by the white crown atop his head.

Royalty.

And was that . . . ?

Niya squinted.

It looked like silver paint sat frozen middrip on his forehead and hands.

"I must ask about your search," the young man said, placing his metallic fingers on Alōs's forearm. "Though I fear what you might answer."

"Then I suggest you do not ask. You have suffered enough this night, Ariōn."

"We both have," Ariōn corrected, looking frustrated. "They were your parents too."

Niya's mind reeled at what she was hearing, seeing.

They were your parents too.

This young man with a crown . . . was Alōs's brother?

Time seemed to stop as her heart froze in a panic, a ringing filling her ears.

But that would mean . . .

No, her mind screamed. *That cannot be possible.*

Alōs was . . . royalty?

"You feel different each time you visit," Ariōn continued when Alōs did not answer. "Your magic . . . it grows colder and colder. You are still doing things you wish you did not."

"Don't," warned Alōs, pulling his arm free. "The past has been written, and I would do every bit of it again."

Ariōn frowned. "Will you never stop suffering for me?"

"I would have suffered greater without you."

"You exist without me now."

"It is not the same."

"No? What is a family if you cannot be with them?"

"Do not argue with me about a time when you were too young, too *sick*, to know consequence." Annoyance flashed through Alōs's gaze. "I made a decision because our parents could not. Despite the price, I ensured both of Tallōs and Cordelia's children lived."

"Yes, lived," Ariōn mocked. "Like I live here? Alone? Unable to leave the palace compound, to step beyond my own walls and walk among our people. I could barely go for a swim without Mother and Father ensuring a horde of medics and healers surrounded my every move. By the lost gods, I've eaten the same meal for almost a decade! If this is living, Alōs, I would rather have died."

A tense silence filled the room.

"You think *you've* been cursed to be alone?" Alōs's tone contained a dark edge of destruction. "You, who were lucky enough to be raised in the sanctuary of our homeland and loved into adulthood by our parents. You have a room of devoted followers waiting in your chambers this very moment, a friend standing beside you now." Alōs gestured to the man in blue robes. "What do you know of alone? What do you know of being forced to start over with nothing and no way back?"

Ariōn wiped at his cheek, as if brushing away a tear, and Niya watched as Alōs's shoulders dropped ever so slightly, a bit of his fury dissipating. His body swayed forward, as if about to embrace his brother. But in the end, he kept still.

"I never asked you to sacrifice so much," said Ariōn eventually.

"You never needed to. We both know you would have done the same if our roles were reversed."

"You are right," Ariōn replied softly. "I'm sorry. I merely . . . miss you, especially today. Which is why I must know. Have you found it?"

"One part." Alōs took a small velvet bag from inside his coat pocket and placed it in Ariōn's palm. The young man spilled out a tiny red jewel, tracing his fingertips over the stone.

Niya instantly recognized the object as the same jewel that had been in Alōs's ring. He had removed it, but why?

"It's so small," said Ariōn.

"Yes," agreed Alōs. "And cost me greatly to reacquire."

"How much?"

"Don't worry yourself."

"How much?" demanded Ariōn.

"Let's just say I am getting used to being banished from kingdoms."

Niya took a step back as though punched, more dots connecting. Banishment . . . was this jewel from his ring the reason why Alōs would be so reckless as to steal *phorria* from the Thief Kingdom? But why? What was so special as to risk one's life and liberty for such a tiny gem?

Where did your biggest red stone go? The question she had asked Cebba. Were these two gems connected? And why would Ariōn need it?

"We are close to finding the rest," continued Alōs. "It's believed to be in the Valley of Giants, placed in the crown of the princess."

"Callista?" Ariōn's brows rose. "A girl of sixteen has our Prism Stone?"

"You are only a year older and will rule Esrom."

"Yes, but I am very mature for my age." Ariōn tipped his chin up, eliciting a small grin from Alōs.

"Extremely."

"Do not mock."

"I'm not."

Ariōn did not appear convinced. "We might not have seen each other in years, but I still know when you're making fun of me. A younger brother will *always* know that."

"I'll be more careful with my tone, then, next time."

Ariōn gave a very unprincely snort in response.

Niya watched the exchange with utter fascination and, if she was being honest, queasiness. It was all so . . . normal. Behavior similar to that of her and her sisters.

To see Alōs—a man who severed heads, commanded thieves, and seduced innocents—act as an older brother, show genuine *affection*, turned Niya's entire world on its axis.

What did you call a monster who was capable of love?

The same name as you, whispered a voice in the back of her mind.

A shiver ran the length of her.

No, she thought. *I am not the same as he!* Yet the conviction felt weak, forced. For she, too, had been called a beast and reveled in it, knowing she could also love.

"But as for your concern about the stone," continued Alōs, bringing her attention back to the room, "no one but us knows what it truly is; plus, when broken apart as it is presently, the Prism Stone doesn't hold any true power."

Niya's mind refocused, hearing his words.

Where did your biggest red stone go?

So this *was* part of the treasure Alōs hunted? A Prism Stone? Niya had never heard of such a thing, but if the rest winked as richly as the small gem in his ring . . .

"I wondered why I didn't feel any power in it." Ariōn touched the jewel again.

"Keep this part safe." Alōs closed his brother's fingers around the jewel. "I will search out the rest. But before I go, I will need something worthy to gift the young princess and something equal in measure to replace the rest of the stone we plan to take."

Ariōn nodded. "Ixō will ensure you part with what you need."

The robed figure, whom Niya surmised was Ixō, came to the young prince's side, taking the jewel from his outstretched hand.

"I will serve however you command." Ixō kissed Ariōn's palm.

The prince gave a small smile. "I know."

Niya watched Alōs regard their exchange, eyes calculating how Ixō's kiss lingered and how his brother did not seem to mind.

"You will succeed, brother." Ariōn turned back to him. "You will put the Prism Stone back together, and everything will be made whole once more."

"Some things, perhaps, but not all."

"I am king now. I will ensure your pardon."

"I'm not sure the people of Esrom would commend you for it," said Alōs sardonically.

"For once, you speak truths."

A high voice brought the group's attention to the bedchamber's entryway. A tall woman in similar blue robes as Ixō's stood at the open door. She had the same silver marking on her forehead, and her long black hair was decorated with matching beads that swayed as she approached. "You will forever be a treasonous deserter to the citizens of Esrom."

"That is not true," countered Ixō, his gaze stern. "There are many in court who understand why Prince Alōs acted as he did. Once the stone is returned, I know they would support a pardon."

"*If* the stone is returned, you mean." The woman looked down her nose at the man. "There is little time left for *Pirate* Alōs to find what he stole," she said, correcting his title with a sneer. "The magic in Esrom grows weaker by the day. It won't be long until we surface, for all the world to rape and pillage. I should not have you arrested but beheaded on the spot for returning here, especially on a mournful day such as—"

"Be silent." Ariōn's voice rang out, sounding much stronger than before. "You shall not speak of my brother's presence to anyone, and if you cannot do as I wish, Surb Dhruva, then you shall be relieved of your tongue."

Ariōn might as well have slapped the woman for the shock she displayed. "But Prince—"

"It is *King* Ariōn now," he corrected.

Surb Dhruva hesitated, a shrewd gleam in her eyes, before answering, "Of course, my king. I am merely trying to uphold the laws that even your parents adhered to."

"I think, under the circumstances, those laws can be ignored this night."

A thick silence hung over the chamber. Dhruva tipped her head up to meet Alōs's scrutinizing gaze before she dropped into a bow. "As you wish."

"You are much the same, Dhruva," said Alōs, his smile sharp.

"And you are much different. Though not in a way that's becoming."

"You never could find compliment in me."

"How could I from a boy who would commit such sin?"

"You know very well why I—"

"Enough," Ariōn interrupted the two, rubbing at his temples. "Enough. I do not have long with my brother, so I ask you to leave us in peace for a few more grain falls. Then we can go back to abiding by all the laws the lost gods laid upon us."

"I would feel I was failing my duty to protect if I were to leave you alone with an outlaw."

"I appreciate your loyalty, Surb Dhruva, but you would be failing your duty by disobeying my command."

Dhruva stiffened. "Very well, my king." She bowed lower this time, and Niya didn't miss the mockery in the flourish. "Surb Ixō, will you walk with me?"

Ixō glanced at Ariōn in question.

"Go; I will call for you again soon."

Ixō seemed pained to leave the young king but bowed in kind and followed Surb Dhruva out.

A new silence filled the room as Alōs and Ariōn were left alone.

"Tell me truthfully," said Alōs after a moment. "How much longer do the High Surbs think Esrom has?"

"The Room of Wells is nearly dry." Ariōn turned to face the bed, his attention dropping to what lay within. "The High Surbs believe we have a year at most."

Alōs's brows snapped together. "Why did you not send word?"

"Does your sandglass not tell you of the time left?" Ariōn challenged. "Besides, I know you have been searching out the pieces of the Prism Stone as fast as you can. Doing whatever you must to find them. Would you have been able to sail the seas quicker knowing this?"

"I might have."

"Even you, brother, cannot slow how fast the grains fall."

"You have *no idea* the things I am capable of."

"Don't I?" Ariōn rubbed the discolored skin on his hands, where brown met silver.

Alōs's jaw tensed. He was seemingly filled with too much of everything to respond.

"Let us not fight anymore," said Ariōn, a tiredness to his words. "You *will* find what we seek in time. I have faith. Then I will pardon your sins."

Alōs shook his head. "After everything, you still remain so optimistic."

"Someone must counter all your sourness." His brother gave him a small smile. "After my coronation, the law is mine to change, and as we discussed—"

"Oy! What are you doing back here?"

A gruff voice rang out behind Niya, and she whipped around. Two guards stood in the hidden doorway at her back. *Sticks!* She had been so wrapped up in what was going on in the room beyond that she hadn't been paying attention to the energy behind her.

Stupid. Stupid. Stupid.

The guards poked her with their pointed staffs, forcing her to walk forward, through the curtains and into the bedchamber.

As Niya neared, she was able to see what she previously could not. Ariōn was blind, his eyes covered in a whitish film. And it was not paint covering the top of his face and hands but skin, metallic in color. Sickly veins ran across the silver expanse, stopping where his brown skin started. She had heard of such a thing from Achak but had never seen it for herself. A marking of death paused.

"I'm sorry, Your Grace," one of the soldiers said at her back. "A servant reported seeing someone unfamiliar slip into your private entrance. We found her hiding behind the drapes."

"Who are you?" The young prince frowned. "I do not recognize your energy."

"She appears to be a spy." Alōs's dark voice curled forward.

Niya's gaze swung to his, every part of her vibrating with the urge to flee, to run, to escape. Instead she kept herself from cowering under the cool fire now blazing from Alōs's turquoise eyes. He looked down at her as if he wanted to take the blade from his hip and slice her clean through. Niya wondered what was stopping him.

"A spy?" Ariōn looked genuinely stunned as the guards grabbed her arms, keeping Niya from her own knives at her hips.

"No, Your Majesty," said Niya, though she kept her attention on Alōs. "I am no spy. I came here with your brother."

A muscle along Alōs's jaw twitched, and she gave him a hint of a smile, one that said, *Yes, I heard everything.*

Now, what to do with it?

Leverage. The word sang triumphant in her mind, despite her current predicament.

"You know this creature?" Ariōn turned to Alōs.

"I've never seen her a day in my life," he replied coolly.

"Liar!" Niya spat. "I am one of his pirates, Your Majesty."

Ariōn raised a single brow at Niya. "Are you? How curious, for I thought Alōs forbade any of his crew to step onto our sacred lands."

"I do." Alōs's voice was a thick rumble of foreboding.

"As I thought." Ariōn nodded. "Take her from here discreetly, Borōm," he instructed one of the guards. "And I trust neither of you will discuss anything, or anyone, you may have seen in this room, yes?"

The unspoken words were there. *You have not seen my brother this night.*

"Of course, Your Grace," answered the guards.

"Very good. I do not want anyone to think Esrom is under more turmoil, after what we have already suffered these past few days."

The guards tugged at Niya, and there was a grain fall when she hung on her indecision about whether to peacefully go with them or to fight and flee.

But then Alōs's commanding voice brought her back to where she was surrounded. "And spy, I would not try any tricks," he said, his tone a cold ice bath of warning. He approached slowly, a storm overtaking the room. "I know you wish to try many," he continued. "Your kind always do. But I shall remind you that Esrom is not large and rests at the bottom of the sea. Wherever you might look to hide, you will not remain undiscovered for long."

Though the gesture was subtle, Niya did not miss how Alōs rubbed the marking on his wrist. Their binding bet his forever connection to her.

She ground her teeth together, her magic a hot coil of energy begging to be set free.

Free.

But Alōs was right.

While Niya could have done many things in that moment, none would erase the memory of her discovery. None would sever her bond to this man who could track her movements if he so desired. And none would save her from his wrath once they were back on his ship.

In resignation, Niya relaxed her stance, her signal that she understood and would behave.

For now.

Still, Alōs's fury did not lessen; instead he leaned closer, his deep voice brushing hot along her ear. "You have overestimated my need for you by coming here, fire dancer. And for that there will be consequences."

Her eyes gripped his as he stepped back, disgust plain in his features. But Niya did not cower. She tipped her chin up as she was dragged away and smiled.

For though she might have been caught, so had Alōs.

And she let him know as her gaze swung to the two figures in the bed between him and his brother.

A couple. Two crowns.

Alōs's parents.

Dead.

Alōs wasn't merely a prince.

Alōs was meant to be a king.

Here lay the leverage Niya was searching for.

And it was in the form of a Prism Stone.

CHAPTER TWENTY-ONE

Niya was growing accustomed to the insides of prison cells. At least, she assumed this was a prison, given the bars. The rest was all rather . . . comfortable.

Standing in the center of the room, Niya took in a spacious cot with a thick duvet, a washing basin with a pitcher of water, and a chair tucked into a corner. There was even a finely woven rug beneath her feet.

It was stars and seas better than her hammock crammed between two pirates inside a pungent hall aboard the *Crying Queen*. Walking to the pitcher, she poured herself a glass, drinking down the cool liquid greedily, and wondered if she might as well take up permanent residence here.

Wiping her mouth with the back of her hand, Niya glanced down, reading the cover of a book that sat beside her washing bowl.

Repent to Replenish: A Sinner's Final Prayers.

Or perhaps not.

Out of habit, her hands moved to her hips but grasped air. Her knives had been taken from her by the guards, which was more annoying than surprising, given she had just gotten them back. But her boots hadn't been removed, nor her clothes switched out for a prisoner uniform.

Her mind spun for what to do next, recalling all she had just learned.

So Alōs is royalty, was born to rule Esrom.

Niya ran a hand down her face, unable to hold in a snort of laughter.

If she had gambled about the truth of such a tale, she would have lost.

Despite her and her sisters being a part of many twisted stories, this . . . this seemed utterly insane.

Alōs might exude princely confidence, but he was a scoundrel, immoral, coldhearted . . . all right, so most royalty carried these traits as well.

Niya shook her head. At least this explained why Alōs's powers felt so deep and ancient. It was because they were.

By comparison, his younger brother Ariōn's gifts felt more like an ember than fire. Niya assumed that had something to do with whatever disease had given him his silver scars. Alōs and Ariōn were part of the most ancient royal bloodline in Esrom: the Karēks.

While not many in Aadilor had ever seen Esrom, all knew who ruled the hidden city. The Karēk family was said to have sat on the throne since the lost gods had still walked among mortals. In fact, Niya couldn't remember any other surname being attached to the crown. Though she'd never been taught who currently sat on the throne, nor whether they had any children. Their father seemed to think such details were trivial when it came to a city that hid underwater for centuries and never traded with any other realm. The name Karēk was all that mattered.

I ensured both of Tallōs and Cordelia's children lived.

So Tallōs and Cordelia were Alōs's parents . . .

But what had happened to cause Alōs to need to ensure their children lived?

The magic in Esrom grows weaker by the day. It won't be long until we surface, for all the world to rape and pillage.

The Room of Wells is nearly dry. The High Surbs believe we have a year at most.

Surb Dhruva's and Ariōn's words replayed in Niya's mind, her foot tapping impatiently as she worked out how to use this to her advantage. She also tried to ignore a twinge of sadness she felt for Esrom and the threat it apparently was under. For Surb Dhruva was right. If such a treasure as this kingdom surfaced, after centuries of hiding from the rest of Aadilor, then it most certainly would be attacked, those who sought sanctuary here destroyed. Rare beauty brought war more than peace, for man was a greedy creature, seeking to master land they felt they deserved despite it already belonging to another.

But such empathy would not help Niya in her task. She had her own problems to worry about. Like getting out of her binding bet and finally becoming free of the insufferable weight of being ruled by Alōs.

Prism Stone, her magic whispered through her veins.

Yes, thought Niya. Whatever this object was, it sounded important and was what had caused Alōs to be banished. But why would he steal from his own people, especially an object that all of Esrom apparently depended on? And how would this have saved his brother's life?

While there was much still to learn, Niya had heard enough to know one thing: Alōs needed this stone more desperately than she had originally thought, and *that* was her leverage.

With a new plan forming, Niya moved to the bars of her cell, grasping them.

She hissed in pain.

They were ice cold, leaving her palms red, nearly frostbitten.

"Lovely," she muttered.

"Better than mine," said a voice from a cell across from her. In the darkness Niya could just barely make out an old man with a graying beard and glowing green eyes sitting on his cot, a book lying open on his lap. "Lightning," he explained, pointing to the bars in front of him. "At least that's what it feels like if I touch them."

"Is there a way past?"

The man laughed. "You think I'd be sitting here if I knew that?"

Niya frowned, reassessing the metal. Now that she was closer, she could make out waves of magic vibrating from the bars. A spell.

"I haven't had company in some time," said the prisoner, shutting his book. "You must have done something awful to end up here."

"Why?" She went to retrieve her own book.

"There's little crime in Esrom," explained the man. "But they still don't bring pickpockets and drunks up here. That lot are taken to a shared room a floor below. You and me, what we've done gets special treatment."

Niya threw her book against the bars. To her surprise, it stuck, ice quickly growing over the cover, before it cracked, shattering to the ground.

"Interesting." She placed hands on hips.

"You'll regret that," said the man, coming forward. "I've read my prayer tome fifty-two times now."

Niya ignored him as she called up the powers that sat hot in her veins. Twisting into a quick dance, she spun her arms out. Flames shot from her palms and blasted against the bars.

The metal hissed, and steam filled her cell. She kept pushing until her limbs ached. Lowering her hands, Niya breathed heavily as the smoke dissipated.

The bars were still perfectly intact.

"Well, sticks," she muttered.

"That's a pretty power you've got there," said the man. "Are you a murderer?"

"Excuse me?" Her gaze snapped to his.

"Are you a murderer?" he repeated.

"Uh. I've killed people, yes."

"Many?"

"Enough."

The man slid her a grin. "Me too."

"I didn't *enjoy* it, though." She frowned, turning from the man to search her cell for anything more she could use.

"I did."

Niya gave a humorless laugh. "Then I see why you're in here."

"I think you enjoyed it too." His glowing green eyes followed her movements around her cell. "With all that heat in you. Yes, I think there are some you enjoyed very much sending to the Fade."

Niya paused as she lifted up her mattress, thinking about that for a moment. "Yes, perhaps some."

The man let out a cackle of delight. She noticed then that he wore the same blue robe as Ixō and Surb Dhruva, yet he didn't have the silver marking on his forehead, only an angry red scar. Niya didn't know exactly what a High Surb was, but she assumed, from the looks of them, that they were some sort of holy order. Every city in Aadilor had its religious sect, people who still gave themselves to the lost gods' teachings, despite their abandonment.

"Are you a surb?" she asked.

His grin held. "Was."

"Where is your silver marking?"

This sobered him. "They removed my chaplet," he said before he spat on the ground.

"Is that what it's called? A chaplet?"

"Where are you from?" He eyed her. "Not here, I imagine."

"No, not here."

"You're strong." It was not a question.

"Is that important?"

"No." The man breathed in deep before blowing a shot of water from his mouth. His bars sparked with blue lightning as his liquid spell slapped against it. With a wave of his hand, he evaporated it all into mist. He met her gaze again. "Strength is not important here."

Niya chewed her bottom lip, sizing the man up again.

"Do all surbs have the gifts?" asked Niya.

"In varying degrees."

She had felt the magic in Ixō and Dhruva, but it was good to know what else she was dealing with. She also saw an opportunity with this acquaintance.

"What can you tell me about this Prism Stone?" she said.

The man's brows rose. "Now, how has someone not from here come to know of such a thing?"

"Why did Prince Alōs steal it?" She ignored his question, pushing for him to answer hers.

The ex-surb's smile was crooked. "I can see why you are now up here with me, destined for the gallows."

Niya did not reply, only waited.

"You ask of history from long ago, girl."

"And you appear like one who might have lived it."

His echoing laugh hit against their stone walls. "Oh, I have lived it and more. Which is why I know we do not speak of the banished prince or the heart of Esrom he stole."

"Heart of Esrom?"

"Aye," said the man with a nod, coming closer to his bars. "The Prism Stone was the last gift the gods gave our holy people before they left. It is filled with their blood."

Niya gave him a dubious look.

"It is true," he urged. "And do you know what pure blood from the gods is?"

"Sticky?" suggested Niya.

"Endless magic," said the man. "And some was contained inside the Prism Stone, which our ancestors placed in the Room of Wells. All the water in Esrom eventually flows through the Room of Wells, where it washes over the stone, collecting power and mixing with the magic of this chamber, before circulating back into our kingdom once more. How else do you imagine we stay safely beneath the waves? Have islands that rise and fall with the tides? A spell of that magnitude is never allowed to grow tired."

Niya listened like a starved child being fed her first meal, greedily taking in every word. "But now the spell does grow tired," she pointed out.

The ex-surb's eyes narrowed. "I can see ideas turning in your head, girl, and I suggest you abandon them. Whatever you seek here, no good will come of it."

Niya ignored his warning, her mind digging through this history and the story of Alōs later taking such a sacred stone from his homeland.

Why?

It was the question that spun around and around and one Niya had no good answer for, besides more proof of Alōs's dark heart.

But yet he searches to bring it back, she reasoned.

Why? Why? Why?

An image of Ariōn and Alōs in their parents' bedchamber, Alōs's concerned gaze as he looked upon his younger brother.

I would have suffered greater without you.

Could it be possible that such a dark soul as he could truly care for another? Sacrifice his own livelihood for another?

Niya's chest burned at the idea, an old scar she had thought faded transforming back into a scab to pick. If Alōs was capable of such emotion, what did that mean for how he had treated her?

Niya's magic hissed with hot revenge through her veins. Her old resolve of hatred toward the pirate captain settling like comforting coals in her heart.

None of this matters, she thought. *The only part that does is the leverage I now have against him.*

But now what?

Sliding her hands into her pockets, Niya pinched her brows together, growing frustrated with her next move. She could of course wait here for Alōs's unavoidable wrath, along with the punishment that came with trespassing in Esrom, but Niya was not good at waiting. She might have agreed to leave him and his brother peacefully, but that didn't mean she was going to lie down and let the pirate, prince, or whatever he thought himself to be walk all over her.

She was Niya Bassette, dancer of the Mousai, for the lost gods' sake. If she was going into battle, she would meet her enemy on even footing. And that meant escaping from this prison and showing Alōs all the talents she brought to his arsenal.

You have overestimated my need for you by coming here.

Well, Niya would see about that.

Alōs needed more help than he let on, and Niya was going to use that for all it was worth.

Niya's thoughts froze as she brushed a finger over a bump in her pocket.

Oh! Her heart picked up its pace as she removed a small pouch. She tipped out a tiny gold ball into her palm. Niya had forgotten she had stuck this into her pocket, so long ago it had been since she had changed from the soiled dress she had worn in Jabari to her current pirate's garb.

A grin curved along her mouth as she took in her seed scoopling. *Thank the lost gods!*

Making her way back to the door to her cell, she crouched in front of the lock.

"No use, I tell ya," said her prison mate, inching closer to his bars but not touching them. "Might as well sit back and share our life stories to pass the grains falling. They like to make you wait before you learn your sentencing."

Niya ignored him. She had only one shot at this.

Delicately, she placed the seed scoopling against the door's latch, holding her breath as the ice quickly crept around it. Right before it closed over the shell, she flicked out a flame from her finger and lit the scoopling on fire.

It gave a little puff of smoke as it caught before it grew in size, oozing black and fighting against the frost attempting to cover it. The seed scoopling won, eating right through the icy lock. A giant dripping hole sat where the latch used to be. The seed scoopling fell to the ground with a slap and began to burrow through the stone floor.

Nothing could stop a seed scoopling once activated. Not even magic.

Niya gave a testing nudge to the cell door with her boot.

It creaked open.

She smiled.

"Perhaps we can tell our stories another time," said Niya to the old man as she gingerly stepped through. "That little guy is going to drop into the next floor soon, and who knows what, or who, might be in its path."

"Wait!" the man called out as she walked by. "Help me. Do the same trick for me!"

But even if Niya wanted to, she couldn't, for she only had that one. The man's shouts faded to echoes of distress as she hurried down the hall, a distant zapping and flashes of light behind her before all fell quiet.

Niya made her way from the top floor, where her cell seemed to be, to the one beneath.

Here she passed more cells, simpler than hers, with only plain benches lining walls. All were crammed with multiple prisoners. They were an odd bunch, wearing varying degrees of expensive-looking clothes. Coats, capes, tunics, and dresses in impeccable shape. The only thing amiss was the strong odor of alcohol.

Well-bred drunks, thought Niya. *How interesting.*

Esrom's main offenses seemed to fall with overindulgence.

And though she felt their gazes on her, a few calling out, she ignored them, senses instead prickling for any nearing guards.

But oddly for a prison, it was so far void of soldiers or watchful eyes.

Niya descended to another floor with little trouble. There, however, she was hit with the sensation of a figure shifting at the bottom of the stairs.

As she crept down, she caught the edge of a guard's uniform, his hand grasping his pointed staff, fingers thrumming along it in apparent boredom.

I'll give you a task to distract you, she thought as she curled her wrists around, gathering her magic. With a flick, she flew out her gifts like an orange fishing line, severing the thin veil of the guard's own powers.

Her thread of magic wound around his head, latching on to his eyes and his mind.

Mine. Her gifts tugged.

Niya sensed the guard grow slack, and as she took the last steps to stand in front of him, she peered into his glassy eyes. "Follow," she whispered, and follow he did.

Niya would be less conspicuous with a guard escorting her.

"Show me the way out," she quietly commanded. The man complied, maneuvering them this way and that through the prison.

Niya's heartbeat grew quick as open windows eventually appeared in a new hall. Early dawn streamed in to paint the white brick around her a soft yellow.

Niya glanced out the glass, glimpsing an empty stone courtyard fortified by a tall wall. There was no splendor here like in the palace, only a platform in the center. An execution block.

Niya did not linger on the scene, instead twisted around a new bend, only to come to a halt as a cool current hit her like a kick in the chest.

Her magic buzzed through her veins, warning bells going off.

She knew this energy all too well.

Alōs was near.

Niya rubbed her lips together, holding steady to the spell that leashed the guard at her side.

She knew she would have to face Alōs eventually, and it appeared eventually was now.

Squaring her shoulders, Niya followed his trail of green energy, which eventually disappeared into a storage room.

She waited by the threshold, peering over the piled boxes that rested inside. The space was full of shadows, save for a sliver of daylight that crept in through a high-cut window.

Though she couldn't see him, Alōs was most certainly there. Somewhere.

Come play, his energy seemed to whisper. *If you dare.*

With her guard in tow, Niya walked in.

Alōs appeared from a darkened corner at the far end like black smoke. His coat swayed by his feet, ebony hair loosely pulled back to make way for the severe angles of his face. His glowing blue eyes were reduced to slits as he took her in. He did not seem surprised to see her outside her cell but rather was thrumming with the same rage as earlier. Alōs stopped at the edge of where the sun ran along the floor, his dark boots toeing the light.

With barely a flick of his hand, the door behind her closed, his magic a cold gust blowing her hair back.

"New pet of yours?" Alōs nodded to Niya's spelled guard.

"If he behaves."

Alōs's response was perhaps more dangerous than his glare. He grinned.

"I wondered how long that cell would contain you," he said, the air tensing between them as he began to circle her in the small space. He was a coiled snake looking for the right time to strike.

"How did you know I would pass here?" asked Niya, remaining still, the guard standing close by her back.

"It's the only way out," he explained. "Plus," he added, bending to whisper in her ear, "you and I know that I can always find the places you roam, fire dancer."

Niya's skin was dusted with bumps as she felt his hot breath along her neck.

"Then why didn't you know I had followed you from the ship?" she challenged.

"I didn't think you were foolish enough to try for me to check. You were ordered to stay on board."

"And you're used to everyone following your orders?" She tracked his every step as he came to stop in front of her.

"You know, I kept the skull of the last of my crew who disobeyed in Esrom," said Alōs, head tilting. "I wonder what I'll do with yours?"

"From what I hear, it is not only your crew with rules to follow when in Esrom."

A flash of something sharp passed through Alōs's gaze. "Careful, fire dancer. You do not want to upset me further, or I won't be responsible for what I do next."

Niya folded her arms over her chest, feigning disinterest, all while her heart beat in anticipation of a fight. "What amusing bedtime stories you must weave for yourself to think your threats would have any effect on me."

"No story will be as amusing as the one I will tell of your death. There will be an encore, to be sure. Pirates of the *Crying Queen* are not keen on being spelled by one of their own."

"How do you know I spelled them?"

"It's the only reason they would allow you to disobey me."

She lifted a brow. "And how do they deal with captains who lie to them? How many know of the prince who poses as a pirate? Or ex-prince, rather. Treason, was it?"

Alōs took a step closer, his energy like ice claws digging into her own as his presence consumed her. "You know nothing of my past."

"I know enough."

"Enough to get you killed."

"Not that I don't find your continued threats entertaining, *Prince*"—Niya shoved her power against his, a red wave of heat hitting a wall of cool green—"but neither of us shall die this day."

"Are you sure? Because you seem like you *really* want to enter the Fade."

"We both know you cannot kill me while I hold this mark."

"That does not mean I cannot get another to—"

"Wha—? Where am I?"

The guard's voice sounded at Niya's back, and she turned to find her spell on him had unhooked when she had momentarily redirected her magic to Alōs. The young man blinked, confused, as he gazed about his surroundings. When he took in Alōs, his eyes widened. "*You* . . . you're . . . by the lost go—"

He was cut off as Niya threw out a punch of her gifts to smack against his head. The guard fell to the ground, unconscious.

Niya turned back to Alōs, smugness in her features. "It is good to remember that I am more useful than most of your pirates, or did you forget how I helped you locate the other piece to your precious Prism Stone?"

He eyed her for a long moment, no doubt taking in what she now might know. "Yes, you are useful on those rare occasions when you follow orders," he began slowly. "Which are few and far between. Your liability has grown tiresome, and tiresome creatures don't stay long alive on my ship."

His words echoed Saffi's.

"You need my help, Alōs."

His brows rose at that. "Your *help* has been mine to command this past month."

"Yes, but as you have just pointed out, you may order me to complete a task, but the result will be *very* different if I do it willingly."

211

A mocking grin grew. "Oh, I know all about your willing acts, fire dancer."

Niya clenched her hands into fists, her magic hissing for her to move, to maim, to burn the man who could so quickly and easily ignite her rage. But that would have been the old Niya, the reactionary Niya, not the one who now waited, planned, thought. It took all her self-control to remain still.

"I am part of the Mousai," said Niya, steering the conversation back to where she needed it to go, "part of the Thief King's favorite executioners. There are advantages I hold in Aadilor that not even a nefarious pirate, or disgraced prince, has. Obtaining my willing help is tapping into *all* my resources and powers. My sisters' included."

Alōs remained silent, which Niya took as encouraging.

"You are right that I don't know much of your past or your history with this Prism Stone, but I do know you need it. *Esrom* needs it. And I can help you get it quicker than any other soul aboard your ship. But while you may command me to do something, even our binding bet cannot force me to tell you all I know or use all of the magic at my disposal. That can change, however. I will give you my full, willing aid to find what you seek, so long as my debt to you is completed upon its safe return."

Niya's plan tumbled from her on the spot. It might have been decent, but she knew it wasn't the strongest hand. She hoped Alōs's desperation to help his brother and save his homeland would outweigh this fact—and would outweigh his current desire to have her killed.

Niya needed to remind him she was worth much more alive than as a skull on his desk.

Alōs studied her a long while, calculation apparent in his glowing eyes. "It might take longer than a year," he said eventually, "which would make your sentence longer."

Niya's heart jumped in relief; this might actually work.

"We both know you do not have longer than a year."

The Room of Wells is nearly dry. The High Surbs believe we have a year at most.

Ariōn's words seemed to fill the silence.

"And if you fail at helping me in time?" asked Alōs, brows drawing together.

"As I remember hearing it, Esrom will then be exposed to all of Aadilor to pick over. Will you really care about anything at that point?"

"Yes."

She weighed her options. "Then if I fail, I will serve a year more."

"You want to make another binding bet?" he asked, disbelieving. "After everything?"

"My odds are all I have at this point."

He watched her closely but did not respond.

"Do we have a deal?" she pushed.

"That depends," said Alōs slowly. "While my crew knows of my old connection with this place—"

"They know you're a prince?"

"They do not know what I seek," he continued past her. "The lost gods know I'm facing enough obstacles in hunting down the other part to this stone. I do not need those aboard the *Crying Queen* getting any ideas regarding trying to take it for themselves."

"While they are pirates, I do not think any of your crew are so idiotic as to steal from you. They all heard what happened to Prik."

"Some treasures breed treason."

True, thought Niya.

"But what of Kintra?" she asked.

"What of her?"

"Is even your quartermaster not to be trusted?"

Alōs glanced away. "Kintra is the exception."

Such an answer shocked Niya, and it took her a moment to soak this in. *Kintra is the exception.* Why did that sting to hear?

Because you weren't, a slithering voice said in her ear.

213

Niya frowned, shaking off the strange emotion clawing hot in her chest. "I did not realize you and she were . . ."

Alōs lifted an amused brow at that. "Were what?"

"Nothing, never mind. I will not tell your crew what we seek."

"Give me your word," he commanded.

Niya frowned but replied, "I give you my word as the dancer of the Mousai, loyal subject to the Thief King, to not tell any pirates of the *Crying Queen* about your hunt for the Prism Stone." She held out her hand. "So do we now have a deal?"

Alōs pressed his lips together, thinking. "Very well," he agreed, though he didn't seem pleased about it. "You *will* give me all your aid in getting back the Prism Stone, and in trade, I will set your binding bet free upon its safe return to Esrom. If not, you shall serve another year aboard the *Crying Queen*."

Niya's pulse quickened in silent victory as they each called up their magic then, winding it around their hands. Alōs unsheathed his dagger and pricked each of their palms. Niya's stomach twisted with anticipation. She had found a way out. She was that much closer to being free. Free of this man. Free of paying for her past sins. Free to finally move on with her life.

Niya gripped Alōs's palm, his touch cold against her heat, their blood mixing as their powers twisted around one another, a fight for dominance.

"*Vexturi,*" they said in unison, and Niya watched their magic spin faster and faster before snapping into their skin.

She pulled her hand free, studying the black mark on her wrist, which was changing along with her new binding bet. Half of it began to fade, lines of her future not yet permanent.

Niya might have made a bigger gamble, but for the first time since meeting Alōs all those years ago, she felt like she had an upper hand. She could not help the triumphant smile edging her lips.

"Let's see how long that grin stays after we return to the ship," said Alōs, opening the door to their closet. "You still must answer for disobeying me, fire dancer, and for spelling my crew. But do not worry. I'll promise to make your punishment quick." His gaze was sharp as he turned, leaving her standing in the dark space.

Niya's feeling of triumph was short lived.

CHAPTER TWENTY-TWO

*T*he sound reverberated in Niya's skull before the pain. The whip cracked across her skin, hot flames against her back. She was being torn in two. But she did not call out, did not give the pirates who watched, their shouts of glee filling the air, the satisfaction of hearing her agony. Especially the man who held the whip.

Alōs stood behind her, cold determination in his eyes to fulfill the sentence his crew had demanded. *Have Red spill red with lashes,* they had called. As Alōs pulled back the leather rope, readying to strike again, Niya turned forward. She squeezed her eyes shut as she dug her fingers into the straps where she was tied to the mainmast. Energy raced toward her, followed by cool air a grain fall before the sharp slice of retribution cut against her spine once more. Her jaw clamped so tight she feared her teeth would crack and shatter to the floor.

Her magic churned up fire in her gut. It screamed to be freed, to lash back. *We can slice him down,* it sang in her blood. *Nothing will be left but ash. We will not even save his bones.* By some miracle, she kept her power contained. Because even in her silent terror, in her desperation to burn each and every person who stood near, she knew she had brought this upon herself. She might be foolish, but she was not dumb. Despite originally believing she had a chance of making it back to the ship with none the wiser, she had sneaked off to Esrom knowing the possible repercussions.

Now here she knelt, before the bloodthirsty pirates.

Saffi had been the one to position her against the mast, her artillery boss's features holding nothing but hurt and rage. Whatever trust the woman might have begun to extend to Niya, she had quickly severed it by spelling her.

Niya had made each of them look weak, helpless. And to a lot like this, that was worse than death.

Still, Niya would not have changed what she had done.

She looked up to her binding bet, which peeked from beneath the ropes around her wrists. Half of it now erased, the other half soon to disappear when she found the other piece of the Prism Stone. Her sentence to this ship would be gone. No more.

Crack.

A gasp left Niya in a whoosh as another blaze sliced across her back, clearing her mind of all thought. Uncontrolled tears streamed down her face, snot from her nose.

She began to shiver.

"Harder!" some of the crew goaded beside her.

"Where are ya powers now, Red?" another shouted.

She would be shown no mercy here.

Not only had Niya made them look like fools, but she had also disobeyed their captain. Any pirate who had acted thus would be punished, *had* been punished, even killed. A flash of Prik being decapitated beside her filled her mind. These were the rules on the *Crying Queen*. And she was part of the *Crying Queen*, whether she liked it or not.

Plus, the law was the same in the Thief Kingdom. She knew because she and her sisters were the enforcers for their king. Torture and punishment were acts synonymous with the Mousai. They might be creatures who spun awake beauty, but it was a mirage concealing a fatal touch. How many souls had she sent to the Fade for their transgressions? Niya shook the question from her mind, for it did not matter. This was the world they all lived in.

Her father had raised his daughters to be brave, ensured they learned not to crumble under pain or heartache, for life was ripe with both, he would say. Niya was determined to make him proud now as well as her sisters.

She could take this punishment as any on board this ship would, as her family would have too.

This was the price of the leverage she had sought.

Niya caught Bree and Green Pea standing silently to one side, and though they did not share in the jeering, their gazes held a mix of emotion—anger, frustration, disappointment, sadness.

A wave of guilt slithered into Niya's chest a moment before another lash fell upon her like lightning. Cold and hot, bone breaking.

HURRRRT, her magic demanded, nearly choking her as it fought to be let loose. But Niya tightened her hold around it, sucking down the eruption of revenge wanting to be freed from every pore on her body. She panted past the consuming pain dizzying her mind and running red rivulets down her skin.

She would prove to this ship of scoundrels that while she might be many things, she was no coward. And if nothing else, that would keep a seed of respect in their detestable hearts.

Hearts she had been on the cusp of connecting with.

Crack.

Niya bowed forward, her cheek slapping against the wooden mast.

She could smell her blood and sweat soaking her shirt, iron and salt invading her nostrils.

Stay in control! she silently screamed at her gifts.

For it wasn't merely her pride that kept Niya from striking out. It was remembering the look on Alōs's face when he'd seen her in his parents' bedchamber. He'd been enraged, to be sure, but he'd also revealed another emotion that Niya clung to: terror. Niya had found more than one weakness in the nefarious pirate's cold, hard veneer this night: his family, Ariōn. She did not revel in the loss of his parents, of course. Niya was not that heartless. But beyond this Prism Stone, for her to know another precious secret of Alōs's, just as he had known one of hers, brought a wicked grin to her lips.

Crack.

Niya bit her tongue. Blood pooled in her mouth as she forced her focus once again on the half-faded band on her wrist. She had found a way out.

She would be free.

Free from this ship.

Crack.

Free from any more pain the man behind her could cause.

Crack.

Pain she wondered if he enjoyed inflicting to hide his own.

CHAPTER TWENTY-THREE

The *Crying Queen* sailed topside, leaving Esrom and entering waters much closer to the Valley of Giants. Despite the days of travel this saved, Alōs sat in his chambers unhinged.

He hadn't felt like this in a very long while.

He hated it.

Alōs could always control his emotions. He allowed very little to get under his skin.

But now it was as if worms wriggled all around.

His gaze loomed over the silver sandglass on his desk, the grains filtering to fill the bottom more than the top. Alōs curled his hand into a fist, holding back the urge to swipe the bloody thing out of his view, to hear the satisfying crash of the glass shattering against his floor, sand spilling out, no longer counting down his failures.

Swiveling his chair around, Alōs looked out to the morning light bathing the azure sea beyond his windowpane. He was being stretched too thin. Too many things to command, to find, to fix, to forget, to hold in. Which role was he meant to play today?

Cold: Cold was the only solace he had, where he could escape within and keep still. Cold allowed him to think clearer. Be solid. Strong.

Though even he knew the problem with ice was how easily it broke under the right tool.

Niya seemed to be the pointed hammer, forged in heat, swinging down again and again.

And he had brought her aboard.

Alōs rubbed against the throb pounding along his temples.

Finding Niya in his parents' bedchamber, so close to their lifeless bodies, his fragile brother by his side, had erupted an anger in Alōs he had never before felt. All in that room were the last bits of his past that kept light in his dark heart. And Niya had been witness.

He had felt raw and exposed standing there, her blue eyes pinned on him, triumphant smile on her lips. It was intolerable and something he had to quickly remedy.

Yet despite it all, he had not enjoyed carrying out the fire dancer's sentencing as he might have suspected. Perhaps it was because she'd so willingly followed him back to the ship, both of them silent in their own thoughts. She hadn't put up a fight, either, as her punishment had been voted upon by the crew, before she'd been turned to take her lashings. Such a powerful creature resigned to her fate. It felt . . . wrong. Even if she had brought it upon herself.

But Alōs *had* to do it. Had to satisfy his pirates. Had to follow the rules that he had set upon his ship. Those who disobeyed were punished. Alōs had killed the last pirate who'd been so foolish as to follow him in Esrom.

And though he had threatened to end Niya's life, he truly did need her help.

Alōs let out a steadying breath as his magic stirred with his annoyance.

Niya was right. She held powers greater than any other of his crew and connections in the Thief Kingdom that could be extremely advantageous come the time Alōs required them. So there Alōs stood, finding himself in the unfortunate position of having to take any advantage he could to regain the other part of the Prism Stone.

He needed Niya's willingness to aid him, not just her obedience. And with her possible shortened sentence, she had her incentive to do so.

But if Alōs was not of a mind to take Niya's life for her breaking his laws, something of equal measure had needed to be carried out for his crew to not revolt. It was also the only way Niya could get back in her peers' good graces and how he could hold his position of power. His pirates would have found their own punishment for her if Alōs had not, bringing chaos in the form of revenge onto his ship. Alōs could not have that. It was better he be the one in control than those who would not stop until she was sent to the Fade.

New crew members were always looked upon skeptically, but one who so quickly played them for fools was as good as dead.

His pirates had wanted blood, so blood was what he'd given them.

Alōs kept it to eight lashes, however, and none strong enough to do severe damage. His restraint while in his rage surprised even him. But just as he needed her help, he needed Niya healthy, not healing once they reached the Valley of Giants. He hoped she understood the lightness of her punishment.

His hands still vibrated from the memory of the whip as it had met its mark. Leather to flesh.

He shook his palms out.

He was changing. Again. And Alōs wasn't sure it was in a way he desired.

Leaning back in his chair, Alōs listened to the slow trickle of the silver sandglass behind him.

He was growing tired. Tired of the chase, the scheming, the race to always be making up for his past. But most of all he was growing tired of cruelty.

And that was a dangerous problem.

He could not survive the life he'd built if he was not ruthless.

Even from birth Alōs had been required to be harder, cerebral rather than playful, for he had been meant to be king. He had to be capable of making decisions many could not. This had produced a certain amount of apathy in his blood from an early age. "To rule with respect," his mother had told him, "one must place a kingdom above themselves, place the fate of many above the sentencing of one."

But now his parents were dead. His younger brother was to be the new king of a homeland on the brink of exposure and collapse. Ariōn would never survive.

The problem with a civilization hiding for millennia under the lost gods' protection was that it grew weak. Why build fortifications or learn to fight when it was not needed? Esrom had grown soft in its comfortable bubble under the sea.

The continuous sound of grains falling echoed loudly in his ears despite Alōs's best efforts to ignore the intricately carved sandglass on his desk. Time lost. Hope lost.

The worst of it was that he was to blame for this race against time. Though he hadn't realized the exact consequence of his actions then. He'd been merely a young boy desperately looking for a solution, a fix for an outcome he couldn't bear—his younger brother's death.

It was springtime in Esrom when Ariōn was born. A time filled with festivals and parties and music in the streets. The palace was abuzz with merriment at the news of the young prince, yet deep in the royal chambers, a somber mood lay hidden. Ariōn had been born too early, too frail, and would not take to his mother's breast.

Alōs stood beside his father as they kept watch on the queen in her bed, the small bundle of the new prince in her arms. She sang a soothing lullaby to the babe. For two nights she did not stop even as the tune grew more haunting, sands slipping away. Alōs watched his younger brother's brown skin grow pale. But it seemed Ariōn had been born with the queen's strong heart, for on the third day he finally turned and latched on to suckle.

That was the first and only time Alōs would see his mother cry.

Yet despite Ariōn's fragile beginning, he persevered. He grew from babe to child to young man, all while ignoring his quickly shortened breaths after the smallest of exertions. Nothing as trivial as fatigue would stop Ariōn from convincing Alōs to partake in every sort of mischief. Ariōn was able to laugh and joke and radiate a light stronger than his future could hold. And Alōs was deeply in love with him.

It was on Ariōn's eleventh birthday that Alōs saw the change. His brother's smile did not quite reach his eyes as they sat opening his gifts. Nor did he touch his cake, which was his favorite: cherry blossom filled with lemon icing.

Later that night Alōs slipped from his rooms to go to his brother's, only to find his parents there first. A chill washed over Alōs as he took in his mother and father huddled over Ariōn's bed, a healer beside them. He listened by the doorframe to his brother's wheezes as the healer spoke the words that would send the first nail of life's cruelty into his heart.

"I am sorry, Your Graces, but nothing can be done."

"That cannot be true," insisted Tallōs. "This is Esrom; we have islands full of rare plants to heal all illnesses."

The medic looked like it pained him to continue but said, "Yes, but not this kind."

"You say it is called Pulxa?" asked his mother while placing a hand on his father's shaking shoulder.

"Yes, my queen, a rare blood disease."

"How are we just learning of this now?" Tallōs began to stalk the room.

"It can disguise itself for a long while," explained the healer. "Especially if those who suffer its pains do not report any ailments."

Tallōs's gaze whipped to the man. "Do not blame my son for you and your staff failing in your duties to find out about this sooner!"

The medic grew red. "Your Grace, I apologize; that was not my meaning."

"We understand," said the queen, gazing down at her son. "Ariōn is a proud soul. He does not like to burden others. But I agree with my husband. We are a kingdom of miracles. There must be something. And if not here, surely a solution can be found in all of Aadilor."

The healer rubbed his lips together, appearing to grow more uncomfortable. "Pulxa can be slowed, yes, but inevitably . . ."

"Go on," coaxed Alōs's mother.

"You see, it starts in the limbs, Your Majesties, before working its way toward the heart, destroying everything as it goes. And I fear the young prince has it very close to his heart by now."

Alōs turned from the scene then, a ringing filling his ears, his own heart stopped as he sought the only people he had been taught could conjure miracles. Alōs went to find the High Surbs.

They sat imposing in their fine cloaks and high-backed chairs within their holy receiving room. Each gazed down their nose at Alōs, who stood before them, desperate and pleading.

"We cannot stop the will of the lost gods," said High Surb Fōl.

"Nor can we keep what the Fade wants." High Surb Zana shook her head. "That sort of magic is forbidden."

"It would be a tragedy to lose your brother," High Surb Dhruva added, her face shining with youth. "But the Karēk line is still safe with you."

"Is that all you care for?" Alōs yelled, hands balling into fists at his sides. "That at least our lineage can go on?"

"You are too young to understand now." Dhruva looked at him with pity. "But with time, you will understand why it is important. Those that are worthy of the crown in Esrom are few. The Karēks are the only royal family in Aadilor to have been present when the lost gods were still among us. It is necessary we preserve that history. That magic."

"And what if I were gone as well? What would you do then with your precious history and future?"

The High Surbs shared a glance before Dhruva spoke again. "But you are not going anywhere, Prince Alōs. You are destined to be our king. We understand the grief you—"

"You understand nothing of my grief! All you understand is upholding laws that no longer have meaning here. The world is changing. Our people leave to explore Aadilor every day, bringing back stories of what lives above us. But all you spout in your lessons is useless history. Do you even remember how to wield your gifts? Or have you grown as lazy as the arses that have molded to your chairs!"

The room rang out with offended gasps, but Alōs cared little as he stormed out.

As their chamber door shut behind him, an echoing click of finality, he screamed, shooting out bolts of his magic and shattering the ancient ceramic statues lining their entry hall. They were depictions of the lost gods. Hōlarax: god of fortune. Phesera: goddess of love. Yuza: goddess of strength. Precious history easily destroyed.

What use was it to believe in gods who had abandoned them? They could not lend mercy now, could not help a people said to be their favorite children. Alōs shook, desperate to destroy more precious items, for the lost gods seemed to be doing the same to his brother.

"Your Grace."

A quiet voice had Alōs turning away from his destruction, his breaths coming out heavy. Surb Ixō stood by a corner at the end of the hall. Alōs did not know Ixō well, only knew he was the same age as he, eight and ten, and not yet a High Surb. "I think I can help."

Alōs followed Ixō into a hidden room, where the surb quickly explained there might be a way to save the young prince, but at a cost.

"I will do anything," said Alōs. "Anything."

Ixō then told of the real reason the High Surbs were desperate to keep a Karēk on the throne: his family's blood was so intricately tied to the magic in the kingdom that they feared what would happen to all the spells protecting the land if their family were to perish.

"I don't understand." Alōs frowned. "What does that have to do with saving my brother?"

"The way to save him is to get rid of you."

"Me? So . . . I must die?"

"Not exactly." Ixō shook his head, his expression grave. "But you would have to commit a sin so horrible that you'd be excommunicated, erased from the family line, making your brother the sole heir to the throne. With your parents too old to sire another child, the High Surbs would be forced to keep him alive by any means necessary, even the forbidden magic they fear."

A life trade, *thought Alōs.*

Perhaps it was his fate calling, the beginning of the thief he'd eventually turn out to be, for Alōs hardly had to think on the matter before he found himself agreeing.

Later that night he set out to steal the most valuable item in the kingdom.

Alōs blinked back to his captain's quarters aboard the *Crying Queen*, his shoulders tight at the memories that had overtaken him.

He had believed then that his banishment, never seeing his family again, would be the worst sentence he'd ever face; he would later learn that the price for disrupting the balance of the Fade was much, much steeper. And the countdown to Esrom's surfacing and exposure was merely one part of it.

Over the years Alōs had traded his heart for one that pumped hollow. If he was to be marked as a villain in Esrom, he might as well play the part in Aadilor.

In the end, his brother's life had been saved, and that was all that truly mattered. He would have stolen the Prism Stone again and again to ensure it.

Alōs merely missed the early days of idly sailing the *Crying Queen* with only the next pillage on his mind. Of drinking with his crew and exploring all the pleasurable corners of Aadilor. His life was never meant to be easy after leaving Esrom, but it had at least been enjoyable.

Since Ixō had given him the news a year ago of Esrom's magic drying out, he was no longer enjoying anything.

A knock rapped against his door, pulling Alōs's attention away from his windows.

"Enter."

"You wanted to see me, Captain?" Kintra stepped in.

"How is the crew?" asked Alōs, turning in his chair to regard his quartermaster as she stopped before his desk. "Are they any better?"

"Most seem mollified after the lashings, though some would have preferred more blood."

"They always do," mused Alōs.

"Perhaps extra chores for her will quiet the rest?" suggested Kintra.

"Whatever you think necessary."

"Aye, Captain."

Kintra waited in silence as he stood, going to the decanter of whiskey on his bookshelf. He poured them each a glass.

"How is she?" he finally asked as she took his offered drink. Alōs did not need to meet his quartermaster's eyes to know they would be studying him.

"Mika tended to her. She's resting below deck."

"The damage?"

"Two of your lashes went pretty deep. There's a lot of swelling and will be a fair amount of bruising but no lasting injury. Mika believes she'll be fine come the storms."

Alōs nodded, swirling the amber liquid in his glass. He hated that this news both relieved him and angered him. *Foolish girl,* he thought. Why could she not follow orders like the rest?

Because she's not like the rest, an unwanted voice responded in his head.

No, she is not, agreed Alōs, though that made him feel no better.

"And you?" he inquired to Kintra. "How are you faring with her behavior?"

She paused before answering. "I said she'd be trouble."

"Aye, you did."

"But you assured she was worth it. So I must ask . . ."

He waited.

"Is she still?"

Alōs took a deep breath in, letting the question settle, a prickling of unease along his skin.

"She now knows my history in Esrom, who I was there."

"We all know you were a prince, Alōs. And just like always, no one cares. Everyone here has a past."

He shook his head. "She also knows of the Prism Stone."

Kintra's eyes went wide. "And yet you did not have her killed?"

"We've amended her binding bet. She's to do all in her power to help me find the other part, and once it's back safely in Esrom, her sentence with us will be served."

Kintra snorted her disbelief. "Surely she cannot be as valuable as that?"

Alōs drew his brows together, not enjoying his decisions being questioned. "She has connections of great value, or do you not remember who showed up to save her? Plus, it is because of Niya we were able to find where the other part of the stone resides."

"We could have found that out without her, and you know it."

"Perhaps," said Alōs. "But not as quickly, nor without making a dangerous enemy out of Cebba."

"We have many dangerous enemies. What's one more?"

Alōs threw back his drink, letting the burn of the whiskey calm his growing irritation. "It's one more I'd rather not deal with." He hated that he felt his quartermaster's inquisitive stare as he rounded his desk. With a frustrated sigh he sat.

"How are you, Captain?"

The question momentarily startled him. No one ever asked how he was. But this was Kintra, he reminded himself. "I'm . . . tired," he answered truthfully, leaning his head against his chair's back.

Their eyes locked, her brown gaze filled with understanding, before she went to retrieve the decanter. She refilled his drink. "I didn't have a chance to tell you before, but I'm sorry for your loss."

Alōs swallowed the discomfort edging up his throat as he waved away the sentiment. He had become an orphan long before his parents had died. "It is nothing more than what most of us have already lost."

"Still, I am sorry for it."

"I imagine not half as sorry as you'll be for what still lies ahead." He sipped his drink.

"I knew that sailing with you would mean many adventures." She smiled, showing a few of her gold-capped teeth.

Alōs laughed at that, the sound foreign even to himself. He used to laugh a lot. "I ask you to remember that sense of adventure once we reach the mist."

"I expect you'll be near to remind me."

Alōs studied his companion, always thankful for her steady way of being. She had shaved new lines into her strip of hair, and a few more gold rings lined her ears. "Tell me honestly," he began, "are you okay with where we sail? We haven't returned to the west lands since—"

"My feelings don't change the fact that we must. It seems we are all revisiting old lives lately."

"Yes, the lost gods test us."

"So let us win."

"I am working on that."

"I know," she said.

Alōs ignored the bit of sympathy in her tone.

"I must ask," Kintra went on. "While I believe you when you say Niya has value, are you sure she can be trusted until the end? There's no denying she's a bit of a wild card. She may end up more in our way."

"With her binding bet ending earlier now at stake," said Alōs, "she will be better behaved."

Kintra didn't respond, merely sipped her drink.

"How about this," said Alōs. "If she's not, I'll let you deal with her. The lost gods know I'm over being her wrangler."

Kintra gave him a grin. "It would be my pleasure."

He snorted at the joy in her tone. If only she truly understood how much of a fighter Niya was. "I cannot wait for this entire bloody thing to be over," said Alōs before finishing his second glass, the burn a strange comfort along his frozen resolve.

"It soon will be, Captain," assured Kintra. "And we will be laughing at the entire memory as we have with all our past adventures."

"This is why I keep you around." He leaned forward to refill each of their drinks, Alōs suddenly desperate to feel numb, to quiet all the responsibilities swirling through his mind. This was the easiest road to get there. "One of us must be the foolish optimist. Now, come"—he raised his glass—"let us drink to laughing at impossible tasks."

"And to seeing how well a wooden ship contains fire," Kintra finished with a wry grin.

Alōs hesitated, remembering Niya kneeling before him, strong and determined and not crying out once as his whip hit his mark. He had seen none of her orange magic seep from her, despite knowing how it must have wanted to erupt and lash back. She had kept it controlled.

She had contained her fire.

But for how long?

Was this still what Alōs wanted from such a powerful creature as she? To cage her?

Alōs shook off his confused thoughts as he sipped his drink.

He waited to feel the soothing warmth down his throat.

Yet this time, the burn held no comfort.

CHAPTER TWENTY-FOUR

Niya smelled like a chamber pot as she knelt, scrubbing the upper deck.

The crew walked all around her, busying themselves in their duties as they sailed through the colder western seas, but none had yet to utter a single word to her.

Though it had been a week since Esrom, since her lashings, it seemed the pirates were still holding strong to the memory of her spelling them. Despite her even being loaded with extra chores on top of her own, all while her back had remained raw and needing to heal.

The only crew to show her any sort of forgiveness was Mika, as Niya had come to him each night in his kitchen. There he'd given her clean dressings and helped her wash the blood out of her shirt, which had inevitably gotten restained each day until her lashes had scabbed over.

"We's a proud sort," he had said to her one night as she'd stood with her back exposed, allowing him to gently clean her wounds. "And we's don't forget easy. But give us time, Red. You'll see more of us comin' around soon."

Niya was still waiting for that "soon."

What sensitive children, she silently grumbled as she sat back on her heels, throwing her scrub brush into the bucket of water at her side. Her fingers ached from the work, and she wiped the sweat from her brow, taking in a deep breath of the cool, salty air.

Though she still did not regret her choice to follow Alōs or spell the crew, she did not exactly enjoy being a pariah on board. She hated to admit it, but she missed Bree's incessant chatter as they lay in their hammocks and Therza's unhinged laughter after she made a rather disturbing joke as they worked together to clean the cannons.

Now there was only silence when Niya drew near, whispers, or backs turned to carry on conversations without her.

It was all rather . . . lonely.

Niya stood with a sigh, stretching her sore muscles before cringing as the movement pulled at her wounds. She still could not sleep on her back, which made finding a comfortable position in her hammock rather difficult to accomplish.

Still, though her skin felt tight, she was thankfully healing, flesh stitching back together to allow her shirt to be easier to wear, her chores not as painful to bear.

Niya had experienced her fair share of bruises and cuts from sparring with her sisters and even the occasional tough beating when their father had joined them in the ring, but she had never experienced such a harsh lashing as this.

It still could have been worse, she thought, gazing out at the churning waves beyond the port side. She could have been whipped *and* not have shortened her binding bet. At least now she had a fighting chance of returning home sooner. She had made a bargain she finally felt she could win.

Niya's mood lifted ever so slightly as she scratched gingerly at the new scab forming on her shoulder.

"I've got some seaweed oil that can help with that."

Niya shielded her eyes from the sun as she glanced over to find Saffi approaching. The stocky woman wore her gray braids twisted atop her head today, a thick brown coat around her shoulders. While the day was bright, these western waters clung to a chilly breeze.

"And what must I do in exchange for it?" asked Niya. As this was the first time any of the crew had spoken to her, Niya was more than skeptical. "Sew up all your trouser holes? Clean the stains from your underwear?"

"First, the holes in my trousers are there on *purpose*," explained Saffi. "Second, I'm merely trying to be nice. But it seems you're only in the business of making enemies and keeping them." She turned to leave.

"Wait," Niya called. "I'm sorry. Nobody has approached in any friendly capacity since Esrom. I can't tell when someone is being kind anymore."

Saffi leaned a hip against the railing beside them. "Then I welcome you to the life of a pirate."

Niya gave her a small smile. "How do you deal with it?"

"Being a pirate? Or not getting on people's bad side?"

"Both, I suppose."

"I try to enjoy this life while also not breaking rules."

"Sounds easy enough."

"Yet it appears rather hard for you to do—at least when it comes to the captain."

Niya's chest heated with silent contempt at the mention of Alōs, her gaze going to the quarterdeck, where his large presence loomed at the other end of the ship, Boman beside him at the wheel. She had not spoken to Alōs since her lashings. Each of them seemed perfectly fine to keep their distance. They might momentarily be on the same side when it came to finding this Prism Stone, but he was still very much her enemy; her deep-rooted anger toward the man remained strong. "What do you mean?" she asked.

"When I tell you to do things for our team, you always comply, rather happily. But it seems painful for you to follow the captain's orders."

Niya shifted her weight with discomfort as she glanced out to the sea rather than meet Saffi's gaze. She had no desire to explain her history of animosity when it came to Alōs.

"He went easy on you, you know?"

Niya frowned, turning back to Saffi. "Excuse me?"

"The options of your punishment for sneaking onto Esrom and using your gifts on us," she explained.

"I was *whipped*, Saffi. And then was given all these chores with hardly any time to heal."

Despite Niya having accepted her sentencing, her pride still smarted at the memory of kneeling before Alōs and all the crew to take her beating.

"Yet the skull of the last pirate to disobey him in Esrom is decorating his quarters," Saffi pointed out.

Yes, well, that pirate obviously didn't have the leverage I have, thought Niya. Plus, she'd like to see Alōs try to take her head. She was quite certain, without the restraint of their binding bet, it would be his severed skull in her hands in the end.

But she didn't say any of this to Saffi; instead she merely shrugged. "So he's getting soft in his old age."

Saffi laughed. "Hardly. It seems he takes different liberties with you. I'm starting to wonder why."

Niya did not enjoy the master gunner's scrutinizing gaze. As she brushed back strands of her hair that had escaped her braid in the wind, Niya schooled her growing annoyance that some of the crew seemed to be watching her and Alōs's interactions more closely than she'd have liked. "I think you're reading too much into things. I was punished like any of you would have been. Besides, you all *voted* for me to be lashed."

"Yes, because of all the punishments the captain put forth, it was the harshest. Death was never on the table."

Niya snorted at how cavalierly Saffi could talk about wanting Niya to be killed. "How disappointing for you all."

"It's just interesting, is all," she said, her eyes still assessing.

"Yes, well, maybe with Prik and Burlz gone, he couldn't afford to lose any more of his pirates."

"Maybe," mused Saffi, folding her arms. "But the crew are talking."

Great. Niya rolled her eyes. "Yes, I'm sure they are."

"Some believe you two share a history. Especially since the Mousai showed up after you were brought aboard."

By the stars and sea, thought Niya. *The last thing I need is the crew poking around in my business or thinking I have some hold over their captain that would afford me special treatment.* It would only have them resenting her more.

Alōs had shown her no favors, no charity. Only agreements and wagers. The only language they seemed to agree on. But she couldn't tell Saffi about that.

"I had a heavy debt to pay," was Niya's only explanation.

"Is that what your binding bet is about?"

Niya kept herself from hiding the black marking peeking out of her shirt sleeve. "Do none of you have something tying you to this ship?" she accused, her magic fluttering in her gut along with her irritation. She was quite over this interrogation. "Or did you all walk aboard free men and women, ready to be commanded and ordered around?"

Saffi studied Niya a moment, letting her sharp retort float away in the breeze. "Did you know this isn't the first pirate ship I've sailed with?"

"Uh . . ." Niya blinked, confused by the sudden turn in their conversation.

"I used to sail aboard the *Black Spider.* Lucia Pallar was her captain."

"I think I've heard of that name," said Niya. "But . . . didn't the *Crying Queen* sink her years ago?"

"With the very cannons we clean every day."

"I thought pirates kill the crew of other ships they commandeer."

"Normally they do," said Saffi, playing with the fine fur lining her coat sleeve. "But Captain Ezra works a bit differently than others, as I'm sure you well know. He's a dirty pirate. Ruthless, to be sure. He cut down Lucia quick. Didn't even give her the rights of last words. But he gave those of us that survived the battle the option to leave. He offered a rowboat and a chance to find a new life in Aadilor, maybe even go back to old ones. Or we could serve him on the *Crying Queen*. But he told us that once we decided to serve and pledged our loyalty to him, the only way out would be through the Fade."

"And you chose to stay?" asked Niya, pinching her brows together. "After he killed your captain, pillaged your boat before sinking it?"

"Aye." Saffi nodded. "But he gave me something Pallar never did."

"A constant headache?"

Saffi grinned at Niya's dry retort but shook her head. "A choice."

Niya drank in the word. *Choice.*

She always believed that choice was a facade. A game of odds. Only a small part of someone's life could be self-decided; the rest was a product of commands by kings and queens or of chaos, a timeline of uncontrollable outcomes. *Choice.* It reminded Niya of the thrill she felt when betting—giving in to life's gamble.

"We all have histories here, Red," continued Saffi. "People we were or planned to be. I never dreamed of being a pirate, but when Pallar came to my fishing village, it was either follow her or follow the rest of my family to the Fade."

Niya's chest tightened. "Pallar killed them?"

"She never wasted time on adults. Said they were already too stuck in their ways. Kids she could mold. Felix over there is from my village, too, not that he talks enough to show if he remembers."

Niya glanced at the thin boy standing next to her bunkmate Bree. She was coiling rope into a pile, chatting animatedly while Felix remained silent, his eyes far away as he sat playing his fiddle. Niya realized the melody he preferred was always a bit somber, but it appeared to be how he best expressed whatever it was he could not speak.

It reminded Niya of Arabessa. She often took to her instruments to deal with her thoughts, preferring bow to string or fingers to keys over talking about what was in her heart.

Seeing the familiar behavior in Felix set a heavy ache in her chest. A quick longing for home.

She took in a steadying breath, turning back to Saffi. "But if you were stolen from your village, why stay when you could leave?"

Saffi glanced to the endless blue water surrounding them. "By that time, the only home I had was the sea. What would I have found if I'd gone back?"

"You could have started over."

"I did." She met Niya's gaze once more. "I started over here. At least on the *Crying Queen* I didn't have to relearn a skill. I was already useful."

"So what are you saying?"

"That our captain does not work in blacks and whites, like most in his position. He acts on reason."

"Yeah, his own," said Niya, folding her arms over her chest.

"Perhaps, but I still wonder . . ."

"Wonder what?"

"What his reason is with you."

Niya watched the curious fire grow in Saffi's gaze, her own frown deepening. She knew such a look—she and her sisters had worn it many times, and it only dimmed when they found what they sought. But Alōs's reason for Niya's presence involved nothing more than her skills and magic—and perhaps he liked to see her suffer. "Well, when you find out this reason," she replied dryly, "please let me know."

Dimples awoke along Saffi's cheeks with her smile. "I will."

"Can I ask *you* something now?" Niya's gaze flowed back to Alōs's distant figure, where he was now in conversation with Kintra. "Do you think he's a good captain?"

"He's the best there is."

Niya shook her head. "You replied too quickly for me to believe you."

Saffi laughed, the sound husky and warm. It also seemed to catch Alōs's attention, for he looked up. As his piercing blue eyes met hers across the deck, Niya's heart quickened, and she turned, gripping the railing.

"Red, you've been sailing with us for over a month," said Saffi. "Can you not see how we feel about our captain?"

"People are capable of all sorts of behavior they do not feel."

"True . . ." Saffi's arms bulged in her coat as she crossed them. "But this I say with honesty. He's the best there is."

Niya felt hot, despite the chill in the air. She did not like thinking of Alōs as a good anything. Captain, son, brother. She needed him to remain cruel, her enemy. To forever be the man who only promised pain. Otherwise he became a person, someone capable of feelings, of *reason*, as Saffi said, and that somehow made everything confusing.

I wonder what his reason is with you.

Niya shook off her unease. She didn't want to think any more about Alōs. All she was ready to admit was that they shared a common goal, and that was to retrieve the other half of this Prism Stone. Then Niya would be free, could leave this for good and be out of Alōs's control. Finally. She would return home, return to her family and her duties, which were far more important than any she carried out here. She would return to that which she had always been destined to become, part of the Mousai.

The only thought about Alōs that Niya needed to retain was that they were enemies with a momentary truce to be allies. Each was using the other for their own gain, and that was how it would always be between them.

"Let me give you that seaweed oil," Saffi suggested again, returning Niya's attention to where they stood along the ship's railing, the midday sun lighting the waves around them in dancing glimmers.

"I could really use a soak more." Niya glanced down at her dirt-covered hands.

"You'll have to wait until we reach the valley for that," said Saffi. "In the meantime, I'll be right back with that oil."

As her master gunner strode away, a shift of energy in the air had Niya squinting into the distant sky. All was as calm as the lost gods napping; not even a cloud graced the blue expanse.

Yet still . . .

There it was: a buzzing of forces churning, gathering. Niya had felt this sort of movement many times before, right before a storm. And from the feel of it, it would be a bad one.

Niya's magic stirred more awake as she turned to warn Saffi, but the woman was already out of sight.

Niya walked toward Bree and Felix. "I think there's going to be—"

Her words were cut off as Bree gave her the cold shoulder with a pout, pulling Felix away.

"Real mature!" Niya called out to their retreating forms. "I guess I'll leave you all to get drenched and thrown overboard," she mumbled under her breath. *If they're still going to hold grudges, why should I warn them of the storm?*

Because I could get thrown overboard, too, Niya silently argued with herself, *if the ship isn't properly prepared.*

While she had been on the *Crying Queen* for weeks now, Niya had yet to sail through rough waters.

If she was being honest, the idea left her a bit on edge, not knowing what to expect. How would her powers respond?

Niya glanced to the horizon again, soaking in the colliding energy lacing the air, which was only growing stronger.

"Sticks," she muttered.

If the crew wouldn't listen to her, she'd find someone who might.

Jaw clenched tight, Niya ignored the itching of the scars on her back, ignored the memory of how they'd gotten there, as she went to talk with the captain.

CHAPTER TWENTY-FIVE

*T*he door to Alōs's quarters stood open, and Niya hovered at the threshold. She had not found him on deck, but as soon as she'd stepped below, she could feel his chill of energy leading here. Yet as Niya peered into his office, it remained empty.

Still, his magic was far too familiar to her now, too enticing as it caressed her own to mistake when he was present. With her senses buzzing, Niya stepped deeper inside, following the residual shimmer of his movements. Her gaze ran over the crammed bookshelves lining the walls, the scattered maps on his desk, and the trickling sandglass and various closed boxes adorning the room. Her fingers itched to shuffle through it all, her thief's habit to search a constant tempting whisper.

The sound of water splashing brought her attention to another half-open door in the corner of the room. It had always remained closed when she was here, but she assumed it was where Alōs slept.

A new tension filled Niya's gut. "Captain?" she called out, drawing closer. "I don't mean to disturb, but—"

Her words dried on her tongue as she glanced inside, taking in a shirtless man bent over a washbasin in the corner of the room. His muscles rippled as he ran a wet cloth over his stomach, brown skin glistening as the sun streamed through a large window behind a nearby bed.

Alōs turned, penetrating gaze meeting hers.

For a grain's fall each remained still, looking at the other.

His hair was wet, as if freshly washed, loose and playing around his shoulders.

Shoulders that somehow appeared much larger bare and fed to a tapered waist.

Niya forced her eyes not to dip lower, where leather trousers sat relaxed on his hips.

A prickling of heat overwhelmed her as past visions erupted in her mind: her hands running over his strong chest, Alōs's lazy smile as he was sprawled across a bed.

Traitor, she silently hissed to her thoughts, blinking back to clarity.

"And once again," drawled Alōs, draping his towel on his washbasin, "the fire dancer goes wherever she pleases, despite no invitation."

Niya straightened with her quickly lit irritation. "Your door was open," she pointed out. "Who washes themselves with an open door?"

"Someone who employs crew who *knock*. Am I to believe my pirates have more manners than a highbred lady?"

Niya pursed her lips. "I take no pleasure in finding you indisposed."

"So you're here to talk of how you find pleasure?" One of his dark brows rose.

Her mouth opened and then closed as she felt a shameful blush fill her cheeks. *By the Fade, he is intolerable!*

"What can I help you with, Niya?" He drew closer, bringing forward more of his cool power, which was only amplified by his well-defined chest. "Something must be very important to have brought you charging in here."

"Don't you want to put on a shirt?" she asked as she warily watched him approach.

"I'm not done washing," he said. "Why put on a shirt when I'll be taking it right back off? Unless you don't mind watching as I finish?" His grin was taunting.

Niya took a step back as he filled the doorframe, her magic spinning in her veins with her unease.

But unease at what? *This is Alōs,* she reminded herself. It wasn't as though she hadn't seen him shirtless before, or countless others in the Thief Kingdom during parties, for that matter.

She needed to quickly do what she'd come here for and leave.

"I came to warn you that I feel a storm coming."

Alōs cocked his head. "You *feel* it?"

"Yes." She nodded. "And I think it's going to be a big one."

His eyes flickered over her shoulder to the windows behind his desk, to the calm waters and blue sky. "Interesting," he mused. "You can sense such a thing even when it's still a good sand fall away?"

"The air . . . there's a particular movement to the wind as storms gather," explained Niya before she drew her brows together. "Wait, you knew we were going to sail into one?"

"Aye." He leaned against the doorframe, arms crossed. "There is always a storm when entering the western waters toward the Valley of Giants."

Niya blinked. "But . . ."

"Yes?"

"Well, everyone on deck seems so unconcerned? Shouldn't they be, I don't know, hurrying about more?"

Alōs smiled at this. "It is not the first storm this crew has sailed through. Nor will it be their last. Though the western storms are notorious for sinking many ships, my pirates still know what to do once they see one on the horizon."

"Oh." Niya frowned, his words not doing much to ease her worry.

"What is it?" he asked.

"Nothing." She turned to leave. "Sorry to have wasted your time."

"Niya," he called, stopping her.

She met his blue gaze. "Yes?"

He rubbed his lips together, assessing her for a moment as his brows puckered in thought. "Wait there," he said. After ducking back into his room, he reemerged holding a small brown bottle. "Here." He extended it for her to take.

"What is it?" She turned the bottle over in her fingers, the liquid inside sloshing.

"Seaweed oil."

Niya's eyes snapped to his, a twist of confusion flowing through her. "It helps with—"

"Wounds," she finished quietly.

Alōs kept his attention on her, his tug of energy wrapping around them both, twisting with her own. "Yes."

She wanted to ask why. Why would he give this to her? Was he remorseful for whipping her? For inflicting the very wounds this was meant to heal? But that would be ridiculous.

Niya had purposefully disobeyed orders, betrayed the crew, and held the knowledge of Alōs needing to save his homeland over his head.

There had been no avoiding her sentence or his wrath.

Niya herself would have punished anyone just the same. Probably worse.

A disquieted confusion ran along her spine.

Do you think he's a good captain?

He's the best there is.

But this is Alōs Ezra, she reasoned. The cold, ruthless pirate who'd broken her heart, held her and her sisters' identities hostage, and blackmailed her king.

Niya glanced back at the bottle. "Saffi said she was going to give me some of hers."

"I see," said Alōs slowly. "Then I guess you do not need—"

"Given the extent of my scars"—she tucked the bottle into her pants pocket and away from his extended hand—"I need as much as I can get."

When she looked up, she caught a flash of something in his gaze, but it was gone too quickly for her to identify. "Yes, well . . . if you need more . . ."

"I'll ask around."

Alōs's features hardened with his nod. He took a step back. "If you want to help before the storm, find Kintra. They do get quite bad, and there's always plenty of crates to tie down."

The tension that had gathered in the room loosened at Alōs's words.

Back were they to their roles of pirate and captain.

Gone was whatever strange moment that had been building.

"Now if you'll excuse me," said Alōs as he turned toward his private quarters, "I'm sure you can find your way out, as you so easily found your way in."

"It's always easy when the door is open!" she called out in annoyance just as his bedroom door shut, removing the image of his half-exposed body.

With clenched fists, Niya stalked from the room, regretting entering in the first place. Because as the bottle in her pocket could attest, perhaps Saffi was right—maybe Alōs *was* a good captain. The idea didn't sit well.

Him being the *best* captain, however, Niya would no doubt deny until her death.

And if these storms were as bad as he said, she might not have long to wait for that day.

CHAPTER TWENTY-SIX

*T*he *Crying Queen* surged over a wave, rain slicing like knives against Niya as she gripped tightly to a rope tied to the mainmast. The sails whipped loud as thunder against the wind. Despite their vigorous preparation when they'd spotted the ominous clouds on the horizon, everyone was yelling, running, falling, getting up, and running more. Ropes were constantly flying free and being retied. The ship tacked back and forth, back and forth, as waves tall as the mainsail smacked against the hull.

Niya now knew the reason why trade was light in the west of Aadilor. She was drenched to the bone. Rivulets of water ran across her face, spraying into her eyes, the taste of salt water filling her mouth. A crack of lightning overhead lit up the ship, the white sails screaming bright in the storm.

She held tight, feeling drunk on the motion. Her body was collecting as much power as it could take from all the movement. There were even moments when Niya fought to not pass out from the pandemonium of energy. Despite the ice-shard touch of the rain, her body was burning with her magic, her skin sizzling for it to be free.

A scream rang out above her, and she tipped her head up to watch Bree hit the edge of her crow's nest and tumble out. Niya whipped up her hand, throwing out bright-orange surges of her power to catch

Bree's falling form. The weight of the small girl tugged at her gifts as they wrapped around her like a coiling rope, bringing her safely down to the deck beside her.

"Niya," breathed Bree, her eyes wide, her skin pale with cold and fright. The rain plastered her short hair across her forehead. "You saved my life!"

"Hold on to this!" yelled Niya as she grabbed a free-flying rope that swung against the mast before them.

She handed it to Bree as an overwhelming sensation hit along her side. She turned to see a large wave surging over the starboard side of the boat.

Spinning, Niya gathered more energy before pushing it from her core, hot surges of power extended through her arms to hit against the wall of water.

The two forces clashed, a glowing red shield blocking the towering churning threat, before it fell away, back over the rail and into the sea. In the next moment, crates broke loose from netting, tumbling toward them, and Niya swung a hand around, knocking them out of the way with a burst of magic. Her muscles screamed at the exertion as well as the exhilaration as more of her power gathered and lashed out at falling debris and encroaching waves.

Niya was fighting with the lost god Helvar, master of the sea, and it felt incredible.

"Here! Tie yourselves in!" she yelled to the pirates who were beginning to crowd around where she and Bree clung to the mainmast. They seemed to think she was the safest place on deck. Niya almost laughed at the irony—only sand falls ago they'd still avoided her like a plague.

Grabbing the extra rope from Niya, they threaded it around their waists.

Out of the corner of her eye, Niya caught Saffi along the port side attempting to push against oncoming waves like she had, her powers coming out silver and thick from her fingers. Though the master gunner was gifted, her magic did little when the giant waves descended.

The water punched onto the deck with an angry roar, surging and knocking most off their feet.

"Saffi!" yelled Niya as the woman tumbled against the deck, before hooking an arm around the wheels of a tied-down cannon.

A breath of relief whooshed out of Niya at seeing the master gunner safe, at least safe enough for Niya to turn her attention to the rest of the ship.

Therza clung to netting near the bow, head thrown back as cackles of delight echoed out of her, as though the storm were an old friend telling her a joke. Another crack of lightning flashed overhead, highlighting the rivulets of rain racing across Therza's round cheeks, but the woman merely laughed harder.

"She's crazy," muttered Niya, wiping hair from her eyes.

Sparks of green had her turning to see Alōs next to Boman by the wheel. A giant bubble of his gifts expanded out and around them, lighting up with every punch of the storm, no rain or wind or wave penetrating in.

As if sensing her watching, Alōs turned to pin his glowing turquoise eyes to hers. A bright beacon in the dark storm.

"Don't fight the waves!" he called to her over the roar.

"What?" She blinked against the rain, which was pelting like hail against her back. Her wounds screamed in agony, but she ignored them.

"It's more energy to fight!" Alōs shot a bolt of magic from his palm, through his shield, to catch the head of an approaching threatening wave. He extended its crest, elongating its neck so it broke on the other side of the ship, back into the sea.

Less damage.

Niya turned back to the bow, watching the front of the *Crying Queen* surge up and up along a mountain of angry sea. The movement had her stumbling back, the ship nearly made vertical.

It would most assuredly break apart on the way down.

Don't fight the waves, Alōs had said.

Swinging herself from the rope tied to the mainmast, Niya slid across the deck and jumped to the bow.

She dug her heels in as the *Crying Queen* angled precariously perpendicular and began to move her body to the sounds of the storm. She rolled her hips to the crashing water, felt the movement of the sea beneath, the waves surging. Niya pushed her arms out and out and out. *Flow more. Flow forward. Streeeeetch,* she told the Obasi Sea. Her skin sizzled with her intentions, steam lifting off her clothes as she wove her magic into a slowly descending bridge that flew from the topside of the wave. The water pulled farther out, tangling easily in the orange liquid of Niya's created current. She was not fighting the storm but working with the energy already in motion, molding it softer. The ship reached the lip of the wave, and it rode along her magic until it glided, almost gently, back into the sea.

They made it through the next wave, one much smaller, and the storm was suddenly at their backs; the *Crying Queen* had sailed through.

Niya breathed heavily, her ears ringing with the echoes of retreating thunder, and peered out at the tranquil gray water and overcast sky that greeted them. If she hadn't been able to turn to see the evidence of the shrinking storm behind them, she would have believed it all a dream.

Though her magic still hummed through her veins, her head still abuzz with the adrenaline of all the recent movement, Niya's shoulders drooped as a swarm of relief entered her chest.

She left the bow to walk along the main deck. The ship was drenched, parts of the banister splintered from the storm, crates broken, sandbags spilling out, one sail ripped. But it was still sailing, still floating. The *Crying Queen* was strong.

"Well, that was fun," said Niya, walking to Kintra, who knelt by the port side, handing Mika bandages as he wrapped the few pirates who were cut and bleeding.

Kintra glanced up at her, a pinch to her brows. "How are you dry?"

Niya glanced down. Her clothes were no longer clinging to her skin from the storm. In fact, they looked rather perfectly washed and laundered. Her hair wasn't a soaked mess, either, but felt warm and full in its braid. Her back even seemed renewed. *Oh!* she thought with surprised glee, looking back at Kintra. "Magic?" said Niya with a smile.

Kintra harrumphed as she stood, her wet boots squashing with the movement. "Mind sharing the gift?"

"All right." Niya rubbed her hands together, gathering her magic into a glowing red ball. She reached up and dropped the mass of heat onto Kintra. It flew down her in a puff, dissipating at her feet and leaving her brown tunic and trousers bone dry, her skin shining like she'd just had a good steam.

"By the lost gods." Kintra twisted around, gazing at herself in wonder.

Niya smiled before the prickling sensation of being watched had her turning to find Alōs standing above them on the quarterdeck.

He was imposing in his black coat, hands gripping the banister before him as the chill of his energy mixed with the already-cool air. His gaze swung from her to Kintra, who stood by Niya's side, then to the gathering group of soaked pirates who were poking the quartermaster's dry clothes like it was a miracle.

When Alōs looked back at Niya, something in his eyes softened ever so slightly, and he gave her a nod.

One that could almost be interpreted as a thank-you.

Despite herself, a warmth seeped into Niya's chest, foreign and uncomfortable, but she didn't have long to analyze these feelings: wet sailors were beginning to line up in front of her.

It appeared she had just been put on drying duty.

Biting back a smile, she waved the first one forward.

Niya had just finished drying off the last pirate when a horn blasted from the crow's nest.

"Prepare yeselves!" yelled Bree from above. "The Mocking Mist approaches!"

Niya walked to the banister along the starboard side, peering out.

She had heard whispers of this mist from the crew, but given they'd still been ignoring her at the time, she had yet to learn what about it had these usually formidable pirates muttering in fright.

Niya watched the mist slowly grow up from the gray water, as if hands from the Fade were reaching to snatch an unlucky sailor into its depths. Vapor filled the air, clogging the view forward and slowly erasing the ship as it pierced into the cloud. The *Crying Queen* no longer sailed through sea but floated in a world of nothing. Niya squinted into the whiteout, hardly able to see two paces in front of her. The wooden boards beneath her feet fell out of existence, as if the lost gods had begun to erase this part of the world.

Green Pea and Felix, who stood nearest Niya, began to back away, frantically shoving their hands into their pockets to retrieve items to push into their ears. Others cupped their hands and crouched into balls on deck before the mist covered them from her sight. Pirates who had just rushed into a storm's mouth now scrambled and cowered away at the enveloping mass.

Kintra approached her, extending two small wax balls. "Best be clogging your ears now."

Niya took them. "This is the Mocking Mist?"

"Mmm." Kintra nodded. "And it is as it sounds, but worse. Now go on—plug your ears. If you can hear me, you can hear *it*, and no one leaves the mist the same if they listen."

Niya glanced over her shoulder, just making out Alōs beside Boman at the wheel. The pirate captain was like a black ink spill in the white abyss, his glowing eyes a hazy blue beacon in the murky air as they peered forward.

Niya caught Boman slipping in his balls of wax.

"What about the captain?" asked Niya. "I didn't see him—"

"Some men need the mist's reminder," Kintra replied simply before she blocked up her ears as well. Niya weighed the balls in her hand.

Her sisters mocked her all the time. Almost incessantly. She was also part of the Mousai, had witnessed many terrifying frights, and had had audiences with the Thief King in all his varying moods. How bad could this mist really be in comparison?

Closing her hand around the wax, Niya decided to wait and see.

The whispers started softly.

They didn't come from one direction but all around, as if the air itself held the voice of thousands.

Hello, Niya, it crooned. *Look at you here, amid this lot. How much you've aged and wrinkled and burned aboard this ship. What beauty has been lost. What a pity, what a shame.*

A tinkle of high-pitched laughter filled her head.

Such hard hands and blistered toes. Scars along your back. Disgusting. Disgusting. Disgusting. And what will your family do once these two years are through? For that's how long you'll be shackled here. You stupid, silly girl. You always bet what you can't win. You disappoint your family. Disappoint. Your sisters will have no use for you now. No use. No use. They have moved on already. Forgotten you. It's been too long. And your father, yes, yes, poor Dolion, he will replace you, find another to be a part of his precious Mousai. So much you must have missed. So many adventures your sisters have gone on without you. Who is Niya? No one remembers.

Chimes of giggles all around as Niya's breaths grew quick as her deepest fears echoed in the air.

You're all alone now. All alone, continued the mist. *But you're used to being alone, aren't you, fire dancer?* The voice took on Alōs's deep drawl, running cool down her neck. Niya spun around, but no one was there, just fog, just mist. *Even when I warmed your bed, you were alone. So naive, so eager to please me. You chose me over your family. Gave me your heart, which I never wanted. Tell me, did you cry after I left that night?*

Do you cry now? His words swam around her, ripping her open, before returning to the high chime of the mist.

You are a fantasy, it said. *They only desire you for what you've spelled into their minds with a turn. A twist. You've feared it, Niya. We know. We knoooow. We know your doubts. You are not clever like Arabessa. You are not kind like Larkyra. No one values you for your mind.* More laughter. *Nonono. Not for you. It's for your body. For your magic. Only for what they want to be theirs. What they long to touch. Who are you without these? What can you offer your family? What can you offer the pirate? Worthless. Worthless and alone. You are the weakest link in your trio. For look how often you disappoint them. If your mother lived, she'd be ashaaaaamed. Ashaaaaaam—*

Niya shoved the wax into her ears, cutting off the vile whispers. She stood shaking. A well of shame was cut open hot in her chest.

Yet even with her hearing blocked, she still made out the cruel words ringing through her soul. *They have moved on. Forgotten you. No one values you for your mind. It's for your body. For your magic. Who are you without these? You are the weakest link in your trio.*

Niya wrapped her arms around herself to hold in another shiver. Her magic had even retreated deep inside her, small and huddled like a lost child in the dark.

Did you cry after I left that night? Do you cry now?

Niya's cheeks burned.

What a horrible place this was.

She would never make the mistake of listening through it again.

After another quarter sand fall, the mist slowly dissipated, bringing the ship back into focus. Nets, crates, masts, a stretch of deck.

Niya saw Therza helping up Bree and Green Pea from where they had sat together, crouched, while others worked out the wax from their ears. A few pirates, Felix being one, remained rocking themselves in corners, soft cries emanating from their bowed heads.

No one acknowledged these individuals as they walked past, merely leaving them to whatever evil still echoed silently in their hearts.

Niya searched out Alōs, wondering what horrid reminders the pirate captain needed to hear, but when she looked at his usual spot beside the wheel, Alōs was no longer there.

CHAPTER TWENTY-SEVEN

*T*he sun was greedy in the Valley of Giants, gluttonous to cover everything, and Niya was hard pressed to find an unoccupied bit of shade on deck. Hugging close to a stack of crates along the port side, she shielded her eyes from the bright day as she studied the land that rose up around her. They sailed through a canyon, its sides painted in slashes of crimson, the sun's relentless heat blistering the towering sandstone rocks, which were what she had learned had earned this place the name of Valley of Giants: the rising rock monoliths.

It had taken another two days to reach the wide river they now floated down from the Obasi Sea, the water here a muddy green compared to the pure azure-blue sky. And though the air was dry, it smelled sweet, as if the sediment held fragrance. The ship's sails were down, for no wind was needed to guide them forward. Somehow the current flowed quickly inland, as if this place knew the destination all visitors sought.

Saffi leaned against the crates beside Niya, cleaning her nails with a splinter of wood, while Therza and Bree rested in the last slice of shadow by their feet.

The crew was tired, but of course they were. They'd just sailed through a storm, only to face the Mocking Mist. Everyone was in need of a drink.

"Captain's making an announcement." Saffi nudged Niya.

Alōs strode to the center of the quarterdeck as they gathered around. Kintra took up her usual spot on his right.

Despite the rising heat, the pirate captain remained in all black. His stance was relaxed but commanding as he waited for his crew to assemble on the deck below. Niya was so used to seeing him at night that she had forgotten how the sun complemented the hue of his brown skin and softened the severity of his features. The breeze filtered through his ebony hair as his sharp gaze took them each in.

"My brothers and sisters," Alōs began, his deep voice echoing through the canyon. "I first want to commend you on your brave work entering the west lands. Not many have survived to see this part of the world, but I did not doubt our success. You may be scoundrels and thieves, but you are the most gifted scoundrels and thieves."

A few hoots came from the group. Niya crossed her arms over her chest, amused at how easily charmed this lot could be by their captain.

"We will soon be met with the people of the valley, and I must remind you that this is *not* a pillaging mission. We come here for rest, to repair what's been broken in the storm, and to restock items in trade for some of our bounty. We cannot make war here, or enemies. This river"—he gestured to the water around them—"is our only way out."

Murmurs filled the air.

"What?" Niya leaned over to ask Saffi.

"Death trap," the master gunner muttered, pointing to the canyon's edge on either side. Niya could just make out piles of boulders clustered together along the top. "No way we'd make it out if under attack. The valley people have ensured it. Push those and *splat*."

"How long will we stay, Cap'n?" asked Bree beside Niya.

"And will we be filling more of our coffers soon?" questioned Emanté, who hung by nearby netting. He was a man who either didn't own a shirt or felt them a useless accessory, for Niya had yet to see him wear one.

Murmurs of shared curiosity filled the group, and Niya waited for Alōs's answer with similar eagerness. She had wondered how he would play off their purpose for sailing here.

"If welcomed by Queen Runisha and King Anup, we will remain here a few days at least," said Alōs. "This stop is for rest, but it's also to acquire information on where we might find some more pretty items to add to our last raid in Cax Island. We collected rumors while in Barter Bay of possible bounty to be found farther west. So you know how to work these visits, my beautiful scum. Keep your ears alert; talk with the people. There are always clues of which nearby cities might be *too* blessed by the lost gods. Plenty of high and mighty that need a bit of rodent infestation to take them down a peg."

Chuckles and hollers filled the air.

Niya rolled her eyes.

"And who knows," Alōs went on. "We all might need to make a stop at Stockpiled Treasure the next time we're in the Thief Kingdom."

The crew laughed before Alōs dismissed them to prepare for port.

"I'll definitely have to stop there," Bree said, turning to her and Saffi, "especially after the Cax raid."

"Wait . . ." Niya frowned. "You really have an account at Stockpiled Treasure?"

This was the most exclusive bank in the Thief Kingdom. Only the richest of the rich held their valuables there. Valuables that were usually tainted by illegal trade or acquisitions, of course, but no less worthy.

"Sure," said Bree. "We all do. Where do you think we store everything we pillage? This ship is big, but it can't hold a vault large enough for all we've grabbed over the years. We're pirates of the *Crying Queen*. Fastest vessel on the Obasi waters. Most feared crew in all of—"

"Yes, yes." Niya waved a hand. "I know perfectly well all of this ship's shiny accomplishments."

"Then it must come as no surprise to learn that many of us own land too," explained Saffi. "Own stores, homes, and support lovers." She winked. "We need somewhere to hold our investments."

"Investments?" Niya lifted her brows. "Who knew pirates could be so financially responsible?"

"Apparently everyone but you," said Saffi.

"Niya," Kintra called to her from where she stood by the stairs leading below deck. "The captain wishes to see you."

"In trouble again already, Red?" asked Saffi with an amused grin.

"Would it be a good day if I wasn't?"

Niya left her master gunner and bunkmate to their laughter and followed Kintra to Alōs's quarters.

Her nerves buzzed with each step she got closer to his open door, the darkness of the hall closing in on her as she moved toward the light. Images of the last time she had come here played in her mind: his glistening exposed chest, his taunting grin, and the offering of seaweed oil to help heal her scabbing wounds. It had been an odd moment of generosity from the pirate captain, which she tried to forget as she entered his space.

Like always the room was swimming with his cool presence, a light-green tinge of his magic possessively covering all.

Niya's own gifts swirled ready in her gut as she took in his large form in all black hunched over his desk as he peered into a delicately carved box. A red glow filtered out, painting his features and angular cheekbones.

"You wished to see me?" asked Niya as Kintra came to stand at her side.

Alōs's bright-blue eyes glanced up, roaming the length of her as he closed the lid with a snap. The ruby light cut off as he sat back in his chair. "Yes, I wanted to discuss what will need to be done while we are visiting the people of the valley."

Niya waited as Alōs ran a finger along the edge of the box on his desk.

"As you know, we learned from Cebba that someone representing the royal family bought the other part of the Prism Stone from her to be made into a gift for the young princess Callista. What we don't know, however, is what sort of gift. Could it have been for a necklace? A bracelet? A scepter?"

"A ring," suggested Niya with a knowing glance.

"Yes, even a ring," said Alōs, eyes narrowed. "Though that would be quite a heavy accessory, given the last part of the stone is quite large."

"How do you know that?" asked Niya.

"Who do you think split the gem up to begin with?" countered Alōs. "Yet despite these unknown details, it's good to assume that however the Prism Stone is kept, it will be in the princess's vault of valuables."

"Assuming she has one."

"All royalty have personal vaults," said Kintra at her side as she folded her arms. The raised burns on her exposed biceps bulged.

"Friends with many royals, are we?" asked Niya with a dry glance to the quartermaster.

"I'm a pirate and a thief. And a good one. I'm friends with any place expensive items are stored."

"Yes, and for us to get to this room," continued Alōs, returning Niya's attention to where he sat like his own royal behind his desk, the large river they sailed in a backdrop through his windows, "we'll need to get into the palace. Which won't be hard, given that when any visitors such as us visit a place such as this, the rulers always demand an audience to make sure no threat to their people is present. We will be gifting the royal family with a hearty peace offering in exchange for our stay. Out of custom they will ask us to dine with them."

"Clever," said Niya.

"We are the *Crying Queen*," explained Alōs. "Clever is merely one of our many attributes."

"Yet humility is not," added Niya. "Do you lot ever get tired of complimenting yourselves?"

"No," said Alōs and Kintra at once.

The pair shared a smile, which caused something hot and uneasy to twist inside Niya's chest.

Kintra is the exception.

Niya pushed through her discomfort. "So once we are inside, then what?"

"Once inside we need to be prepared for all things. But ultimately we will find the Prism Stone and replace it with a fake."

"A fake?"

Alōs swiveled the box around on his desk and clicked it open.

A large red stone glowed out of a bed of white satin. It was uncut and crude but no less a glorious gem. It was about the size of her fist.

"This is a fake?" asked Niya, stepping closer. "It's so . . ."

"Beautiful?" said Alōs as he shut the lid. Niya blinked at the sudden loss of glamour that had momentarily filled the room. "Yes, it should be, given it's from Esrom's own royal vault," he continued. "It may not be part of the Prism Stone, but it certainly has value."

"So where do I fit in with this plan?"

"Once Kintra and I assess the situation in the palace, you'll ensure our next steps go smoothly. That we get back the other half of the stone no matter what. However we might need you to help, you will. Spelling guards, distracting guests, *dancing*," he finished with a sharp grin. "You'll need to be prepared to do it all. As you promised."

Niya held the pirate captain's piercing gaze, her heart beginning to beat faster. Whether at the anticipation of the heist or for the man she stood before, or both, Niya couldn't help but feel a thrill rush down her spine. She was getting closer to her freedom. "Yes." She nodded. "I'll do as promised."

"Good." Alōs leaned back into his chair. He steepled his fingers over his wide chest, assessing her.

Though Niya hated his scrutinizing gaze, she kept still, chin up. *Two can play this game,* she thought. Silence stretched between them before, keeping his eyes trained on her, he opened a drawer to his right.

"I have debated whether to return these to you," he said, revealing her blades and holster. He placed them on his desk, his hands remaining possessive over the carved hilts.

Her heart leaped at the sight of them. She had thought they had been forever lost when taken from her in Esrom. Niya's fingers twitched at her sides to snatch them up. *Ours,* her magic cooed.

"And have you come to a decision on whether you will?" She lifted a brow, feigning indifference.

He smiled. Not fooled. "I have. But I warn you, if they fall into my possession again, I will not be so generous in their return."

"It is not only Kintra who is a skilled thief in this room," said Niya, eyes narrowed. "If they fall into your possession again, you won't notice when they fall out."

"Nor will you," said Kintra to Niya. "You seem to be careless with your belongings, Red. I'd be a much better master of those blades."

"Care to make that threat more real?" Niya turned to the quarter-master, magic jumping in her gut.

Kintra's hand slipped to the long knife sheathed to her thigh. "Gladly."

"All right, you two," said Alōs, raising a hand. "While the thought of watching you both black and blue one another is amusing, I have far too many valuables more important than either of you in this room to break. If you feel like a fight, do it later, and outside. Now take these"— he pushed the blades toward Niya—"before I change my mind."

Niya cut Kintra a last narrowed glance before retrieving her knives, slipping the holster around her hips.

She held in the contented sigh at the familiar feel of them.

"One last thing before you can go," said Alōs.

"Yes?"

He paused for a grain fall. "I wanted to thank you."

Niya blinked, momentarily blindsided. "For . . . what?"

"Helping as you did in the storm. I saw you guide the bow."

Niya didn't know how to respond, to feel, so unaccustomed to genuine compliments from this man. "Yes, well, as promised. I give my full aid."

"Yes," said Alōs, holding her gaze. "As promised."

Niya shifted her weight. She did not like him like this, she realized. *Nice.*

She needed Alōs to remain mean, cold, loathsome.

All the easier to keep her wall of hate, of revenge, fortified and standing tall.

He used me, she reminded herself, again and again. *And blackmailed my family. He's using me now.*

Just as you used him, a small voice echoed in her mind.

"Is that all, Captain?" she asked.

Hearing the use of his mastering title over her, without mockery or sarcasm, something in his eyes sparked. Another reminder of their momentary truce in place.

"Yes, pirate," said Alōs. "That will be all. For now."

The people of the Valley of Giants revealed themselves like flowers in bloom. There were few at the start, popping up behind rocks on the canyon's rim, standing sentry at the edge, until they gathered along the beach at the end of the river near where the *Crying Queen* anchored.

They wore hooded robes, dyed shades of burnt orange, which camouflaged them into the sandstone surroundings. Bows and arrows were poised at the ready, blades and spear tips reflecting the sun's light.

Kintra ordered the pirates to load trunks pulled from the bowels of the ship onto boats before the forty-odd crew members rowed to shore.

The two groups stood along the bank, each eyeing the other with distrust, a tension added to the thick, hot air.

Alōs stepped forward, throwing his sword to the sand, followed by a hidden blade in his boot.

Niya looked to the pirates around her as they did the same.

She sighed. *Of course, right when I get my knives back.*

"It's for show," whispered Saffi beside her, noticing her hesitation. "We'll pick them all back up in a grain fall. You'll see."

Niya turned back to watch a tall woman step out from among the people of the valley. She had black skin and a shaved head save for a single strip of hair and two ears lined with gold rings.

Niya instantly glanced to Kintra, who stood slightly behind Alōs, her styling so similar. The quartermaster's shoulders appeared stiff, and Niya could sense her tight energy. She knew Kintra was from Shanjaree, another western city, but perhaps it was closer to the Valley of Giants than she'd originally thought.

Alōs greeted the woman. *"Paxala,"* he said. *Peace this day.* "My crew and I have sailed for many days. We come for rest and to see the wonders of the Valley of Giants for ourselves. Nothing more."

The woman angled her head to the side, eyes narrowed, in a trickle of tense silence, before she broke out in a wide grin. "Alōs Ezra," she said, clasping hands with their captain as though they were old friends. "Your entourage has grown, and so have you."

He smiled in kind, nodding to the soldiers behind her. "The same could be said about you, Alessia."

"Your lot are not the only scoundrels who have dared the western storms these past years. Our army has doubled."

"Really?" inquired Alōs with raised brows. "I see there is much to catch up on."

"Which we shall," said Alessia. "But first, come. I shall take you to our queen."

The beach became alive with movement. Niya was thrown her knives by Saffi as the master gunner bent to retrieve her own blades. Kintra yelled to the pirates to pair up and haul the trunks as they marched in a line, following the people of the valley into the thick, dry brush.

On their journey Niya quickly learned two things about this land. One: the heat was intolerable and the insects unnaturally large. Two: it was wild. Their current path had been made by years of trekking over the same area rather than being paved.

It was a grueling hike through brush and rock, full of sore feet and labored breaths. None of the valley people talked with the pirates or vice versa. Despite the pirate captain and the commander seeming to know each other, it remained a game of sizing up, of watchful eyes and skeptical brows.

By the time their group reached the carved city situated along a high plateau, Niya was covered in sweat. Leaning against a boulder, she wiped her forehead and took in the splendor before her.

A multitude of soaring columns of sandstone rose to the sky. Cathedrals of rock carved to make homes in the sides, ladders and roped bridges connecting them together. As their procession continued on, twisting through the streets, the citizens came out to stand in doorways, stopping their purchases among vender stalls, all to watch them pass. They wore finely beaded and embroidered wrap dresses, trousers, and tunics. All dyed a variety of reds, oranges, blues, and greens. Their skin was a variety of shades, from dark to the palest white, all accented in swirls of gold paint and piercings, as if celebrating the glimmering hue of the land they were born from.

A fair-skinned girl hid behind her mother's legs, staring up at Niya as she walked past where the pair appeared to have stopped to collect water from a spigot. She probably was no older than six, but half her right ear was already covered in piercings. Niya smiled at the girl, and she ducked farther away.

This city was as sprawling as it was tall, a tangling mix of dwellings built beside or on top of shops. Eventually they entered a wide main thruway, which led to a rising stone monolith at the end. At the base were stairs that went up, up, up, up, up. Niya craned her head back to take in a massive palace at the very top, carved out of the rock's face.

Twirling columns supported an intricately carved roof in half relief, where the sun glistened over the sandstone, making it appear as though thousands of diamonds were embedded in its surface.

"We're to go up *there*?" Niya all but whined. "There must be two thousand steps."

"I'd rather sail through the Mocking Mist without my ear wax," grumbled Boman beside her, dabbing at the sweat along his neck. It was a useless gesture, given his entire shirt was soaked through.

"Come on, you old cows"—Saffi nudged them both—"or do you want me to tell Kintra you've volunteered to carry one of the trunks the rest of the way?"

Niya's eyes widened. "You wouldn't dare."

Saffi merely smiled, inching to where Kintra stood at the front of their procession, beside where Alōs was talking with Alessia. The two were engaged in an amusing story, while Kintra remained stone faced, glancing to their surroundings with tense shoulders.

"Come on, Red." Boman took Niya's arm. "Best not test her. In my experience, she'd do anything for a laugh."

It felt like a miracle, but Niya made it up the towering steps to enter a cool, shadowed hall, smelling of desert jasmine and yucca, a tangy sweetness.

Giant bowls of fire lined the way forward, peppered between massive stone columns that held up a beautiful mosaic ceiling.

The patterns were geometric and elaborate, reminding Niya of some of the stained glass windows found in the Council buildings in Jabari.

At the thought of her home, a sharp ache seized her heart.

How she missed her city of birth. The tight alleys that held memories of her and her sisters running through them after dark. Larkyra and Arabessa would certainly enjoy the splendor she walked through now. At the thought, Niya was gripped by a desperate wish to see them. If only for a moment so she might tell them all that had happened since they'd been parted.

Niya moved with the wave of her crew as they were guided down another grand hall, tall doors opening to usher them into a throne room. Like many courts Niya had seen, this one was lined on either side with court members, curious gazes wrapped up in fine clothes and fluttering feather-woven fans.

At the very back, three figures sat atop a dais in high-backed chairs made from a mixture of wood and stone. This was where their group halted, lowering their trunks, as Alessia approached the royal family, whispering something low.

Queen Runisha, who sat in the middle, peered down at them. Her garb was a dusty hue, cinched tight at the waist, which accentuated her rigid posture. Her black hair was teased and gathered tight into multiple twisting buns, where a similar crown as her husband's, a branch-like creation curling around sapphires and orange citrine, rested. The pair also shared similar green eyes, but while King Anup looked upon them bored, hers were alight with curiosity and intelligence.

She waved a hand as if to say, *Go on.*

Alōs swept forward, bowing low onto one knee. The crew followed in an awkward wave of pirates attempting to show chivalry. Taking in the scene, Niya smiled in amusement but did the same.

"Your Graces," began Alōs, looking up to the three figures, "we thank you for welcoming us into your beautiful city. We have traveled far to reach the wonder the rest of Aadilor calls the lost gods' gold. Though we are lowly rats of the sea, our visit is one of peace and rest."

Listening to Alōs, Niya was quickly reminded of how silver tongued he could be.

"We come offering gifts in exchange for hospitality," continued Alōs as he signaled at nearby crew. They brought forward and opened their trunks. Piles of sparkling riches shimmered from the cases: jewels and silver coins. Appreciative gasps and murmurs filled the hall from the court members. Saffi had explained that it was a portion of the pirates' pillaging, taxes of a sort, saved for times like these, when they needed to stop in friendly waters to refuel. Treasure in trade for food and rest.

"Rise, pirate." Queen Runisha's voice vibrated deep in the hall. It was a husky, pleasing sound. A mother's hum. "We do not see visitors here often, especially not of your variety. But the storms and mist have let you pass, as they have once before. Yes, the land remembers you, Lord Ezra, as well as a few of your companions." Queen Runisha's gaze brushed past him and landed on Kintra. "It is good to see you have proved again to be worthy of an audience. Now tell me: While your gifts are welcome, it is your words I wish to validate. Have you truly come in friendship?"

"We have, Your Grace."

The queen remained skeptical.

But Niya's attention was pulled from the exchange when a flash of red caught her eye.

Princess Callista sat to the queen's left, silent, obedient, learning. And while she certainly was a vision with her smooth brown skin wrapped in a dusty-rose robe, it was her gold crown that had Niya's heart jumping into her throat. The hall fell away, the crew, the court members, the words spoken between Alōs and the queen. For all Niya could see, could taste, was the brilliant red stone resting in the middle of Princess Callista's diadem.

The Prism Stone.

Niya's magic flooded her veins at her jolt of shock.

It was here. Right in front of her. In front of everyone. A round oval of purity, glimmering red and bright, like newly spilled blood, amid a wrapping of gold leafing in the young girl's crown.

Niya fought every urge to snatch it and run.

This is it, her mind screamed.

What caused Alōs's desperation.

What Esrom needed.

What promised Niya's freedom.

It's here!

Niya felt torn in two, from knowing she needed to remain still and uncaring among her companions yet desperately wishing to point to the stone and yell, *Mine!*

She looked to Alōs at the front.

Has he seen it? Nothing in his stance gave it away. But then, *there.* In the intensity of his gaze as it held on to the young princess. It was the look of a wolf finding its prey.

Callista blushed under the attention.

Niya had a moment of empathy for the girl, for who knew the depravity the pirate lord would stoop to so he could reclaim what he had suffered so greatly to find.

"I will put to the test your words of peace, Lord Alōs." Queen Runisha's voice returned Niya to their exchange. "And when I say 'test,' I mean it. We will extend our hospitality, but know my soldiers outnumber your crew tenfold."

"May I assure you, then," he said, charmer's grin present, "any test I've been given I've passed with flying colors."

Queen Runisha smiled as well, a game seemingly now afoot. "Then, great people of the valley"—she turned her gaze to her subjects—"come forth and meet our new friends, for tonight we will be dining with pirates."

The hall erupted with movement as the gifted treasures were carried away and servants slunk from shadows to guide the group of pirates to where they would be staying within the palace.

Niya's magic jumped along with her haste as she squeezed through bodies to get to Kintra. Had she seen the Prism Stone as well? Niya's mind spun, plans forming for how they could take a crown from a royal's head without them noticing.

But when she was only a few steps from the quartermaster, a touch of magic, strong and familiar, caressed the back of her neck.

Hello, it seemed to say.

She spun, brows pinched as she searched the cavernous hall.

Who's there? she thought.

And then, as though the lost gods smiled down on her this day, she saw them.

They stood amid an animated conversation taking place between a group of court members, but they paid them little mind as their violet eyes clung to her, a crooked smile on their lips.

Niya's heart gave a leap.

Achak, her old friend, was here.

CHAPTER TWENTY-EIGHT

*D*espite the excruciating voyage to the Valley of Giants, Niya decided she quite liked this kingdom. For so far, since arrival, everything was going according to plan and more.

As Niya reclined deeper into the hot spring, where she and the rest of her female crew members bathed within the mountain palace, she looked across her secluded pool to Achak.

Steam scented with jasmine and honey rose around the sister's black, luminous skin, her bald head glistening with water droplets.

"I've missed baths," sighed Niya. Letting her overworked muscles relax into the warmth.

"And they very much appear to have missed you," said Achak, scrunching her nose. "You reeked badly, my dear."

Niya splashed water at Achak, but it merely hit up against an invisible barrier of their magic. The sister hadn't even moved a finger to create it.

"Show-off," muttered Niya.

"Jealousy is a quick sign of weakness."

"Yes, well, so is mortality."

Achak raised her brows. "How wise you've become in this short time."

"I would not describe my time so far aboard the *Crying Queen* as short." Niya pursed her lips, a twinge of annoyance digging into her chest. "Every sand fall feels like a lifetime."

"Then be glad of that. The alternative makes moments meaningless."

Niya studied her friend. "I still cannot believe you are here."

"Every creature deserves a holiday," explained Achak, resting her head against the rim of their pool.

"Holiday? From what?"

"Our lives, child. Queen Runisha is an old friend of ours. Plus, the people of the valley hold some of the best parties in all of Aadilor. We try to visit often."

Niya took an offered bar of soap from a passing servant, whipping up suds in the steaming water. "I didn't realize your life was so stressful it required holidays."

"We've helped raise you Bassettes, have we not?"

Niya gave a snort. "Are you sure it's not the other way around?"

Achak grinned. "My brother fights to say his piece, but it would be improper for him to be here, among all these naked ladies."

Niya listened to the echoing laughter flowing around the high-ceilinged bathhouse. Therza had dunked Bree into the waters of a nearby pool, the young girl wasting no time to kick her companion's legs out from under her so she would fall in too.

"Say something else that will annoy him," urged Achak. "I'm thoroughly enjoying this."

Niya looked back at Achak. While she was close to her sisters, to be so close as to share one body and hear them constantly in her mind seemed a quick recipe for madness.

Nevertheless, she played along. "I think it's time he trimmed his beard. It's looking like a bear has taken up residence on his face."

Achak's body twitched, but the sister tensed her muscles and stayed present. She laughed, the twinkle a mixture of voices.

Niya settled into the familiar sound with a contented sigh, so long it had been since she had seen a familiar face. "I'm happy you're here," she said with a smile, turning to run soapy water down her shoulders. "It has—"

"Child," Achak cut her off with a frown, the bath rippling out as she slid to her side. "What happened?" She traced one of the red welts on Niya's back.

Niya's cheeks burned, and not from the steam, as she scooted away. "What it probably looks like. I misbehaved."

Achak's face morphed quickly into the swirling features of the brother before snapping back to the sister. A dual voice spoke. "And who shall we be sending to the Fade tonight?"

"No one." Niya shook her head. "At least not tonight, anyway. Alōs has unfinished business."

"Your captain did this." It was not a question.

"I disobeyed an order."

Achak studied her for a long moment, the splashing sounds of the other women around them filling their tense silence. "What kind of order?" the sister eventually said.

Niya played with the bubbles in front of her. "Evidently, an important one," she said, hot shame filling her chest at the idea that this would get back to her family. They didn't need more reasons to believe she could not do as she was told. That she was merely all fire and reaction.

"Mmm," was Achak's only response, the sister's eyes remaining narrowed as she settled back into the bath.

"It is in the past." Niya pushed to move on.

"As were many of your problems which still affect your future."

Niya snapped her brows together. "I am trying to do better."

"Your new wounds prove otherwise."

"They were worth the bargain," she ground out.

"More bargains?" Achak's eyes widened. "I thought you said you were trying to do better."

"I *am*. This one I shall win."

Achak shook her head. "Famous last words of many a gambler."

"You may condescend all you like, but I know what I'm doing." She raised her arm to display her binding bet, which now sat half-removed.

Achak studied the black lines before meeting Niya's gaze again. "I suspect this has something to do with why the *Crying Queen* has come to the valley. Tell me, what is your purpose here?"

Niya hesitated, glancing to her shipmates in the other pools. While she had promised Alōs she would not tell them about the Prism Stone, she had said nothing about sharing with those off the ship. Plus, this was Achak, not just any passerby. Slinking closer to the sister, Niya lowered her voice as she shared all that had happened since sailing upon the *Crying Queen*. It felt good to unload, to be in the confidence of an old friend. When Niya was done, Achak's gaze was far away as they looked out to the cavernous bathhouse.

"We wondered when this would happen."

"What do you mean?"

"The issue with the Prism Stone."

Niya stared down her companion. "You knew about this?"

"We have roamed this world longer than most. We know many things. The stolen Prism Stone was no secret to those like us."

Her magic was a flutter of shared shock. "Why did you never tell us about it, then? About Alōs being royalty? That Esrom could rise to the surface within a year if it is not brought back?"

"A litany of questions."

"All deserving of answers," she said in annoyance. "I shared my knowledge—now you must share yours."

"You could never retain all that we know, child."

"*Achak,*" Niya said with a huff, her temper a quickly fed flame.

The ancient one waved a hand of indifference at her tone. "Alōs's past was his story to share," explained Achak. "You never asked of his lineage before, so we didn't see reason to bring it up. Plus, who he was, not to mention this stone, did not matter to the Mousai."

"It mattered to me!" said Niya loudly, drawing a few curious eyes.

Achak held her gaze, her eyes' violet hue assessing. "Yes, but at the time would it have changed the outcome of your relationship with the pirate? If you knew him to be a Karēk, a banished prince, would that have helped you resist his seduction? As we know you, once you are set on a decision, you follow through, consequences be damned. Young love is like rain; it falls fast and doesn't care who it hits in the process."

"I was *not* in love," Niya hissed. But *of course* she had been, or had thought she was. A dumb, foolish, naive love. Achak was right. None of it would have mattered. If she had known Alōs to be a prince at the time, and a banished one at that, it would have had her infatuated with him further. What an imbecile she was. Might still be now.

"Whatever you need to call it," said Achak, "it has brought us to where we are now. Our paths are paved forward, child, not back. There is no use in questioning what might have been."

Niya didn't respond. She wasn't done pouting.

"But the stone, the other half is here, yes?" asked Achak.

Niya sighed. "The princess wears it in her crown."

"Of course," Achak laughed as she shook her head. "Life is never boring when a Bassette is around. That is an obstacle to be sure. We look forward to the following entertainment. We assume there is a plan?"

Niya moved her hand in the water, watching as the ripples spilled away from her. "I am meant to talk with Kintra and Alōs before the feast tonight. Evidently, they are hatching this plan now."

She was still annoyed at Kintra for brushing her off earlier in the throne room. She'd approached the woman regarding what they were to do next, given the other half of the stone was sitting a mere few steps away.

"The captain and I will reconvene and let you know," was all the quartermaster had shared before she had stayed behind with Alōs as he'd continued to talk with the royal family. The rest of the crew had been shuffled out to wash and prepare for this evening's events.

"And are you not to help with this scheming?" asked Achak.

"I help by being at their disposal," said Niya, trying to keep the annoyance from her voice.

"Mmm, an agreement which is part of this new binding bet, I imagine?"

Niya was tired of discussing binding bets and actions still to come. So instead of answering, she asked, "What I want to know is why Alōs would have stolen such an item from his people if it would put his kingdom at risk of surfacing."

"Perhaps he didn't know that would be the outcome."

"But he was banished because of what he did, wiped from the royal line."

"He must have had a very good reason, then."

Despite the price, I ensured both of Tallōs and Cordelia's children lived.

Alōs's words to his brother surrounded Niya, along with images of the scars of Ariōn's sickness across his hands and face.

"You know the full history," Niya challenged. "Why won't you share it with me?"

Achak rose from the pool, rivulets of water sliding down her sleek body as she reached for her discarded robe, which sat folded on a nearby stone. "Some history is meant to be told by others. During a time when the past fits better with the present."

Niya huffed, irritated. From the years of growing up around her companion, she knew when they were done revealing knowledge they believed better suited for another to share. "You ancient ones are always filled with useless riddles."

"Yes, but at least we come bearing gifts."

Niya perked up at that. "Gifts?"

"We had a feeling we would be crossing paths on one of our journeys. We have been carrying a message for you." Achak removed a small gray rock from her robe's pocket. The center pulsed with a faint white glow.

"A memory stone?" asked Niya.

"From your sisters."

Niya's throat tightened, and she took the stone. "Thank you."

"They miss you."

They miss you.

Three words Niya was starved to hear. Starved to say.

"I miss them," she said. "Very much."

"Come to me after you've broken it. We can capture one for them in return."

"Have I mentioned that you ancient ones are my favorite?"

Achak smiled. "Not nearly enough."

That night, Niya dressed for the feast that was to be held within the palace. In the quarters she shared with the other female crew members, they were brought a rack of clothes to change into. While many grumbled that they were too "delicate" to be useful, Niya's skin thrummed with excitement at the prospect of wrapping herself in such finely woven garments. It had been far too long since she had been pampered, and her soul hungered for every bit of luxury she could slip between her fingers.

Picking a soft frock that wrapped at the waist and was dyed an ombré of yellow to red, Niya ran her hand down the material as it hugged her form. Her feet were bound in soft leather sandals before young girls came to do her hair and paint her skin, as was customary to celebrations in the valley.

Niya sat, enjoying the tickling of the brushes over her brows and along her arms, the warm glow of nearby fire in brass bowls bathing her in comfort. The room they occupied held no windows, but the ceilings were tall, keeping it from feeling claustrophobic. And drapery hung from corners, creating a tented atmosphere over beds.

"Do you like, miss?" one of the girls asked as they stepped back.

Niya peered at her reflection in the mirror before her.

Her skin looked luminous with the added gold paint swirling over her features, her hair in soft loose waves to her waist. Niya smiled, a flutter of pleasure running through her. She had not felt this beautiful in a very long while.

"I love it," she said. "Thank you."

The girls bowed before collecting their items and slipping out of the room.

"You coming, Red?" asked Bree from where she stood by the door with Therza.

It appeared they were the last of their lot still in the room.

"I'll catch up with you in a bit," said Niya. "I have a few more details I'd like to add to my outfit."

"You're covered in details," said Therza. "Any more and you'd be hidden away."

"Nevertheless, I'll see you there," she added, patiently waiting for her companions to finally make their exit.

When alone, Niya turned back to her dressing table, where her robe from the bathhouse was folded up on the side. She dug into the pocket, taking out the memory stone.

Her heart leaped as she brushed a thumb over the smooth, glowing surface, and then with a whack, she broke it open on the table.

A cloud of smoke rose from the cracked center, swirling into a tight ball as two figures came into focus as if captured in the fog.

"Niya." It was Larkyra, her white-blonde hair up in braids as she sat beside Arabessa's darker form on their veranda in Jabari. "We hope you're alive to get this."

"Otherwise it would be a dreadful waste of our time," added Arabessa.

They were looking straight at her, as if they were in a portal through the mirror in front of her. Niya ached to respond, to reach out and touch their hands folded in their laps.

"Achak thinks they'll be seeing you soon to give you this," explained Larkyra.

"And you know if Achak believes something to be true, it must be," said Arabessa.

"Have you gotten us into more trouble?" asked Larkyra.

"She can't answer us, dear, remember?" admonished Arabessa. "We just have to talk *at* her."

"What a novel idea," mused Larkyra, thumb to her chin. "Niya unable to talk back?"

"Shall we say words to incite her?"

A spark of mischief lit up in Larkyra's gaze as she said, "I hope you don't need us to come save you again."

"Or pay any more of your debts."

They each grew quiet then.

"We do hope you are well." Larkyra leaned forward, brows coming together. "And that you haven't singed too much of Alōs's ship with your fire."

"Or not enough of it."

"Oh yes," said Larkyra. "I like that better. Burn it all down and come home! The house is too quiet without you."

"The kingdom not nearly as dangerous."

"Father won't let us perform."

"Which is best."

"Yes." Larkyra nodded dutifully. "It wouldn't be the same without you."

"But as soon as you're home . . . ," Arabessa added.

"As soon as you're home," echoed Larkyra.

Niya swallowed, tears threatening to break free. She wanted to gather her sisters in her arms and never let them go.

"Darlings?" a deep voice called from out of frame.

"We are on the veranda, Father!" Arabessa turned, looking through a faint door behind them. Niya could just make out the manicured bushes that lined their glass doors.

"My songbird, my melody." Her father walked into view. "I was seeing if you girls wanted to come with me to—oh, Achak, I didn't realize we—"

"We are making a memory stone for Achak to give to Niya," explained Larkyra. "Say hello, Father."

Niya couldn't stop the tears now. They streamed, unchecked, down her face. She'd known she missed her family, but she hadn't realized just how badly until she saw them. Saw them, but could not touch, could not hug.

Dolion bent down between the girls, face bulging forward at where Achak must be sitting tranced and listening. "The flame of my heart," he said. "I hear you have gotten yourself into quite the pickle with a pirate."

"Father, you needn't be so close to Achak." Arabessa tugged the large man back. "Just sit right here, between us, yes, like that. Perfect."

All three of them peered at Niya then, Dolion squeezed in between her sisters. They looked happy. Niya pushed away the prickle of jealousy. She'd be with them soon enough.

This was the first time Niya had seen her father since her betrayal had been revealed. A wave of shame and longing flowed through her. What did Dolion truly think of his careless daughter who'd broken the only rule they ever were meant to follow?

"I am not angry with you, my flame," said her father, as if reading her thoughts. "I know any punishment or disappointment would be nothing compared to what you have already put yourself through for all these years. I merely wish you had come to us earlier. I taught you girls to take care of yourselves, but that does not mean you need to do everything alone."

Alone. But that was how Niya always found herself. Alone in a room. Alone with her mistakes.

"When is your magic most powerful?" he asked the group.

"When we work together," Niya replied in unison with her sisters.

"Indeed," said Dolion. "Now, my flame, I hope you're keeping your wits about you. Your head held high. Pirates, especially aboard the *Crying Queen*, are a slippery lot. They are ruthless and cunning, and while they can grow to be your friends, do not forget who their captain is. Lord Ezra is duplicitous, to be sure, and has a very, *very* long history of doing whatever it takes to get whatever he wants."

"I know," Niya couldn't help muttering to the empty bedchamber.

"But you know this." Dolion leaned back. "Just remind yourself often."

"We love you, Niya," said Larkyra, her gaze pained.

"Very much," added Arabessa. "If Achak does end up crossing paths to give you this, force them to make another for us."

"Oh! And the next time we are together," Larkyra added, "remind me to tell you about Arabessa walking in on Zimri—ow! Father, did you see Ara just hit me?"

"You had a spider on you," Arabessa said coolly.

"I *like* spiders," said Larkyra, trying to slap Arabessa back.

Dolion pulled them apart. "See what happens when you leave, my flame?" He laughed, his arms bulging to restrain his daughters. "We all know these two only have ever enjoyed fighting with you."

The echoes of their banter faded as the ball of smoke dissipated with the memory ending.

The room hung quiet.

"Niya?" a deep voice asked behind her.

Caught off guard, Niya stood. She hadn't been paying attention to anything but the words and image of her family.

Alōs was by the door, regarding her from across the dimly lit room. His large form was wrapped in a finely sewn navy tunic and trousers, blue-and-green embroidery detailing the edges. He looked nothing like a nefarious pirate lord and everything like the prince he'd been born to be. The king he had been meant to become.

"Yes?" she asked, quickly wiping the tears from her eyes.

"I noticed you were lagging behind the others." Alōs touched the marking on his wrist. "Came to see that you weren't getting in your usual trouble."

"Stupid leash," muttered Niya, pulling her hands behind her, as though hiding her binding bet would momentarily remove its existence. "I'm coming," she added louder, her voice overly bright. "Merely needed a few moments with my outfit."

Alōs studied the space where her family had just been. When his eyes returned to her, they held questions. "Are you . . . all right?"

Niya blinked. Alōs *never* asked anyone, let alone her, such a thing. "Why wouldn't I be?" she asked.

Alōs's brows creased, his gaze making her believe he wanted to say something else, but he merely replied, "We'll be making the switch tonight."

A flutter in her stomach.

"I hope there's more of a plan than that one statement."

"There is." Alōs glanced behind him, out the door to the sound of passersby. He slipped farther in, shutting it quietly. "At dinner I will be gifting the princess with a diadem, which out of decorum she will hopefully replace her current crown with for the remainder of the evening. Kintra is to follow where they take the crown with the Prism Stone and report back to us."

Niya watched the pirate approach as he explained their plan. And though they'd been alone before, now that the door was shut, the air felt charged, dangerous. Niya became acutely aware that nothing but soft beds and lounges filled the space. The last time they had been alone in such an opulent bedchamber, Niya had given up her identity, her freedom. The memory had her muscles tensing, her walls of protection rising.

Fight. Her magic stirred silky in her heart.

"Much seems to be riding on propriety," she pointed out, folding her arms over her chest.

"The diadem I'll be presenting is rare and beautiful," explained Alōs. "The people of the valley value these two traits more than any other. I have no doubt the princess will want to show it off."

Niya pursed her lips, not knowing what else to say but, "Then it seems you and Kintra have everything under control. Are you sure you need me tonight?"

Alōs raised a brow as he came to a stop a few paces away. "The night has barely begun, and already you want to fight with me. Must I remind you that we are now on the same side, Niya?"

She scoffed. "The only side you are ever on is your own."

"The same could be said of yourself," he accused.

"Only because someone taught me long ago the consequences of trusting another."

"Oh, come now." He smiled. "It wasn't *that* long ago."

Niya's grip on her arms tightened. *Buuuurn,* her magic sang to her. *Burn him like he burned you.*

"No cutting response?" Alōs stalked closer. "Something *must* be wrong."

With wariness, she watched him approach, his contained power slowly wafting out, cool to the touch along her hot skin. His energy felt different tonight, languid, like it often was in the Thief Kingdom. She had almost forgotten what it was like to be on this side of his charms. She had become so used to the pirate captain, the stern commander. She preferred that version. It was easier to separate their past from their present when he was nothing but business.

"I am in no mood for your games," she said.

"Niya—"

"Stop saying my name."

"But you hate my nicknames," Alōs pointed out. "Am I to call you *thing*, then?"

"Please stop." Niya suddenly felt tired. She rubbed at the new throb along her temples.

"Stop what?" He was now directly in front of her, glowing blue eyes peering down.

"Stop doing whatever *this* is." She gestured toward him. "You no longer hold my identity over my head. There is no more reason to tease and poke as you do. You do not need to pretend that you know me. I am merely part of your crew, and until all this is over, let us leave it at that."

"It is not pretend," he said, his gaze holding hers. "I *do* know you, fire dancer. Despite how you might hate it. I know you more than you probably know yourself."

His words slithered uncomfortably along her skin. An echo of ones he had once begged of her in the past.

Let me know you, fire dancer.

Niya tipped her chin up, steadying the magic that continued to swim with threats in her gut. "Highly doubtful."

"I know you despise corsets."

"Every woman despises corsets."

"I know you prefer night to day," he continued, undeterred, "and can't turn down a gamble. I know your vice for eating honey and apples after a performance. I know, above all else, you care for your family and wear a mask of indifference too large for your empathetic heart to handle. And those are merely the things I've gathered from watching you. Shall I share what I know from touching you?"

Niya sucked in a breath. "You bastard."

"You've met my family," countered Alōs with a sharp grin. "I am many things, but a bastard, you very well know, I am not."

"Why do you do this?" asked Niya, her body thrumming with her mixture of growing rage and frustration. "Why do you hate me?"

He blinked, the question appearing to catch him off guard.

"From the moment we met," she continued, "you have been scheming for the upper hand. And even after you get what you want, you still go out of your way to elicit my anger. Why?"

Alōs was quiet for a long while, so long Niya was about to leave when he finally responded. "I do not hate you."

She laughed, the sound harsh to her ears. "Fine, whatever you say. But know I am done with it. Done with all of it. Our past, our present. And if you try to anger me in the future, I will not rise to it anymore. Do you understand? I am here to complete our bargain, and that is all. You have broken your plaything. Go find a new one."

Niya stomped past him, but he snagged her arm, stopping her.

"You want to do this?" asked Alōs, his body so close she caught his scent of midnight orchid and sea. "You wish to finally air out the truth of our past? Then let's." His eyes blazed as they drank her in. "But know it was never hate driving my actions. How could I hate someone I did not know?" He dropped his grip from her arm, but the brand still lingered along her skin. Niya breathed quickly. "I was after leverage when I first met you. I no longer had a home or a family. Everything was business to me, a transaction for a better standing in the pecking order. That first night I came to the palace, I searched for the most valuable thing in the room and saw you, Niya Bassette, dancer of the Mousai." His gaze roamed the length of her, assessing, appreciating. A chill danced along Niya's exposed flesh in its wake as Alōs's magic began to seep from him unchecked, a green mist. "I sought what you hid so thoroughly, knowing the leverage it would bring me. I hurt you in the process. I know. But as we've seen, I came to require that bargaining chip. I am not sorry to have done it. I would do it again. Regret is for cowards too weak to make amends in the present."

Niya's heart beat loudly in her ears, her own red haze of power tangling with his. They stood trapped in a cocoon of their own creation. "Is this your attempt at making amends?" she asked, glaring daggers up at him. "An explanation for your behavior over an apology? Because I can tell you, it is not working."

"You were raised in the Thief Kingdom," Alōs snapped. "You are a part of the Mousai. Do not pretend to be innocent of cruelty and sin."

Niya took a step back, attempting to sever herself from his pull. His pull that always curled deliciously, but with warning, around her. Too similar. They were too similar. Beast and monster clashing for dominance. For control. "I never have claimed to be innocent of such things," she began. "But it is one thing to break someone's heart, and it is another to continuously bully them so they can never forget. Yes, your charms worked on me. Yes, we shared a bed. *Once.* But I have had many lovers since you, pirate. So please, be done with me! For I am certainly done with you."

Alōs's stare danced like the center of the nearby flames. "If my memory serves," he said, "*you* have been seeking *me* out since that night. Not the other way around. I made sure to avoid you at all costs after our . . . encounter, but I always knew when you were near. I feel your energy as you feel mine, fire dancer, as soon as either of us step into a room."

"I sought you out because I had been trying to kill you!"

Alōs smiled sharply. "It sounds, then, like it is you who hates me."

Niya groaned her frustration. "Of course! You held my life in your hands after that night. My family's! Threatened us every day forth."

"An outcome I did not force from you. You always had a choice that night. Do not hate me because you made the wrong one."

Niya felt crazed, dizzy in her cacophony of emotions. She wanted to scream and cry and burn everything down because she knew deep in her heart Alōs was right. He might have played her for a fool, but she had not been raised to be an innocent; she should have known better.

The enemy Niya had hated for so long was herself.

Her magic burned like fire in her veins as she forced herself to ask, "Why, then, did you not leave the moment you saw me, knew my name? Why did you stay the night?"

They remained a touch apart, and Niya watched Alōs's gaze drop to her lips. "Because"—his voice came out a husky rumble—"you offered yourself. And it wasn't just your identity I had grown to want."

Niya felt her body betraying her, felt it sway forward, closer to the beast whose cold magic made hers feel that much hotter. Memories of that night swam through her mind like a forbidden dream.

Alōs's hands were cool against her cheeks as he studied every inch of her newly exposed face. "Niya." His voice was rough as he said her name for the first time. "So beautiful," he whispered before angling her lips to his. Niya had been kissed before, stolen ones by young gentlemen in Jabari. But none had been like this. Alōs's mouth was soft, his form solid. Having a man who held such power yet could be so gentle with her was intoxicating.

Niya wrapped her arms around him, letting out a moan of greed, of desperation. She knew revealing herself was a risk, but after hiding herself away for so long in this palace, the forbiddenness of taking off her mask for another—the rebellious freedom in it—was too great. Especially with Alōs's pining so devoted, his passion overwhelming, his words perfect. He never said he loved her, but how was this not love? Niya ran her fingers through his thick hair as she pulled back. "Take me to my bed," she whispered. His blue eyes sparked at her words, his grip on her hardening as he bent to kiss her again, but he did not move them from being pressed into her dressing table, where they hid in her private rooms beneath the palace in the Thief Kingdom. "Alōs." Niya rubbed impatiently against his thigh, her breast pressing against his chest. "I want to feel how much you cherish me. Take me to my bed and show me."

"Are you sure?" Alōs asked.

Niya ran her hand down to where he was hard and strong.

He groaned.

"Is this answer enough?" she asked.

With that, Alōs easily lifted her and walked the short distance to her bed. That night their magic danced with gives and pulls, of lust that reduced every sensation to a breath, a moan, a rake of nails along a back, Alōs's dark skin contrasting beautifully against her pale—

"And as I remember"—Alōs's husky voice brought Niya back to the present, to the bedchamber within the mountain palace—"you were very glad that I did."

Niya was shaking now, her shame and rage and current confused longing too much to handle.

She held Alōs's consuming stare, felt his pressing power. He overwhelmed her. Always had. He was his own form of a gamble, she realized, for he made her feel more alive than any spill of dice or flip of cards. He made her feel as though she could burn as hot as she needed and he would merely stand there, soaking in her heat. But Niya was sick of always running hot, sick of forcing stakes high to feel alive. For this was where all that had gotten her. She was constantly running from lenders, currently separated from her family, and wrapped in a binding bet attached to another binding bet to the man she had been trying to escape yet had stalked for years.

She needed to end it. She needed to move on. She needed to leave this room.

"Perhaps I was," said Niya. "But I am no longer that girl."

"As I am no longer that man."

"And who are you now?"

"I am someone much worse." Alōs's glare bore down on her. "So you can keep hating me if that gives you solace, but we have fought as enemies for a long while, fire dancer. Perhaps it is time we see what happens when we work as allies."

"I could never be your friend."

"No," Alōs agreed, his stare darkening, eliciting more unwanted heat in her belly. "Friendship was never our fate. But you promised me your absolute cooperation. So you might find it easier to point your hostility elsewhere until promises are fulfilled."

Niya watched him a long moment. "Very well. Until bargains are complete. Then we are done."

"Then we are done," said Alōs.

Niya pushed past him, striding from the room.

As soon as she entered the hall, she breathed easier.

The last piece of the Prism Stone was here. They would get it, and then this horrible game would be done.

Tonight, thought Niya. *I merely need to get through tonight.*

After which she'd be that much closer to home.

And then Niya would never have to see Alōs Ezra again.

CHAPTER TWENTY-NINE

Niya was surrounded by merriment and laughter, but her mood was similar to that of the stuffed and cooked pig on the table before her: rather annoyed to find herself here. The banquet hall was boisterous and warm, a spicy incense mixing with music and the echoing of guests. The pirates of the *Crying Queen* now mingled easily with the people of the valley. The endless fine spirits no doubt a tool in the loosening of suspicious walls. Exotic fruits and steaming vegetables passed quickly under Niya's nose where she sat between Saffi and Achak at a table toward the back.

Yet in contrast to her two companions, Niya slowly sipped her red wine and hardly touched her plate of food as her gaze continued to fall to where Alōs sat amid the royal family at the front of the room.

The young princess was on his right, appearing to suffer the same affliction as Niya had once had at her age.

Callista's cheeks flushed anytime Alōs turned to engage her in conversation.

There was no denying Callista's beauty. Her dark skin was luminescent under the firelight, her prominent cheekbones complementing a long, graceful neck. Her hair was teased out with a plaited braid zigzagged in the middle, her outfit made of the finest silk. And her crown, no doubt the focal point of all of Alōs's charm, glistened as she angled her head close to his, the red of the Prism Stone a flashing temptation in the center.

Despite the age difference, Niya couldn't help but admit the pirate lord and the princess looked good together. Callista's pureness balanced Alōs's wicked allure.

Both born to rule.

Niya suddenly felt even more wretched, and she wasn't exactly sure why.

Perhaps seeing such an innocent beside the pirate reminded Niya of her younger self.

She knew all too well how intoxicating it felt to draw the gaze of such a powerful man, to have Alōs's sole attention in a room full of splendor. It was like a drug. Once you experienced the gentle touch of his glowing eyes, the heated curve of his grin, the prickle of his cool magic, you needed it like your next breath.

She watched Alōs's gaze slip up to the Prism Stone as Princess Callista tipped her head back, laughing at something he'd said. A desperate hunger seeped into his eyes then, a glint of pure danger.

Everything he had searched for, had been banished for, was a mere touch away.

What was he feeling? How much strength was he using to control his urge to rip the stone from its setting in her crown right then and there?

Niya almost wished he would; the binding bet along her wrist tingled at the thought. She absently rubbed the mark with her finger. *Freedom,* it whispered. So close, yet still out of reach.

"Kintra!" Achak's deep voice brought Niya back to where she sat beside the brother. He raised a large hand, flagging down the quartermaster as she walked past their bench. "Come sit with us a moment," said Achak, gesturing between himself and Niya.

Kintra studied the tight space, which was mostly taken up by Achak's ostentatious robe. "I don't want to intrude."

"Nonsense!" said Achak, his gold-painted brows glistening as he moved over. "This one has been a complete bore." He nodded toward Niya. "Hardly spoken a word since she's sat down. You would be saving Saffi and I from any more of her dullness. Move over, child."

Niya was forced to scoot to the side as Achak pulled Kintra down between them.

"So, my love"—Achak turned to Kintra—"have you seen any friends since you've arrived?"

The quartermaster frowned. "Thankfully, no."

"It has been a while since you've been back here, yes?" asked Achak. "Queen Runisha told us it might be close to four years."

"Six." Kintra reached for a glass of wine that sat on the table, taking a hearty sip.

Niya pinched her brows together, confusion swirling. "You know the queen?"

"We know *of* each other," Kintra clarified.

"Forgive me for assuming," said Niya, "but I thought you were from Shanjaree."

"She is," said Saffi on the other side of Achak, stabbing a large slice of pork on her plate.

"I *was*." Kintra eyed her shipmate. "And I'll tell my own past, thank you."

Saffi raised her hands, forkful of food included.

"Yes, I was from Shanjaree," Kintra continued, her posture tightening as she stared into her drink. "But my only affinity now is with Alōs and the *Crying Queen*."

Niya glanced at Achak over Kintra's shoulder, but the brother raised his brows as if to say, *Ask her, not me.*

"So . . . how did you come to know the people of the valley?" asked Niya.

Kintra's gaze went to the pirate lord across the room, still wrapped in conversation with the young princess. "It's not really a tale suited for dinner conversation."

Saffi snorted before talking through a mouthful of food. "We are *pirates*. When have we ever abided by conversational decorum?"

"It's okay," began Niya. "If you don't want to share—"

"No, it is just that . . . the king of Shanjaree, King Othébus, was . . . not a good man, you see," said Kintra, playing with the stem of her glass. "He took many wives. And as he got older, the wives he chose got younger. My family are members of court, or they were the last time I saw them. No one wanted to bring their daughters to the palace, but the king demanded he know the families of each of his courtiers. I must have caught his eye, for I was chosen to be his tenth wife. I was thirteen."

"Oh dear," breathed Niya.

"My parents tried to dissuade him," continued Kintra, her gaze growing unfocused. "They told him I was not a good match. Too strongheaded, with opinions of my own, but King Othébus would not hear it. And because he was our king, they had to obey. I had just gotten my markings." Kintra ran her fingers over the five scarred welts on one of her biceps. "It was how the king remembered each wife's number in line," she explained. "My binding to the king was meant for the following day when I met Alōs.

"He must have heard me crying, because he found me hiding in a street behind the palace, not wanting yet to go home. The burns, they hurt too badly, and I couldn't allow my family to see me upset. Alōs asked why I was sad, and normally I wouldn't have spoken against the king to a stranger, but at the time I was so angry and scared, and I wanted everyone to know my rage. It wasn't until it was all said and done that I would come to learn the consequences of such an act." Kintra smiled to herself then. "The king was murdered later that night."

Niya's pulse quickened as she listened to Kintra's story, a chill running through her at her last words. "Alōs killed the king?"

Kintra nodded. "Evidently Uréli, the king's firstborn heir, had been organizing a coup for some time. Alōs's appearance was more than coincidence—it was planned. He wasn't much older than myself at the time, but Alōs's reputation had already spread far in Aadilor, and Prince Uréli requested he come for an audience. I've never been sure how much of my story persuaded Alōs into his next actions, but when he met with the prince, he agreed to bear the sins Uréli could not commit himself. He agreed to kill the king for Uréli, so long as Othébus's wives were freed and taking child brides was banned.

"That night, the streets were in chaos," Kintra went on, now seeming unable to stop her tale. "I still can hear how the horn blasts seemed to come from every treetop as soldiers forced discipline on any who openly celebrated the assassination. Alōs came and found me in my home, slipped right into my bedroom window like the shadow of a lost god. I had no idea how he knew where my family lived, but there he was, quickly telling me that he was the pirate captain of a ship called the *Crying Queen*. He offered me a place with his crew. I'm not sure what made me do it, but I went with him that very moment. I only left a note for my family, telling them that I loved them and I was not dead. We sailed immediately here, to the Valley of Giants, seeking sanctuary for a time. Apparently there had been a secret peace treaty between the people of the valley and Uréli. I guess the young girls at court were not the only ones threatened by the old king's leering eyes. Many girls of Shanjaree sought refuge here, and it appears"—Kintra caught the gaze of an older woman sitting across the room—"many have not left."

Silence fell over their small party as the commotion of the dinner continued to swim around them.

"Did the captain ever tell you why he searched you out later that night?" asked Saffi. "To ask you to join his ship?"

Kintra breathed out a sigh. "He said I reminded him of someone he had once cared for."

Ariōn. The name hung unsaid, but an image of Alōs's younger brother swam forward in Niya's mind.

She sat beside the quartermaster, lost for words, as her convictions regarding the pirate lord echoed in confusion.

Protector, heartbreaker, liar, savior, friend, thief, murderer, monster, companion, defender.

How could Alōs have so many contradictions?

Because so can you, a voice whispered through her.

Niya glanced to Alōs's dark form at the front of the hall. He was made up of cool shadows yet burned with such life, such conviction in his mission.

As Niya did with hers.

Her duty to her family, her king, was everything she had. Everything she believed in and would fight for. That meant sometimes committing monstrous acts in the name of good.

She suddenly felt very hot, her magic twisting in her gut as it sensed her flash of panic. She realized with a flood of dread she would have done exactly as Alōs had, to her or to anyone else who got in the way of what she was after, especially if it was to save her family, her home.

She would have broken a thousand hearts, betrayed a kingdom of people, to protect those she loved.

And there was no denying Alōs loved his brother, was still duty bound to Esrom despite his banishment, and, as evident from these stories, cared about the pirates aboard his ship.

He *cared*.

Niya felt far away at the thought, as though everything in the room now glistened with new meaning.

We have fought as enemies for a long while, fire dancer. His earlier words to her echoed in her mind. *Perhaps it is time we see what happens when we work as allies.*

295

Had he truly been attempting peace? Peace that he perhaps had wished they could have built had they met on a different day under different circumstances?

If my memory serves—Alōs's voice from earlier continued to burn through her resolve—*you have been seeking me out since that night. Not the other way around.*

I sought you out because I had been trying to kill you!

It sounds, then, like it is you who hates me.

You who hates me.

Something shifted, hard and uncomfortable, in her chest.

Dare Niya admit that she now understood Alōs? All his motives and intentions toward her. He had been on a mission to destroy any threats in his way in order to heal from a past that still haunted him, still had his heart splintered and bruised. Niya had been a threat to him.

It wasn't just your identity I had grown to want.

Niya's throat felt gripped tight, unable to swallow against what this possibly meant.

Her gaze swung to Alōs's at the front of the room.

As though the pirate could sense her pulse of panicked energy even from this distance, his attention shifted off the princess, and his glowing blue eyes locked onto hers.

Niya's heartbeat sounded loud and uncontrolled in her ears.

It wasn't just your identity I had grown to want.

There was a roomful of guests between them, heady music filling the air, but for a grain fall it was just her and him, fire and ice steaming the air.

"Would you ever go back?" Saffi's question to Kintra sounded muffled in Niya's ears, but it pierced through her bubble of spiraling emotions enough for her to tear her gaze from the pirate lord.

"No," said Kintra. "I see no point in it."

Saffi glanced down to her plate. "No," she echoed. "No point."

"Where you are born only defines your blood," said Achak as he sipped his wine. "And even that is too easily spilled. Your home is where you're happiest, and that, my children, can be anytime, anywhere, and with anyone."

The sound of forks clinking against goblets had the commotion of the room quieting.

"Your Graces." Alōs stood, and heads and bodies twisted toward where he bowed to the royal family. "I want to thank you," he said, "on behalf of myself and my crew, for such a warm welcome. My sailors know it could not have come at a better time. Believe me when I say they were starting to look at one another like the food they have so ravenously devoured on their plates."

Laughter filled the hall as Niya continued to feel numb and far away.

"In a show of our deep gratitude," Alōs continued, "we would like to present your lovely daughter with a belated birthday present."

Boman approached the table and handed Alōs an ornately carved coral box.

In shocked pleasure, Princess Callista held her hands to her mouth as Alōs placed the gift before her and opened the lid. Her delighted gasp echoed through the room.

"It is beautiful! Mother, look how beautiful it is."

Callista lifted a silver-spun diadem from the box. Five spiraling and interlocking tips covered in glistening sapphires and diamonds.

The members of court chittered in awe as Queen Runisha leaned in to inspect the tiara.

"Yes, my light," said the queen, her intelligent eyes sliding to Alōs, who sat back down beside her daughter. "It is extremely breathtaking. How thoughtful of you, Lord Ezra, to part with such a rare treasure. I believe this alabaster silver is only found in Esrom?"

The queen was showing her cards. *I know where your origins lie,* her look seemed to say.

Alōs merely smiled. "Shall we see if it fits?"

Princess Callista's attending ladies approached, removing her current crown and placing the new one atop her head.

Niya hardly took in the next events as she watched the old diadem with the Prism Stone be placed on a plush pillow. Two armed guards came to stand on either side of the attending lady, who held it carefully a step behind the princess's chair.

"Oh, I love it." Callista's smile was radiant as she gazed into the mirror one of her other maidens brought forth, tilting her head this way and that. The diamonds sparkled like her youth. She placed a hand on Alōs's arm. "Thank you. I shall wear it the rest of the evening!"

The guests clapped before the music started up again. It was a new, quicker beat, filled with drums and the pleasant mixture of male and female voices.

The king stood, extending a large hand to his wife. With a laugh that brought a gentler light to Queen Runisha's eyes, she followed her husband to the center of the room.

The hall filled with cheers of delight before others were moved to dance.

Usually Niya would have joined in on such a moment, but she now forced herself to the task at hand, her attentions only on one event this evening.

Niya watched as the old crown was carried, guards in tow, from the hall.

Her gaze flickered to Kintra. A shared look before the quartermaster stood, excusing herself.

Niya's pulse thumped a new beat of readiness, an unknown patience keeping her seated and waiting.

She hesitantly allowed herself to glance at Alōs. He was once again in conversation with the princess in her new diadem.

His smile was charming, but there, edging the corners, was the twist of a jackal's grin.

Their old games might have ended, but new ones had just begun.

CHAPTER THIRTY

*A*lōs waited in the shadows of an alcove, a spiral column his separation from the plush-rugged hall that stretched out on either side. The royal wing sat quiet, save for the pacing guards: groups of two every quarter sand fall.

His breaths were even, but his cool magic twisted quickly through his veins along with his growing anticipation. This was it. This would be his final act to allow him to sever his responsibilities to the kingdom that had banished him.

He could dare to dream of sailing untethered, a truly free man, into the open waters.

Yet even at the thought, Alōs winced, feeling that never-ending tug deep in the center of his frozen heart.

Ariōn, it whispered. *You could never truly leave Ariōn.*

Couldn't he, though? *I have done far worse,* he thought.

The sudden weight of guilt that fell upon his shoulders was momentarily distracted by the black line of the binding bet along his wrist growing hot. As it always did when she drew near.

There was a new jump in his magic, readiness solidifying as a blur of red hair slid into the alcove where he stood. He inhaled the scent of honeysuckle as Niya pressed herself in close beside him, sharing his shadows as the soft material of her wrap dress brushed against his hand.

Alōs was momentarily dashed back into her shared bedchamber from earlier tonight, where they'd stood alone in a sea of plush bedding. He had caught the tail end of the message from her family, saw the track of tears on her cheek. Something heavy and rather uncomfortable had shifted within his chest then. For he was quite certain he did not like it.

Despite their tumultuous history, Alōs had never seen the fire dancer cry.

Not even when he'd known he would be breaking her heart.

Or had come to collect for the secrets he knew of her.

Or had been forced to lay a whip to her skin.

Niya had remained a statue of contained power, a lost god staring him in the eye, silently promising her own retribution greater than any pain he might have laid upon her that day.

It was enough to take anyone's breath away.

Bring a lesser monster than he to his knees in a plea for forgiveness.

But Alōs had not been seeking to be forgiven, only to be forgotten.

"Did any see you approach?" he asked Niya, his attention returning to where they claimed shadows deep within the mountain palace.

"Would I be standing here if they had?" she asked, her blue eyes dancing, alive and excited as they met his. "You're not the only one who can hide behind columns."

Alōs ignored her jab. "The guards appear to be on double patrol tonight."

"A smart order," said Niya. "Since pirates do roam about."

"Yes," mused Alōs. "But their caution forces ours. We must be quick and quiet. Kintra said the crown was brought to the princess's quarters, which are down the hall to the left. Two guards stand outside at all times."

Niya nodded. "That shouldn't be a problem."

"No," he agreed, "but we don't know where it is kept within her rooms. It could be in a safe or simply sitting out on her dressing table."

"Shall we place a bet on where we'll find it?" Her white grin gleamed bright even in the dark.

Alōs shook his head and, despite his earlier somber mood, found himself smiling in return. "You truly are your own worst enemy."

"Says my actual enemy."

His eyes found hers once more. "I thought we had made peace, fire dancer?"

"Yes, but habits are hard to break."

"So I am your habit?" Alōs arched a brow. How impossible she made it not to flirt.

"Don't flatter yourself," she said. "Now, shall we talk more or finish this?"

"How close do you need to be to trance the guards properly?"

"I could do it from here," said Niya, "but it's best if I can see them first."

Alōs peered out of their alcove. The hall extending to the princess's wing remained empty. Large flaming bowls lined the way on either side, dancing light and shadows along the painted murals. There would be no columns to hide behind after this. They would be prey running across a barren field.

"All right," Alōs murmured. "Let's get closer."

Alōs moved from their safe, shadowed corner and slid silently down the corridor, Niya quick on his heels.

He had left the party at its height, the dancing and music growing quick and heady. The princess was spinning about with lords and ladies of her court, and the king and queen had long since gone off to bed. All parties properly distracted from Alōs and his whereabouts as he disappeared from the banquet.

"Wait," whispered Niya, coming to a stop beside him. "I think I feel someone approach . . . a group."

Alōs cursed. "How close?"

"Close," said Niya, beginning to retrace their steps. "They must have come from the princess's rooms. I wasn't able to sense their movements until now. The stone walls are thick in this mountain palace."

Alōs looked down the hall behind them. They had traveled far from the alcove.

"They're almost here," said Niya, fire flickering alive in her palms. "We won't have time to run back the other way. We'll have to fight them."

"No. We cannot risk raising any alarms." He pulled them beside one of the flaming bowls. "Can you trance them?"

Niya's gaze went out of focus for a moment, her magic slipping from her, orange mist testing air. "Yes," she began, "but . . . I fear a few have the gifts. I don't have time to make it subtle; they will know something was done to them once my spell breaks."

Alōs could hear a rumble of approaching voices now, see forms turning into their hall from the far end. A foreign sense of panic seized him as he locked eyes with Niya.

By the stars and sea, he thought, *I must be mad for attempting* this. But it was the quickest way he knew how to hide in plain sight. "Don't hurt me," he warned, crowding Niya until her back hit up against the wall.

The flames beside them reflected in her startled eyes.

"Hurt you? Why would—?"

"I'm going to kiss you, okay?"

Her eyes snapped wide, palms pressing against his chest. "You most certainly w—"

"We have to," he quickly urged, hearing their guests getting closer and closer. "Lovers are never considered threats, while roaming pirates—"

"*Lovers?* You've lost your—oy! *Don't touch me there!*" she hissed, knocking away the hand angling for her waist.

"I have to." He placed his slapped hand on the wall beside her head instead, his large form enveloping her further. "As you said, you cannot currently spell them without them learning of it later, and we *cannot* fight, for that will surely raise alarms. So unless you can think of another way to get out of why two pirates are in these very off-limits quarters of the young princess—"

"You there!" a voice called toward them as Niya's eyes held his. Time stilled as he watched a barrage of thoughts and feelings tumble through their blue depths.

But Alōs had not gotten this far, gone through so much, to be caught. He would not be stopped this night. Niya had to understand this. Her own fate hung in the balance as well.

"Please," he whispered. His last attempt.

"Halt! You are not meant—"

But the rest of the guard's words were lost as Niya pulled Alōs down to her lips.

They were soft and full, just as he remembered, yet her body was seized in tension, her grip hard on his arms, nails digging into his skin. Alōs held steady. They were two roaring waves fighting for dominance. But this time, Alōs no longer wanted to fight.

She must have noticed, sensed his submission, for her hands loosened and her mouth parted, sending a delicious tongue to sweep across his own.

A wave of pleasure flowed through him as he took the invitation, just as he had those four years ago. He wrapped his hands around her small waist, pulled her supple form deeper into his hard chest, and devoured her.

And though this was a kiss of farce, nothing in the way his body responded to her was pretend. Alōs only hoped, as he claimed her lips, magic purring, Niya wouldn't notice.

CHAPTER THIRTY-ONE

*I*t was Niya's nightmare all over again. Because it was exactly like her dreams.

Alōs's ministrations were exquisite, his lips full and skilled. His hands were steady, strong, as he held her against the wall. He tasted like rich wine and experience.

Goose bumps were dusted across Niya's skin.

A betrayal.

In the back of her mind she knew everything about this was wrong, horrible, that she should shove her knee swiftly into his groin. But they were trapped with guards nearing.

Please.

The one word that had done her in. The plea that had shredded through her resolve. His need for her, and not just physically. No, it was him knowing that she held his future in the balance, and it sent an intoxicating wave of power through her.

Please, I am at your mercy.

And what separated her from him was that she was strong enough to give it.

Niya had leaned into what was already happening, a sick part of her reveling in it, wanting it. She'd melted her tightly spun energy, letting it pool beneath her feet, and tugged Alōs into a kiss.

A deep rumble of approval came from him as he pinned her harder to the cool wall. He was pure muscle and soft caresses. The heady scent of sea and midnight orchids filled her nostrils as she inhaled, and suddenly she was four years younger, alone with him in the privacy of her Thief Kingdom dressing room.

Niya was seated in front of her looking glass, tucking a piece of escaped hair into her headdress. She was adorned in a gold silk costume, preparing to leave for one of the many soirees happening in the palace that night, when she felt his cool energy, a chilled kiss beneath her covered neck.

In the reflection of her mirror, Niya watched a painting at the far end of her chambers edge forward and a tall, imposing man step out.

"You're not meant to be in here," said Niya, watching his dark form prowl close.

Alōs remained quiet as he came to stand behind her, his glowing turquoise eyes drinking in her costumed form.

Niya's body filled with a cool wind of anticipation.

Alōs was so beautiful. So consuming. So commanding. So untouchable.

All at court wanted to be near him. And she knew many had invited him to their beds.

But night after night the pirate lord had sneaked into her chambers, not theirs.

Niya's vanity glowed at the thought, preened at the temptation to give in to his loyalty to her and finally allow his skin to brush against hers, uncovered, bare, exposed.

"Were you hoping to catch me without my costume on?" teased Niya.

Alōs's grin sparked in the candlelight. "I'm always hoping to catch you, fire dancer."

They were an arresting sight, reflected in her mirror. Niya, in her shining gold-studded headdress and mask, her crown of pearls. Alōs, in his devastating beauty wrapped in darkness, brown skin smooth in the glow of her candelabras.

He leaned down, warm breath playing over her thinly veiled ear. "Do you think tonight will be the night when ice can finally play with fire?" he mused.

"Oy! Lovebirds!" A shout cut through Niya's memory, heat and haze dissipating. "You cannot be here."

Alōs released his hold on Niya, his soft mouth leaving hers in a cooling whoosh, as he glanced to their intruders.

"Excuse me?" asked Alōs, his voice calm, not at all matching the pounding beat Niya felt in her chest. She placed a steadying hand against the wall as the gazes of the guard and two servants roamed over where she and Alōs were still partially embraced.

"You need to leave," said the guard, eyes narrowed. "This wing is for the royal family and those who serve the—" The man cut himself off, eyes widening in recognition as he took in Alōs fully. "Sir." The man bowed quickly. "Forgive me. I did not recognize you, but I'm afraid you are still not allowed in this part of the palace."

"Oh?" Alōs straightened, bringing Niya with him as he curled an arm around her. She blinked, shaking off her momentary fluster to play along. She draped herself against Alōs's side. "I do apologize," he said. "I don't even know where exactly we are."

"This is Princess Callista's private wing," explained the guard. "No unaccompanied guests are allowed here."

"Of course, of course." Alōs nodded. "We weren't paying attention to where we were walking. I was merely looking for a quiet place to . . . well, you saw." He gave the guard a conspiratorial grin.

One of the servants chuckled before swallowing the sound after a stern scowl from the soldier.

"Of course, Lord Ezra," he said.

"They could try the library," the other servant suggested.

"Barneth," admonished the guard.

"What?" Barneth shrugged. "We all know it's always empty, and it's not only guests who have been known to frequent its . . . seclusion."

"It sounds perfect," said Alōs. "Where can we find this library?"

The guard still appeared unsure, as if it was against his duties to show where one might be able to snog another.

"I beg of you," said Alōs. "It would be a tragedy to have my night with this one end so early."

Niya dug her nails into Alōs's back as his hand lowered to her hip.

Alōs merely grinned wider.

The guard assessed Niya, his gaze lingering on her more ample parts.

Look longer and we'll see how well you'll see tomorrow, she thought.

"I suppose it wouldn't hurt," the man said slowly, "but you mustn't disrupt any books."

Alōs placed a hand to his chest. "We will not go close to a single one."

The guard nodded, seemingly mollified. "We can show you the way."

"Oh, we would hate to take up any more of your time," said Alōs. "Merely point us in the right direction, and we shall go there promptly."

The group walked the long way back down the hall, passing the alcove where they had hid, and halted where the corridor split into many paths.

"Take the stairs at the end there." The guard pointed to where a doorway led to descending stairs. "The library will be at the bottom on the right, through the double doors at the far end."

"I am in your debt," said Alōs. "See, my love?" He pulled Niya closer against him. "I'll be able to finish what you were begging me to start."

Niya wanted to cut off each and every one of his fingers.

"Enjoy yourselves," the servant, Barneth, whispered as they passed.

Niya and Alōs watched the group leave, pretending to turn toward the library before quickly doubling back once the guard and servants were out of sight.

Niya shoved Alōs away from her as they strode down the corridor to the princess's rooms, a good deal quicker this time. "If you *ever* try something like that again," she hissed, "I will melt the skin from your body."

"You should be thanking me for the suggestion," said Alōs. "We were about to be caught."

"I'll thank you to find a better alternative next time."

"As I remember it, you were not offering up any viable options yourself that wouldn't have raised alarms. But I'm flattered my kiss appears to have affected you this much." Alōs's smile dripped smugness.

"The only thing it affected was my dinner threatening to be expelled."

They quieted as they drew closer to the far corner. Niya sneaked a quick glance around the bend.

Two guards stood in the middle of the hall, guarding the large double doors of Callista's chambers.

"They are not blessed," said Niya as she pressed back against the wall.

"No," Alōs agreed. "Remember we need them pliable, not knocked out."

Niya nodded before taking a deep breath in. Rhythmically fluttering her fingers, she sent red tendrils of her magic along the ground. They traveled like silent serpents on the hunt.

With a quick twirl of her hand, her powers wrapped around each guard.

Their wills gave a soft tug of resistance before sighing to sleep.

"They're mine," she said, pulse quickening.

The soldiers didn't move at their approach but merely stood rigid, eyes forward.

"What did you do to them?" asked Alōs.

"I made their minds blank."

"How long will it last?"

"After I remove the connection to my magic? About a half sand fall."

Alōs nodded as he shot out his own green magic through the lock in the door.

A soft click sounded, and they quickly slipped inside.

Niya took in Princess Callista's cavernous chambers. They stood in a massive receiving room made up of dusty-rose-and-orange detailing. Five other anterooms appeared to split off from where they stood. With a nod, she and Alōs turned from one another to search separately.

Time seemed to fall too quickly as Niya ran hands over rough painted walls, looking for a trick latch, and pulled books and moved away hanging tapestries, hoping one would reveal another hidden room or safe, something cloaked where valuables would be stored.

The fear of more servants or guards entering set her nerves on edge, especially since the walls were so thick in this caved palace, cutting off her senses from motion beyond what was closest. She felt like half a person without these aspects of her gifts, and she hated it.

It was like only being able to take in half a breath, rather than a large, satisfying inhale.

"In here," Alōs called softly from Callista's bedroom. Niya found him in the back of the princess's large wardrobe, where rows and rows of beautiful garments were folded and hung at either side. Alōs stood before a heavy gold door set into the back panel.

Niya's magic pulsed with her whoosh of relief.

"You found it," said Niya, coming to his side.

"Not necessarily. But whatever is in here holds value. I only hope that includes the Prism Stone."

Niya glanced to the round-dialed lock beside its handle. It gleamed with complicated markings—a spelled lock. Crisscrossing fingers wove together, appearing to each need to be individually opened for the clasp to give.

"Will this be a problem?" asked Niya.

"Thankfully, no." Alōs crouched before the door, taking out a leather pouch from his pocket and opening it on the rugged floor to display an array of thin metal picks. Alōs bypassed the snake rake, long hook, and other standard lock-picking devices that Niya knew to select a thin straight rod that pulsed white at the tip.

"Is that a magic lockpick?" asked Niya.

"It is indeed." Alōs grinned as he placed it next to the dial. "A mirror pick, it's called. It can get through most locks."

"Where did you get such a thing?"

Turquoise eyes glanced up at her, a mischievous twinkle in their depths. "I'm a pirate, Niya. And captain to the most notorious and successful ship—"

"Oh, by the love of the lost gods," she breathed in exasperation. "Never mind. Just get on with it, will you." She waved an impatient hand.

A soft chuckle rumbled out of him as he turned back to his task. Alōs's attention refocused as he placed the glowing tip close to the interwoven locks.

Niya dared not breathe as she watched him angle the tip into the first latch, his adept fingers twisting and curling it to bend and weave into the second and then the third, down the row of entwined fingers.

Her nerves cascaded down her skin, too convinced someone would enter the princess's chambers at any moment, see the stunned guards at the door, and raise the alarms.

All they had done to get here, her kissing Alōs, it would be for naught. They would never get the stone and—

Clink, clink, clink.

The individual locks snapped open one by one. Alōs stood in a whoosh beside Niya and pulled the door open.

All her tension fell from her like leaves dropping in autumn as utter splendor replaced her worry. "By the lost gods," muttered Niya as she stepped into a small room lit by a hanging chandelier.

Every inch, shelf, and hook sparkled with treasure. Diamond necklaces. Gold leaf masks encrusted with sapphires. Niya ran her hand over rows and rows of jeweled bracelets, the softest leather shawls that slipped through her fingers like water, and earrings woven out of silver spider silk. Niya's mouth watered. The part thief that she was itched to have a few of these items find their way into her pockets.

Niya turned from her shelf of fine treasure to find Alōs approaching the far end, his attention pinned to a crown on a plush white pillow. Even at this distance she saw the brilliant red glow from what was resting in its center.

Her heart gave a thrilled pulse as she went to his side, each of them staring down at the gleaming Prism Stone. It was an alluring red siren in the center of the gold-tipped crown.

This was it!

Niya smiled wide as every part of her wanted to spin and twirl and dance in the utter elation.

Her freedom rested a touch away.

Her home, her sisters, her family—everything was wrapped up in the glistening jewel before them.

And no one was around to stop them from taking it.

"It's ours," whispered Niya as she glanced to Alōs. He had not moved or uttered a sound in some time. He stood rigid, tense, as though . . . but no, why would he be frightened? He finally had what he had hunted for so long. The final piece of the Prism Stone. "Alōs . . . ," she began, pinching her brows together.

"We must be quick," he said, shaking off whatever ghosts had clung to him.

With nimble fingers, he removed a new pouch from his pocket, revealing the fake red gem his brother had given him. Though rough, it was just as red and rich in sparkle as Niya remembered from when she'd first seen it in his captain's quarters. But now with the real one in front of them, Niya could see, right there in the center, it didn't gleam with a hint of power and history like the real Prism Stone.

She watched as Alōs studied the gem in the crown before holding up the fake. He shot a stream of icy-green magic from his fingertip, deftly carving the rock down to become an exact replica.

"Hold this," he instructed when he was done, handing Niya the imitation gem. She turned it between her fingers. It was just as rough along the surface, but more oval now. A smoothed purpose to its shape.

Using a thin blade, Alōs bent forward to carefully pop out the Prism Stone and, spreading a bit of sticky durberry paste in the empty pocket, took the replica from her hand and settled it into the crown. He stepped back, admiring his work.

If Niya hadn't seen the switch, she wouldn't have known it was done.

She leaned close to Alōs as they each studied the prize in his palm. She had a strong urge to hug him in that moment, not out of any comradery but because it was done! They had it! Her magic soared through her veins, a warm barrage of triumph.

Alōs remained quiet, pensive, as he turned the stone over and over.

"What's wrong?" she asked.

"This isn't all of it."

His words were a cold ice bath to her joy.

Nonono, she thought quickly, *he's forgetting.* "Of course it's not all of it. The stone in your ring fits into this part here." She pointed to the small groove in the side.

"No." He shook his head, brows pinching in. "There's another cut . . . at the back. See?"

Niya leaned in; a sizable chunk was missing on the other side. Her stomach twisted, the small amount of food she'd had at dinner threatening to come up. "So . . . what are you saying?" she dared ask.

Alōs's hard gaze met hers. "This isn't the final piece of the Prism Stone."

312

CHAPTER THIRTY-TWO

Niya felt like a ghost as she accompanied Alōs back to his private chambers—unfeeling, a specter of motions as they stole quickly away from the princess's rooms.

Kintra was already waiting for them by the warmly lit fireplace. She stood as they entered, a question in her gaze as Alōs went straight to a decanter of wine, finishing the glass in one go. He refilled it again.

"Did you not get it?" asked Kintra.

"We did," answered Niya.

"Then why does it feel like a funeral in here?"

Niya looked to Alōs, waiting for him to explain, to remove the Prism Stone from his inside pocket and show his quartermaster what was missing, but he remained silent, staring into the jumping flames of the fireplace.

With a frown, Niya divulged what had happened. With each word, her skin trickled with more fury and frustration. For when she was done, the question that hung silent in the air, that none wanted to ask or mention, was if the part missing was truly only *one*. The chunk cut from the back was sizable, almost as large as a silver coin. If someone had been willing to cut that out, perhaps they'd then split the third piece a dozen more ways. And was it the work of Cebba or the people of the valley? The endless possibilities were paralyzing.

"What do you want to do, Captain?" Kintra turned to him, worry etching deeper into her features as Alōs once again remained mute.

Niya had never seen him like this before. Reserved. Almost . . . defeated.

It unnerved her.

He could at least be angry like she was, for anger held energy that could be molded into something useful. Complacency was next to uselessness.

Niya had no time for inaction. And neither did he. His home was on the line, for the Obasi Sea's sake. She couldn't sit idly by while an entire nation was unmoored!

Niya's thoughts froze.

When did I start to care about his *problems?*

She swallowed back her unease. *It's because of the people who live in Esrom,* she silently reasoned. If Esrom surfaced, a war against the hidden treasure would be imminent. Too much lore surrounded the city, too many whispers about how its people thought themselves better than the rest of Aadilor. Other nations would surely try to claim it. And then there was Ariōn. So young to his new responsibilities as king. Alone in that palace. Hadn't he experienced enough hardship with his illness before losing his brother and then parents? He did not deserve such a tragedy as this to end his short reign.

Plus, Niya wasn't a heartless snake. The Bassettes might have been thieves, her sisters part of the Mousai, but they never stole from the less fortunate, never punished the innocent. They struck and helped where they felt they were most needed.

Niya was needed here.

"We're going to figure out what happened to the rest of the stone," said Niya to Kintra. "We'll find where it is, and we'll get it back."

Alōs snorted his disbelief from where he remained by the fire.

"Do you have something to add?" She turned to him.

"No, you lie quite beautifully for the both of us."

"It is not a lie. It is a plan, which we need, *Captain*. Or have you forgotten that's still who you are?"

Alōs met her gaze, a flickering spark of his old self in his eyes' depths, before it fell away and he returned to staring at that blasted fire.

Say something! Niya wanted to scream. But she didn't. It was apparent he still needed time. She only hoped it wasn't more than a sand fall, for even that was too much to spare at the moment.

Niya looked to Kintra. "We should get whatever rest we can before tomorrow's breakfast. Make sure he sleeps"—she nodded to Alōs—"and if that's by getting him more drunk, so be it. I'll figure this out."

"How?" Kintra's brows drew together.

"I don't know yet," admitted Niya, "but . . . I will."

With that Niya headed back to her shared rooms to crawl into bed.

She lay awake for a long while, the rumbling, drunken snores of her lady shipmates a backdrop to her turning thoughts.

This was all becoming a bloody, muddy mess.

Her new convictions in caring for Esrom, for the pirates who slept around her; her new truce with Alōs; their recent kiss. Things were changing. She was changing.

But is it for the best? she wondered as she idly ran a finger over the mark around her wrist.

All she currently knew was that Alōs needed to snap out of it. He was useless as he had been in his rooms earlier. Licking his wounds like a defeated dog.

Where was the ice-cold energy he always carried? Where was the impertinent, stubborn beast who welcomed a challenge with a sneering grin? She needed Alōs fighting again. Being ruthless again.

Niya pushed out of bed. She could sleep when all this was over. Currently she needed to figure out a plan.

It wasn't until servants came to wake them that she finally felt one forming.

The morning spun honey-yellow light over the large terrace where the next day's breakfast was taking place. Niya stepped onto the balcony, taking in the sandstone buildings of the valley, which rose like proud fingers of giants in the distance. The pleasant aroma of fresh-baked sugar rolls and delicately sliced fruit wafted toward her from a nearby table, but she ignored the rumble in her stomach that begged her to fill a plate. She was on a mission this morning, praying to the lost gods that she would succeed. Food could come later.

The lively commotion from the night before was reduced to snail movements as she twisted through the guests, glancing to her crew, who nursed hangovers on low sofas placed in the shade of olive trees. Saffi was still dressed in her silk pants and tunic from the past evening, eyes closed with a wet towel over her forehead, while Boman sneaked bites off her plate. The old man seemed spry compared to the rest of the lot, no doubt immune to hangovers by now. His thick gray beard shifted upward as he grinned at her.

Niya nodded in return but did not stop to talk.

She approached a tucked-away section of the veranda that was beside a twisting wall of jasmine, the sweet fragrance enveloping the area in a gentle mist. This was where Niya found King Anup sitting beside Achak and an elderly woman who looked like a folded-up napkin.

The guards blocking them patted Niya down before allowing her entrance to the group.

"Child," greeted Achak from where the sister lounged on a low sofa. "It is good to see you have survived the debauchery of last night." She turned to the king and the elderly woman. "Your Majesties, let me introduce Niya Bassette, second daughter to Count Dolion Bassette of the second house of Jabari. My brother and I are old friends with her family. Niya, you know King Anup, of course, and this is the queen mother, Murilia."

Niya bowed. "Your Grace, on behalf of the *Crying Queen*, I want to express how grateful we are for your generosity these past two days. The lost gods knew we needed rest after sailing through those storms."

"I must admit"—the king's brows rose—"I have never heard of a lady who sails with pirates. Please, join us for some food and tell us how that came to be."

Niya bowed again before a plate of dates with a warm roll was handed to her by an awaiting servant. With thanks she took a seat beside the old queen, who merely kept eyes forward, withered hands folded like fragile pieces of paper in her lap.

"I'm sure it's a story like any other aboard the *Crying Queen*, Your Grace," answered Niya to the king. "I was in the right place at the wrong time."

"Aren't most of us?" He smiled. "Now, tell me more of our western storms; have they truly gotten as bad as they say? It has been some time since I've sailed through them myself to know."

"It was my first experience, Your Grace, so I have no past to compare, but I can say the waves matched the height of your canyons, and if it wasn't for the skill of our captain and crew, our ship would be splintered to pieces at the bottom of the sea. The entrance to the Fade would now be very busy with a surly lot of disgruntled pirates."

The king laughed, the sound a soft rumbling of boulders. Unlike his wife, King Anup seemed open with his energy, friendly. Which was what allowed Niya grow her confidence to continue in what she was after.

"That *is* a fright to hear," he said. "I must come to the river and see what damage still lingers on your vessel. Though my wife tells me most of the wreckage has already been repaired with the help of our people."

"You and Her Highness have our thanks."

"Don't be too grateful," tutted King Anup. "Your captain paid handsomely for the assistance."

The old queen beside her reached over and grabbed a wrapped date off Niya's plate.

"Mama," admonished the king. "I'm sorry, Lady Niya; I fear my mother is quite fond of that particular snack. She ate every last one from my plate as well."

"I eat in her lands," said Niya. "This food is always hers to take."

"Your flattery is wasted on her, child," Achak explained as Niya held her plate steady so the old queen could eat a few more. "Queen Murilia hasn't been able to hear in a decade, at least."

"But I can still read your lips, ancient one," croaked Murilia, eyes narrowing.

"And still keep us on our toes," said the king with a chuckle, patting his mother's shoulder.

"You have a blessed family," said Niya. "Your daughter will be a great leader with such lineage in her blood."

"Yes." The king's expression grew warm at the mention of his daughter. "Callista has outwitted us all on many occasions. I'm sure my wife will find herself handing over her crown soon enough and without even realizing she's doing it."

Niya's nerves buzzed, seeing her opening. "I must say, in all my years gazing upon the splendor of Aadilor, I have never seen crowns as beautiful as you and your family's. Were they forged here?"

She could feel Achak's questioning gaze on her, but Niya kept her attention on the king, her features smooth.

"They were," he said. "We have some of the best metalworkers in the west. Each of our crowns has been made by the Dergun family for decades."

"How amazing. We Bassettes are no royalty, but I know my father would be flattered if I brought him home a gift made by such hands. Are the Derguns' services only reserved for the royal family?"

"They take commission from any who can pay. In fact"—the king glanced beyond their section—"I think the wife and son are here now. I can introduce you to them later, if you'd like."

Niya controlled her sweep of joy at finding out this information to a mere smile. "I would be forever grateful."

The king nodded. "Of course."

"I do love learning about such trade," continued Niya after a moment, daring to push for more. "Metalworking is an art form, to be sure. How the Derguns can manipulate such strong material to curl so gracefully around jewels is astonishing. I truly could not stop admiring the princess's. And that red jewel within." Niya shook her head in awe. "I have never seen its equal in color or size."

She was toeing a dangerous line, Niya knew, her magic awakening in her gut at her surge of adrenaline, but the king appeared an over-sharer, and she didn't have time to play a longer game. If there were extra answers to be gained, she needed to acquire them fast.

"And no matter how many more kingdoms you visit, you will not," said King Anup proudly. "Such a stone is a rare beauty, like our Callista. And my mother, of course."

"Your mother?" Niya tightened her grip around her plate. "Does she have a crown of it as well?" She glanced at the woman, but no such sparkling adornment sat atop her head.

"A pendant," the king clarified before sipping from his goblet. "My mother and daughter share the same month of birth. We had the stone split to be made into a gift for each."

A ringing filled Niya's ears then, all her attention zeroing in on the old queen once more, searching through her many drapes of purple and orange clothes. Queen Murilia's hair matched her son's; long gray braids draped over her shoulders and lay coiled in her lap. But nowhere could Niya find a necklace made with the Prism Stone. Was it in her rooms like the crown had been in Callista's? Could it truly be here?

Hope began to bubble up in her chest. *Please, by the lost gods, for once let everything I seek come easier.*

"Of course, she lost that within a fortnight." The king sighed.

Niya blinked over to him, feeling the color drain from her face. She struggled to keep her breathing even. "Lost it?" she asked, forcing as much of a casual tone as she could muster, when what she really wanted to do was scream and shake the old bird beside her. *How could you lose it!*

"Can't recall where she put the necklace," he explained. "Which is why you might notice she doesn't wear anything precious now. She'd misplace it as soon as she put it on." The king put his hand beside his mouth to hide his words. "Her hearing isn't the only thing that's gone. Her memory isn't what it used to be either."

Niya vaguely nodded, no longer listening, as her thoughts exploded into a mess of panic, hopelessness, dread.

Lost. It's lost. She lost it.

Was this really how it was to end?

Coming up short.

Esrom handed to the wolves. Niya chained to the *Crying Queen* for another year, at the mercy of a pirate who would no doubt blame her for everything. The fragile peace between them shredded on the spot.

"I'm often forgetful." Achak's voice broke through Niya's downward spiral. "Which is the only reason I enjoy having my brother around. He can always recall my *forgotten* memories."

Niya met the ancient one's intent stare.

"Forgotten memories are inevitable when the fountain of youth fades," the sister went on. "And though you are still young, Niya, my sweet, you must not take for granted your *fountain* of youth."

"Yes," said Niya slowly as certain words began to click in place.

Fountain . . . memories . . .

A calm settled over her as she held Achak's knowing purple gaze, a new plan awakening.

"This all said by a creature who never ages," said the king. "Not that you'd be any less magnificent if you did."

Achak smiled. "My dear Anup, since you were a young boy, you were always an incorrigible charmer."

"How do you think I got my wife to marry me?"

"We presumed it was because of your heavy dowry."

The king laughed long and hard. "Yes, well, that certainly helped keep her open minded to a ruffian like me."

As the conversation continued, no one noticed Niya's hand slip behind the old queen's back. Her heart felt like it was pounding in her throat, her senses on high alert as she twirled her finger once, twice, thrice, before a flame flickered on the tip.

Her pulse was a stampeding beast in her veins as she smiled and nodded along with Achak's story, which held the king's attention, the sister shifting into her brother.

And well, no one could look away when the twins came out to play.

With a quick slash, Niya singed off a small piece of the old queen's braid. The nub fell into her palm, and with a single fluid motion she tucked it safely into her pocket.

Her eyes darted around the veranda, seeing if any might have noticed such a small movement from her, but the space remained idly lazy. She allowed herself a sigh of relief.

Niya remained with the group for another half grain's fall before she made her apologies and stood to leave. Before exiting, she made sure to give Achak a quick kiss of thanks on the cheek.

"Safe travels," said Achak, now back in the form of the sister, a twinkle in her violet eyes.

Niya strode back across the veranda, ignoring the calls from Bree to join her and Green Pea, and waved away Therza asking her to get her more food. Niya felt like a hound in a fox hunt; there was only one person she cared to find.

And find him she did. Alōs stood on the other side of the balcony beside Kintra. They conversed with the queen and the princess. Callista still wore her gifted tiara from Alōs. Still smiled up at him like he was the rarest of gifts.

Alōs, however, seemed to have forgotten his charms this morning. Though he appeared engaged with the group, his posture was straight, tense. His gaze far away.

Still moping, thought Niya. *Moping while I do all the work.*

Charging past them, she made a point to meet Alōs's gaze and inclined her head just so.

We need to talk.

Niya paced beside the doused fireplace within Alōs's rooms, her magic churning with impatient energy in her veins. *Move,* it shouted. *Get going!*

She glanced to the sandglass on the mantel. Why wasn't Alōs here already? Didn't he know time was not on their side? Didn't he know—?

The door to his chambers opened and closed.

"The old queen had a necklace made with the other part of the Prism Stone," she blurted, striding toward Alōs.

He paused, hand still on the doorknob, an array of emotions running through his gaze. "What do you mean, *had?*"

"She lost it. Can't remember where she put it. But—I know how to find where it might be."

"How?"

Niya reached into her pocket and pulled out part of the queen's braid.

Alōs scrunched his nose. "Is that . . . hair?"

"Yes," said Niya. "But don't you see? We can use *this*"—she shook the nub—"to find the answer in the Fountains of Forgotten Memories."

"The Fountains of . . ." Alōs's brows drew together. "In the Thief Kingdom?"

Niya nodded, a grin edging along her lips. "In the Thief Kingdom."

CHAPTER THIRTY-THREE

No longer by days or grains through a sandglass, time was now measured by destinations.

After traveling back through the Mocking Mist and surviving the western storms yet again, the *Crying Queen* sailed endlessly over open waters. And Niya now knew why pirates were a surly lot.

Each day brought new weather, from ice rain to balmy sun to hailstorms that left dents in the deck the size of peach pits. Being at sea for so long, her sense of reality became reduced to sensations. Hunger, thirst, fatigue, boredom.

A deadly combination for a group that lacked strong morals.

The only thought that kept her sane was the promise of what was waiting for them at the end of their journey. The Thief Kingdom. Though this did nothing to stop her impatience to get there, her magic a continuous churn of mirrored eagerness in her veins.

Home, it crooned. *Mischief,* it begged.

My sisters, Niya added.

While she'd been unable to find Achak before they'd officially set off from the Valley of Giants, she only hoped the twins would be able to get word to her family of where the *Crying Queen* was sailing next.

Niya's chest swelled with longing and uncontained excitement at the prospect of Larkyra and Arabessa being there when she arrived.

As land rose on the distant horizon, it appeared Niya was not the only desperate soul craving the kingdom or solid ground, for a dozen pirates rushed starboard, gripping the railing to take in the view.

There were a few ways of entering the Thief Kingdom, but Niya had never sailed in through one of the marina ports.

A small strip of beach sat in the middle of the sea. Not even a single palm tree marred its horizon. The only feature that rose up in glaring strangeness was a freestanding waterfall cutting through the middle. It rained down from some invisible source in the sky.

Niya looked up as the ship slipped through, the loud roar of water parting like a drape, none on board getting wet. And then the *Crying Queen* entered from wide-open sea into the dark cave of the Thief Kingdom.

Niya's energy sang as she took in the spectacular hidden world. Cool mist rose from the waters, slowly revealing the twinkling lights of the dark city's edge. Colorful puffs of smoke from chimneys curled around the massive stalactites and stalagmites, and hanging glowworms covered the cave's ceiling, the stars of this world.

In the distance the imposing onyx castle loomed like a guardian in the center of the cave. Its pointed turrets gleamed like liquid ink in the night as spits of fire escaped their tips, beacons for the wicked to come play.

Niya breathed in deep, savoring the damp but sweet air, a cacophony of familiarity.

If she were one who easily cried, she would be now.

She was home.

Home.

Despite what still lay ahead, Niya felt a huge weight lift from her shoulders. Somewhere within this city might be her sisters, and within the castle, seated above a river of lava, was her father. Her magic tingled along her skin, desperate to be reunited.

"Oy, Red," called Saffi. "Mind helping the rest of us?"

Niya jolted from her thoughts, turning from the view to join the crew as they rushed about, readying the ship for port. After settling into a tight spot among other vessels, they dropped anchor and lowered the sails before making their way below deck to put on their disguises.

Stopping by her bunk, Niya fished out a leather mask that Kintra had given her. It was worn, stained in odd places, and nothing like the disguises she was used to wearing here. But it would do.

"Coming?" asked Bree as she waited by the stairs. Her small bunk-mate had on a red, feathered mask that was a bit too big for her face.

"Yes." Niya slipped on her disguise. Though it was not hers, it still settled along her skin like a familiar hug. She was back in the king-dom where anyone could be anything. With a wide grin, she ascended topside, standing back as her crew members passed by, hauling heavy sacks on their shoulders, their collected bounty from past raids they'd be depositing at Stockpiled Treasure.

Despite the grueling journey, the mood of the pirates had instantly lifted when they'd entered the Thief Kingdom, and Niya understood why. There was much promise before them for the next few nights: spirits, gambling, reunions with lovers. Their responsibilities to this ship could be forgotten as they lost themselves in the promised debauchery of this caved world.

If only Niya could have been as lucky as they. Yes, she was back, but a part of her knew she would be tied to Alōs, committed to the duty of her binding bet. Still, her mood remained high, for she only hoped she could entertain a few grain falls away from him and with her sisters.

Finding Alōs and Kintra by the gangplank, where they exchanged quick words with various pirates as they left the ship, Niya went to their side. Per usual, Alōs wore no mask. His dark, devastating beauty on full display. Niya now understood the only place he truly feared being seen was in Esrom. That was where he hid, keeping to shadowed outlets or empty passageways. In the rest of Aadilor, Alōs stood confidently in the open, wanting to be known as the infamous pirate lord. The more cities and realms that knew him as his current role—thief, scoundrel, murderer—the better. It was easier to hide trails to a past when so many led away.

"I assume we are going straight there?" Niya asked Alōs as the last of the pirates descended to the docks below.

"You assume correctly," he said as he set off down the gangplank himself, her following on his heels. "Kintra will meet us once the rest of the ship is secured."

"Could we grab a bite first?" asked Niya. "The lines at the fountains are always horrid, and I can guarantee I am much more cooperative when I'm not starved."

"You must be starved often, then," he said before turning to have a quick word with the port master, who stood at the edge of their dock.

Niya huffed her impatience as she went to wait on the boardwalk for him to finish.

Leaning against a lamppost, she watched the stream of citizens strolling by. The docks were filled with the sweet fragrance of honey pies and coffee from a nearby vender. Niya's stomach grumbled loudly.

"This is maddening," she mumbled, marching away and straight up to the nearest masked merchant. "I'll take three pies, and don't even bother wrapping one of them up."

She paid with what little silver she had acquired as part of the *Crying Queen*'s crew and hardly took a breath as she devoured the crumbly delight. "By the lost gods," she moaned, savory flavors exploding across her taste buds. Niya was about to open her bag for the next pie when the tingle of familiar energies played over her skin.

Swiveling around, Niya searched the crowd, her heart picking up speed.

The world seemed to stop as she saw them. Two figures walked toward her. One wore an immaculate purple three-piece pantsuit with a black cloak and top hat, while the other was wrapped in a pale-green dress that flared dramatically at the waist, a matching veil covering her hair. Each had on a marble black eye mask, and together, arm in arm, they appeared like a genteel couple out for a stroll.

Despite their disguises, Niya would know them anywhere, for their energy was her own.

Niya ran toward them, her food forgotten on the street as the three collided with squeals of delight. Well, Arabessa didn't quite squeal as much as Larkyra and Niya.

"Achak got word to you?" Niya hugged them close, inhaling each of their scents. Lavender and rose.

Home.

She was home.

They were her home.

"Achak did," said Larkyra, pulling back to look at Niya. Her blue eyes shimmered behind her mask. "And we've been strolling the docks every day since, waiting for the *Crying Queen* to come to port. Oh, sister, look how much of a pirate you've become! You're practically freckled all over."

Niya's heart was overflowing, almost painfully, at finally being reunited with her sisters. She hardly knew what to say, do. "New shoes?" she deflected, glancing down at Larkyra's silver-heeled boots.

"A gift from the duke." Larkyra pointed her toe out. "Do you like?"

"He spoils you."

"As he should."

"I miss new shoes." Niya sighed. "And being spoiled."

"I'm glad your vanity has survived your sentencing," said Arabessa.

Niya shot her eldest sister a grin. "All my glowing personal attributes are still much alive. It's my physical ones that I'm afraid have been threatened."

"Yes." Larkyra flapped her hand under her masked nose. "You smell rather . . . fragrant now."

"And my hair is a rat's nest."

"Well, it has always been in the mornings."

"And my hands are dry and scabbed."

"At least they now match your feet."

Niya swatted Larkyra on the arm, but despite the insults, Niya laughed. The sensation was freeing as it burst from her lungs. It had been far too long since she'd laughed like this.

"I think the real difference is in your energy," Arabessa mused, her blue eyes assessing beneath her mask. "You now seem . . ."

"Tired?" Niya suggested.

"More mature," finished Arabessa. "You've seen much in these few months."

Niya waved away the seriousness in her sister's voice. She did not want to go there. Not yet. "Few months? It has been at least three hundred years since I've last seen you," she corrected. "I mean, look"—Niya pointed toward Arabessa's coiled black locks—"is that gray starting to sprout at your temples?"

"Nice try," said Arabessa haughtily, smoothing back her perfectly tucked-up raven locks. "Whatever has happened," she continued, "I'm glad your travels have led you here, my love. We were sure it would be a full year until we saw you again."

"With the way things are going, it might have been two," she found herself admitting.

"Two?" Larkyra's gaze widened behind her disguise. "You must tell us everything. Achak was rather vague in their information."

"Lord Ezra," Arabessa announced, the group turning to find the pirate approaching.

"Ladies." Alōs inclined his head. "It is good to see you both looking so well."

"And it is good to find our sister still in one piece."

"With her aboard, I fear it is my crew you should have been more worried for."

"Indeed," agreed Arabessa, assessing the pirate. "I can hardly believe your boat does not display a single singe mark."

"It seems your sister chose to leave her mark by relieving me of a few of my crew instead."

"Truly?" Arabessa glanced to Niya. "I guess she always has fancied herself as valuable as three or four men combined. She probably did not see them as a loss to lose."

"Yes," said Alōs with a grin. "On that we can agree. She does think rather highly of herself, doesn't she?"

"I thought we were in a hurry." Niya glared between her eldest sister and the pirate. "Or would you like to stand around all day sharing more of my faults?"

"If that is an actual option . . . ?" asked Larkyra with a smile.

The sound of Alōs's husky laugh did nothing to improve Niya's suddenly declining mood. It was one thing for each party to poke at her from their separate corners; it was another entirely to find the odd pairing commiserating together.

"I leave you three to it, then." Niya turned, heading up the cobble road to town.

Alōs was by her side in two long strides. "I thought you were more cooperative when you had food. Or do you still need to eat the other pies you bought? Though I fear they aren't as good now on the ground."

She chanced a glance, catching his amused grin.

It only made her frown more.

"And I thought we were to go to the fountains *immediately*."

"We will accompany you there as well," said Arabessa as she and Larkyra caught up to them. "And you will not argue, Lord Ezra." She raised her hand, stopping his interjection. "It is the least you can do after taking away our dear sister."

"As much as I wish to argue against your point," he began, "it has been a very long voyage, and I don't desire this day to be wrought with any more difficulties."

"Wise man." Arabessa nodded. "Now let us hurry. It is midday, which means there is bound to be a line forming."

The Fountains of Forgotten Memories were at the center of the Gazing District, where an array of beautiful temples lined the streets. The fountains were the most ornate, however, in an exposed marble pavilion with dozens of columns holding up a stained glass dome. The scenes above were said to have been childhood memories of the architect. It was a mixture of serene blue skies with blooming flowers and dark stretching forms looming over the fields as if soon to cover them completely in shadows. A multitude of glowing pools lined the rotunda, where indeed queues, four to be exact, curled around the space. Keepers stood at the helm of each pool, attending customers one by one.

It took a full sand fall for them to finally reach a Keeper of the Cup. Theirs was a round figure whose identity was hidden beneath drapes of white robes, their hands wrapped in gauze. They sat on a cushioned pillow before their small glowing basin of water. Alōs stepped forward and placed two silver coins into the jar by their feet, which was already brimming with past payments.

"Who will be drinking?" asked a raspy voice.

"I will," answered Alōs.

"You have skin, bone, nail, or hair?"

"Hair." Niya pulled forth Queen Murilia's small gray braid, handing it to Alōs.

The Keeper dipped a ladle into the glowing blue water, sending ripples across the surface, and poured the liquid into a large goblet resting on a side table. They took the braid from Alōs, lit it on fire, and dumped the ash in the drink, swirling as they did. "Drink." They extended the chalice to Alōs. "All of it," they urged as he pulled away, choking on the flavor.

Niya had visited the fountains once before, when she and her sisters had been gifted a lock of their mother's hair by their father for one of their birthdays.

The experience of living through some of their mother's memories had been amazing, but the drink had been disgusting.

"Sit there," the Keeper instructed, pointing to a carved stone bench where others were slumped, eyes closed behind their disguises. Some twitched and moaned. All still in the trance of memories.

Alōs complied, settling into the small space as Niya and her sisters crowded around him.

She wondered if Alōs knew what he was in for. How memories could be an extremely overwhelming experience.

Niya drew her brows together, that wiggle of discomfort again that any part of her was beginning to care for any part of him. Her main concern was meant to be about this working; otherwise she was out of options. Her next year aboard his ship as good as solidified.

"Is something supposed to happen?" asked Alōs after a moment.

The Keeper didn't answer, merely watched from his perch as Alōs suddenly gasped, his eyes rolling back to white. He collapsed against the bench.

"You may wait over there," the Keeper told Niya and her sisters. "Depending on what he seeks, it may take some time."

The girls stepped to the side, where others waited for their companions to wake from walking through forgotten memories.

"So tell us," said Larkyra, drawing close to Niya. "Why are we here? What is it Alōs searches another's memories for?"

Niya glanced to the unconscious pirate across the way. He was so vulnerable like this, she realized. Tranced, unable to wake until the thoughts he swam through released him.

Something akin to guilt tugged at her chest at the idea of speaking his secrets to her sisters when he was in this state.

Of course, she had no bind *not* to tell them of the Prism Stone, but . . .

"He searches for an item that was lost," explained Niya vaguely.

Larkyra huffed a laugh. "Well, of course, isn't that why all go searching forgotten memories, to look at things lost?"

"What I mean is"—Niya turned back to regard her sisters—"he is trying to find a particular gem that has gone missing."

"A pirate searching for treasure?" asked Arabessa. "How boring."

Niya smiled at the sentiment, for she had said something similar herself when first learning of the Prism Stone.

"Yes, boring," Niya echoed.

Her eldest sister eyed her from beneath her mask. "I have a sense that is not the entire truth," she accused.

Niya shifted on her feet, her resolve slipping. *I have no loyalty to Alōs,* she reminded herself, *merely a momentary truce.* And she was kidding herself that she could ever keep such a secret from her family. Not after she had hidden what Alōs had known of them for so long. That omission was what had gotten her into this whole mess to begin with. And though she hated to ask for help, this time Niya decided she would try leaning on others for a change.

"I can't get into the details here," she began in a whisper, forcing her sisters to angle closer. "But it's a gem that is very important, very powerful," she added. "It belongs to Esrom and has been lost for some time. And if not found soon, the magic holding the kingdom deep underwater will relinquish, and their world will surface."

Larkyra and Arabessa were quiet for some time, seeming to take in her words. "What do you mean . . . surface?" asked Arabessa. "As in . . ."

"Esrom will be at the mercy of Aadilor after centuries of hiding away as a sanctuary."

Both girls drew back.

"By the stars and sea," breathed Larkyra.

"But why is Alōs seeking it?" asked Arabessa. "To hold it ransom from his old kingdom for payment?"

In an unwanted shock, the accusation against the pirate stung Niya.

While she did not know the exact details regarding Alōs's first reasons in stealing the stone from his kingdom, she knew it was connected to Ariōn, knew it had helped the young king at the time, helped Alōs's parents. He had stolen it for them and now was searching to return it for them as well. Of course, her sisters wouldn't have known any of this, only saw him for the nefarious pirate lord Alōs wanted all to see him as. The heartless man Niya was still trying to believe him to be.

But despite her past convictions, something in Niya was changing, forcing her to open her eyes to the true motives behind all of Alōs's sins. Her animosity toward the man was dimming, and she wanted her sisters to understand what she was growing to realize herself.

"Alōs," she began slowly; "he's not actually as he may seem."

"What does that mean?" asked Larkyra.

"It's complicated to explain, but the intentions of his actions are far more similar to our family's than at first glance."

Niya watched Arabessa and Larkyra share a look.

"I think you have a lot more to tell us, then, dear sister," said Arabessa.

"Yes." Niya nodded. "A lot more, but—"

A gasp burst from behind them, and Niya spun to find Alōs sitting up with a start.

He bent over, wheezing to catch his breath, glancing about with frantic eyes, as if unsure when and where he was.

Niya rushed to his side. "Breathe through your nose," she advised.

"Niya?" Alōs whispered, unfocused gaze landing on her.

"Yes." She placed a gentle hand on his shoulder, a flutter in her belly at hearing the vulnerability in his voice. "And you are Alōs Ezra, remember? Infamous pirate lord. Captain of the *Crying Queen*. You are in the Thief Kingdom. You also owe me six silver."

He sat farther up with a grunt, clarity returning to his features. "Nice try."

"Every word is true," she assured, hiding a smile. "It's the side effect of the drink. Short-term memory loss. You'll remember the bit about the six silver soon."

He looked back at her then, his expression growing strangely soft with his amusement.

Something in Niya's stomach twisted as they regarded one another, and she stepped back. "Did you find anything?"

"I did." Alōs rose to his feet, raking a hand through his hair.

Niya's pulse jumped with hope. *"And?"*

His brows knitted. "I know where the last part is."

"That's great!"

"It is and it isn't."

She watched him carefully. "Don't tell me it's back in the Valley of Giants. I'll pawn all my precious jewels in Jabari to buy us a portal token before I sail through those storms again."

"It is not in the valley," he assured.

"All right, then, what's worse than that?"

He let out a tired sigh. "Hallowed Island."

"The land of the cannibals?" asked Larkyra from where she stood behind Niya.

"*Giant* cannibals," clarified Arabessa on her other side.

Niya's shoulders drooped. "Wonderful," she grumbled.

She should have known better than to ask.

CHAPTER THIRTY-FOUR

Alōs needed a drink, and fast. The bitter flavor of the forgotten memory clung to his tongue like needles on a bramble bush. Only a strong whiskey could clear his palate as well as his fogged mind. Stopping at a corner illuminated by a single streetlamp, Alōs took a moment to breathe in the cool cave air. He felt Niya and her sisters at his side, sensed the inquisitive gaze of the fire dancer as she waited for him to elaborate on what he had seen. But he still needed a moment to collect himself.

Being inside the old queen's memories had not been pleasant. Her thoughts were erratic, distracted, and slow compared to his own. It had felt like an eternity for him to focus on what he had come to search for. A gifted necklace. The old queen, it turned out, had been given many.

Memory after memory flipped by. He experienced her receiving a plethora of fine jewels, from other kings and queens, from subjects and scoundrels like himself. Alōs did not know how long it was before he got to the red stone that gleamed like fresh blood, dangling from a long chain. He clung to that memory's thread until it led them to travel through a portal door to a hilltop on Hallowed Island. She was there to help the valley's alchemists collect rare herbs. As she bent over to pluck lavender berries into her basket, the chain's clasp came undone, and the necklace slipped into the thick brush.

If Alōs weren't specifically looking for the moment the necklace had become lost, he would have missed it entirely. Especially since immediately after, a muffled roar of a far-off beast had the old queen glancing up, her pulse quickening. Her guard's hand came down on her shoulder. "Time to go, Your Highness," they said.

As quickly and silently as the group had entered through their portal door, they slipped back through. But before the portal had closed, the old queen had looked back at the hilltop on Hallowed Island to watch a giant, green skin with rippling muscles, bend down to retrieve the glowing red stone from the grass. The gem's strong gleam had distracted the beast from the scene of the group vanishing with a snap through the portal door, retreating safely back to the Valley of Giants.

The screeching of rickshaw horns blasting nearby, the drivers weaving precariously through the clogged streets, returned Alōs to where he stood within the Thief Kingdom. The Gazing District was a distant tangle of structures now blocks away.

His eyes met Niya's beneath her brown eye mask.

Well? her gaze seemed to say.

But Alōs wasn't about to divulge the particulars with Larkyra and Arabessa nearby. Finding all the pieces of the Prism Stone was getting more and more impossible, and he didn't need what was left of the Mousai to compete with. He could picture it now, the pair running back to their king to give him a clear path of revenge for Alōs blackmailing him and his precious pets.

"Perhaps your dear sisters could give us a moment?" He lifted a brow.

Niya shared a glance with the two girls, each puckering her lips in displeasure before retreating to the far corner of their sidewalk to wait.

"So what are we going to do?" asked Niya.

What indeed? thought Alōs as he scratched his chin. He felt the scruff he had been too preoccupied to shave on their final leg to the

Thief Kingdom. "I'm not entirely sure yet," he admitted. "I see no way around visiting Hallowed Island to search for the stone."

"We'll have to search the *entire* island? That seems an impossible task. Especially with these cannibal giants lumbering around."

"Hopefully it won't come to that. In the old queen's memories, she saw a guard find the necklace. If my knowledge serves regarding their kind, they are extremely loyal to their chief, who is a collector of rare and beautiful artifacts. The guard would have brought it to him."

"So we are to infiltrate another royal's home?"

Alōs frowned. "This is the difficult part. Hardly any who make port on Hallowed Island ever make it out to speak of it. Over the years the giants have made it quite clear that they do not enjoy visitors or being disturbed."

Niya crossed her arms over her chest. "Then why, by the stars and sea, was Queen Murilia even there?"

"The island is rumored to be ripe with rare but strong healing herbs," explained Alōs. "It appears the people of the valley went there on a foraging mission."

"Still, that seems like an awfully foolish place to go to snag some berries," Niya pointed out. "If I had a grandmother, I would never let her step foot on such an island."

"If she was anything like you," Alōs found himself saying, "you'd have little choice in where she went."

"If she was anything like *me*," Niya added, chin tipped up, "she would have known the exact moment such a precious gem fell from around her neck. Then none of us would be in this position to begin with."

Alōs smiled down at the fire dancer before catching the scrutinizing eyes of Arabessa and Larkyra, who had slowly slunk closer. They now stood a couple of paces away.

They did not trust him.

As well they shouldn't.

Alōs was beginning to not trust himself.

Especially around Niya.

He had always enjoyed her company, of course, even when she out-wardly despised any breath they might have shared, but since the valley . . . since that kiss and her burning determination to keep looking for this stone, something had fissured open in Alōs's chest.

Something he had made sure to drown at sea.

Compassion.

The word coiled with disgust through his mind.

But he could not deny it was now being resurrected, though Alōs was not yet prepared to face what that might mean.

"It seems your sisters are over waiting." Alōs nodded toward the girls. "We can discuss what's to be done about the other part of the stone later. You can call them back over if you'd like."

As he watched the three women regroup, immediately chatting ani-matedly about what was happening in Jabari and a recent trip Larkyra had taken with her husband, he saw a spark in Niya's eyes return, a spark that he realized had been dimming these past months.

Thoughts of his younger brother filled his mind. He and Ariōn had not been given the gift of growing up together. Their time had been stolen early by the inevitable injustice of this world. But he knew the power behind a chance to one day remedy their lost past. To build a relationship that should exist among siblings. The idea almost left him breathless, a painful, sharp-as-a-knife yearning in his chest.

It hit him hard then just how happy Niya was to be reunited with her sisters and just how unhappy she must be aboard his ship. The true weight of being chained to him, of all the bargains she was fighting to win. Though she stood strong, he caught the signs of tiredness in her worn clothes, which were stained and wrinkled compared to her sisters' well-sewn disguises. She even had a bit of dirt on her cheek peeking out from beneath her mask.

His crew was all having a night off; she deserved one too.

"This might be a fool's question," he heard himself say before really thinking about the consequences of saying it. "But what are the chances the Mousai would be performing tonight?"

Three sets of surprised eyes landed on him.

"Excuse me?" asked Niya.

"I know these events usually are planned farther in advance," he went on, "but given how long it's been since the kingdom has had the pleasure of the Mousai's talents, I'm sure the king could arrange it."

"You . . . want to see the Mousai perform?" Niya regarded him suspiciously.

"It was not lost on me how quickly the crew fled our ship," he explained, wanting to clarify his intentions. "And given the heavy amount of sailing we must push through next, I know they'd be a less disgruntled lot after such a night as one fueled by the madness of the Mousai. But if you do not think it possible—"

"Anything is possible," Arabessa cut in. "It only depends on the price."

"I have plenty of silver to help pay for—"

"I refer to the price a particular dancer would owe for slipping out of her duties to you, even for a night."

"I ask for no price," said Alōs. "I think we all deserve a bit of revelry tonight."

The girls seemed to consider him a moment, Niya's gaze the most curious, the most questioning.

What new scheme is this? her silence seemed to ask.

Alōs pushed away the discomfort of asking himself the same question.

"Well." Larkyra rocked back on her heels. "Let's not weigh a gifted pig and all that. We have to see about getting the Mousai back together."

With that, the three ladies set off immediately, Alōs remaining to handle a few other pieces of business, like acquiring a map of Hallowed Island.

Though he had many tasks to accomplish in the next few sand falls, he found himself remaining on the corner of the street, watching the group's retreating forms, eyes always seeming to fall to the redhead in the center.

With unease, Alōs realized he was beginning to feel a strange kinship with the fire dancer. One that existed beyond attraction or goals but came from an understanding that each had a tether to a duty they'd been born into rather than chosen. A duty to family that, despite the weight it often placed on their shoulders, they could not and would not walk away from. And while he believed this to be a weakness in himself, he found he admired it in Niya. She did not hide what she cared for but burned hot and in the open for her convictions. How freeing that must be.

Something nagged in Alōs's gut. *Careful,* it whispered, his magic stirring in agreement.

Careful.

What Alōs wasn't sure of, however, was if the warning might be too late.

CHAPTER THIRTY-FIVE

*A*lōs glided through the halls of the dark palace, senses on high alert at walking in a space where he knew very well he still was not welcome. His banishment might have been lifted, but his presence at court was far from reinstated. He was only allowed entrance tonight through a personal invitation from the Mousai. With attention locked forward, he ignored the red gaze of the stone guardians standing sentry as they turned their heads, following every one of his steps.

The palace was busy tonight. Court members lined the high-ceilinged space, tucked between protruding onyx spikes that rose from the ground or dangled dangerously from above. Their disguises dripped their usual extravagance. Exotic fur-lined coats, suits of scales, and woven silk lace over plush feathered gowns took up all corners.

Yet despite how opulent they appeared, all eyes were on him this night as he strode through the crowd.

Here walked the man who had been hunted by the Thief King and survived.

"Captain Ezra." A stout bloke in a silver-studded mask slid to his side, hurrying to keep pace with Alōs's long strides. "We did not think you'd grace these halls again."

"And why was that?" he asked, not stopping to give this man, or anyone, his full attention.

"Because of the bounty on your head, of course. Are you here to talk with our king?"

Alōs held in a long-suffering sigh. He had no desire for peacocking tonight.

"That depends," he began. "Are you willing to hear the answer in exchange for your tongue?"

The man laughed as though Alōs had told a great joke. "As always, you surpass your colorful reputation, my lord."

"And as always," Alōs replied in kind, "you have no reputation for me to recall at all."

Alōs left the frowning man behind, staring down any other brave fools who might dare approach.

The cavern where the Mousai usually performed was in the lower bowels of the palace, and Alōs could hear the roar of attendees before he pushed through the doors.

The space was already ripe with a heady mix of debauchery. Overperfumed bodies moved like a school of fish, rhythmically twisting from the tables of steaming food to the chairs and lounges to grope one another as strong spirits were poured in mouths through holes in their disguises. The circular balconies overflowed with a similar scene.

It appeared the rumor of the Mousai performing after so long had spread quickly and was greeted ravenously.

Alōs recognized the disguises of most of his crew amid the crowd, already heavy in their cups. They gorged themselves on plates of decadent treats, sprawled over furniture as companions of every shape and size rubbed up beside them.

He caught a glimpse of Achak on a balcony above. The twins were surrounded by an adoring audience. A young man tipped a goblet to their lips before licking away a bit of wine that spilled at the corner of their mouth.

Alōs pushed through the mass toward where his quartermaster stood, tucked away in a corner. Kintra wore an orange-beaded eye mask and long-sleeved tunic, which covered her markings, but he would know his friend anywhere.

"Tell me good news," said Kintra as Alōs came to her side. She snatched him a goblet from a passing server.

"The old woman lost the jewel on Hallowed Island."

Kintra was quiet for a beat. "I suppose that is good news."

"Giant cannibals are good news now?"

"You could have told me you didn't find anything in her memory."

Alōs took a sip of his drink, savoring the sweetness against his tongue. "I never knew you to be such an optimist."

"A trait that appears to have rubbed off from our redheaded friend. The dedication that one showed in the valley was rather reassuring. I might even be beginning to trust her."

"A dangerous idea," muttered Alōs, more to himself than to her.

"Really? And here I thought you'd be pleased to hear it. After all, you seem to put a great deal of trust into her. Where is she anyway? I assumed she would have arrived with you."

Before Alōs could reply, the lights dimmed and a spotlight lit up the center of the room. Guests began to clear out of the way.

"My cue to leave." Kintra drained her drink before setting it aside. "I'll see you later on the *Crying Queen*?"

"I do not see why not."

Kintra left him standing among the gifted to take a spot with the giftless, who were strapping themselves to the wall.

Alōs handed his cup to a server as his magic swirled awake in his veins. He had been to many of the Mousai's performances, but even he was hard pressed to contain his thrill of anticipation.

The trio always had a different spectacle to perform, disguises to astonish. It left so many starved to take in the next overwhelming delight they had in store for the crowd.

His attention held to the center of the room, which now lay empty, as the low hum of male voices filled the cavernous space.

Guests shifted beside him, angling their heads for a better view as a group of large, fur-clad creatures pushed a stage to rest under the spotlight, chanting all the while.

In the middle of the dais stood three forms, dressed head to toe in tassels. Beastly fanged headdresses sat like crowns above their golden masks. They were wild even in their stillness, with a circling of drums around the tallest.

The chanting grew in height, the fur beasts stomping their feet until abruptly stopping.

The cavern rang out with anticipatory silence as the attendants slunk into shadows, leaving only the Mousai in the light.

Alōs watched, vibrating with the same tense energy that filtered across the crowd as the tallest Mousai lifted a hand, angling for the drums before her.

Thump thump.

She began to beat out a rhythm.

Thump thump.

The spotlight shifted from white to orange.

Thump thump.

Orange to red.

Thump thump. Thump thump. Thump thump.

Her arms floated through the air, moving across the stretched skins, pulsing out a trance.

Slowly a voice entered the rhythm, alto and soprano at once. Larkyra spun a chorus into her sister's beats.

Then finally, as if everyone had been holding their breath for the final Mousai, Niya began to dance.

Her movements started low, a stomping of feet and quick twisting of hips to catch the heady beat. The tassels lining her costume jumped and spun, her magic spilling like bloody mist into the air to mix with her sisters and cover the crowd. Alōs kept utterly still as he sensed the group's spell wash over him, the icy barrier of his own magic swimming to the surface of his skin to both shield and moan in delight.

Beautiful, his gifts whispered.

Play with us, the Mousai's magic crooned.

Steady, Alōs commanded.

The room was slowly being captured. Bodies swayed next to him and voices rose behind, attempting to match the level of euphoria searing the space.

Tonight the trio spun magic so potent he didn't dare take a breath.

The beat was a trance. The song an overdose. The dance carnality.

The Mousai performed unhinged, angling to take all present as their prisoners.

The only cure was to give in.

Alōs curled his hands into fists, unable to look away as Niya ran her fingers over her silhouette, twisting to the beat.

His heart pounded loudly in his ears as she moved off the stage. With growing dread and traitorous hunger, he watched her slink nearer.

Guests took careful steps back, all while still reaching for the fire dancer, scared and desperate at once.

Alōs understood such temptation.

Niya glided and twisted, creating a pocket of space as she moved.

And just when he believed he had himself in control, beneath her mask, blue flames met his through the crowd, their eyes colliding.

It took all of Alōs's strength not to take a step back.

Niya was locked onto him, approaching like a lit fuse to a bomb.

She rolled her hips, around and around, parting the mass of fawning and frenzied onlookers with her ripple of powerful magic, until she was a mere grain's distance away.

Waves of her heat licked over his clothes, sending cracks along his frozen shield to finally seep into his skin. Alōs bit back a groan; he felt as if he were being unwrapped, dipping naked into a steaming pool.

His power responded to her power with a purr.

Yes, his magic crooned in treachery. *More,* it pleaded, bending to her will.

Alōs clung desperately to the thin strands of his lucidness, clenching his jaw as his gaze ran along Niya's curves, watching as her gifts continued to pulse, lush and giving, from her body, red ripples in a pond.

She was magnificent.

She was consuming.

She was also testing him. Teasing him. Pushing him as far as she dared.

Here was the creature he had bound and collared aboard his ship.

She'd been given a night of freedom and was now angling to soar.

Alōs could not blame her. After months of being chained to him on his ship, of course she would burn the brightest once home. He had wanted this. To give her a night of freedom. He now realized his earlier warning to himself had been too late. For he was not sure he would survive until tomorrow as Niya continued to cover him with her magic. Her searing spell battling his icy tundra of strength. A wall of steam. Of dares.

She did not dance for the crowd this night. She danced for him.

Alōs was the only one responsible now for bringing himself back.

So he did it the only way he knew how.

Alōs turned and forced himself to walk away.

CHAPTER THIRTY-SIX

Niya struggled to stand still as her sightless maids loosened and unclasped her costume. Her skin continued to buzz from the performance, a red haze of her magic circling her like hungry bees in a flower field. She wanted to keep moving, keep dancing. Oh, how she felt so alive!

It had been too long since she had moved so freely, had captured a roomful of souls and sent their minds spinning. Niya had allowed her worries of what still lay ahead with the Prism Stone to fall away. She had wanted to dance unbound, and her sisters had met her energy. The Mousai had truly outdone themselves this night. The kingdom would be talking about it for months.

Niya smiled as she thanked and dismissed her maids before slipping into the warm bath they had prepared for her.

With a sigh she let the warm water massage through her tired muscles. Honeysuckle filled the air as she lathered her body and worked her fingers through her scalp. For the first time in a long while, she felt at ease, relaxed.

She never wanted to leave her chambers.

Her private dressing room was covered in plush pillows and hanging floral tapestries. Candelabras burned in the corners, creating glowing pockets of warmth. At the back, her large circular bed was calling to her. Once she was done bathing, Niya planned to curl up in it and revel in its softness.

She and her sisters were scheduled to have an audience with the king later, but she had enough time to enjoy a little more lazy pampering.

I deserve it, she told herself, *especially after spending months aboard a pirate ship.*

Niya did not want to think just yet about how she'd be sailing away soon. She didn't want to think about the black mark on her wrist or the responsibilities that were still bound with it. She didn't want to think about anything.

Slipping under the water, Niya relaxed her whole body. Her magic settled gently into her veins, the sinking of wet leaves.

She held her breath for as long as she could, enjoying the quiet that filled her head.

When she resurfaced with a gasp, goose bumps rose on her bare arms; a new chill filled the empty room.

Niya was no longer alone.

The bath sloshed as she dipped lower into it.

"I know you're here," said Niya to a shadowy pocket in the corner.

He stepped forward from the dark as though carrying it with him.

Alōs's sapphire gaze was bright against his brown skin, his angular features cut hard.

He stopped at the foot of her tub, standing before her like an eclipse.

Niya's entire body tingled as his gaze slipped to what she hid beneath the suds.

When their eyes met again, his expression was unyielding.

"The servants' passage to your chambers is still not well guarded." His tone was casual, almost friendly compared to his coiled energy.

Niya raised a brow. "As I can see."

Silence.

"Is there something I can help you with?" she asked.

Alōs's eyes brushed the tops of her breasts, skimming the surface of her bathwater.

Niya felt a wave of hot panic as he shrugged out of his coat, but he merely draped it over a nearby chair and sat.

"I came to congratulate you on your performance," he said, crossing ankle over knee.

"How kind of you," she replied slowly, continuing to eye the pirate, every part of her body aware of every part of him, ready to act before he did. Alōs merely leaned farther into his seat as if they were sitting together for tea rather than her being naked in a bath.

She loathed him for forcing such an upper hand.

But Niya also knew she had pushed him tonight. It had been the most satisfying thing to watch desire flood into Alōs's eyes, desire she had placed there.

He had been on the verge of being controlled.

By her.

And then he had walked away.

Alōs could not handle her, and knowing this filled Niya with carnal delight.

She was not one to ever be *handled*.

"While compliments are always welcome," she went on, "I do not see why they couldn't wait until another . . . more appropriate time to give them."

"You never complained when I paid you visits like this before." He angled a brow. "Do I make you uncomfortable?"

He was pushing her as she had pushed him. As they always seemed inclined to push one another.

"Perhaps you should get naked and I dressed and see if such a reversal would make you as disagreeable as I."

White teeth flashed with his grin. "I would only find fault in that situation because we were not both naked together."

Niya pursed her lips, the familiar irritation he prodded awake in her rising to the surface. But she was beginning to understand this game. "Why are you really here, Alōs?"

He regarded her for a long while, the gentle sound of the candles flickering in the room the only backdrop to their moment.

"The next part of our journey might be the hardest part yet," he eventually admitted. "And while you have certainly proved your dedication in helping me find the pieces of the Prism Stone, I find when those in my crew do not trust one another in moments of importance, things go awry. When we get to Hallowed Island, it will only be you and me searching out the stone. Kintra will not follow."

"Your point being?"

"You do not trust me."

Niya snorted. "Of course not."

"I'd like to remedy that."

"And how, by the lost gods, do you intend to do that? You are a horrible person."

Even as the words escaped her, she knew them to no longer be entirely true. But she had acted on reflex, according to how they'd always spoken to one another. Biting, caustic, enemies.

Niya was still unsure how to navigate being allies with Alōs, despite beginning to care about completing this mission for entirely different reasons than acquiring her freedom. She could not allow the people of Esrom to suffer such a fate, could not allow Ariōn to be at the mercy of the wicked creatures that filled the upper parts of Aadilor. Niya herself could be grouped into that lot, as well as Alōs.

Every world deserved a sanctuary. What would Aadilor become without theirs?

"I do not argue you that point," said Alōs, tone hardening. "Yes, I have done horrible acts, and I will still. But there are . . . reasons my life was set on this path, a path I have accepted."

"And pray tell, what were those?"

"Ariōn."

Gooseflesh danced along her arms at hearing him speak his brother's name. Would he finally share what she had been wondering since Esrom? Niya waited, quiet, despite sensing the bubbles in her bath thinning.

"Arion was born in the spring, during a moon letting," said Alōs, gaze growing cloudy with memories as he looked to a corner of the room. "A day that was said to be a blessed time to bring new life into our kingdom. But he was born weak and thin, carrying a sickness, our healers said. Yet he was alive, breathing in my mother's arms. As soon as I saw him, I loved him fiercely. He was my younger brother, and I knew in that moment my role, more important than the king I was meant to become, was to protect him. Ariōn . . ." A wistful smile fell to Alōs's lips then. One Niya had never seen mar his features before. "Well, if you believe *me* to be stubborn, Ariōn beat me there tenfold. I was surprised our healers did not catch on sooner that whatever they told him he should not do, he would. Ariōn loved to swim and would pull me to our private beach almost daily to float in the waves. He was so curious about Aadilor, too, then. We'd look up at the sky, knowing despite the clouds there was an entire ocean between us and the rest of the world. He loved to ask me what I thought was up there. What was so scary and bad that Esrom kept hidden and afraid in our bubble. I admitted that I did not know, but our parents and the High Surbs were wise and had their reasons. Little did I know then how many threats truly lurked topside. That one day I would become one of them." Alōs grew quiet, Niya watching him idly rub the area where his pinkie ring had once sat. Her heart ached at his story, knowing in a way what came next. "He was eleven when we learned of his rare blood disease," said Alōs, his voice coming out rough. "*Pulxa,* it's called. By the time real symptoms arise, it is too late, or so my family was told. 'Nothing can be done.' 'We're sorry.' That's all our medics said. *Useless,*" Alōs bit out with a frown. "But I couldn't accept that. Ariōn was so good, filled with such compassion and joy for life; how could he be the one meant for the Fade over me?" He looked at Niya then, his burning gaze imploring her to answer a question that seemed to have haunted him for years. A wash of helplessness ran through her. "Ixō in the end is the one who told me the way to possibly save my brother," Alōs went on to explain. "What would allow both of us to live. I had to commit such a traitorous crime that I would be eradicated from Esrom's history, removed from the royal line as the next king. This would force the High Surbs to call upon ancient and forbidden magic to save my brother. Pause death so he could then be king, the Karēk line saved and all the spells that are so tightly wound to Esrom from the centuries of our family's rule intact. I hardly had to think about my options. That very night I stole one of the most important things in Esrom. I took the heart of Esrom and left. It wouldn't be until years later, after the Prism Stone had been divided and sold for some time, that I would learn the price for cheating the Fade of a soul it desired."

"Esrom's magic was fading," said Niya in a whisper.

He met her eyes and nodded. "Yes, and now it's not just my brother's life that is threatened but all of our people's and those who seek the sanctuary of our shores. So you see, while I do not deny the monster I have become, none of us enter into this world meaning to be bad."

Niya held the pirate's gaze, taking in what he had just shared. The water in her bath had grown cold, but she hardly noticed as her mind spun along with her thumping heart.

Despite how she fought against it, she *did* feel for Alōs.

He'd been barely a young man when he had decided to steal the stone to save his brother. Everything since that moment had been about survival. Survive so his brother could live. Sin so his homeland could be saved. Take so he was not left with nothing, again.

These were convictions Niya understood, actions she would have mirrored if any of her sisters' lives were in danger, behavior she most likely had already done at one time or another for her family, for her king. For love and loyalty very rarely could be separated. Not for her.

But even as she let all these thoughts settle deep into the missing grooves of who she had always believed Alōs to be, a buzz of frustration, of warning, swam to the surface.

He has spoken such pretty lies before, a dark voice said in the back of her mind. *He has tricked you into trusting him, just as he is now. Trust him for more leverage over you. Trust him so he can take what he needs and leave you bare and exposed. Look how he has approached you in your dressing room, when you're most vulnerable. Tricks,* the voice hissed. *Tricks.*

Yes, she thought, her breathing growing quick at her sudden anger. Even though she knew his story to be true, what did that matter? He wanted her to trust him, but why? She already had agreed to help. What would trust do except allow him to betray her as he had before? Go to this Hallowed Island and help him find the last piece of the stone, only for him to then leave her to the cannibals when she least expected? All for reveling in perpetually having the upper hand. Tricks, tricks, tricks. Niya was no longer that naive girl. No longer easily swayed by a sob story. She had seen her fair share of thieves employing beggars in the streets, drawing in innocents so they could pick pockets for more silver. *Look this way so you cannot see me attack from behind.*

No! she silently shouted. She had been doing just fine as she was, keeping those aboard the *Crying Queen* at arm's length, the captain especially. Only fools repeated mistakes of the past.

Tricks. Triiiiiicks.

"Damn you," Niya bit out, unable to contain any more of her thoughts. "I will not let you manipulate me. Not again."

Alōs blinked, as though this was the last response he had expected. "I am not trying to manipu—"

"Of course you are, and the worst part is you can't even tell anymore. You come here, ready to intimidate me when I'm most vulnerable, then you spout your good deeds so I trust you enough, care enough, to risk my life for your goals. I will help you find the final piece of the Prism Stone, Alōs, but know it is *only* so I can get rid of this"—Niya lifted her wrist from the water, baring the mark of their binding bet—"and be free of you and the entire lot on the *Crying Queen*. I will cooperate because that was our agreement, nothing more."

An odd look passed over Alōs's face, and if Niya hadn't known better, she'd have thought it was sorrow. "I truly did a number on you."

Niya's rage burned higher. "Don't flatter yourself," she scoffed. "I am what I am because of what I know this world to be. You were merely my first lesson."

"So there is truly nothing I can do to remedy the past?"

She laughed, cold and hard. "Why try? Like you said, we could never be friends. Let us remain what our destinies have handed to us: companionable enemies."

He watched her a long moment. "How extraordinary."

"What?"

"You're scared."

Her chin jutted out. "I certainly am not!"

"You are. You are scared of what a true alliance between us would create."

"I may have fears, Alōs, but they no longer involve you." Niya stood from the bath. She would not be forced into a corner any longer.

Her nipples hardened in the cool air, rivulets of water running over her skin as she exited the tub.

Alōs froze, his gaze locked onto her nakedness as she stalked toward him. There was a hiss of steam as she bent low, their two powers clashing, her breasts lightly grazing his chest. She caught his intake of breath.

"Who is scared now?" cooed Niya before pulling free her robe draped on the corner of his chair.

She shrugged into it, but Alōs grabbed her wrist, keeping her from cinching it closed. His gaze burned. Engulfed her.

"You," he all but growled, "play too well with fire."

Niya was in his lap, his lips upon hers, before her senses had registered what was happening.

Niya would like to believe she resisted then, that she twisted his arm back to free herself. She easily could.

But she didn't.

While Niya's convictions were screaming to push away, to stop this madness, her body, the betraying bastard, leaned in. Despite all her hateful words, her mistrust, she wanted Alōs; her magic desired his. Two opposites destined to collide.

It was utter insanity!

But as his mouth worked against hers, she found herself opening to him, parting hers in kind.

With a frustrated groan, she wrapped her arms around his neck and pulled herself closer.

It was like settling into the calm eye of a storm, a moment of exhausted relief.

Alōs tasted like midnight and sea, his skin cool to her warm, and it sent treacherous shivers up her spine.

She might not trust him, but she could no longer deny how he made her feel.

Alive. Soaring. Unstoppable.

And now here she was, kissing the man again, letting him kiss her—and not because it was an act, a way to escape the suspicion of guards, but because she wanted it.

She bloody wanted it, so have it she would.

If only for a night.

With that resolve settling inside her tumbling sensations, Niya did what she usually did in these moments. She fell into the chaos.

Pressing her breasts against Alōs's hard chest, she continued to claim his mouth as he claimed hers. They were two crashing waves, finally able to drown their victims, to send them spinning in their surge.

Their hands were everywhere, in each other's hair, down arms, over shoulders. Alōs kneaded along her exposed thigh, deliciously close to where her robe was split.

She wanted more. She wanted everything.

Twisting in Alōs's lap, Niya straddled him, running her fingers up his strong arms, through his hair.

A carnal growl came from the pirate's throat as she ground against him. The most sensitive part of her finding the hardest part of him beneath his trousers.

His grip tightened, hands cupping her backside, following the rhythm in her movements.

Niya's thoughts were no longer. She was only sensations, reactions, desires.

But this time she was not fooled regarding the expectations of after. She would have Alōs, but this time he would not be taking any piece of her.

Not again.

She would give her body but not her heart.

Alōs's fingers parted the material of her robe to bare her chest.

"By the stars and sea." His voice was a rumble of reverence. "How I've dreamed of touching these again."

He ran a gentle finger under the curve of her aching breasts where they sat heavy and wanting. He captured her gaze while he took one of her nipples into his mouth, a light nip of his teeth.

She let out a groaning sigh.

Her body was the center of the sun, and Alōs flew uncaring toward the burning flames.

He kept his attention on her as he sucked, played, cherished, his energy held tight, controlled.

Niya was angling to shatter that control.

She leaned into him, drunk under his skilled attention.

A strong arm circled the small of her back, the other running up her neck to hold her cheek as he kissed her again. It was a gentle but possessive gesture, a king careful with his treasure.

"You are a lost goddess," he said between their kisses. "You have me, fire dancer."

He tipped her head back so he could look her in the eyes again.

She didn't want that. She didn't want to see him.

But he forced her to.

He forced her to see what she had done to him, what she was doing to him. Alōs was a monster on his knees; he was a coil of desire, of desperation, waiting for her command. "Do you understand, Niya?" he continued. "You can take whatever you want of me."

You can take whatever you want.

The words pierced her heart, a well-aimed arrow.

He was giving himself over. Giving her his powers tonight.

This was different from then, from that night four years ago. Everything about how he looked at her now, touched her, *didn't* touch her, said all the difference.

"Niya," he rumbled, his voice the deepest part of the sea. "I am yours to command."

Niya realized then just how dangerous it was to finally get what you wanted, because often you ended up wanting more.

CHAPTER THIRTY-SEVEN

Alōs was drowning in madness. For everything he was saying to Niya he meant.

He had been his own master for so long, fighting against any who would dare disrupt his power, his independence, his safety behind walls, that he had forgotten what it was like to truly feel another. Touch another. He was tired of being a frozen island.

Despite Niya's good or bad intentions, she was the only one who had ever properly threatened to melt his cold veneer. The only one who had strong enough heat to thaw the layers of ice in his veins.

But what truly drove Alōs to accept the crumbling barriers between them was finally accepting that their partnership was more powerful when stitched together.

They were unstoppable together.

Perfect together.

Just like they had been on his boat, fighting back the storm side by side.

And the Valley of Giants, working in tandem.

Just as she felt perfect in his arms now.

Niya had consumed him from the moment he'd seen her those four years ago. He'd known then that she was more than his equal: she was his superior. Which was exactly what had made her his threat. His enemy. Alōs had already lost too much after Esrom. At that time he could not allow any other distractions or weaknesses into his life. Niya, he had instantly known, could destroy him.

So he had angled to destroy her first.

But now . . .

Now he wanted her forgiveness and trust more than he knew. It burned across his skin like the deepest craving.

He wanted her to always look at him as she was now, with desire and strength. He wanted her to laugh with him, as carefree as she was with her sisters, with his crew.

He wanted . . . her.

Tugging her closer, tasting the honeysuckle that clung to her skin from her bath, he finally pushed himself headfirst into her flames.

He didn't deserve any part of Niya, but he would take whatever she was willing to give.

As he ran hands over her softness, he recalled her at the Fountains of Forgotten Memories, her gentle touch to his shoulder when he had fought for clarity after being in the old queen's memory. Niya's perseverance in the Valley of Giants to locate the last stone when he had been defeated. Her fight to save his ship in the storms.

After all he'd put her through, Niya had every right to carry her disdain for him to the Fade. Yet there she had been, helping. Binding bet or no, Alōs knew she would have acted similarly anyway. Because that was who she was. She might be a thief and a mercenary, but at the core, Niya was good.

Whereas he was rotten.

And Alōs was determined to make things right between them.

So he did it the only way he knew how.

He worshipped her.

Angling her chin, Alōs pressed kisses along Niya's neck. He raked teeth over her shoulder, eliciting a tantalizing moan from her lips.

But it wasn't enough.

Alōs wanted her panting, soaring, as untethered as she made others feel when she danced. He wanted to give her the crazed euphoria that she gave to her audience—that she gave to him.

Her continuous rocking against his cock sent more madness through him, his control breaking. Gathering Niya up in his arms, he brought them to her bed.

She lay sprawled over the soft sheets as he stood above her, her robe open, displaying her pale skin, the fullness of her breasts. His gaze dipped to the patch of red hair between her legs, his entire being alight with all the things he wished to do to her.

Niya's eyes were glassy as they looked up at him, yearning, wanting. Yet this time, he felt not like the hunter but like her willing prey.

He would not touch her again, not without her command.

A spark appeared in Niya's gaze, as if she understood this, for she finally demanded, "Touch me."

"Where?" His voice came out a husky whisper.

Alōs watched as her bold, magnificent hands ran down to her most sacred of places, through her curls of red. "Here."

Alōs was on his knees instantly.

He glided his fingers up her inner thighs, savoring the softness before spreading her open. He paused for one aching moment, his eyes meeting hers over the hills of her breasts.

"Yes," breathed Niya. "There."

His mouth was upon her.

"Alōs," she groaned, raking hands through his hair. She kept him right where she wanted him, needed him.

He was drunk on the taste of her, on the warmth flooding through his veins, as her magic filled the room, fogging the mirrors. And though Alōs could, he did not fight her energy with his own. He settled into it, letting it melt away his walls.

Niya thrashed under his ministrations, rocking against him.

He kept steady, focused, as he slipped a finger in.

With a cry, Niya arched up, her body shivering, before she settled back into the sheets, satiated.

Alōs knelt back, unable to do anything but stare.

Niya was glowing, resplendent in her relaxed state. And he had done this to her. No longer was she coiled and fortified behind her hate for him but spread out, open.

Slowly her head rolled to the side; her blue eyes found his.

They were filled with something he could not read.

"Come here," she said, extending a hand.

Alōs quickly unbuckled his sword's sheath and kicked off his boots before lying beside her. Niya started on his buttons. Alōs kept perfectly still as she slid the material away; her palm smoothed over his chest, down his abs, before slipping beneath his trousers.

He closed his eyes with a groan as she gripped him, running her hand up and down his length. Still he did not move.

"Such restraint," Niya teased.

He looked at her, only truth in his next words. "I am yours to command."

A flash of something dark fell across her features, but then it was gone. "Do you want me?" she asked.

The question startled him, given she held the proof of how much he wanted her. But then he realized this question was a test. It made him feel uneasy at just how desperately he wanted to pass. "I want whatever you are willing to share."

She studied him a long moment as she continued to caress him. He felt his restraint fissure. His body was boiling for her, to take, consume, have. But this was exactly what she was waiting for, expecting, and what he had to prove he would not do. He would no longer take anything from her, especially not this.

"I want you to show me how much you want me," said Niya.

It was all Alōs needed to hear.

He bent to claim her mouth and then licked along her neck, pleased with the goose bumps that rose on her skin, the sigh that escaped her lips.

She began to tug at his trousers, almost impatient, and he chuckled, helping.

As he freed himself, lying naked before her, a satisfied purr came from her lips, her eyes hungry as they perused his body.

Her magic reached for him, red tendrils of smoke caressing his skin. *Mine,* it seemed to whisper, and Alōs couldn't help grinning, thinking the same as he beheld Niya.

Mine.

Settling on top of her, Alōs was drunk on the way her skin felt against his. She was a warm blanket of silk, of temptation, and she was giving herself to him. Trusting him. If only for tonight.

The thought made him want to savor every grain fall. Capture every moment, sound, and graze in his memory.

He cupped her breasts, taking one of her nipples into his mouth, sucking as they began to grind against each other.

Niya was wet and needing, and he felt crazed with the knowledge.

"Yes," she whispered. "Yes."

Alōs held her gaze and slipped himself inside her. They both moaned, foreheads touching.

He held steady for a moment, savoring her heat and the way she fit around him.

"Alōs." Niya squirmed, restless.

"Easy, my fire." He captured one of her wrists, pinning it to the mattress. "You told me to show you how much I want you, and I shall, but I intend to be thorough in my demonstration."

He kissed her full lips, swallowing her cry as he began to slowly move his hips, going as deep as he dared.

"Yes." Niya turned her head to gasp. "Yes."

Alōs created a rhythm that Niya quickly matched, their bodies dancing, a gathering of tension.

Before either of them lost themselves too soon, Alōs rose, sitting back on his heels. He tugged Niya by the waist to settle her exactly where she needed to be around his hips. He wanted to see her fully, watch as he slipped back into her.

Her blue eyes were the stars during the darkest night at sea. Bright, guiding, home.

"By the lost gods," he moaned as he filled her, over and over, his body shivering around her warmth.

Niya cried out with her own desire, her head rolling to the side.

Her hair was a fan of red on the sheets, her cheeks a rosy glow.

Alōs pulled her hands toward him, which angled her breasts high. They were full and perfect as they moved with every one of his thrusts.

He was lost in her.

Ruined by her.

Though they had slept together before, this was nothing like then. Not to him. Then, Alōs had been thoroughly untouchable, young and filled with anger at the world's injustice. He had been concentrated only on his task, what he needed from Niya—her identity—and what he would gain: unmeasurable leverage. He had not allowed himself to properly be in the moment. Though he had made sure to please her, to Alōs it had been a night of scheming with an added bonus.

But now . . . now, each of Niya's moans shattered the ice casing around his heart.

He wanted to decimate that young man of the past.

As Niya preened under his touches, the red haze of her magic radiating from her skin like a flower in bloom, her supple curves there to study, to devour, he realized that nothing about her should ever have been taken for granted.

Niya pulled herself up, straddling him so Alōs lay on his back.

He became entranced as she rode him.

Her breasts jutted forward; her ruby locks cascaded down her back; her hips flared deliciously wide as she moved.

She was magnificent.

She was commanding.

She was a queen.

His queen.

The thought momentarily stunned him.

But Alōs drowned whatever fears were creeping into his mind by tugging Niya down for a kiss. He lost himself in her thoroughly. Spun dizzy with his desire.

They were sin this night, carnality finally giving in.

Alōs was changing by the grain fall, *had* changed, and it was all thanks to the woman in his arms. He wanted to be better, wanted to be what she needed. He wanted one of the most powerful creatures in Aadilor to *need* him, and not because she was bound by a bargain but because her desire wouldn't have it any other way.

With this new goal burning, Alōs sought to bring Niya to new heights, to awaken every thread of her pleasure. He wanted to tie her euphoria so tightly to himself that no other being would satiate her.

As the night slipped forward, he had her falling into wave after wave of release.

It wasn't until she begged him to find his own bliss that Alōs finally pulled himself free and spent himself on the sheets before collapsing, his body racked with shivers of satisfaction.

They breathed heavily beside one another, their skin dewing with sweat.

The room buzzed in the following silence, tinged orange from their intertwined magic.

Alōs turned toward Niya where she lay on her stomach. Her eyes were clear, unguarded as she looked at him. It sent a strange ache through his chest.

But then his gaze landed on the marks along her back, fading but nonetheless there, and a new pain slashed sharp, guilt gripping him.

"I'm sorry for these," he said, lifting a hand to gently trace the remaining lines.

Niya tensed, but after a few more of his caresses, she eased back into the mattress. "They are not your fault. It is not you who spelled the crew and clearly disobeyed orders."

"No." He frowned. "But I still am sorry."

"Why?" She lifted her head, placing it in her palm as she leaned on the bed. "This is our world, Alōs. People seek vengeance when they are wronged. It's understandable that your pirates wanted my blood for making them look weak. And you needed to punish me in front of them to hold your power on the ship. I have no delusions regarding what was done to me. You forget who my king is. I have seen and done far worse." She played with the sheets under her. "And so have you."

Though he knew her words to be true, they did not help him feel any better.

They each had been scarred by their roles here, numbed to the wickedness that roamed Aadilor. Had each become such creatures themselves when necessary.

"But let us not think on all that now," she went on. "I don't know about you, but I'm quite content to float in this cloud a bit longer."

When she smiled, a real smile, he smiled back.

It felt odd, this moment, as they lay naked beside each other; they weren't touching, and yet this felt more intimate than their recent act. Talking to one another, openly, honestly.

How quickly would it all fade once they left this room? When Niya remembered she still did not trust him? Returned to her resolve that he was the same man who had betrayed her and broken her heart?

Alōs forced his darkening thoughts away as he gathered Niya into his arms, tugging the sheets over them. As she settled against his chest, he held her protectively, as if that could slow the sands of time. Just for tonight. Just for them.

He had not intended on falling asleep, but Niya was so warm, so comfortable in his embrace. A comfort he had not felt in a very long while. Alōs let his eyes close, chasing away the fatigue of tomorrow. Yet even in sleep, he knew the false promises brought by peaceful dreams. For when Alōs awoke, he was not surprised to find he now lay alone.

CHAPTER THIRTY-EIGHT

Niya was late to meet her sisters.

The reason for which still tingled along her body and burned in her magic as she swept through the dark halls of the palace.

I am yours to command.

Alōs's words caressed her memory like melting sugar, a sweet temptation. The image of the pirate lord, submissive and wanting, strong and thrusting, sent a bolt of heat through her core.

She had slept with Alōs.

Again.

Had let him touch her, everywhere.

Again.

But this time, Niya had awoken not regretting a single grain fall.

Something had shifted tonight, a changing of power.

Niya finally felt in control.

And not just of herself.

In a heady, drunk way, she truly believed she had been in control of Alōs.

I am yours to command.

How dangerous those words were to her.

How tempting.

If she was not careful, she'd actually find herself thinking she could trust him.

"There you are." Arabessa's voice cut through Niya's thoughts, refocusing her attention to the end of the hall that she approached. "We were about to go in without you."

Her sisters waited outside the Thief King's private chambers. Their disguises matched hers: the black hooded robes and gold masks of the Mousai. It had felt like loosening corset strings when Niya had slipped on the familiar mask, feeling it hug her skin like an old friend.

"Sorry," said Niya. "I fell asleep and forgot to ask a maid to wake me."

"Has something happened?" Larkyra tilted her head beneath her mask. "Your energy . . . it feels—"

"Let's not have our king wait any longer." Niya waved a hand as she pushed past them, grappling to control her gifts, which jumped along with her nerves. The last thing she needed was for her sisters to suspect what had just happened between her and the pirate lord. Especially when she was still sifting through her own feelings on the matter.

The Mousai stepped over the threshold of the Thief King's chambers, and the door behind them closed with a sealing click, a dozen locks bolting and shifting back in place. A veil of impenetrable magic.

The Thief King's identity was the most sacred secret in any kingdom, in any realm, in fact. Which was why his personal chambers were buried deep within the center of the palace, behind walls of guards and spelled doors. Even Niya and her sisters, his own daughters, had agreed to a Secret Sealer regarding his identity. Larkyra's husband, Darius, did not even know what other role his father-in-law slipped in and out of.

Yet though he was the King of Thieves, Dolion's private chambers were rather modest, especially compared to his soaring throne room. The receiving hall was small, followed by a long hallway that led to a sitting room, the space made up for comfort rather than spectacle. Sturdy furniture to support a sturdy man and soft, worn rugs to ease feet carrying the weight of endless responsibility. A large fireplace and pockets of standing candelabras lit the room warmly.

"You three are late." Zimri stood in an archway that led to a dining room.

Niya's chest lightened at seeing him, a smile forming. "What a delightful greeting to a sister you have not seen in months," she said as she approached, removing her mask before planting a kiss on his cheek.

Zimri had always been the definition of impeccable, from his combed-back hair to the shine on his onyx alligator shoes. The only thing that put him off this evening was the bit of scruff on his usually smooth black chin.

"Zimri is *not* our brother," countered Arabessa from behind them as she folded herself into a chair by the fire, removing her own mask in a flourish.

"And thank the lost gods for that," said Zimri as he followed Niya to sit among her sisters. "I feel enough responsibility for you lot as it is. The weight of being an older brother would drive me to madness."

"You and Arabessa are the same age," Larkyra pointed out, placing her disguise on a low table that sat between them. "So you'd only be the older brother to Niya and me. That should lighten the cause for insanity."

"On the contrary," said Zimri, brows raised. "I am exactly two months older than Arabessa. Which is a blessing—I could not order her about as easily without the advantage of age."

"There are no advantages in the world that would allow you to order me about," said Arabessa as she glanced at her nails in boredom.

"I could think of one." Zimri's grin taunted.

Arabessa's eyes whipped to his, a pinch to her brows. "And I could think of one which would permanently remove that smile from your face."

"Oh, please, do not do that," said Larkyra. "I am rather fond of Zimri's smiles."

"As am I," added Niya. "You would be ridding the world of one of its beauties."

"If that insufferable grin is considered beautiful"—Arabessa crossed her arms tightly—"then I have a very different definition of what pleases the eye."

"Really?" Zimri leaned back in his seat, hands clasped over his chest. "Then I must ask. Do you consider yourself beautiful?"

"Excuse me?" She frowned.

"When you look in the glass, do you see beauty? No, Niya and Lark, I do not care for either of your opinions on the matter." He raised a hand to stop them from interrupting. "I'm asking Ara. Do you find yourself beautiful?"

"What a foolish question."

"That you seem scared to answer."

"I am hardly scared." Her gaze narrowed on him. "Only if I answer one way, I will seem self-loathing, which I am not. And if I answer the other, I will appear vain, which, again, I am not."

"You aren't vain?" Niya raised her brows.

"*No*, I am not." Arabessa cut her a glance. "But I *am* growing tired of this line of questioning. I do not see the point in it."

"The point," said Zimri, "is that I see beauty. When I look at you."

Niya watched as Arabessa blinked over to him, a tense silence filling the room as they regarded one another.

Niya found Larkyra's twinkling gaze, suppressing a grin as her sister wiggled her eyebrows up and down.

"So?" Arabessa eventually asked, the annoyance in her voice faltering.

"So," Zimri continued, "if you do, too, then our definition of what pleases the eye is not so very different. Which would mean you *do* find my smile to be beautiful, because I find my smile quite beautiful too."

Niya bit back a laugh as she watched her older sister struggle in her response. But whatever the red-faced Arabessa was poised to say—or do—next was interrupted by the entrance of their father.

All stood.

Well, except Niya. She ran straight toward the man.

Despite him being in the midst of shrugging out of the ornate alabaster uniform of the Thief King, still permeated with the ancient magic he forced into his role when on the throne, Niya could not stand on decorum in this moment. He was unmasked, his blue eyes shining bright beneath their rim of black soot.

"Father." She threw her arms around him, savoring his mixed scent of sun-soaked hay and smoke. His braided beard tickled her cheek as she rested her head on his chest. "I'm so sorry."

Dolion did not respond right away; he merely held her tighter. "I know, my flame. Now come"—he pried her loose—"let us sit and hear of what has transpired."

Niya felt as though she was finally able to breathe. Now in the privacy of her father's contained quarters, her family all around, she unloaded everything: her visit to Barter Bay, the journey through the Mocking Mist, the storms that protected the far-west lands, and the beauty of the Valley of Giants. Finally she shared the purpose of the *Crying Queen*'s travels, the item Alōs searched for: the Prism Stone. Why he had taken it in the first place: to save his younger brother's life. She shared all this in the hopes that they could help in some way. A lesson learned from when she had failed to ask for their help in the past.

"My, that is a tale," breathed Larkyra once Niya had finished. "I hadn't realized Alōs had a brother. Who knew I could actually feel pity for the pirate?"

"Are we sure all of this is true?" asked Arabessa, brows pinched in with suspicion.

"I had my own doubts at first," admitted Niya, "but all the pieces seem to fit. Alōs most certainly was born to be the king of Esrom. And

I overheard their holy order speak of the stone and the magic leaving the kingdom. As far as King Ariōn, I have seen the markings of his illness for myself and watched him with Alōs. There is no denying the affection between the two. Alōs still very much feels duty bound to help Esrom."

"Still," began Arabessa, "I—"

"What Niya says is true."

All eyes turned to Dolion. He sat closest to the fire in his high-backed leather chair, the white disguise of the Thief King now hanging at his side, leaving him in a plain tunic and trousers, though he still filled the space like a commanding force.

"You *knew*?" Niya blinked, a wave of shock going through her.

"The Thief King knows the history of all who become part of his court," Zimri answered for her father.

"You knew *too*?" She swiveled around to meet his brown gaze.

"Who do you think gathers the information?"

"But why—?" she spluttered.

"Why didn't we tell you?" said Dolion. "Because, my child, the identities and pasts of our court members are for the king to hoard, not those who serve him."

"Yet Zimri knows." Arabessa's glare was a prick of ice.

"And I have been bound by a Secret Sealer to only discuss the specifics with the Thief King," Zimri countered.

Dolion affirmed this with a nod. "But who Alōs Ezra once was had no standing in our lives. As far as I was concerned, any interaction with the man was with him as he is now, the pirate captain of the *Crying Queen*. I hadn't realized there were any intimate . . . connections until his ransom with you, Niya."

Niya felt her cheeks redden, the familiar shame for giving away their identities resurfacing.

"Now, regarding this issue with the Prism Stone," Dolion continued. "This is a new development to me. While I was aware of the stories of Alōs taking it, I hadn't realized how truly important this stone was, nor that the pirate lord would care enough about the kingdom which banished him to want to get it back." Her father met her gaze. "But it appears he cares a great deal."

"Yes." She nodded. "It's all he cares for, really."

"Which is why you must continue to be careful with him," said her father. "Despite Alōs's selflessness in the past, we all know the man he has grown to be. He has acquired the title of notorious pirate lord for a reason. And as the sands fall, he will only grow more desperate to find the stone. And desperate men are dangerous."

Niya swallowed. Her father's words landed like blows, even though they were the same convictions she had reminded herself of earlier tonight. Earlier, before she had slept with Alōs, again. Before she had watched him submit to her, worship her; before she'd lain in his arms and listened to his breaths as he fell asleep.

Tonight he had been different; she had *felt* different with him. Powerful. In control.

Could she believe in these new feelings?

Niya's thoughts were momentarily distracted by a reflection on her father's shirt. There was pinned the compass brooch of her mother's.

She said when she touched it, it helped ground her. It allowed her to find her way.

Niya swallowed. *I must find my way,* she thought as she stared at the weaving gold that made up four different points. Four different directions to take, but in the center rested a shining sun. Her focus.

You must continue to be careful with him. Her father's words echoed in her mind. *Desperate men are dangerous.*

With a heaviness to her chest, Niya knew her father was right; she could not yet trust Alōs.

Not until all of this was said and done. How Alōs acted after he got what he wanted would be the real test. Whether his words to her tonight would remain sound. It saddened her to realize this, but it did not stop her from knowing she must keep him at arm's length until then. Keep her walls high.

"Yes, Father." Niya tore her gaze from the compass to meet his gaze. "I understand."

Dolion's expression softened, as though he knew where her attention had just been—on the pin that sat above his heart. "Yes, by now I'm sure you do. Yet . . ."

"What?"

"Tell me, how is it the mark of your binding bet is already half-filled when your time on the *Crying Queen* is not nearly half up?"

Niya looked down, realizing she had taken off her long black gloves and had been twisting them in her lap. The mark on her wrist sat exposed. "I have struck a new agreement with the pirate lord."

"Here we go again," groaned Arabessa.

"I have a *new* bargain to obtain my freedom *quicker*." Niya shot her sister a scathing glare.

"And what is this new bargain?" asked Zimri, leaning forward.

"As soon as I help find the final piece of the Prism Stone and it is returned safely to Esrom, I can return home."

"But that could take longer than your year sentence," Larkyra pointed out.

"It can't."

"But it could."

"It *cannot*."

"Why not?"

"Esrom doesn't have that long."

Silence.

"All right," said Arabessa slowly, "and what happens if you don't return the stone in time, for you, I mean?"

"Why are you so pessimistic?" Niya frowned.

"I'm a realist."

"A real pessimist."

"*Niya,*" interjected Zimri. "What would that mean for you?"

She was hesitant to meet any of their gazes. "Another year aboard the *Crying Queen.*"

"Another year!" exclaimed her sisters.

"But it won't come to that," Niya added quickly. "We know where the final piece resides. You heard Alōs say it himself." She turned to Larkyra and Arabessa. "It's on Hallowed Island. He thinks the chief there might have it."

"By the lost gods." Zimri sat back in his chair. "Are you certain?"

"Quite," said Niya, glancing at the concerned expressions around the room. "I know they are giants, but they can't be as bad as all that . . . can they?"

"What do you know of giants?" asked Zimri.

"They are slow and dumb."

"Storybook nonsense," replied her father. "They are giants; one of their steps is ten of ours."

"And dumb?" Niya dared to ask.

"They are about as clever as they come, especially with their food. Like a cat with a mouse. They play before they eat."

"Wonderful." She folded her arms across her chest. "Let me guess: they are also gifted."

"No, giants do not hold magic," said her father.

A wash of relief flowed over her.

"But that hardly matters when not even your own powers will do much against them," he added.

"How is that possible?" Niya drew her brows together. "I'm part of the Mousai."

"Yes, and they are *giants,* my dear," said Dolion. "The larger the creature, the more gifts needed to control them. And they are *very* large indeed. You would need a handful of gifted souls to go up against one; otherwise it's like a fly trying to fell a human with the wind from its wings—useless."

Cold dread settled in her chest. "Well, sticks."

"Zimri, can you retrieve one of our maps of Hallowed Island?" Dolion sat forward, clearing the low table between them. "If you're going into a den of giants—"

"Giant *cannibals*," corrected Larkyra brightly.

"Smart, fast, immune-to-the-gifts, giant cannibals," added Arabessa.

"Yes, thank you," grumbled Niya.

"You should be as prepared as you can," Dolion went on. "I think one of our maps has the location of their village."

Zimri stretched out a chart of the Obasi Sea. A small island rested in the center. Scratches of information marked over its land.

"Yes, here." Her father pointed to a cluster of buildings right in the middle of the island. "Now"—he breathed—"let's figure out the best way for you to get in and out without being eaten."

CHAPTER THIRTY-NINE

*A*lōs stood at the banister of his quarterdeck, looking through his spotting scope at Hallowed Island—a thick, tangled mass of green on the horizon. Clouds of smoke drifted from a volcano at its center. This unpredictable beast was what made the spit of land so precious. The soil on Hallowed Island was rich from centuries of eruptions, causing an overwhelming abundance of rare foliage. The plants found here were rumored to be powerfully healing or fatal with one twist of a petal. A combination that made courageous fools of many, for to steal even a small sprig of the right specimen could fetch heavy coin in any kingdom's underground market.

This very fact created the perfect excuse for sailing these waters. Alōs had hoped that giving his crew a task that promised riches would have them cooperating without question. He knew he had been pushing them these past few months, but there was no way around it.

Time was falling too quickly, and he was growing desperate to catch up.

Alōs collapsed his scope with a snap and tapped it on his palm, thinking.

He had ordered the *Crying Queen* to anchor a good deal away from Hallowed Island, so the ship would appear no bigger than a speck to any who might look out from its shores. Though giants were not known for keen eyesight, the sun was high, and Alōs would not chance being seen. They needed to breach the island safely and quietly. Alōs planned for them to approach by nightfall.

"I've instructed the crew of what's to come once the sun sets." Kintra appeared at his side, her gold earrings winking in the bright day.

"How much guff did they give?"

"Not much, which was surprising. But perhaps the reputation of the island's inhabitants silenced anyone who might be annoyed at staying on board. A few still question how valuable the plants truly are, though, to have sailed nonstop for the past fortnight. Especially when none of us are lacking for coin."

"We have not become the most profitable pirate ship by being lazy," Alōs pointed out with a frown. "So now they complain of being too successful?"

Kintra leaned a hip against the railing beside him. "I think they are tired. And honestly, I was going to wait to say anything, but . . ."

A prickle of unease ran through him. "What?"

"A few have grown suspicious regarding our random choice of destinations over the past months," Kintra explained. "Even you must admit our usual pace of travel is never like this."

Great, thought Alōs, *exactly what I need right now, a ship full of pirates asking questions.* "Yes, well, usually we are not hunting down an object that continues to slip through our fingers," he bit out, a new tension setting in along his shoulders.

"Usually *you* are not," Kintra clarified.

He met his quartermaster's brown gaze. "So what do you suggest, then? It's not as if I can change where an old lady has dropped a necklace, Kintra."

"No," she agreed. "But perhaps it is time we tell the crew."

He slammed his brows down, her words threatening to push him back a step. "Are you *mad*?" he hissed, glancing past her to make sure there were no nearby pirates.

"I don't mean every detail," said Kintra. "Merely that you need to find an item lost that holds importance to your old kingdom. Despite what you may think, many of us aboard this ship care for you as you care for us. I truly believe they would assist their captain in a task that was important to him. After all, you have helped many of us at one time or another. Or have you forgotten?"

Of course Alōs had not forgotten. Many of those deeds were what had had those aboard agreeing to become a part of the *Crying Queen*. But still . . . what Kintra suggested was madness. Wasn't it? Alōs glanced to the island in the distance. There were already too many unknown variables ahead; could he really add on the unpredictability of pirates learning what he was after? An item he needed more than the ship beneath his feet or the entire lot of them.

Despite his crew knowing his old standing in Esrom, this particular secret he had held so close for so long he did not know how to even begin to set it free.

"It's too risky," he found himself saying.

"More risky than a crew no longer believing in their captain?"

His magic chilled along his skin at her words. "That is not what is happening."

"Not yet," said Kintra before raising her hands in submission at his sharp glare. "I merely ask you to think about it."

Alōs sighed, his sudden rage leaving him like the waves crashing away along the side of his ship. "I have no energy for this today."

"I know." His quartermaster drew closer, in the way that a friend would to comfort another merely by letting them know they were there.

"Saffi said you wished to see me?" Niya's voice sounded from behind him, and he and Kintra stepped apart, turning to watch her approach from the main deck. Her hair was pulled back into its usual braid, tinged rust colored in the open air, and she was back in her weathered outfit, her blades strapped to the holster at her hip. She was again a soldier of the sea.

He and Niya had interacted little since their time in the Thief Kingdom, and what words were shared did not touch on what had happened there.

Still . . . Alōs knew neither of them had forgotten. He caught the flame of the memory in her gaze whenever it met his across the deck, the way she lingered on him and he on her. Their opposing energies also no longer pushed against one another but circled, a heated glide of two apprehensive beasts finding the other now familiar. But were they now friend or still foe?

Alōs knew his answer, but he was patiently waiting for Niya to reveal hers.

"Yes." Alōs looked behind Niya, to the furtive glances from Therza and Boman as they walked by. *A few have grown suspicious regarding our random choice of destinations.* Kintra's words played through his mind. "But let us go to my quarters," he said. "I have no patience for eavesdroppers today."

Once below deck, Alōs leaned into his chair, letting his muscles dissolve into the hardy wood.

By the lost gods, he was tired.

Kintra and Niya stood waiting while Alōs ran his gaze over the map spread out on his table.

Niya had returned to the *Crying Queen* with it, along with a litany of information regarding the island. The best shore to row into, the quickest path to the giants' dwellings. He knew she had been called to see the Thief King but had been less than pleased to learn she had told him what they sought. And more so that he had helped.

"You had no right to tell him," growled Alōs as she presented him with a map of Hallowed Island.

"We need all the help we can get," argued Niya.

"Not from him. By the lost gods, Niya, what keeps him from retrieving this piece of the Prism Stone for himself to hold at a higher ransom?"

"He will not do that." She shook her head.

"How do you know?"

"Because I do."

"Reassuring."

"He is my king, Alōs." Her hands fisted at her sides. *"If he asks me a question, I cannot lie."*

"And I am your captain; you swore your loyalty—"

"To regain all of the pieces of the Prism Stone at whatever cost. This helps us, so it is worth whatever we must pay." She slammed down the map she had been holding on to his desk, unfurling it. *"It's not much, but it's better than that sad old map you've got. You should be grateful."*

Alōs ran his gaze over the detailed markings of her map, details that had most certainly been lacking on the one he had acquired in town when in the Thief Kingdom. His mood plummeted further. *"That's my point."* He looked up at her. *"Now we are indebted to him."*

"You are a fool to think you ever were not." She stepped back, regarding him through narrowed eyes. *"He did you a favor by removing the bounty on your head for my identity. Those who blackmail the Thief King only ever end up screaming in his dungeons before begging for the Fade. I know. I've put many there. We both are in his debt. But if you do not want to use this stupid piece of parchment—"*

"Leave it," he said, stopping her from rolling it back up.

Niya gave him a long look then, one that ended with her lips curling into a satisfied smile as she said, *"Aye, Captain,"* before stomping out of his quarters.

Now this same map lay between them, their only real lifeline. Niya had been right.

It had helped them plan which side of the island to anchor near, which plants his pirates could busy themselves pruning while he and Niya sneaked off to travel the straightest path to the giants' dwellings.

Whatever the Thief King might want in return for this, Alōs decided he would worry about later. For as it was, the lost gods knew he had enough on his plate at the moment.

Steepling his fingers, Alōs took in Niya and Kintra before him. "You each know the task ahead," he began. "And the threats. But I'd like us to go over everything one last time. Niya, if you want to start?"

"As long as you don't interrupt me like you did last time," she said, smiling a bit too sweetly.

"I won't need to if you get the details right."

Her grin flattened before she stepped forward to point at the map on his desk. "After nightfall you and I, along with Kintra and another small boat of the crew, will bridge the beach on the western shore. There are watchtowers rumored to be on the four corners of the island, so we must be sure our boats remain out of their glow. While Kintra and the crew pick along the foliage growing here"—Niya slid her finger to a dense area circled with various markings and names of plants—"you and I will slip off to enter the path said to lead through the forest here." She indicated a thin line that twisted and turned toward the center of the island. "Once we get to the giants' homes, we'll start our search first where the chief resides"—she tapped a finger on one of the larger buildings drawn—"and then pray to the lost gods we find the Prism Stone right as we walk in so we all can sail away to live happily ever after." She stood back, plunking a hand on her hip, pleased grin present.

"Cute," said Alōs dryly.

"She does have a point," said Kintra. "The next part of the plan is all rather . . . vague."

"I think the word you are looking for is 'nonexistent,'" suggested Niya.

"The next part of the plan," said Alōs pointedly, "is to be adaptable. If we don't find what we're after with the chief, we'll reassess."

"Reassess to what, though?" asked Niya. "To search every giant's dwelling on the island? Track back to where we *think* the old queen was when the necklace fell from her?"

Alōs let out a frustrated sigh. "I don't know yet. I just—"

"Um, we're about to have more company," interrupted Niya as she glanced to his closed door. "*A lot* more from the feel of it."

A knock sounded.

What now? thought Alōs in annoyance.

"Enter," he commanded.

"Captain," greeted Boman as he stepped in, before Saffi and Bree and Emanté and Green Pea and Therza and—by the Fade, who was still on deck sailing his ship? "We don't mean to disturb," continued his helmsman as the group filled up his quarters.

"But it appears that you do," said Alōs coolly. "What is this about?"

"Well, sir, you see . . . the crew . . . we've, uh . . ."

Alōs stared Boman down. He had never known the man to mince words, which showed his nerves. But nerves regarding what?

"Spit it out, old man," said Alōs in irritation. "Or have one of your companions do it, for surely they are here for similar reasons as you."

"We know we ain't here for no plants," said Therza beside Boman, before quickly adding, "Cap'n, sir," as she took in his piercing glare.

Alōs leaned back in his chair, invoking the forced composure he often displayed for his crew. "And?" he asked.

Therza shared a quick look with Boman. An encouraging nod was given. *"And,"* she said, "we feels we've gots the rights to know the real reason we've sailed like the possessed to this island. We've all heard the rumors of the giants who live here, using human rib bones to pick their teeth."

"I hear they like to eat us raw," added Green Pea from where he stood crammed between two other crew members. "Pluck us straight from the ground, like ripe tomatoes, they do, and toss us in their mouths. Crushing bone and skull and guts, slurping us down."

Murmurs of anxious agreement flowed through the group of pirates.

"So we's wondered," continued Therza. "Why would our cap'n sail to such a place? And like a storm be chasing us? We knows something went down in the valley. Not all of us were in our cups the entire visit. And we's pirates, of the *Crying Queen*; we can smell scheming riper than when Mika passes wind. Normally we leave you right be with this business, Cap'n, you know that. But then we's come to thinkin', why is Red in on it but not the rest of us?" The stout woman pointed a finger at Niya, who stood off to the side with Kintra. "Especially when she's the guppy on board?"

Niya's gaze swung to meet his, a ripple of unease in the air.

"What about me?" asked Kintra with mock offense, folding her arms. "Do you not care that I might know what's going on?"

"Pshaw." Therza waved her hand. "We all know you and the captain are thicker than lard from a pig's rear. Ain't nothing new there. But Red, here . . ." She pursed her lips, assessing her. "Changes have been afoot since you've stepped aboard, girl."

"I would hope so," said Niya coolly. "Most of you didn't know how to properly use soap before I arrived."

Despite her line of questioning, Therza responded with a chuckle.

"We don't ask many questions of ya, Captain," Boman chimed in, seeming to have now found his words. "You've never led us astray to need to. And we trust whatever's brought us here is for a reason, an important one. More important than some silver gardening weeds can fetch us. We want ya to know ya can tell us, and that we can help."

Silence followed as Alōs slid his gaze over his crew, each waiting for his reply. Some twisted their caps between their fingers, others glanced to the ground, and a few brave souls looked him square in the eye.

It had taken courage for them to come here, and a part of him was damn proud of that. He did not employ cowardly pirates. But at the moment he could have done without all of it.

Yet still, the usual rage he would expect himself to feel from such insubordination was void.

Instead he only became more exhausted.

More confused.

Despite what you may think—Kintra's words from earlier awoke loud in his mind—*many of us aboard this ship care for you.*

His eyes roamed over his crew once more, an odd feeling slithering in his chest as he took in the men and women he had lived beside for years now. He knew most of their scars, warts, missing teeth, and individual odors better than any of the people from the kingdom he'd once called home.

They were now his family.

The thought unsettled him. Despite how long he might have known it. Silently, in his cold, dead heart, for this way only lay more duty, more vulnerabilities.

Could he risk letting these pirates get any closer?

Despite what Kintra declared, could those like himself really put aside their own ambition to care for others?

The riffraff. The abandoned and banished. The immoral and selfish.

The monsters.

Alōs looked to Niya then, a now-familiar warmth blooming in his chest.

Yes, a voice whispered in his mind. *Here is proof someone like yourself can care about another.*

A vision of Ariōn swam before him next, then his kingdom.

All these pieces he had seen as weaknesses, but for the first time Alōs now understood how they were strengths. They were reasons to burn bright, mighty, just as the fire dancer did so openly for her family—for they were people to fight for. Purposes to live for.

We want ya to know ya can tell us, and that we can help.

Were his pirates searching for this purpose? A family to protect, a reason beyond treasure to remain sailing the endless sea? Or had they already found it? And Alōs was the last of their kind to see clearly.

It was a lot to reconcile, years of calluses to soften from the fated aftermath of the hand he'd been dealt, but nevertheless he found himself turning to his awaiting pirates, and whether it was from these new realizations or because he truly was at the end of his rope, Alōs threw away careful planning in substitute for what felt right in the moment.

Which was a version of the truth.

"You really want to know what brings us to these waters?" asked Alōs, leaning forward. "Fine, I'll tell you lot, but I *can't* tell you everything. And I don't want to hear any sniveling about that." He looked each one in the eye, receiving quick nods of understanding. "And when I'm through telling you what I deem enough, I don't want any more questions. Perhaps in time, if events turn out, I will, but for now this isn't story time. You hear?"

The room was filled with *aye, Cap'n*s.

Alōs stood then, and as he did, he sent a wave of his cool magic through the space. A bite of cold, of intimidation. *Remember who's in power here,* the gesture silently said.

He turned to look out his window, to the blue expanse lit by the morning sun. The water glistened brightly, a merry dance of light that sparkled in stark contradiction to his somber thoughts. "I look for an item that is important to Esrom," he began. "Important to prevent a death that I cannot let happen. I may no longer live there, but this I am duty bound to fix more than any other atrocity I have ever committed in Aadilor." He turned to look at his pirates. "And you all know what sort of actions I am capable of."

He watched Bree and Green Pea share a glance, shifting feet.

"My time is running out, however." He gestured to the silver sandglass on his desk, to the never-ending trickles of grains counting down his failure. "Which is why we've been sailing like storms were chasing us, as you put it, Therza." He looked to the woman, who stood listening intently. "The item is said to be on this island, and since we are no longer standing on pretenses, I of course will not ask any of you to come ashore. But I must, and will, alone. Well, alone, except for with Niya."

All eyes turned to her then, which she met head-on. A warrior.

If Alōs were in a different mood, he would have smiled.

"As you know, she is blessed with the lost gods' gifts, as gifted in powers as I."

One of her brows arched as she met his gaze. "I'd beg to argue a bit *more* gifted in powers than you."

"Yes, you would beg that," he replied, knowing silent amusement danced in his features, before looking back at his crew. "So she has the abilities needed to get what I seek. She has been brought here to help," he explained. "In ways unfortunately none of you are able. This is my burden to fix, you see. I have merely hoped to find advantages for all of you along the way. Once this is done, well, if you want off this ship, I will not stop you. But know all that I have spoken is true, and currently it is all I can share."

The room filled up with silence then, a tense vibration of blinking eyes and steady breaths.

Here it was—the most Alōs had ever confided in his crew, the most he had ever put on the line in front of them.

His heart pounded with uncertainty the longer everything hung in silence. But he was used to starting over, if that was what his current actions caused, having his pirates sail all over Aadilor for his needs and his needs alone—so be it.

To find the rest of the Prism Stone and save Esrom from surfacing, save his brother from what this cruel world had in store for him, Alōs would start over again and again and again.

"How precious are these plants again?" asked Boman, the first to speak.

Alōs met the old man's dark eyes, a hint of a smile in them, of understanding.

The look set off a wave of shocked relief.

"A single stalk of most would pull in a clean bag of silver, others maybe two," answered Kintra.

Therza whistled. "My, my, perhaps that is worth a trip to the beach, despite any hungry giants lurking about."

"Aye," said Emanté from where he hung in the back of the group, his massive shirtless form taking up the width of two men. "I've never cared about what's between me and more coin. Anything to add to my investments, I am happy to oblige."

A few more of the crew nodded and mumbled their agreement.

Alōs took it all in, silent, amazed.

Dare he even say grateful?

Kintra had been right.

They care.

As you care, a voice replied from deep inside him.

Alōs drew his brows together. How much he was changing.

"We thanks ya, Captain, for this opportunity." Boman brought his attention back to the group. "I'll be sure to prepare the boats for whoever still wants to go pull some weeds tonight. And understand if you and Red here go looking for more rare ones deeper in." His eyes glimmered with silent words. *We still stand with you.*

Alōs held his helmsman's gaze. He, who had helped steer his ship through many storms, was doing it now.

"That sounds good, old man," he said with a nod. "And do remind those aboard that we wait for no one. If they are not ready when we are to push off, they miss out on collecting any bounty."

"Aye, Cap'n." Boman tapped his heels together before barking at the group to push out of the room.

As the door shut behind them, Alōs stood for a moment, barely taking in what had just happened.

"Well," breathed Niya, pushing from the wall and striding toward him. "That was unexpected."

He shook his head. "Annoying is more like it."

"I believe it went exactly as I thought it would."

Alōs turned to lock eyes with Kintra, an unsettling sensation running through him. "Did *you* put them up to this?"

"I put no one anywhere." She held up her hands. "It's not my fault if they took my gruff response about them stopping gossiping like bar hands and taking whatever questions they had up with the man himself."

"By the Fade, Kintra!" Alōs growled.

"As I see it," she said, unfazed by his temper, "now we all can get on with plans and stop with the tiptoeing. This ship is a family, whether you like it or not."

Family.

Alōs ran a tired hand through his hair, letting out a sigh as he sat back in his chair.

He'd barely survived the first family he had. This lot would surely do him in.

Still, he would be lying if he said a part of him wasn't pleased by the turn of events. Cautious but pleased.

"Speaking of plans," said Niya, gesturing to the map on his desk. "Our plans for tonight are still rather rubbish."

Alōs glanced to the spread-out papers, thoughts of what still lay ahead resurfacing along with the throb in his temples. "Yes," he agreed. "But they're the only ones we've got."

CHAPTER FORTY

*T*he moon was a silver crescent in the night sky, the peeking voyeur to the pirates who slipped quietly through dark waters below. Their rows were timed to the rhythm of crashing waves on the distant shore, their pants of exertion no louder than the whistling of sea air.

Sitting at the bow of one of the boats, Alōs studied the bonfire glow coming off the farthest-west cliffside. Its twin to the far north. Watchtowers.

An island with eyes.

Yet he and his crew, three boats full, slithered directly in the middle, through their blind spot.

That night they breached land where few who stepped on ever stepped off.

All were silent as they set to their tasks. Giddy glimmers in gazes as they plucked forth blooms edging the forest entrance. Children with the heady promise of shiny treats when done with their chores.

No one spoke of what had been shared in his chambers. Only moved like the accomplished thieves they were, focused on the task at hand.

Alōs found Kintra across one of the sand dunes, watching the scurrying pirates like a mother to children. Her shadowed gaze met his, with a winking of gold from her earrings against the faint glow of the moon.

His heart beat a quicker rhythm as they each gave a nod, and he and Niya split off from the group, carving their path north.

"This is where I think we are meant to enter." Niya pointed to a tangle of dark trees crammed between severe cliffs. "We can reach their camp fastest on this trail, but we'll have to cross those two rivers." She glanced back to the map she had unfurled. Its markings were barely visible in the night, but he had studied it enough to know she was right.

"Crossing rivers won't be an issue," said Alōs, stalking forward.

Niya caught up to him, tucking the map inside her vest. "Says the man who can walk on water. But what about me?"

He glanced down at her. "Can you swim?"

"Of course . . ."

"Then we enter here."

A wet growl echoed from inside the jungle as they approached.

Niya paused, studying the unknown darkness. "Rivers may not be an issue," she began, "but other things not drawn on maps might be."

"There *will* be other things," assured Alōs. "But we must get to their camp while it is still night. I don't know about you, but I would rather not sleep here unless forced."

Alōs walked on, and as he stepped beneath the black canopy, he allowed his eyesight to adjust. Barely any moonlight fell across the forest floor, but thankfully, as they continued deeper, pockets of firebugs and glowing shrooms began to light their way.

Alōs pushed aside thick vines draping from branches. They twisted around one another like the island's veins. The air grew damp and heavy, and Alōs's magic purred contently from the mist, feeding off dewdrops that collected on his exposed neck.

"It's beautiful," whispered Niya, reaching out to stroke a purple glowing bud. It opened at her touch.

"And deadly," added Alōs.

"What do you mean?" She frowned over to him.

"'For the plants that glow, into the Fade the eaters will flow.'"

Niya tugged back her fingers, wiping them on her pants. "Maybe lead with that one next time."

They climbed over felled trees, used their blades to cut through thick foliage, and carefully avoided hanging nettle.

"This place," said Niya, as they entered a meadow twinkling alive with firebugs, "it reminds me a little of . . ."

"Of what?"

"Esrom."

"Yes," he agreed, pushing away the sudden ache that realization caused. "It has similar qualities."

"Do you miss it?"

His brows drew together. "Esrom?"

"Yes. Do you miss having it as your home?"

He was silent a long while, only the buzzing of nocturnal creatures mixing with his thoughts. "At first, it was like living without being able to breathe. But now . . ."

"Now?"

"It is a pain I've grown so used to it has become a strange companion."

Niya was quiet for a spell, the soft crunching of their footsteps the rhythm of their path forward. "Some memories, I think," she eventually said, "are worth the pain they bring. They remind us that whatever we had was real. And knowing it was true, remembering, well, it can sometimes offer a comfort, even amid all the hurt."

Niya's eyes were two pools of blue sapphires in the glowing night as he met them. Open, like they had been so many days ago when she'd lain in his arms. A new pressure weighed against his heart, but it had nothing to do with memories of his old home.

"Niya . . . ," he began.

"We've reached the first river." She pointed forward.

The canopy of forest broke to reveal fast-flowing waters dancing like quicksilver in the reflecting moonlight.

Niya strode toward the bank, leaving Alōs alone in their shared moment like a child releasing a floating lantern into the night.

"Do you think it is deep?" asked Niya.

Alōs came to her side, looking at the flowing river. "Only one way to find out."

"Can't you work your magic so we both can walk on water?"

"If you allow me to carry you, then yes."

This seemed to give her pause. She bent to test the water. "By the Fade," she hissed, shaking out her hand. "It's freezing."

"I'll meet you on the other side, then?" Alōs spun out a spell, gathering his magic in green clouds beneath his feet, before stepping right above the river's surface. He could feel the power of the water beneath him, a rush of energy that fed into his gifts to keep him floating.

"Wait," called Niya.

He turned to look at her on the bank. "Yes?"

"Carry me."

"You'll have to repeat that," he said. "The river is quite loud."

"You heard me just fine." She fisted hands on hips.

"I promise I did not," he said, feigning innocence. "Something about cranberry tea, was it?"

"Carry. Me."

He arched a brow. "Was that a command? Because given the circumstance, I believe the situation warrants more of a grateful, humbling request. Don't you?"

She glared daggers at him, obviously unaware that such a look only fueled his actions further. He bit back a grin.

"Carry me, *please.*"

Such sweet satisfaction, he thought.

"Why, of course, my lady." He returned to her side before quickly scooping her up.

"Wait. No. I can ride on your back." She wiggled in his arms.

"As if I am some common pack mule? I think not. Now stop struggling, or I might lose my hold and have you topple into the *very* cold river."

Niya stilled, looking wholly awkward as he carried her in his arms. The river continued to rush beneath them as they slowly made their way over it.

"You can put them around my neck," he suggested.

"What?"

"Your hands. For a better grip."

"I'm gripped just fine."

"That you are." Alōs held her tighter so her hand fell flat to his chest.

She plucked it away.

"Interesting," he mused, his mind instantly going to the last time she had touched him there. When it had been skin against skin. Despite their current surroundings, a wave of dark desire washed over him.

"What?"

"Well, you were not so skittish about laying hands on me the other night. Yes, I'm bringing it up," he said in response to her widening eyes. "How shocking. The lost gods know we have both been thinking of it since."

"Speak for yourself."

"Okay, speaking for myself, I'd like to do it again. Many times, in fact."

Alōs knew it sounded crass, but by the Fade, it was the truth.

Niya surprised them both by laughing, the warm sound vibrating through him.

"That amuses you?" he asked, looking down at her.

"Thoroughly."

"And why's that?"

"Who *wouldn't* want to sleep with me again?" She gestured to her ample bosom and devious curves.

"My, my," tutted Alōs as they drew closer to the opposite riverbank. "How arrogance suits you, fire dancer."

"Yes, I think so," she replied smugly.

Despite himself, Alōs laughed in kind, a deep chuckle that was met with Niya's inquisitive stare.

"What?" he asked.

"I think that might be the first time I've heard you laugh."

"Nonsense. I laugh all the time."

"Not like that."

Alōs shifted her slightly in his arms, a ripple of unease going through him. "Like what?"

"Like you were actually happy for a grain fall."

Her words fell like blows. But rather than pain, they only had him settle deeper into his growing warm resolve regarding the fire dancer.

"Yes, well"—his eyes held hers—"it appears I have found more moments to actually be happy in."

He watched as her cheeks turned pink, a rare occurrence of shyness that Alōs found he enjoyed thoroughly.

When he placed Niya down on the other side of the river, he realized at some point her arms *had* wound around his neck.

For a breath, they remained there. A tingling of awareness shot between them before Niya stepped away, letting a cool whip of wind replace the heat of her touch.

"If you must know," Niya eventually said as they headed into the next stretch of dark, damp jungle, "yes, of course I enjoyed that night, but it changes nothing."

"What does that mean?"

"Just because we find pleasures with one another, just because we have this . . ."

"All-consuming sexual tension?" he suggested. "Unstoppable power when together?"

"*Thing* between us."

"I preferred my description."

"Doesn't mean I have forgotten our past," she went on.

Alōs held back a frustrated groan. "Niya, how many times must I explain myself?"

Her jaw set in stubbornness. "Many times, it seems."

He shook his head. That familiar weariness gripping him, as it did when he'd held her in his arms those nights ago. That no matter what he said, she would never forgive him. Never give him a chance to prove that he was not the same man, that he was no longer the same pirate, despite how she might have witnessed him opening up to his crew earlier on the ship. An act he *never* would have done before she had come aboard, before her burning fire had worked its way into his heart, keeping it from ever truly being able to freeze over again. "I know what I did to you was ruthless, but you of all people must see *why* I did it, understand. We each live in a ruthless world."

"Of course I know the world we live in," she said in a huff. "And I might now empathize with your past, yes, but—"

"But nothing. If I were to judge your entire character on a single action in your life, like those souls you have danced into the Fade as a performance piece, I would say you were a vain, heartless monster."

She flinched as though hit. "Those prisoners were *killers themselves*! Traitors to the—"

"But I *don't*, Niya," he said, cutting her off. "Because we are all a complicated tapestry, a tangle of decisions and actions. I have seen your good along with your evil. Where you let some people in and push others out. We have experienced enough together by now that I would hope you would have found similar nuances in me."

The sounds of the woods buzzed around them. Niya's lips set in a firm line.

"What exactly is it you want, Alōs?"

"Isn't it obvious?" asked Alōs. "You."

Niya blinked.

"You may never forget our past," he went on, "but let us move beyond it. We will always find reason to fight, you and I, but let it not be as enemies."

"Alōs—"

"Why do you resist this?" He stepped toward her, sensing her magic as it skittered confused along her body, a red vibration. A wall. "Why do you resist what you know is possible between us?"

"Because," said Niya. "Just because it feels good doesn't mean it is."

"You still do not trust me."

"How can I? You're *you*."

It was as if she'd spiked him through the chest.

So there it was. She truly could not see anything beyond the ruthless pirate. The selfish man. The worst of it was he could hardly blame her. Alōs had made sure his reputation preceded him.

"I see." He spoke coolly, feeling the cold veneer from the past reforming along his bones, locking tightly across his muscles. His suit of armor despite his newly thawed heart. "So the courageous fire dancer will deny what burns between us because she fears repeating the past?"

"It would appear so." Her chin tilted up. "Because even I know the hottest of flames are the quickest to burn out."

They traveled the rest of the distance in silence, Niya deciding to swim the final river rather than be carried, then using the heat of her magic to dry herself quickly when back on land. Alōs was glad of her choice. He didn't need to feel her against him, hold something close knowing he could never touch what lay inside.

She did not trust him, nor forgive him, and Alōs believed she truly never would. His life's work seemed to only involve seeking clemency for past actions. And he was tired of it. Once all this was done, he would set himself and his pirates to sail a new course, search for fresh waters. Once all this was over, he and Niya could finally go their separate ways. He was not about to force the fire dancer to remain with him any longer than he already had because of their binding bet.

"By the stars and sea," said Niya, her words bringing Alōs back to where she had stopped to peer over a thick tangle of bushes.

He pushed aside a branch and looked upon a cutaway section of the forest.

It sprawled endlessly, deep into a gorge.

And there, spilling out wide from the center, was the home of giants.

Massive buildings with expertly thatched roofs and neat, brick-laid streets.

"It's all so . . . large," breathed Niya.

"Yes," said Alōs, his resolve returning to what had brought them here, what he prayed lay within this beast. He hungrily took in the city, his gaze landing on the largest of the homes at the very back, a hulking four-story dwelling. "And we're about to be its mice. Now"—he looked to Niya—"let's go steal some cheese."

CHAPTER FORTY-ONE

The first thing Niya noticed as she and Alōs wove through the sleeping streets, pressed up against towering buildings like skittering cockroaches, was the beauty.

Niya would be the first to admit that in her imaginings, the dwellings of giant cannibals would be filled with piles of picked-over bones, body odor mixed with the tang of feces. Their homes would be archaic. A wet, dripping cave would suffice, where they'd sleep curled together like wolves. What Niya witnessed now, however, was a hard lesson in her own prejudice.

The brickwork was intricate and symmetrical, built by expert hands. Doors were decorated in complex carvings, and massive torches flanked their sides, lighting the streets warmly. From where they crept, she and Alōs had shrunk to a fourth of their size, the large buildings seeming to go on endlessly.

The second thing Niya took in was the smell. The city was wrapped in floral fragrance. Glancing up to windowsills, Niya saw why. Flower boxes overflowed with dripping blooms of white plumeria or pink gilia, grown to be plucked by a much larger hand than her own.

Despite their circumstances, Niya's excitement soared as she took in what very few ever had.

Oh, how she hoped they'd see a giant soon!

She could feel them asleep in their dwellings, hear their snores vibrating through the walls.

They must be very large indeed, she thought, for though they hardly moved, their energy still felt like a bag of bricks against her skin.

It was utterly fascinating.

How envious her sisters would be when she told the tale of how she had stolen from giants and survived.

The last bit coming true was the most important part, of course.

The farther they roamed, the more Niya gave in to the one thing that would put any Bassette on a misguided path: curiosity.

"Stick close," hissed Alōs as Niya began to wander into the middle of the street.

"That is a sewer drain." She pointed to a large grate set into the cobblestone street.

"Yes, I can see that."

"That means they have plumbing here, Alōs. *Plumbing.*"

"Your deductive reasoning is astonishing. Now get back here," he urged from where he pressed against the edge of a building.

"We don't even have that yet in the Thief Kingdom."

Alōs shushed her as they slid along more homes before turning into a large square. Storefronts were boarded up for the night, and the sliver of moon directly above cast its faint glow across the quiet space. Something winked silver in the center.

"That's a sundial!"

"By the lost gods." Alōs tugged Niya back against the wall. "Is this how it is to be the entire time?"

"How are you not as astonished as I? No one has spoken of the things we've seen here."

"For a reason," he reminded her. "They're all dead. Can you focus now? We have to make it to the chief's home before we find out if any of your fawning over giant architecture has woken anyone."

"They do seem to be deep sleepers," she mused, glancing to the shut doors around them.

"And thank the lost gods for that. Now come on," said Alōs. "I think that building there must be his." He pointed to a distant dwelling that loomed over the town, its facade twinkling with finer stone than any of the others.

"Well," mused Niya as they crept forward. "That does not bode well for the rest of our journey."

"Why do you say that?"

"I've found whenever the first part of a task is easy, the second part is near impossible."

"Better than it being near impossible the entire time."

"But not as good as easy throughout."

"Nothing worth having is ever easy." Alōs's glowing gaze seemed to consume her as he glanced back.

A flapping of wings erupted in her gut, his words from earlier flying forward in her mind.

So the courageous fire dancer will deny what burns between us because she fears repeating the past?

Niya watched Alōs duck forward, leaving her standing alone.

Niya was not fearful. She was terrified.

Because she knew if she were to trust him again and he were to break that trust, it would not be Alōs she could never forgive. It would be herself.

And that was one gamble she could never bet upon.

Shaking herself out of her thoughts, she hurried to catch up with Alōs, who was now an entire block away. As they skirted corners and hung back, waiting to see if the rumbling of giants sleeping would change to the pounding of them rising, heavy feet on stone, an entire sand fall seemed to pass. But the city slept soundly, the heavy weight of the giants in their homes still. It was obvious these creatures had no fear of unwanted visitors, for who would be fool enough to come seek beings many times bigger than they, rumored to enjoy eating them for breakfast?

Niya and Alōs, it appeared.

Breathing heavily, they finally approached the towering home that Niya hoped was the chief's. Her gaze traveled up massive stairs, each lip as tall as she, to a soaring wooden door at the very top. Large burning bowls of fire flanked its sides, and carvings of flowers and leaves decorated the stone exterior.

Now that they were closer, she could pick up the echoing thump of music from within.

Niya's magic stirred, nerves awakening. "It appears not all are asleep," she said.

"No," agreed Alōs, his gaze studying the structure before them. "And by the sounds of it, they won't be for quite some time. It changes nothing, though. We have to get in there."

He began to pull himself up each step.

"Wait," grunted Niya as she followed, her arms aching with the climb. *By the Fade, there must be over a dozen steps.* "You can't seriously be thinking of walking straight through the front door?"

"Of course not," whispered Alōs as he made it to the final landing.

Niya bent over on her knees, wheezing slightly. "Then what was . . . the point . . . of that?"

"We are going to *squeeze* straight through the front door." He pointed to a gap by the door's hinge. "One advantage to our size." He flashed a smile before stepping forward.

"Alōs," she hissed, tugging at his coat. "Can we wait just a moment? What's the plan once we squeeze through?"

He turned, glowing eyes meeting hers. "The plan is we come up with a plan. But we won't know anything more standing out here."

"I can feel them inside, Alōs," she said, pulse quickening while she kept on his heels as he shimmied into the crack. "And I fear there are quite a lot."

He said nothing as they pressed tight into the space. Niya could just barely make out a glimmer of light beyond Alōs's large form. She did not like being pinched like this; in fact, her breathing grew panicked along with her swirling magic. *Lost gods, what if someone tries to open the door with us in here?* The thought had her scooting faster until soon she was pressed tightly behind Alōs where he'd stopped, right at the opening.

Delicate harp music mixed with the pounding of drums hit up against her, boisterous chattering and laughter along with passing shadows of large forms. But most of all, there were waves after strong waves of movement. It almost caused Niya to take a step back.

"What do you see?" she asked, angling for a better view over his shoulder.

"There's a party going on," Alōs whispered. "But there's a flower bed right by the door we can duck into. Ready?"

"Yes."

Like rodents, they scurried in and dropped into a long bed of plants. Niya clutched against a stalk, ducking under petals. They appeared to be in a flower bed that was dug down from the stone floor and lined a long entrance hallway. Niya peered left, then right, but could not see an end to the foliage where they hid. A forest of plant stems went on endlessly.

The ground shook beneath Niya's feet as the thumps of footsteps walking down the hallway hit up against her.

Still, Niya's heart leaped with a mix of anticipation and relief at not being seen. *We made it inside!* And giants roamed all around.

With her pulse quickening, she shifted the white petal right above her head and peered out at the scene. Her eyes flew wide.

While the outside of the building was all stone, the inside was a green jungle. Vines climbed walls like live wallpaper, and captured firebugs fluttered in clear jars, lighting the expanse of the soaring hall. And there, filling up all the air, were giants. Massive green- and blue-skinned creatures with thick muscles that bulged from sleeveless wraps and barely there tunics. They mingled with one another, talking and drinking from goblets as large as horses.

Now that she was among them, no longer separated by thick walls, their energy of movement was even heavier than she had first felt, like being crushed by a roomful of sand. Weighted. Oppressive. Paralyzing.

It took her breath away.

She now knew why her father had said her magic wouldn't do much against them. Her gifts were powerful, yes, as were Alōs's, but with so many . . . it would be like a drop of water trying to extinguish the sun.

She ducked back down, her thoughts racing as a new panic overtook her.

It was not merely locating the Prism Stone that they were up against tonight. No, she had truly underestimated what they would find here. Impenetrable stone walls in the form of giant cannibals.

"Are you all right?" Alōs drew close.

"Their movements are like holding a city on my back." She met his eyes, saw the worry in them. "Alōs, our magic cannot save us here. Not against them."

The crease between his brows deepened. "No, perhaps not *against* them, but our gifts are called gifts for a reason, fire dancer. There is always a benefit to be found in them. Now, let's get out of this hall. I am not sure why yet, but something is telling me to follow this flower bed to wherever it leads us to down there." He pointed right. To the endless flower forest with no distinguishable end.

Finding her bearings, Niya forced herself on, following Alōs forward and careful not to disturb stalks as they remained crouched under leaf and petal.

"I see an end approaching," said Alōs after they had walked for some time, the party and pounding of giants around them their beat to keep moving.

Coming to the end ledge of the flower bed, they peeked over its lip to look into a domed chamber. Its floor was made up of a mosaic stone pattern swirling into a point in the middle, the roof a curved masterpiece of stained glass, more depictions of plants. Yet despite its size, which Niya would have thought would be the perfect area for the giants to mingle in, it was empty, save for one.

While his height was not so tall as to reach treetops, it still was that of five or six men. His black hair was pulled back into a tight ponytail, revealing facial features that sat plump and heavy, as if a bee had stung his brow, nose, and lips. He leaned against a wall on the other side of the room, picking at his nails with a stick.

A stick that looked an awful lot like a bone.

Niya swallowed. "Do you think he's a guard or guest?" she whispered.

"I think all guests are guards here."

"What should we do?"

Alōs didn't answer, his brows drawn together as he peered toward an entryway that sat across the domed room.

"What is it?" she asked, inching closer to him, trying to see whatever it was he did.

"I can feel something."

"Yes, so can I. It's the giants stomping about."

Alōs shook his head. "No, it's similar to what I've felt around . . ."

"Around *what*?" Niya pushed impatiently.

"The other pieces of the Prism Stone."

Niya's heart stuttered, her grip tightening on the ledge they crouched behind. "You feel it here? Are you sure?"

"Not entirely, but . . ." His gaze turned toward her, a spark of light, of hope. It was a look that was enough to send her own optimism soaring. "I'll be more sure if we can search whatever is in that hall over there."

Niya glanced back to the open door across the room. The hallway looked similar to the one at their back, except it hung in silence. She could sense little movement down its length. But she no longer entirely relied on her senses here. The waves of movement coming off these giants discombobulated her bearings.

"The distance isn't far," she said. "But there is nowhere to hide to reach it."

The long flower bed ended where they crouched, nothing but stone floor in front of them. Not even a pot or statue to hide behind.

"Then we'll have to be true thieves tonight," explained Alōs. "If we stay quiet and move slowly, we should be able to make it past with him unaware."

Niya frowned. It wasn't really the best plan, but what so far had been? And what other options did they have? Their magic was useless against such a creature. She could almost imagine how drained she would become, and how quickly, attempting to penetrate such thick skin and hulking muscle with a spell.

Beside her Alōs began to grab handfuls of dirt by their feet, slathering it over his face and coat. "To hide our smell," he explained when he met her concerned look. "Just in case."

"This keeps getting better and better," she grumbled, bending down to do the same.

Once properly dirty, they climbed out of the flower bed, pausing with backs flat against the curved wall to their right.

Niya's heart seemed to ricochet against the ground, every one of her senses heightened as she waited. *Fight,* her magic hissed, not understanding why she kept it contained, suppressed. She continued to ignore its demands as she watched the giant take no notice of the two mice wedged in tight across the room. He merely moved from cleaning his nails to picking his teeth.

Alōs glanced her way and gave her a smile before sliding forward, one slow step at a time.

He looked strangely endearing covered in dirt, she realized, his usual impeccable state lost under smears and smudges.

Niya's gaze swung erratically between the new hall they approached and the giant on the other side of the room. *We are nothing. No one. Tiny bugs not even worth squashing.*

They were now only ninety steps away.

Seventy.

Fifty steps.

The giant looked toward them. Niya sucked in a breath and froze, Alōs now motionless beside her.

The beast sniffed the air, and Niya pressed tighter against the wall, as though the effort might have the stone swallow her whole.

She felt like a sitting target. The giant was looking *right at them.*

What had they been thinking, walking into the middle of this room? It was madness!

Everything inside Niya screamed to move, run, spin a spell that would at least buy them time to retreat.

But she remained still. As did Alōs. As did their magic, which she could sense wanting to jump from the pirate's skin as much as hers, a contained vibration beside her.

By some miracle the beast turned back to his task.

She and Alōs slipped forward once more, but not until they had successfully rounded the corner into the next hall did she let out a relieved breath.

"By the Fade," she whispered. "That took years from me, I'm sure."

"Better a loss of a few years than the giant taking them all if he had seen us."

Niya held back a shiver. "Where to now?"

Alōs drew his brows together in concentration, peering down the long hall. It had no windows, but the twinkling lanterns woven into the tapestry of vines lit the stretching path. Six open doorways, three on either side, patterned its length.

"It's stronger here," he said, "but we should search each room before moving on."

They hurried forward, entering into rooms that twinkled with captured starlight or were covered in the softest glowing moss. And when Niya sensed giants approaching, the pounding of their footfalls hard to miss, they ducked into the thick vines carpeting the walls. After another half sand fall of exploring, Niya noticing Alōs's growing frustration, she began to fear that perhaps whatever he sensed might merely have been a phantom of hope. The place was enormous, with many spectacular items waiting for them in each room.

Especially when they stood before two glowing green orbs, no bigger than apples, that circled each other endlessly. They floated above a plush pillow, the only two items in one of the rooms.

"What are they?" she asked, watching the balls spin around and around, as though drawn to one another but unable to touch. Magic was assuredly trapped here. *Is this what Alōs felt?* she wondered with dismay.

"Connection stones," said Alōs, the green before them lighting up his face. "I have only ever seen these in Esrom."

She frowned, looking back at the orbs. She had never heard of them before.

"What do they do?"

"Their magic can bind two beings together. When split up, either party can summon the other. I hear to refuse the call can be painful. Like splinters in your blood until you meet again with whoever holds the other piece. Connection stones do not like to be separated for long."

"Sounds dreadful. Who would ever bind themselves like that?"

Alōs did not answer, only stared at the spinning orbs, his gaze growing distant.

"Alōs?" She stepped closer, but he turned from her, walking from the room.

Niya glanced back to the connection stones, confusion swirling at what he had seen that she didn't, before following him out.

They continued searching in a tense silence, sensing that their time here was almost up, until Alōs suddenly set off down the hall in a jog.

Niya's nerves buzzed as she chased after him. "What is it?" she asked as he skidded to a stop by the last open door in the hall.

"In here," he said. "I can feel something—"

But his words died on his tongue as they both peered into the room.

"By the Fade," whispered Niya.

They stood before a room of horrors.

Shelves lined the walls, displaying people from all over Aadilor, taxidermized and frozen. A group of men from the northeast lands of Hultez was positioned on their knees, looks of terror on their faces as they held up shields. Two women from Shanjaree hugged one another, their features pinched in heartbreaking sorrow. Even children were displayed but were made to smile.

Niya's blood ran cold.

"Do you think . . . ?"

"Yes," said Alōs, stepping deeper inside. "These are all who have died here. It appears we've found the chief's trophy room."

As if she were tranced by the gore, Niya walked the rows, a buzz filling her ears. Creatures of all kinds filled the cases, not just humans, and on some she began to take note of a difference on a few of their plaques. "What do you think this symbol means?" She pointed to a cluster of stars stamped on the metal nameplates. These stuffed trophies, compared to all the others, were always situated at the front, as though they were the jewels of the collection.

"I think"—Alōs came to her side, studying the hollow eyes of a woman whose arms were raised up, as though she were pushing out something from within—"that means they were gifted."

Niya blinked. "What? With magic?"

He nodded. "It appears they are their favorites to eat."

Niya backed away, her throat growing tight. "We have to get out of here."

But as she turned into the next row, a rumbling growl vibrated the stone at her feet.

Niya froze.

If it weren't for the gently swooshing tail, Niya would have thought it was another stuffed trophy.

A large feline lay curled by a lit fireplace a stone's throw away. Its head rested on thick paws while its slit hazel eyes stared straight at them.

Niya was seized with cold panic, just as her nose instantly began to itch. *Cats.* She hated cats. Especially abnormally large ones.

The feline lifted its head then and gave a sleepy yawn. Sharp teeth, the length of Niya's forearm, gleamed like ivory daggers in the firelight.

Niya's heart lurched, but not because of the toothy daggers, but because there, dangling from the cat's collar, in the center of swirling metal, winked a red gem.

"Alōs—"

"If you're going to make a joke about me referring to us as mice earlier," he said from where he remained motionless behind her, "you can save it."

"No, *look.*" She jutted her chin forward. "At its collar."

"The Prism Stone," whispered Alōs before his tone turned annoyed. "Decorating a *cat?*"

Despite the tension gripping her entire body, she found herself rolling her eyes. "I think you're concentrating on the wrong part here, pirate. We *found it.*"

"On a beast that might be worse than a giant."

Niya's magic crashed against her sides, a rippling of anticipation as she studied the creature who studied them. "It's not so big."

"Yet one roar could alarm all the guests to come running."

"Not if it's too tired to make a sound," she suggested, the beginning of a plan forming. "And it already seems awfully tired."

Approaching slowly, Niya ignored Alōs's hiss of warning as she began to sway her hips.

The feline's ears pressed back as it watched her approach, its back arching in readiness before she pushed out her magic in a puff of red haze. *Relax.* She sent her intentions soaring through the air, covering the cat like a warm blanket.

Its eyes drooped.

Sleep, she instructed, moving her fingers as if she herself were petting the beast instead of waves of her magic.

Slowly the cat lowered its head back onto its paws. Vibrating purrs filled the room.

She glanced to Alōs with a grin, satisfaction radiating through her. "See? Sleepy. Now come be a proper thief and steal your jewel while I keep him drowsy."

Alōs stepped to her side, eyeing the cat suspiciously. "How do you know it's a he?"

Niya shrugged. "He feels lazy."

Alōs gave her a dry glance. "Nice."

Turning back to the cat, he let out a deep breath, squaring his shoulders. The jeweled medallion on the feline's collar was now half-buried beneath where its head rested. Alōs would need to dig under its chin to pull it free.

Though Niya felt like a twisted-up tangle of nerves, she continued to twirl her wrists in a soothing rhythm. She could sense the strength of the beast under her fingertips, though this animal appeared already half-domesticated. But even the gentlest of cats could scratch at random. Another reason she loathed them. Distrustful creatures.

Niya watched Alōs step over one large paw, knocking into a whisker. Niya sucked in a breath as the cat shifted, belly up, bringing Alōs with it.

He now sat straddling the beast, the pendant directly in front of him. He kept still.

Niya forcing her rapidly beating heart steady.

Calm, she breathed into her gifts. *Gentle.*

Sleepy purrs emanated through the room once more.

A sigh of relief.

Alōs's gaze became marble then, eyes trained on the winking red gem a reach away.

He pulled one of his daggers free, silver gleaming in the firelight.

With a barely audible pop, he lifted out the red stone. It winked as he turned it over and over before his glowing eyes landed on her, a triumphant grin beaming.

"It's here," he said. "It's all here."

A rush of relief and elation threatened to knock Niya to her knees.

We did it! By the stars and sea, we did it!

The last piece of the Prism Stone.

Esrom would be saved.

She would be free.

Alōs slid down, returning to her side, and with her buzz of adrenaline she hugged him.

His strong arms held her tight, their blue gazes colliding as they pulled away.

The moment felt oddly perfect.

His eyes dipped to her mouth, setting off new flutters in her stomach.

Niya held still as he leaned in, knowing and wanting what was about to happen.

And then she sneezed.

CHAPTER FORTY-TWO

Niya could now attest that being chased by a giant cat was an overrated experience.

She and Alōs careened around the corner leading from the trophy room back into the hallway just as another roar of the beast shoved them from behind.

Niya's breaths pumped harsh in her lungs as the heavy movements of the animal fought with her own as she sent a blow of her magic toward the feline.

A wink of red sparked out of the corner of her eye, Alōs shoving the Prism Stone into his pocket before he twisted, pushing out green pulses of his powers.

But the damn cat was nimble. Because it was a *cat*, and it pounced away from each surge of their spells.

Niya wondered then if animals held the Sight or if they could merely sense magic, as they could sense other oddities humans could not.

But Niya's musings were soon stolen from her as the stone floor began to rumble with new meaning.

"Giants!" she cried as she and Alōs turned to find five of them crashing down the hall behind the cat who chased them.

Normally she could gather and use the motion around her, but this was too much. Everything charging toward them only made Niya feel like she was drowning in her gifts rather than controlling them.

Alōs cursed. "Stop using your magic," he rushed to say as they continued to flee back to the domed room.

"But why?" she shouted. Even if she could not do much against the giants, hopefully it could buy them a little time.

"Because we've seen how they treat those gifted," Alōs said hurriedly. "It will almost ensure our deaths."

His words sank in, adding to the weight already pushing her down. They were not going to escape.

For her father had been right—in a few quick strides the giants were upon them, more arriving at the other end.

They were trapped.

Niya scurried to the wall of the hall along with Alōs, attempting to bury themselves into the vines, but then large hands swatted down, ripping out plants in violent yanks.

She was knocked unsteady, the thick motion of so many moving at once dizzying her bearings further. Somewhere at her side she heard Alōs call her name, but her head spun, and in the next moment she felt a force like boulders shove her from the wall, and she was dropped into a large glass cage.

She hit against the hard surface, bumping into Alōs as it was turned and twisted until finally righted. She collapsed onto the wooden bottom, Alōs beside her, as they were swiftly lifted up and brought eye level to a circle of toothy-grinning giants.

A distant meow could be heard far below.

"Visitors," one rumbled, his breath fogging the glass.

"And at this late hour," tsked another.

"Our chief will not be pleased," a female pointed out. "But once they're cooked up with some of his favorite seasoning, he'll be happy."

"So you *are* cannibals," Niya couldn't help blurting out from where she crouched.

The giant holding them spun the cage, causing her and Alōs to fall back.

"How odious you smalls always are," he said. "Cannibalism would mean we eat our own kind. You most certainly are not our kind."

His companions laughed as they made their way forward, parading her and Alōs past all the other giants. They drew quite a long procession as they entered a throne room.

A twinkling canopy greeted them, more firebugs hanging from jars, while thick trees stood like columns leading up to a pillowed dais. On either side, Niya glimpsed more beasts gathering in the dim light, their green and blue skin blending into their environment.

The giant who carried them stopped a few paces away from the front of the throne room as drumbeats pounded out.

Niya's heart thumped along with the heavy rhythm, fear prickling over her skin as Alos stepped closer to her. A brush of a finger ran along hers. *I am here*, the touch seemed to say. While she was grateful for the reassurance, Niya had entered many throne rooms before, stood before the oppressive gaze of the Thief King, and because of that, she had learned how to bury deep her dread and stand tall before all.

She might have been small compared to those in the room, her gifts trapped under their weight, but her courage matched them in size.

With a hardening gaze, she clenched her hands into fists and trained her eyes on the new giant who entered. He walked with a hunch, as though he were a tired mountain, a thick layering of necklaces weighing down his front beneath a silver beard.

Settling into the pile of pillows on the dais, he rubbed his drooping eyes. "Tell me, Dthum, what was so important to summon me from sleep and those of us who were still making merry?"

"Sire, I caught some night crawlers." Dthum placed their cage on the ground before the chief's large feet. "They had made their way into the manor."

The crowd rumbled with the news as the old giant blinked his eyes clear, leaning forward to peer at them through the glass.

"It has been some time since we have had smalls here," he said, curiosity lighting his features. "Some time indeed. What herbs have you risked your lives to come for?"

Alōs stepped forward. "We have stolen no plants, sire."

"Of course you haven't," said the chief with a wave of his hand. "To steal means you have already successfully absconded with the items. You haven't successfully done anything. But you are here. In *my* manor. Which means you risked your life for a reason. So I shall ask again: Which herbs have you come for? Mystical Moss? Make Me Fly Ficus? We may not be gifted creatures, but we are collectors of many magical items and know how to harvest some of the powers the lost gods took with them. And we only keep the most rare in the manor."

"We do not care for your botany."

The chief threw back his head, letting out thunderous laughs, soon echoed by his subjects. "Of course you do," he assured. "You smalls are all the same. Always taking, never giving. Do you know what it is like to be constantly stolen from for centuries? We have found ways to quiet the ships on our shores, however. Islands with monsters are much more peaceful than one would think." The chief displayed a row of file-pointed teeth.

"My companion speaks true." Niya stepped forward. "We are mere explorers who have heard of what lives on Hallowed Island. We are not here to take anything but to observe. Look at us for the truth. We come only as two and carry no purse or sack for looting, merely the clothes on our backs. We have come to see for ourselves if rumors of the cannibal giants were accurate. We can now see how unjust Aadilor has been to your kind. You are much more than that. You are great creatures, with intelligent minds and beautiful horticultural skills." She gestured to the lush, leafy room. "Let us leave, and we can carry tales of your wit and engineering. We can help give you trade rather than thieves."

The old giant studied Niya from his perch, an amused spark entering his dark eyes. "Well spoken, small female. If such words had been given in times past, they may have moved me. But you see, we have grown comfortable in our isolation. In fact, we have thrived in it. While your intentions may be sound, we know the tales of war and greed of your kind. Peace is never long at hand. I fear your trip here will end the same as all the others. The only question which remains is who would like to be eaten first."

A true pang of fear entered Niya's chest then, and she looked toward Alōs.

Was this really it?

Had they made it so close to the finish line for it all to end now?

The idea of her death had always been a faraway vision. Inevitable, to be sure, but never now. And certainly not here, eaten by giants.

A shiver ran through her, and whether her magic was useless or not, she would not go down without a fight. Her powers swirled ready in her gut, a growing ball of fire. If she could not burn these thick-skinned giants, surely she could burn the plants that surrounded them.

She waited for Alōs to give the word, a nod, some signal for them to start their final dance.

But he appeared unmoved by the chief's words as he dusted off the bits of dirt from his coat and shirt. "Doesn't such monotony bore you?" asked Alōs.

The chief's brows lifted. "Does eating exotic, well-seasoned meat ever bore *you*?"

This elicited more chuckles from his subjects.

"Of course not," said Alōs. "But what I meant was, Doesn't the way you always kill our kind bore you—just as our kind always bores you with our thievery? It sounds like a tedious existence. I would think clever creatures such as yourselves would want more sport from your meals. Especially if you will eventually display us as trophies."

A dangerous smile edged the old giant's lips then. "I see you have traveled far into my manor, small one. So tell me, what sport has your skin adding more value to my collection?"

"Let us play for our freedom or to be your food."

"A game?" the giant mused.

"Yes." Alōs nodded. "Some entertainment before your possible supper."

The chief's eyes shone with delighted curiosity. "And what game is it you'd like to propose?"

"A hunt," said Alōs. "Set us loose with a quarter–sand fall head start. If we reach the beaches before getting caught by your subjects, we can leave. If we fail, we fill your belly."

An excited murmur flowed through the room.

"Are you mad?" hissed Niya, stomach dropping. "We would need a half sand fall, *at least*, to beat their strides."

The pirate did not look her way, only kept his gaze on the chief, waiting.

"A hunt?" the old giant mused. "Between us and your tiny kind? That is an amusing prospect. But I can think of a situation *far* more exciting."

Niya swallowed. *What could be more exciting for him than a hunt?*

"You fight each other for your freedom."

"Fight each other?" repeated Niya with a frown.

"Yes, my simple one. No weapons but hands and fists, I think. A way to tenderize your meat for us."

The room tittered with laughter.

"Whoever knocks down the other first is set free and can tell whatever tale they'd like of our island. But don't forget to share what happened to your companion who lost . . ." The chief patted his belly.

"That's a horrible game." Niya folded her arms over her chest.

"Worse than you both being eaten?" asked the chief.

Niya didn't reply, for she realized with a wave of cold dread that she didn't actually know the answer.

"Do we have your word on this bargain?" asked Alōs.

"You cannot seriously be entertaining this?" Niya swung her gaze to him.

But again, he would not look at her.

"Alōs," she demanded, actually stomping her foot.

"Do we have your word?" he asked the giant again.

"You do," assured the chief. "My oath as the ruler of my people. The winner will safely be allowed to leave this island."

"Then you have a fight," declared Alōs.

The hall erupted in noise and movement, sending Niya's head momentarily spinning from such large waves of energy.

They were dumped from their cage and then pushed apart.

"Alōs!" She stared in disbelief, entire body vibrating with uncertainty. "What have you done?"

His blue gaze locked on hers, cold and determined. "I have saved one of us."

"I will not fight you."

"You must fight, little one," the chief said from his padded throne beside them. "We have a bargain. A gracious one on my part. I could eat you both, right now, but your companion promised sport, so sport is what you shall provide."

A wall of giants surrounded them. Eyes blinking down with vicious glee. She saw wooden chips go from hands to pockets, wagers. With her throat tightening, she realized this might be the first bet she had no desire to get in on.

Her gaze settled back on Alōs, standing tall and imposing in front of her. Somewhere in the folds of his clothes was the last piece of the Prism Stone. Their joy of victory had been fleeting.

"Alōs," she said again, a plea this time.

This could not be their only choice. Every bad situation had many doors to exit through. Arabessa had taught her that. Thinking of her sisters twisted another blade of uncertainty through her. She could not die here. She could not! But neither could she allow Alōs to.

He had Esrom to save. His brother to aid. A ship of pirates to command.

Niya didn't know what to do. She was stuck, cornered. And at the thought, a ferocious wave of anger rose within her. She loathed being forced into any situation. Somehow she had to regain control.

"Come on, fire dancer, you always talk a big game. Why not show me what you've threatened to do to me for so long?" Alōs's cool words brought her attention back to him, where he began to circle her. "Or is it that when it comes down to it, you lack the conviction to ever really finish what you've started?"

Icy annoyance prickled over her skin. "What are you talking about?"

"You have told me many times how you hate me; now is your chance to show me." He spread his arms wide.

"Stop this." Niya frowned. "I know what you're trying to do."

"Prove that you are the weakest of the three?" Alōs's features remained a frozen lake. "The one with the most liability? Tell me, have your sisters ever put your family in as much danger as you have?"

His words fell like lashes to her heart. But she wouldn't rise to the bait. He was trying to anger her so she would make the first blow. But she couldn't. *They couldn't.* There had to be another way out of this. "Don't." She shook her head. "Whatever you are—"

"Did you know"—Alōs prowled closer, a whisper of his breath along her ear—"when I left your rooms those four years ago, after you gave me so many, *many* precious pieces of you, I immediately sought the bed of another."

Sharp anger erupted, ferocious, through Niya's body. Her clenched hands heated.

But she couldn't reveal her magic. Not now. Not yet. Still, Alōs was toeing too close to a forbidden line. *Lies,* she thought. *These are lies.* But the doubts still crept into her heart, wrapped like bladed wire to puncture deep.

"You see," he continued in a purr, "while you certainly were a delight, my darling, there are some pleasures virgins cannot satiate in a man."

The room disappeared as a roar broke free from Niya, her fist connecting to jaw.

He stumbled back, head whipping to the side as a distant crowd cheered their excitement.

Niya gulped in breaths full of rage as Alōs rubbed his chin, his turquoise eyes bright, consuming, behind his mask of cool as he glanced back at her.

"You call that a punch?" he taunted. "No wonder you rely so heavily on"—his gaze roamed her body—"other things."

"Stop!" Niya stomped forward, shoving him. "Don't do it like this. If you want a fight"—Niya pushed again—"then fight back!"

"But I would win entirely too quickly that way," crooned Alōs. "It appears I share a similar trait with our audience: I like to play with my food."

The chief's laughter echoed toward them. "Who knew our unwanted guests could be so very entertaining!"

His subjects shouted their agreement.

Niya shook her head, trying to clear away her surging desire to burn. But it spun hot, searing deep into her belly. Reactionary fire. *Let us out,* her magic crooned. *Let us cook him, burn him, eat his flesh from bone.*

"I wonder if any of my crew will even notice your absence?" Alōs taunted. "So many thought you useless, after all."

"*Lies,*" she ground out through clenched teeth. "You are filled with nothing but lies this night!"

"And you cowardice," he spat back. "Tell me, honestly, have you ever been able to find another who fills you with as much feeling as I? Or who has filled you so *thoroughly* as I?"

The echoing of crude jeers erupted all around as Niya finally snapped. She landed a new blow, then another and another. Left cheek, right, upper jaw. None Alōs attempted to block.

"Hit me!" screamed Niya as she pounded against Alōs's chest, broken skin along her knuckles stinging. "Who is the coward now? Hit me!"

"I am, my sweet." He looked down his nose at her. "I'm hitting you with the truth. The truth of how inconsequential you are."

"More lies!" She spun, kicking him in the side.

He stumbled.

The room held its breath along with Niya.

The first to fall.

"No!" Niya grabbed his arm, steadying him. "Stand up and fight back! Why will you not fight back?"

"Because," said Alōs, displaying crimson-covered teeth with his wicked grin, "you were hardly ever a proper opponent to begin with. How many times have I bested you now?" He gripped her wrist hard, raising her binding bet between them. "I'm starting to lose count."

Niya growled her frustration, shoving him away.

"Tell me, Chief." Alōs turned to the old giant. "What seasoning will you use on the female when you cook her?"

The chief's grin was ear to ear. "Oh, she looks like she'd be good spicy."

"Right you are," agreed Alōs. "But you see, I've tasted her and can also attest to her sweetness."

All thought drained from Niya, her gaze tingeing red as she charged him, spin kicking Alōs across the face.

Alōs's head snapped back, but his returning smile was maddening as he wiped the blood dripping from the corner of his mouth, only to lick it from his finger. "And I suggest you save her most ample bits for last," he went on, staring straight at her. "I could have savored her breasts for sand falls."

"You bastard!" Niya's vision warped, pulling in all her magic to converge into her booted foot as it connected with his chest.

Alōs soared, landed on his back, and stayed there.

The room exploded in cheers as the faint sound of the chief's voice declaring her the victor filled her whirring head.

Niya blinked, her rapid anger knocked away as the reality of the situation slammed down upon her like boulders from a mountaintop.

"Alōs!" She ran to him.

His face was cut and bleeding, one eye already swelling shut as she cradled his head in her lap. Niya had done this to him. Claws of guilt gripped her throat, threatening to strangle it closed.

"Why?" demanded Niya, her voice breaking. "Why did you not fight back?"

Alōs's one good eye locked on hers, the center of a flame still burning. "Because, fire dancer, how do you fight someone who is no longer your enemy?"

It was as if someone had squeezed her heart so it could no longer beat.

"But we were meant to." Niya shook him in frustration. "You forced us to."

Alōs's pained features softened. "Yes, and it was far more important that you win."

Win.

The word felt gross and heavy. This was no win. Everything about this screamed loss.

"You are more valuable on this plane than I, fire dancer." Alōs touched her cheek, and she leaned into the soft caress, so different than her pounding fists. "Your sisters need you. The Thief King needs you. I could not allow the Mousai to end this night."

"You *fool*," she cried. It was as if the very air around Niya were drowning her. "This is not the time for you to become a martyr. What of the *Crying Queen*? Esrom? We can run. Fight. Now, we can—"

"No." Alōs trapped her shaking hands, which had begun to glow. His gaze darted to the giants, who were moving in around them. "You must find control. If you show you have gifts, they certainly will not let you leave. Deal or no."

"I don't care!"

"Listen to me, Niya," Alōs said, speaking past her. "If there's one thing I ask of you, it's that you finish this. Take the pieces back to Esrom and finish it."

Everything inside her was cracking and shattering. "Alōs, stop—"

"Kintra knows what to do once there. She will be captain now. Do you understand? I know you still do not forgive me for what I have done to you, and I will take that to the Fade, but please say you will do this for me."

Niya's vision blurred, but she refused to let a single tear fall. "I *do* forgive you, Alōs. I do. But we will both take it back to Esrom."

"Stubborn until the very end." He smiled before wincing in pain.

Niya's heart clenched as she wiped strands of hair from his face. "I refuse to have this end this way."

"Then let us remember it differently."

Alōs pulled Niya down to him and kissed her, his other hand gripping her hip. He tasted like iron, but Niya didn't care about the blood, because she also knew he tasted like the first cool glimpse of stars at night, the piercing white dusting of infinite possibilities.

Niya realized in a horrible desperation that a world without Alōs Ezra would be a terrible one. A boring one. And if there was one thing Niya despised most, it was boring.

Large, rough hands pulled them apart. Niya was pushed into a cage.

"Thank you for visiting us here on Hallowed Island," said the chief as she was lifted. "It was most entertaining."

Niya pressed against the glass, staring down at Alōs bleeding on the stone floor far below.

"Finish it!" he called to her. "Finish it and be free."

And then all Niya could see were the backs of giants as she was carried away, and her surroundings ceased to have meaning.

Niya was deposited at the edge of the jungle.

She didn't even know if it was the right part of the island.

Nor did she care.

Her entire body was overtaken with rage. Desperation. Anguish. Her magic swam dark. *Go back,* her powers coerced. *Let us see how tasty their meat is. I bet it burns easy. I bet it burns bright.*

Enough! she silently commanded.

The only thing keeping her from obeying was the lump in her pocket. She had felt Alōs place it there when they'd kissed, his last graze of fingers against her hips.

Stumbling through brush, she stepped onto the beach and collapsed in the cool sand, pulling the stone free.

The last piece of the Prism Stone felt small and insignificant in her palm. The dark red matched the dried blood staining her shirtsleeve. Alōs's blood.

She looked into the creeping dawn on the horizon, a barely discernible speck of a ship in the distance.

Finish this.

Alōs's last words seemed to echo in the crashing waves hitting shoreline and the boat that had been left there.

Finish this.

And be free.

Niya would.

But not yet.

CHAPTER FORTY-THREE

Niya's hands ached as she climbed the ladder on the side of the *Crying Queen*, leaving her rowboat tied and fighting the waves that smacked against the side below.

"They're back!" called Bree to the rest of the crew as Niya landed on the foredeck.

"Where's the cap'n?" asked Boman.

"Did you see any giants?" questioned Therza.

"Did you get back what the cap'n needed?" wondered Green Pea.

Niya answered none of the pirates as her gaze momentarily met Kintra's above her on the quarterdeck, before she strode past the group toward the captain's quarters.

"Keep back, rats," instructed Kintra behind Niya. "I'll get all the gossip to satisfy your appetite."

Niya pushed through the door at the end of the dark hall, only to stop as the lingering sensation of Alōs's magic enveloped her. The cool threads danced over her body. Covered everything in the room. A chilled whisper of power. *Mine.*

Niya hated how comforting that whisper now felt. How it brought welcome goose bumps to her skin, followed by sharp dread.

Niya forced herself forward, rounding Alōs's desk. The early sunrise streamed through the paned glass at her back, painting the wood in a honey finish.

"Where is he?" Kintra stood in the doorway, watching as Niya fumbled to open his locked drawers. "What's happened?"

"We were caught. He's to be eaten."

"What?" Kintra shut the door behind her.

"I know you have the keys to this." Niya kicked the sturdy desk in frustration. Her magic couldn't do so much as loosen a hinge.

"Niya, stop," said Kintra, approaching.

"You don't understand!" Her gaze swung to the quartermaster. "We don't have much time. I must get help."

"Get help?" Kintra frowned. "Look around. We are help."

"Pirates will not help here. We need magic. *A lot* of magic." Niya strode to the bookshelf, pulling out spines, searching behind them.

"By the stars and sea, *will you stop?*"

Only because she had never heard Kintra raise her voice before did Niya obey.

"Thank you," huffed Kintra. "Now, tell me what you are looking for."

Niya ran a hand through her hair, a tangling mess coming out of its braid. "A portal token. I know Alōs must have some in his personal bounty, which he keeps in this room, yes?"

Kintra eyed her suspiciously. "Perhaps."

"And you have the key to it, being his most trusted second-in-command."

Kintra didn't answer.

"Well?" Niya shoved out her palm. "Don't just stand there like a statue for the birds—hand it to me."

"You truly must be off your sails if you think I'm to give you Alōs's treasure with barely an explanation."

"Didn't you hear me? He's to be eaten!"

"By giants?"

"Who else would be able to stomach such a sour soul? Yes, *giants*. We found the final piece." Niya fumbled in her pocket, her fingers trembling with barely contained magic as she revealed the small shard of the Prism Stone. "And then were caught."

Kintra stared at the gem, the red reflecting in her dark eyes. "You got it."

"Yes, we got it."

"It's over."

"Not quite. Kintra, *please*, where does he keep his bounty?"

"But you escaped? Not Alōs."

"It's complicated."

Niya felt Kintra's quick movement, the singing of her blade as she unsheathed it.

"What are you doing?" Niya spun, placing the desk between them.

"Do you think I am a fool?" Kintra's gaze was an aimed arrow as she held her knife at the ready. "You want a portal token to escape after feeding Alōs to the giants."

Niya slammed her brows down. "No. That is not—"

"You cannot kill those who hold your binding bet with your own hand, so you found a way around it. And to think I was beginning to believe you were one of us."

"Kintra, listen to what you are saying," Niya said in an exasperated breath. "If I were planning to walk away now, why would I have told you about the Prism Stone? Why would I have come back here at all?"

"Because it's the only way to leave."

"We don't have time for this!" Niya threw out her hands, frustration boiling over. "Alōs could be getting chopped to bits right now!"

Kintra glanced to Niya's wrist, to where her debt was inked. "No, unlucky for you, my captain still lives."

Niya hadn't thought of her band disappearing as a sign of Alōs's death. With a fresh shot of panic, her powers vibrated along her veins. Another unknown sandglass flipped over.

"Kintra, I do not want to use my powers on you, but I will if you do not shut up and stand down."

Kintra lunged at her, but Niya knocked away her daggered hand. Spinning, she jumped atop the desk and pinned the quartermaster to it.

But Kintra was a pirate of the *Crying Queen* and easily slipped from her grip.

She attacked Niya again.

"I'm . . . giving . . . you . . . one last . . . chance . . . to stop," Niya warned, blocking blow after blow, making a point not to extend any blows back. She had inflicted enough pain this day.

A vision of Alōs's bruised and bleeding face filled her vision.

Niya's desperation soared.

"You know," said Kintra while attempting an uppercut, "he was beginning to trust you too."

"And *you* know what?" asked Niya after dodging it. "This is growing tedious."

Spinning like a gust of wind, she shot out a red wave of her magic. It blazed against Kintra, sending her flying against the bookcase.

Heavy tomes fell, plunk, plunk, plunk, atop her head as she slid to the ground, unconscious.

"I'm sorry." Niya crouched beside her, feeling under her clothes. "But I did warn you."

She pulled a chain from around Kintra's neck. On it dangled a group of small keys.

"One of these should work." She tugged them free.

Rounding Alōs's desk, Niya began to unlock drawers, rifling through them as her desperation climbed. But then her fingers stilled, heart lurching, as she found one with a false bottom. Sliding it to the side, she revealed a heavy onyx chest.

She let out a shaky, hopeful sigh, but as she grabbed the box, a consuming cold burned her fingers.

Niya hissed, dropping the chest.

A defensive spell.

"Clever, pirate," said Niya before pushing flames awake along her palms, protective gloves of sorts, to grasp the box once more.

This time her hold held, sending steam sizzling through the air as the conflicting magic collided. Fire fighting ice.

She settled the chest on the desk with a heavy thunk, quickly trying each key again on the chain. Finally an unlatching click as the lid swung open. "By the lost gods," she breathed.

Atop Alōs's desk an array of precious gems, gold coin, and silver winked out like a temptress. Niya opened a felt bag resting on top, finding the other pieces of the Prism Stone.

She swallowed down the rising ball of anguish as she added the final one. They each glowed bright for a grain fall, a whispering sigh of relief to be reunited, before fading to dark.

It was done. The pieces were collected. But Niya's sense of accomplishment was void. There was much still to do.

Pushing aside the bag, Niya fingered through the rest of the bounty, searching for the one thing she needed more than any of the riches before her. "Please be here, please be here, please be—aha!" Snagging up a silver portal token that swirled black in the middle, she kissed it. "Always a sight for sore eyes."

Pulling one of her daggers from her hip, she pricked her finger. Then, holding the token with a smear of blood, she whispered a secret into it, one she'd only recently realized she carried, and flipped the coin into the air.

Before it hit the floor, a portal door rose up.

And Niya ran through.

CHAPTER FORTY-FOUR

*I*n a remote part of the southern sea, a sandglass hissed the passing of time while a pile of treasure winked, vulnerable, atop a captain's desk. A portal door glowed open in the center of the room while a pirate slumped unconscious in the corner. A strange sight indeed for any of the *Crying Queen*'s crew to have found, had they dared enter. Luckily for Niya, the pirates hardly desired to go near their captain's lair when summoned, let alone when they were strictly not allowed.

So the room held quiet, an unmoved spectator as the sun slowly rose higher outside the paned windows, sending rays of light stretching along the floor and walls.

A commotion barreled into the calm as three figures in black hooded robes and gold masks slipped in through the portal.

"Darius will not enjoy me missing another dinner," grumbled Larkyra.

"You'll be back before he'll notice you've left," assured Niya, snatching up the portal token.

The door to the Thief Kingdom disappeared with a snap, and Niya turned to regard her sisters, disguised as the Mousai.

It had taken longer than she would have liked to gather them both together, and her nerves continued to buzz chaotically through her veins.

Go. Run. You are out of time.

"I think it will be hard to miss his wife gone from his bed when he wakes," pointed out Larkyra, eyes narrowed behind her mask.

"Then perhaps you should have told him goodbye upon your leaving," suggested Arabessa, straightening her robes.

"I left him a note. I didn't want to wake him after last night."

"What happened last night?"

"Let's just say he put in a very thorough perform—"

"Never mind." Arabessa held up a hand, stopping her. "I just ate breakfast."

"Niya." Larkyra studied Kintra's body beneath the bookshelf. "Who is this?"

Niya glanced to the woman, relieved to find her still unconscious. "Our quartermaster."

"Is she dead?"

"No, but help me tie her up before she wakes."

Without question her sisters aided in securing Kintra to the metal hook bolted to the floor.

Niya didn't miss the irony, in that she had once been bound to that very spot, kneeling, bruised, and bloody, and now was tying up another to save someone she had left bruised and bleeding.

"All right." Niya stood. "Now to take care of the rest of the pirates."

Niya pulled open Alōs's door, gliding down the hall with her two sisters in tow.

As soon as they stepped on deck, the echoing sound of metal singing, blades being pulled from sheaths, quickly told her they had been seen.

A ship full of armed pirates circled them, more still hanging above from ropes and clinging to masts. All eyes beady and ready for a fight. Saffi stood the nearest, her gray magic a haze around her as her gaze was pinned to Niya's.

"We didn't realize we had the pleasure of visitors aboard," said the master gunner. "Especially ones as esteemed as you three."

Though her words were cordial, her tone was anything but.

"How would you like us to handle this?" asked Arabessa from behind Niya. She could sense the vibration of each of their gifts gathering.

But the last thing Niya wanted or needed was to waste any more time with a fight.

"We have come to retrieve your captain," said Niya, deepening her voice slightly. These pirates had been around her enough to most likely know her tone by now. "We were told he is in need of help. We are not here to harm any of you, but if you try to fight us, we will. Now stand down so we can pass."

The sound of the sea hitting along the ship and the screech of gulls above were the only responses for a beat.

"Our captain has sent for you?" asked Saffi suspiciously. "Where's Niya? And Kintra?"

Frustration gripped Niya then; she had no time for explanations! This could be sorted out later.

"We have no time for this, pirate," said Niya. "Now will you part and let us pass? We merely wish to get onto the island."

Saffi glanced to the crew then, and Niya watched each of them grip their weapons, smiles spreading. "If our captain be needing help," said Saffi, eyes shifting back to Niya and her two sisters, "it is we who will give it."

Stupid prideful creatures, cursed Niya silently.

"As you wish," she said. "But know it is *you* who asked for this, not us."

The master gunner frowned. "What—?"

But she was cut off as Niya spun, shoving out her magic to send Saffi flying.

"Knock them out!" shouted Niya to her sisters. "But try not to hurt them."

"It is impossible not to hurt someone if you want to knock them out," explained Larkyra as she ducked and twirled from Boman and Emanté charging her.

"Then don't hurt them *too badly*," clarified Niya in a huff as she sent another wave of her magic into Green Pea and Bree.

She hated shoving her friends away, watching their heads smack against wooden crates before they slumped unconscious, but it needed to be done.

They'd wake up eventually, she reasoned.

Larkyra began to sing a tune of the sea from behind her, a lullaby that spoke of rocking waves and sleeping babes. Yellow tendrils of her gifts curled around pirates, glazing their eyes to eventually droop closed.

Arabessa knocked a fiddle out of Felix's hands, snatched the bow from the air, and strung out an accompanying tune.

Mika charged her from the side, but Niya watched her sister twirl out of the way, not even missing a note as she continued to play.

The rest of the scuffle went fast then, with the ship being doused in the conjoined serenade of the Mousai, their powers a thick shimmering of red, yellow, and violet to send every last pirate to sleep.

Niya regrouped with her sisters along the port side as their performance drew to a close. She stood by the railing, breathing heavily under her black robes as she took in the scene of bodies slumped about all over deck.

"Well, that was fun," said Larkyra. "We've never taken down a whole ship of pirates before."

"Yes," agreed Arabessa. "And this fiddle was even an out-of-tune mess."

A twist of guilt gripped Niya at her sister's words, given she had actually done this once before to this very crew. A crew who had only *just* begun to treat her with kindness again.

They don't know it's me, she reasoned.

Plus, when they woke up, especially once their captain was back, all could be sorted. Currently, however, Niya couldn't have any of the crew trying to follow and getting in her way.

It would assuredly have them all ending up meals for giants.

"All right." She turned, pushing away the nagging of remorse to stride past her sisters. Gripping the railing, she peered over, down toward the rowboat still tied far below. "Who wants to help row to shore?"

Niya crouched in the shadows of a thick bush atop a hill, Arabessa and Larkyra at her side. Their gold masks now removed, they looked down into the massive sprawling city of giants in the center of a gorge, three serpents coiled as they planned their strike. As it was morning, however, it was an altogether different scene than what Niya had experienced last night. The town was now alive with the massive green and blue beasts. The rumbling of each of their footsteps echoed against the valley walls, their deep voices carrying far in the wind.

"This place is extraordinary," whispered Arabessa.

"Wait until you see inside the chief's home," said Niya, unable to disagree. "The entire thing is a pristine garden."

"How fascinating."

"Yes, fascinating." Larkyra stifled a yawn.

"Oh, I'm sorry," snapped Niya. "Is sneaking into a city of giant cannibals boring you?"

"I told you," said Larkyra with a frown. "I was kept up late. It is not my fault I didn't predict you'd be pulling me from bed mere sand falls later."

"I still do not understand why we are even here," added Arabessa, letting go of the branch she had been holding down, covering up their view of the giants' city with a whoosh. "Isn't it a good thing if Alōs dies? Your binding bet would end immediately, and so would all of our headaches regarding the insufferable man."

Niya chewed her bottom lip, uncertainty swirling. "Things have changed," she admitted.

Arabessa narrowed her gaze. "Changed how?"

"They just . . . have."

"Nope. Not good enough." Arabessa crossed her arms, sitting back on her heels. "You dragged us all the way here, without us putting up a fight or peppering you with questions, I might add. We understand the need to find this final piece to the Prism Stone, but why must we save Alōs in the process?"

A flutter of nerves ran up Niya's spine. "Uh, actually there is something I haven't mentioned yet, about the Prism Stone . . . well, we actually found it."

"That's great!" said Larkyra, clutching Niya's arm.

"Yes," agreed Niya.

"Why do I sense a *but* coming?" asked Arabessa.

"*But,*" began Niya, "it's back on the ship, with the rest of the stones. I put it there before I went to get you both."

Her sisters blinked, tense silence stretching, before Arabessa abruptly stood, retracing their earlier steps back into the woods.

"Wait!" hissed Niya as she chased after her, Larkyra following on her heels. "We still need to save Alōs."

"No, we don't." Arabessa ducked under a vine. "Your mission is done. Once you return the pieces to Esrom, your oath to him will be complete. The city will be saved."

"And how do you suggest we *get* to Esrom?" Niya reasoned. "No one on board the *Crying Queen* is from there to give us access to the kingdom."

Alōs had told her that Kintra knew the means necessary to take them to Esrom in case he didn't return, but Niya wasn't about to admit that to her sisters. Not now.

Arabessa waved a hand. "Father will know someone."

"Arabessa, *please*"—Niya tugged at her sister's robe, forcing her to stop—"I can't let Alōs die!"

Her demand echoed into the treetops, sending birds into flight.

Arabessa regarded her with raised brows. "By the Fade," she breathed. "You've fallen for him."

Niya drew back, defenses rising. "No, I have not."

"Don't lie to us. We are your sisters. We *know* when you lie."

"Niya," said Larkyra gently, coming to her side. "Is this true? Do you . . . have feelings for Alōs?"

Niya felt like a cornered animal as she glanced between her two sisters. She wanted to hiss and claw away their confused expressions. Panic swirled around her, her magic spinning with her terror, but instead of lashing out, she did something even she was not prepared for.

She covered her face and cried.

And it wasn't a gentle cry. No, Niya let loose ugly, gulping tears that racked her entire body as every emotion she had grappled with for the past few months surged out of her.

She hiccuped a breath as arms suddenly wrapped tightly around her.

Larkyra and Arabessa hugged her, which only seemed to set off more tears.

But by the stars and sea, it felt good.

Even as it pained Niya to be so vulnerable, it felt like the first real breath she had taken in so very long.

"Get it out." Arabessa stroked Niya's hair.

"Yes, all of it." Larkyra's arms tightened. "Arabessa doesn't mind getting snot on her robe, do you, Ara?"

"I'm sorry." Niya wiped at her face, stepping back. "I don't know what's come over me."

"You've been through much this year," said Arabessa. "And it appears much more has come to pass between you and the pirate since you stepped aboard the *Crying Queen* than we had originally thought. We had our suspicions when we watched you both in the Thief Kingdom but were not quite sure what to make of it."

"Neither do I," admitted Niya.

"I mean, after all that he's put you through, threatened our family with," said Larkyra, "we didn't think it possible that you'd . . . but of course now, understanding his past with his brother's sickness, yet still—"

"He saved my life."

Larkyra's brows drew together. "Excuse me?"

"With the giants," said Niya. "You know how we were forced to fight for our freedom?"

Her sisters nodded.

"Alōs didn't lift a finger to hurt me. He just stood there, letting me hit him. Over and over." Her fists ached at the phantom memories of them connecting with his jaw. "He sacrificed himself so I could go free."

"He . . . he did?" Larkyra blinked.

"Are you sure?" asked Arabessa.

"Quite."

"Well then . . . ," breathed Larkyra.

"That does rather complicate things," admitted Arabessa.

"Yes," said Niya. "But it also can't. He and I . . ." That familiar pain in her chest again. "Beyond what connects us with this binding bet, our duties afterward do not lie on the same path." She shook her head. "So it doesn't matter how things might have changed. The only importance right now is that we find him, preferably *before* he dies, so he can save Esrom as he is meant to."

Her sisters watched her a long moment, no doubt wondering whether that speech had been meant to convince them or her.

"So what's our plan?" asked Arabessa.

A wave of relief fell over Niya. "We have to find where they are holding him."

"And how do you suggest we do that?" asked Larkyra. "Their city is huge, with huge citizens lumbering about."

"Yes," agreed Niya. "But I have a good hunch that he'll be kept in the chief's manor, which is at the edge of the town. We just need to—"

Niya's words died away as a shiver of cold caressed along the back of her neck.

She swiveled around, gazing into a tangle of trees.

But the jungle stayed quiet. Shards of sunlight pierced through the canopy, highlighting dancing pollen and creeping phlox.

"What is it?" asked Arabessa.

The cool touch ran along Niya's neck once again.

"That bastard," she muttered, stomping into the forest.

"Where are you going?" asked Arabessa as she and Larkyra scrambled to follow her.

"To kill someone," Niya growled.

"That seems counterintuitive." A silky voice wafted through the forest then. "Seeing as you came to save my life."

Alōs stepped from behind a moss-covered boulder, his large form not at all diminished by his surroundings. Despite his bruised face, he still moved like the prince he was, beautiful and dangerous and utterly sure of his standing.

Certainly not at all concerned that he was meant to be caged inside a giants' city just a few paces behind them.

Niya's entire being fought with a cacophony of emotions at seeing him here, alive.

"Lord Ezra." Arabessa spoke first. "We were led to believe you were about to be the centerpiece of a giant's barbecue."

Alōs's gaze moved from where it had been pinned to Niya to take in the eldest Bassette. "I was. Until I wasn't."

"Should we be preparing to run, then?" asked Larkyra.

"Not unless you desire exercise. I walked away a free man."

A bird called in the distance, filling the dubious silence as his words slammed against Niya.

"'Walked away a free man'?" she repeated, incredulous.

"Yes. With a rather warm send-off, in fact."

"No." Niya shook her head, confusion swirling. "No."

"I think it's true," said Larkyra. "He's standing right here, after all, and no giants appear to be giving chase."

"I don't believe it," Niya insisted.

"How can you not believe what you see?" asked Arabessa.

"Because!" yelled Niya. "We were forced to fight for our freedom. I bruised up your face! You were to be eaten. Why, then, would they merely *let you go*?"

"Perhaps they realized he'd taste gross?" suggested Larkyra.

"It's idiotic!" Niya threw out her hands, irritation soaring along with her magic. *Tricks,* it whispered. *Tricks.* "You're telling me I made Kintra my enemy, summoned my sisters from the far reaches of Aadilor, fought the entire crew until they lay unconscious, and then sneaked back to this horribly humid, giant-infested island in an attempt to save you, just for you to walk away a free man?"

A softness settled into Alōs's features as he held her gaze. "I'm flattered you went to such lengths, fire dancer. But yes, it appears so."

A frustrated growl ripped from Niya.

But instead of shoving him with her coiling powers, Niya found herself throwing her arms around him instead.

Alōs stiffened beneath her, no doubt just as caught off guard, but then his hands slipped across her back, hugging her tight.

"Hello," he said softly.

Niya breathed him in, savoring Alōs's cool sea breeze hidden under a layer of dirt. Her gifts swirled around his, hot and cold reunited.

He was here.

He was not dead.

He was—

A throat clearing pulled Niya from the moment.

She stepped quickly back. Cheeks no doubt ruby red.

"Well," began Arabessa. "Now that we've had that . . . reunion checked off, shall we return to the ship? I'd rather not dawdle while hungry giants roam behind us."

As they walked toward the beach, Alōs fell into step beside Niya, washing her in his cool presence. She did her best not to meet her sisters' stares. Stares that she all too easily felt aimed at her back as they kept close behind.

You've fallen for him.

Arabessa's words twisted up in her heart.

You are more valuable on this plane than I, fire dancer.

Alōs's pained gaze as he'd stroked her cheek, bleeding in her arms, gripping her tight.

She *had* fallen for him. How could she not? He had proved just how much he had changed from the young man who had once betrayed her. He'd put her life above his own. Had trusted her to complete the final part in saving his home, his brother, without him. He had given her everything as he'd lain on the floor in the giant's throne room, spoken his heart as he'd held her in her bedroom within the thief palace.

Yet still, did it change anything?

He was still a pirate captain, bound for the sea and treasure raids, just as she was duty bound to her family, to the Mousai and her king.

The emotions she was feeling—relief mixed with anger, joy mixed with confusion—muddled her thoughts even more. All she knew was that something had shifted inside her, had moved out of the way, but she didn't know what to do about it. What she *could* do about it.

She looked up then to find Alōs watching her.

He smiled, a gentle expression that set a warmth sizzling along her skin.

"You do realize," she began, wanting to push away from her confusing emotions, "you have not yet shared how you were able to walk away?"

"Yes, that—well, I demonstrated my powers."

Niya frowned up at him. "But you insisted that we didn't."

"Yes." He nodded. "And I still stand by that."

Niya let out a tired sigh. "Please, Alōs, I have used up my patience today. Speak this next part plainly."

"Of course. I apologize." Amusement danced in his glowing eyes. "After you were taken away, I was put in their kitchens. And let me tell you, that place made their trophy room look like a relaxing bath house. As I stood there watching their cook sharpen knives and mix spices, I decided one thing: if I were to die by their hands, it would only be after the biggest fight of my life. So when the cook was turned, I froze my glass jar, shattering it. As you could probably guess, the cook came running. I knocked him down, however. Their eyes," Alōs explained, seeming to notice her dubious expression. "They don't have such thick skin around their eyes. The trick, of course, is reaching them. But yes, I got that one bent over, howling in pain, only for two more to enter, then three. The entire kitchen was taken up by their massive forms as I tried to outmaneuver them, make it to some crack or opening to escape." He lifted up a vine for her to duck under. "By the end, the entire kitchen was practically covered in ice. I was exhausted, could barely stand for draining my energy so thoroughly. I had been prepared then to feel their heavy palms squash me like the pest they no doubt believed me to be. But then nothing happened, the kitchen was silent, and that's when I realized the giants were still. They have never seen ice before, you see. Have never felt such chill as what I put into the air. As you know, this is a hot land, made of eruptions in fall and humid summers. Cold is an entirely new invention for them. This is when I saw my in. I was brought before the chief, where I quickly explained my gifts, the benefits of ice—how it helps keep food from spoiling, can feel refreshing on the skin—but what really did the trick was chilling his cup of ale. I have never seen such a large, childish grin. He was utterly charmed. So I made a bargain: my services in exchange for my freedom."

"Why not just keep you prisoner to cool them forever?" asked Niya.

"Their chief had a similar idea. But I quickly showed how long I'd last as a prisoner."

Niya studied the red cut Alōs displayed along his neck. "You were prepared to take your life."

His silence was answer enough, and Niya frowned as a sliver of distress ran through her, thinking of him in such a desperate situation. "That was a risky gamble."

"I had nothing left to lose."

"I did." The words were out of her mouth before she even thought to say them.

Sapphire eyes snapped to hers.

Held hers.

A tension of longing filled them.

If they had been alone, Niya knew Alōs would have reached out to touch her then. A flutter filled her stomach; she wished he would anyway.

"What bargain did you make, Lord Ezra?" Larkyra's voice chimed in from behind. "That would satiate such greedy giants?"

Alōs dug into his pocket, revealing a green glowing orb.

"A Connection Stone?" Niya blinked up at him. "But you said—"

"Twice a year I must return and refill their ice supply or be summoned if I fail to do so," he interrupted her. "Such pain seems a trifle, really." He shrugged. "For my freedom."

Freedom.

But was it freedom if he was now tied to this island indefinitely? At least with a binding bet, once it was paid, it went away. This, well, this was meant to be forever. A burden he would have to fulfill even when old and unable to sail across such waters. What then?

Niya looked over at Alōs, wishing to ask, but something in his hardened gaze told her he did not want to speak of it.

Perhaps because he had already come to such conclusions.

Sacrifices. These were things Alōs knew. Continued to make.

Her feelings for him swelled then, blossoming like a midnight orchid under a full moon. He thought her life more valuable than his. For such a notorious pirate, he was far more selfless than any could know.

But *she* knew.

And something about that pulled the man walking beside her deeper into her heart.

A dangerous sensation, for in the end, both were held to responsibilities that would lead them elsewhere.

As their group stepped from the shade of the jungle and onto the beach, the aggressive sun had Niya shielding her eyes. The warm breeze was a welcome whip along her sweating skin. In the distance the *Crying Queen* sat like a black smudge in the otherwise-pristine blue sea.

Alōs came to her side, and together they stared out to what would bring them to their final journey.

"I could have left without you," admitted Niya after a moment.

"Yes," answered Alōs. "You could have."

But I didn't, was her unspoken response, which seemed to fill the silence.

But I didn't.

Once this was all over, however, Niya knew she would.

CHAPTER FORTY-FIVE

Daggers and knives winked along with sharp snarls as a ship full of pirates stood at the ready.

The sight momentarily amused Alōs as he slid from the banister to the wooden deck.

"What a lovely greeting this is," he said.

"Captain!" Kintra pushed forward. "You're alive."

"Sorry if that disappoints."

"We were coming to save you."

"Save me?" Alōs raised his brows. "What nonsense. Pirates are not in the business of saving anyone."

"But Niya said you were to be eaten by giants, and then the crew said the Mousai showed up—"

Her words faded as the aforementioned creatures swung over the banister behind him. Black robes swirled by their feet, hoods pulled up, faces shrouded in gold masks.

As they floated to his side, his crew tightened the grips on their blades.

Boman spat onto the deck between them. "How dare you return to this ship, cretins!"

"We assure you," came Arabessa's cool reply behind her disguise, "we are as thrilled to be back here as you are to see us."

"Then why don'ts yous jump back overboard?" Emanté suggested. "Or would yous rather we throw yous instead?"

"I'm sensing some tension here," Alōs observed.

"These lackeys of the Thief King knocked us all out," grumbled Boman.

"They can't do that, Cap'n!" cried Bree.

"Yet it appears that we did," said Larkyra.

Though she was masked, Alōs could hear the smile in the youngest Bassette's voice.

"Nobody takes on the *Crying Queen* without consequences!" Saffi shouted.

His pirates rumbled their agreement.

"Then by all means." Alōs stepped to the side, revealing the Mousai. "Seek your revenge, but know Niya called them to help with similar intentions as all you."

"As we *told* them we were," said Arabessa. "But I'm afraid you employ dim-witted souls, Lord Ezra; they forced us to fight."

"We didn't force anyone—"

Alōs raised placating hands, cutting off Saffi. He was too tired for this. "Please, while I'm flattered that so many of you care enough to want to save me, as it turns out, I didn't need it. I saved myself. Which, can any of you really be that surprised to hear?" He raised a brow.

"No, Cap'n," said Saffi. "But . . . that means"—she turned to Kintra, who stood beside her—"Niya was telling you the truth. She did fetch aid like she said she was gonna. I *told you* she was one of us."

Kintra did not reply, merely kept her narrowed eyes suspiciously trained on the black-robed trio.

"Where is that girl anyway?" asked Alōs, breaking the tension and feigning to look around the deck.

"We don't know, Cap'n," answered Bree.

"We searched everywhere," said Therza.

"She wasn't on the boat when I woke up," Kintra explained.

"Woke up?" Alōs looked to his quartermaster. "My dear Kintra, you must not have been that concerned if you were able to take a nap before my rescue."

"*Sir*, that is not how it happened."

"No? Is that nasty bump on your head how it happened, then?"

"It is part of it," said Kintra through grinding teeth. "Yes."

"Well, why don't you tell me all about it after we set sail?"

"Set sail?" asked Boman. "Does that mean you found what yous was looking for, Cap'n?"

"Aye, which means we must prepare the ship for Esrom." He strode through the group, which parted easily as he made his way toward his captain's quarters. He needed to wash his face and change his clothes and pour himself a drink. No, an entire bottle.

"Sir." Boman placed a hand on Alōs's arm, momentarily stopping him.

He glanced down to it in surprise—his crew never touched him—before meeting his helmsman's gaze.

"I'm glad to hear you got what yous was after," he said, the earnestness in the old man's voice settling uncomfortably in Alōs's chest.

He still wasn't sure how to feel about his pirates showing him empathy. It seemed a contradiction to, well, them being pirates.

Thankfully Boman turned from Alōs, freeing him from a need to respond.

Kintra came to his side next. "Are we waiting for Niya before we set sail?" she asked. "And what of these three?" She nodded to the Mousai, who stood poised, watching the scurrying crew with curious gazes. None of his pirates dared to get too near. The trio were like carved statues meant to scare away pigeons. And Niya, hidden in the middle.

Alōs drank in her shorter form. And as though she felt his gaze, from beneath her gold mask, blue eyes collided with his.

It was like coming home.

She had come back for him. Had called her sisters to help. Something sharp and hot cut open his heart at the thought. Did he dare hope this meant she now trusted him? Cared for him? As he cared for her. Every muscle in his body was coiled to remain in control, when all he wished to do was pull her into his sleeping quarters and find out. Interrogate her with his mouth and caresses until she was so drunk on her desire for him that she'd be helpless but to answer truthfully.

As it was, however, he could do none of those things.

So he shook the desire from his mind, turning back to Kintra.

"Portal doors are useful for making trades," he explained. "I have a feeling Niya will be returned once they are."

"It was generous of the king to extend such help after everything." Kintra held his stare. "He will expect the action to be reciprocated."

"Yes," agreed Alōs. "I suspect he will have many tasks for me once all this is done."

"And it will be done?" she asked. "The final piece . . . Niya showed me—"

He nodded. "It will be done."

An ever-present tension in Kintra's shoulders appeared to ease then. A well of emotion filling her amber eyes.

They had been on this journey together for a very long while.

And yet, Alōs realized, he still felt no relief with the promise of its end. For it meant the finishing of another.

CHAPTER FORTY-SIX

*T*he portal door glowed bright, an image of a captain's quarters on the other side, as Niya stood beyond its light in the Thief Kingdom. The dark city twinkled temptingly below her and her sisters, gathered on a ledge rimming the caved world. Cool air collected in her lungs as she took in her first breath of relief.

"I truly cannot thank you enough," said Niya as she handed Larkyra her Mousai disguise of black robe and mask. Underneath she had kept on her pirate uniform, which remained worn and dirt stained from her time on Hallowed Island. She knew she smelled but had now grown used to such characteristics of living aboard a ship among scoundrels. No longer did it bother her. Much.

"There will come a time when you can repay us, I'm sure." Larkyra smiled, tucking Niya's disguise under her arm.

"For now, though," began Arabessa, who stood beside Larkyra, her gold mask still on, "take care of the rest of your journey swiftly and safely. You are almost done, sister." She stepped up to clasp Niya's hands. "We hope to see you back in Jabari soon."

Niya nodded, the thought of returning home now an abstract desire. The acute ache that usually accompanied the thought no longer as great. But she forced away what that possibly meant as she said, "I will be back as soon as I am able. And tell Charlotte she better have a basket full of sugar rolls waiting for me when I return."

Arabessa huffed a laugh. "I'm sure she and Cook will have all of your favorites piled high in the kitchen."

"Good. It will take a proper month to rid my body of the slop I've had to endure on that pirate ship."

"I'll be staying in Jabari until you return as well," said Larkyra. "I would not be a proper sister if I wasn't there for your welcome party."

Niya's chest tightened, tears threatening to break free once more. She was becoming a right emotional mess these days. "Thank you," she said, hugging each of her sisters.

"One last thing," said Arabessa as they stepped back, glancing to the awaiting portal door. "Regarding your pirate."

"He's not *my* anything," corrected Niya pointedly.

"Don't be daft. You both are keen on one another, and it wouldn't take a *senseer* to know that," explained Arabessa. "Just be careful there, okay? Before you fall too deep, it might be best to know his intentions when all this is said and done, and what you are willing to give up to meet them. Our lives in Jabari are flexible, but remember, our duties here are not."

The sharp grip to her heart again. "Yes, I know."

"He is different than Larkyra's husband. He's settled in one place, whereas a life of a pirate—"

"By the lost gods, Arabessa," breathed Niya in horror. "*I'm not going to marry anyone.* Now I must go, before you insult me further."

"I just—"

"Nope!" Niya covered her ears as she backed toward the portal. "You've officially ruined this farewell. I will look forward to you making it up to me later. Now, goodbye!"

She turned, slipping from the Thief Kingdom and back into the warm cabin aboard the *Crying Queen*. Scooping up the portal token, she slammed the portal door shut behind her.

Two sets of eyes and the muffled sound of lapping waves greeted her.

"Welcome back," said Alōs from where he sat behind his desk, amber glass in hand. Through his windowpanes rested a dark sea, the moon only a crescent of light.

Kintra was in one of two chairs across from him, ankle on knee, sharing a similar drink.

She eyed Niya suspiciously as she drew near.

"Come, sit with us." Alōs poured Niya a glass from the bottle on his desk, sliding it toward her.

She took it, slipping into a chair.

Alōs was freshly washed, his inky hair sweeping his shoulders, pristine black shirt rolled up at the sleeves and hugging his broad chest.

The blank line of their binding bet was now reduced to a mere square on the top of his wrist. Niya forced herself not to look at her own, to see the last mark that bound her to this man.

Free.

Soon she would be free.

The word no longer seemed to hold its sweet allure.

"We are having a celebratory drink," said Alōs. "Also one of clemency, for it appears there might be some . . . retained hostility between you two."

Niya raised her brows, looking at Kintra. "If there is anger in the air, it is not coming from me."

"You used your magic on me, *again*," said the quartermaster, fire in her brown eyes.

"Yes, because you were trying to skewer me with your knife. I told you the truth about trying to help Alōs. It is not *my* fault you wished to not believe me. If anything, it is *I* who should be angry with you."

The quartermaster snorted her incredulity before tipping back the rest of her drink and slamming it onto Alōs's desk. She stood. "I find this useless, Captain. Can we just agree that she and I will not be chumming it up anytime soon? Plus, she'll be leaving. There is no point in it."

There is no point in it.

The words hit up against Niya, tangling with her own uncertainties regarding her and Alōs.

I'll be leaving. There is no point in it.

A squeeze to her heart.

"Listen, it's obvious my presence offends you," she said to Kintra. "But perhaps it has less to do with me and you and more to do with you and Alōs."

Kintra glared down at her. "And what does that mean?"

"Well, it's obvious that you two . . ." She waved a hand between them. "Share a history. As I am to leave soon, like you reminded all of us, it is not my intention to get in the way of past lovers."

A thick silence filled the room. The trickling of the sandglass on Alōs's desk the only reminder of time passing.

And then the quiet was drowned in laughter, from both Alōs and Kintra.

"Lovers?" Kintra held her side as the word gasped from her. "By the stars and sea, can you imagine?" She looked toward Alōs.

He had leaned back in his chair, regarding Niya with mirth and a strange spark of pleasure.

"What?" she said, irritation flaring.

"Niya," began Alōs, "what in all of Aadilor gave you the impression Kintra and I were ever lovers?"

"Well . . ." She looked from one to the other. "You said . . . you said Kintra was the exception. And it's obvious you are close. Closer than any others on board."

"Because she is my second-in-command," he said. "Kintra was one of the first to become a pirate aboard my ship. Our history runs long."

"And?" Niya frowned, an unwanted spark of jealousy overtaking her as these facts only fueled her theory.

"And I like women, Red."

Niya blinked over to the quartermaster. "So?" she said. "I like women too."

Alōs tilted his head. "You do?"

"Sure. Women have warmed my bed as much as any man."

"Well," began Kintra, "I find many things not to like in a man. So many that I only take women to *my* bed."

Niya let her words settle. "Oh."

Kintra raised a brow. "Yes, *oh*. I am very fond of the captain, but not in the sense that, well, you might be." She held Niya's gaze. *Yes, I know more than you think,* the look seemed to say. "So no, my annoyance with you has *nothing* to do with my *friendship* with Alōs."

"Then what does it have to do with?"

"Perhaps you're just not that likable," she challenged.

Niya snorted her disbelief. "That's impossible. Everyone likes me."

At this Kintra smiled, "Well, I am not like everyone. And you came aboard this ship with your own intentions, which were very different from all of ours. I would not be doing my duty if I became as charmed by you as everyone else."

"Everyone is charmed by me?" Niya perked up.

Kintra rolled her eyes. "What I mean is, I'm the captain's right-hand woman. I'm meant to distrust others for his best interest. You did not appear to be in his best interest."

"Me?" Niya jutted her chin out. "I fear you forget it was *you all* who kidnapped me and started this entire mess of a journey, *not* the other way around."

"Yes," agreed Kintra. "But time has a funny way of changing intentions. And plans."

"Careful," warned Alōs.

His quartermaster met his hard stare, something passing between the two that Niya could not read.

"But I'll leave you both to figure that part out," she said, glancing back at Niya. "If you'll excuse me, Captain, I'll inform the crew we are to sail to Esrom presently?"

He gave her a nod, his eyes trained on her all the way out of his quarters.

A new tension filled the room as Niya now sat alone with Alōs.

She met his gaze, his contained power behind his desk palpable as he took her in.

"How do you feel?" he asked. "Now with your binding bet almost paid?"

The question stirred up a mixture of replies. Happy. Distraught. Proud. *Confused.*

Niya felt it all but instead said, "I'm sure close to how you feel with being so near to returning the stone."

He watched her a long moment. "Yes," he said. "Indeed."

"You did it, Alōs." She gave him a small smile. "You saved Esrom."

"From a threat I created."

His quick reply had her frowning. Would he not give himself any reprieve of responsibility? Of guilt?

"You did not create your brother's sickness," she said.

Alōs did not respond, merely looked into his glass, which now sat empty in his hands.

"What will you do after the Prism Stone is returned?"

He gave a shrug. "Whatever my pirates want to do, I suppose. I owe them much after they've followed me through this mess of a voyage."

"Your actions may have served you, but they were always for another," she reminded him. "You're not as selfish as you might want others to believe, you know?"

His turquoise gaze met hers. "And what do you believe?"

That I care for you more than I want to.

"I believe that I might actually trust a pirate now." She smiled. "Despite what trouble that might land me in later."

His responding chuckle warmed her. "And it only took me nearly dying to finally convince you."

"I am not a prize won by simple favors." She arched a brow.

"No." His features grew serious. "And even then, you are not a flame meant to be contained on anyone's mantel but your own."

If Niya had not been sitting, Alōs's words would have set her back a step.

She held his stare, gooseflesh dancing along her arms.

Dangerous, her magic whispered.

This man was too dangerous.

She did not trust herself to remain alone with him any longer. After everything she had done today, survived, she needed a moment alone. She needed to collect herself, away from the all-consuming presence of this pirate. She needed to figure out what she wanted. And perhaps more importantly, how much she could afford to want.

"I should get cleaned up," she said, standing abruptly. "And I'm sure you have to help Kintra get us to Esrom."

Alōs watched her back away toward the door. "Niya—"

"I'll see you topside," she interrupted, nerves jumping to run, to flee, before he said anything to make their parting more painful.

But as Niya strode from his quarters into the dark hallway of the ship, she knew this man already held the power to break her heart again.

Yet this time, she also held the power to break his.

CHAPTER FORTY-SEVEN

Alōs knelt before his brother in the Hall of Starlight. Guards surrounded him, blue-sparking spears aimed to kill. It had been the first time the *Crying Queen* had ever docked at Esrom's main harbor. The first time in six years that Alōs had walked through the capital, Silver City, to enter the palace. Citizens had stared in disbelief; court members had thrown insults, many spitting at his feet. Alōs was the Betrayal Prince. The traitorous son who'd stolen their precious Prism Stone—a holy relic of the lost gods given upon their final parting. Had they known the true power it held, that it kept Esrom safely in its bubble under the sea, he no doubt would have been hanged as soon as he'd been seen placing boot to ground. Luckily that particular secret was kept tightly within the palace walls.

Now here he was, bowing to their new king in an attempt to reverse time.

His magic churned in anticipation, a cold veneer around his heart his last attempt to contain the coil of hope he dared allow slip in, the hope that all he had suffered would finally come to an end this day.

"You have created quite a stir, showing up as you have after so many years," said Ariōn from his white coral throne. He was flanked on either side by the six High Surbs. Alōs noted with satisfaction that Ixō stood the closest. "As well as bringing pirates to our shores, no less. A bold move for the most wanted man in this kingdom."

"My crew knows not to breach land, Your Grace. Though I cannot account for their actions if any of your guards attack first."

"*My* guards are trained in peace," said King Ariōn. "A novel concept, I'm sure, for your lot. Now tell me quickly why you have shown your face here. My High Surbs tell me you have returned in the hopes of a pardon for your treason."

"I come seeking only a moment of your time, Your Grace. If my sentencing still stands afterward, so be it. I will not return to these lands again."

"If your sentencing still stands, pirate, you will be arrested and executed."

Alōs looked into Ariōn's foggy eyes, and though his brother was blind, he felt the passing of understanding and excitement in the young king, despite his threat, to finally find his older brother kneeling here.

Soon our past will officially be behind us, so we may start a new beginning.

Yes, thought Alōs with a pang of longing. *Let us hope.*

Though the silver drippings of his brother's sickness stood out prominently across his brown skin, Ariōn filled his throne well, with his shoulders back and chin tipped up with regal grace. A spark of pride shot through Alōs as he took him in. Ariōn made a great king.

"Yes, Your Grace," replied Alōs, bowing his head once more. "I understand."

"It was risky coming here, knowing your possible fate."

"Suicidal," added High Surb Dhruva, her ruthless gaze pinned to Alōs.

"Which has me begging the question," Ariōn continued: "What would grant such magnanimous forgiveness?"

"I have brought back the Prism Stone." As Alōs reached into his satchel, guards stepped closer from where they flanked him, spears poking into his back.

"Stand down." Ariōn raised a hand. "Let us see if he speaks true before we fill him with holes."

Alōs gently laid out each piece of the red gem on the tiled floor.

They winked richly against the white marble, a whispering of their power churning in each of their centers.

"Come, pirate," sneered Dhruva. "You think us fools to believe your lies, your pirate tricks. My king, he has not brought back the Prism Stone. He lays at your feet useless shards of—"

"*Silence,*" commanded Ariōn. "That is the second time you have spoken out of turn, High Surb Dhruva. I highly suggest it be your last."

"My apologies, Your Grace." The old woman bowed her repentance. "I merely want to make sure you could see what—"

"I see more than any of you do."

The hall filled with a chill of wind as the young king summoned forth what power he could afford.

Alōs drew his brows together. He knew such an act would drain his strength quickly.

"Yes, Your Grace." Dhruva bowed low once more, lips pursed. "Of course."

Ariōn settled his cloudy eyes back on Alōs. "Hand me the stones."

The throne room swam with tension as Alōs approached his brother. They were a study in contrasts. Alōs wore shadows, his form large and imposing. Ariōn's slender body was wrapped in delicate white spun fabric.

Alōs met Ixō's gaze, a gleam of relief in the surb's expression, as he placed the pieces into his brother's delicate hand.

Ariōn closed his eyes as he felt over the shards.

And then a small smile edged along his lips.

"You have indeed brought us back our Prism Stone," he said. "I feel the whispers of the lost gods within, but will it provide us with what it once did, broken like this?"

Alōs held the young king's gaze. "Let us put it back together and see."

They stood in the Room of Wells, a cavernous chamber deep within the center of the palace. Alōs remained flanked by guards, but he paid little mind to their spears at his back. His thoughts had tumbled to the past, to the last time he had been here, in this ancient room where hundreds of waterfalls poured from the rocky walls. He had been a young man, possibly still a boy, creeping onto the thin walkway that floated above a liquid abyss. His eyes had been trained on the dais at the end, where the Prism Stone floated like a red sun under the thinnest of the waterfalls—the Weeping Waters. It cascaded from an opening in the ceiling. The epicenter of their protective bubble under the Obasi Sea. As the water hit the stone, it refracted into rainbows, powerful magic filling the wells far below, veins threaded throughout Esrom. He had been told at a young age how the Room of Wells was the beating heart of his kingdom, where the air sparkled with healing wet mist. Where the pure energy of the lost gods could be felt.

It had stolen Alōs's breath then.

Now his hung still.

The Weeping Waters fell uselessly over an empty dais. No sparkle or refracting colors in the air.

Alōs could only sense a thin veil of magic clinging desperately to fading power. A dying soul.

"Even if this works, pirate," whispered Dhruva at his side, "your sins against this land will never be forgotten."

"If this works, surb, then I am glad to have sinned, for my actions to save my brother were not in vain, when you and your holy order did nothing until I forced your hand. I will never forget *that*."

Dhruva's lips thinned as she joined her council at the top of the walkway near the king.

What a useless lot of hot air, Alōs thought, studying the group.

Well, except one.

"Ixō, will you do the honors?" Ariōn nodded toward the white-haired surb, who stood with him closest to the round dais at the end. Ixō was never far from the young king.

"Of course, Your Grace."

Ixō stepped up to the dais, uncovering the three pieces of the Prism Stone.

"Alōs," Ariōn called to him. "Will you stand beside me?"

"Your Grace," cautioned one of the High Surbs, "I do not think that wise—"

"If my brother's intentions were less than honorable, he would not have come to us so openly. Now please, give us space."

Alōs ignored the surbs' scathing glares as they backed away, allowing him to pass through and approach Ariōn and Ixō.

"You have done it, brother," said Ariōn with quiet triumph as they stood side by side, facing where Ixō waited before the single waterfall sifting through the dais.

"Let us see what happens before you start congratulating," replied Alōs.

"Even if it does not work, the actions you've taken for our people have been noted. We will deal with the consequences together."

Our people.

Together.

Alōs could have reminded his brother that, no, it would only be Esrom's king to bear the burden of this kingdom going topside. That if this did not work, Ariōn would have no other choice but to order his execution. A very public one, no doubt. But Alōs was tired of thinking of life's cruel realities, so he said nothing. *Let Ariōn have a moment to hope,* he thought, for it had been so very long since he had been allowed.

The Karēk brothers stood shoulder to shoulder as Ixō sent tendrils of blue magic into the air to lift up each shard of the Prism Stone and float them. The surb spun his hands and worked his fingers as if he held the pieces himself, fitting the three together before the thin trickle of the Weeping Waters.

Alōs held his breath, the pounding of his heart an echo in his ears as the fate of his life and his brother's kingdom hung on a slipping of red stones coming together.

For a grain fall nothing happened. The Prism Stone remained a dull, dead red, hovering above the High Surb's hands. Alōs realized then just how much he had been wrung dry by life's disappointments, for a part of him was not surprised. A numb acceptance.

And then—

"Look, Your Grace!" Ixō called.

Above him the seams within the jaggedly cut rock glowed red hot, fissures resealing what was broken, until the stone leaped high. It spun dizzily in place, and Alōs sensed what little magic was left in the room getting sucked into it.

Wind whipped through the cavernous chamber, sending a few High Surbs toppling to the thin walkway behind them. Alōs pulled his brother close as the room shook, and Ixō quickly ran to them, wrapping his arms around the young king as well, becoming another layer of protection over Ariōn.

Bits of moss and rock fell from walls as water soaked their clothes from the waterfalls being blown about. Alōs turned up his gaze to watch a liquid arm reach out from the central waterfall above the dais. It snatched the spinning, glowing stone from the air, pulling it into the Weeping Waters with a snap.

Magic and colors exploded.

The Prism Stone was finally home, and it screamed its relief, shooting out every thread of energy.

Alōs crouched farther over his brother as magic spun hot, cold, rough, and silky across his skin.

And then as quickly as the chaos had ensued, everything fell quiet, the final note a relieved sigh.

Alōs felt Ixō's hesitant release as he stood. Alōs lifted his head, blinking to clear his vision.

And a gasp rattled from him.

The room sparkled diamonds. The air turned sweet as it was filled with the lost gods' misting magic. The Prism Stone was now wedged high above in the Weeping Waters, out of reach of any greedy hands. Rainbow threads poured from beneath it, once again bloating the water below, filling it with magic. The Room of Wells was restored. And thus, so was Esrom.

Ariōn stood at Alōs's side for a moment before leaving him to pass Ixō and step toward the dais.

He wanted to reach out and pull him back, to shelter him from any other possible harm that still lingered. But Alōs remained still as the young king approached the end of the walkway, his silver crown reflecting the multicolored waterfall as he came to a stop before it, the Prism Stone pulsing bright above. Ariōn ran fingers through the cascading water and let out a breath of sensation.

When he turned back to Alōs, his smile was radiant. "Now can I congratulate you?"

Alōs shook his head, and though the moment was indeed a relieving one, he could not share in his brother's grin. "I do not deserve praise in returning what I had taken."

Ariōn frowned at his words as he walked back to his side. "The burden of what you did sat with both of us." He placed a hand on his shoulder. "But it is over now, Alōs. You've done it. And I am honored to welcome you home, brother."

How long Alōs had yearned to hear those words. He'd traveled to the ends of Aadilor in the hopes of one day being led back. Now here he stood, no longer hiding in shadows but openly beside Ariōn, both given a chance to make up for the years they'd lost.

Alōs looked to the Prism Stone, glowing red and strong, feeling far away from a moment that was most assuredly meant to be a triumphant one.

The item he had stolen burned euphoric at being back where it belonged.

Was it truly done?

Could he finally stop running to make up for his past?

At the thought, Alōs's wrist began to burn. He did not look down at what he knew he would no longer find: his binding bet.

Done. It was all done.

Despite the release he knew he should feel, the relief, Alōs's chest remained tight.

There was something taken still left to return.

CHAPTER FORTY-EIGHT

*I*t was night, but no one in Esrom slept.

Within the palace, Niya stood by the open window of her guest room, the kingdom alive with uproarious celebration below. Lanterns lit the streets like firebugs, casting warmth over the dancing citizens as flutes and drumbeats echoed in the air.

Word of the Prism Stone's return had spread like shooting stars across the islands, along with the truth of why the Betrayal Prince had stolen it—to save his dying brother. A strategic political move by the king and his council, no doubt, now that everything was back in order.

The citizens of Esrom were hungry for a bout of good news after such a long succession of sorrow within the royal family. They were quick to forgive the elder prince's sins.

It appeared Alōs was to get all he desired.

Wrapping her arms around herself, Niya held in a chill that filtered through the window.

She was still in her robe, her outfit for tonight untouched on her bed. She was meant to dress and join the party, her pirates somewhere among the merry crowds.

Although, Niya thought, frowning, she supposed they were no longer *her* pirates, now that she was free of her binding bet to their captain.

Her chest grew heavy as she peered down at her wrist.

Empty.

Pale.

No trace of the mark that had once bound her tightly to a ship, its captive turned crew.

She was free.

Then why did this not leave her elated?

Because, a voice whispered, *you have found another sort of freedom aboard the* Crying Queen.

With an uncomfortable twist, Niya let this thought sink in, knowing the truth in it. Though she loved her family and her role with the Mousai, she had found she was able to test and explore new corners of her strengths and weaknesses with these pirates. She had fought to sail through storms, worked side by side under countless days of heat and sailing, survived the wrath of a ship full of angry crew, and lived through pain and homesickness she'd thought might break her. Aboard the ship they had their own rules, unbound by queens or kings, sisters or brothers, cities or kingdoms, but created from what kept them alive as they sailed toward the endless sea's horizon. Then there was the captain, Alōs, who welcomed her blaze of heat as he met it head-on with his cool. Alōs, whom she'd believed was her worst adversary, had ended up being a mirror to her endless possibilities.

But it was all over now.

Tomorrow they would sail topside, her final leg aboard the *Crying Queen* before they returned her to Jabari. Where she would resume her life, her duties.

A knock sounded at her door, and before she even called for them to enter, with a flutter in her chest, she knew who it would be.

"It appears I am destined to always find you indisposed," said Alōs as he drank in her robed form from where he stood silhouetted by the light cast from the hall behind him.

"Or perhaps there is never a good time for us to be alone." She turned fully toward him, a buzz of treacherous anticipation awakening.

She had been avoiding him since they'd arrived in Esrom, not that it had been hard to do. Alōs had been ensconced by his brother and people, always surrounded. Still, she knew, despite how she might try to twirl from his grasp, he would eventually find her. He always did.

And perhaps because of that, she decided to finally stand still. To face their parting head-on and bear the consequences later. As she had learned to in the past.

"Interesting theory," he mused. Closing the door behind him, he approached slowly. "How do you suppose we should test it?"

Niya momentarily closed her eyes. "Alōs . . . ," she began.

"Yes?" His voice was a challenge as he stopped beside the roaring fire. His shadow stretched toward her over the plush carpet. Still a distance away, and she could feel his delicate touch of cool. *Say what is on your mind, fire dancer,* his gaze prodded.

"What brought you to my room?" asked Niya instead.

A flash of disappointment before his reply: "The crew were wondering why you were not celebrating with them. I came to find answers."

"Any of your pirates would have done that for you."

"Yes, I'm sure they would have if I had asked."

"Why didn't you?"

He gave her a look then, as if to say, *You and I both know why.*

"Niya," he said as he stepped closer, until he was directly in front of her, his glowing turquoise eyes taking her in, his features a study in beautiful angles. Niya's belly twisted with desire as she inhaled his scent: sea and midnight orchids. "We should talk."

Dread filled her. "Talking is far too overrated."

A small smile on his lips. "Normally I would agree, but presently I think we have something to discuss."

She turned back to the window, stared out into the night lit by celebration.

"What is there to discuss? It's over," said Niya. "Esrom is saved, and I have paid my debt to you."

"And this upsets you?" His breath was warm along her shoulder.

She squeezed her eyes closed. "No." *Yes.*

"Then what troubles you?"

Tomorrow, she answered silently as she slipped away from his crowding form, moving toward her bed. She ran fingers over the silk wrap dress that had been laid out for her.

A roar of a group's laughter filtered up into her room from the streets below, the joyous beat of a new melody being spun into the air.

"Esrom is happy tonight," said Niya, still not looking at him as she changed the subject.

"They will be celebrating for many days," agreed Alōs. "My brother has decreed today a new holiday."

She smiled at that. "I'm glad the king has found happiness. The lost gods know he has had a hard start in life. You both have."

Niya could feel Alōs studying her from where he had remained by the window, could feel the desire in his energy to move toward her, reach out and touch her. Again.

And by the Fade, how badly she wanted that, too, which was exactly why she was fighting it. She was terrified of this passion she felt for him. Passion greater than anything she had known before. It surpassed her old anger, her need for revenge. It soared higher and gripped her harder than any performance she had danced. Her sisters always said she burned hot, and it appeared it was true even in love.

Love.

Was that what she was feeling? A surge of panic overtook her.

"My brother wants to meet you," said Alōs, his words bringing her back with a jolt. "Officially this time."

"Me?" Niya spun to regard him. "Why?"

"Perhaps to apologize for throwing you into our dungeons."

"As I recall," she said, "that happened because *you* called me a spy."

He lifted a brow. "And are you not?"

"Not *always.*"

"Were you not spying on me that night?" Alōs approached her carefully, as though trying not to scare away a wild thing.

"I was following you, not spying on you."

"Ah, I see. Thank you for clearing that up."

"You know"—Niya frowned, watching him draw nearer—"you can be quite annoying."

Alōs grinned as though the insult were a compliment as he stood before her once more. Tentatively he lifted a hand to brush loose strands of her hair behind her ear. Niya remained perfectly still, the gentle caress sending shivers all the way to her toes. "Niya," he began softly, "my brother wants to meet you because I told him how you helped me find the pieces of the Prism Stone. He wants to meet you because I told him how important you are. To me."

His words penetrated through her, restarting her heart so it would no longer beat the same.

Niya stood breathless.

When she had first been brought aboard the *Crying Queen*, she had been so clear in her task: survive however long it took to be free once more.

But then she had warmed to the pirates, even found friendships among them. Her eyes had been opened to a new kind of adventure, and that included this man.

Alōs was Niya's ultimate foolishness. She had given him another chance to stand in the center of her life. And he'd proved worthy by choosing instead to stand at her side. Alōs had filled Niya's mind with words of their strength together, not animosity. Even shown her that he believed her life more important than his.

What was Niya to do with all that?

She no longer recognized her next move.

Especially when her only path was paved for her to return home.

"Stay," said Alōs. "As part of the *Crying Queen*."

Niya blinked, his words rocking her back a step.

"What?"

"Stay with me, Niya. We do not have to sail you back to Jabari tomorrow."

She shook her head, brows drawn together. "You know that's impossible."

"Why?"

"Well, for starters, your crew would not take kindly to you suddenly playing favorites. For if I were to stay, I can assure you, I would *not* be sleeping in the hold smashed between those flatulent pirates."

"Of course not." His gaze darkened. "You'd be warming my bed."

"Alōs—"

"My crew would take kindly to whatever makes their captain happy, Niya."

"I"—Niya faltered—"I make you happy?"

"You make me many things, fire dancer. Happy is merely one."

Niya's breathing felt ragged along with her racing pulse. "You know why I cannot stay, Alōs. It's for the same reason you must always go. Different lives and responsibilities call for us to return. You have the sea, the *Crying Queen*, and your pirates. I have my duties to the Thief King and my family. Our paths may move around one another but can never be long beside each other."

A crease pinched between Alōs's brows, shadows falling across his features.

"And I am not saying this to be cruel," she went on, even as the pain wedged itself deeper into her chest. "We both know I speak true."

"Yes," he said after a moment. "But I still had to ask."

Her throat felt tight.

There, laid out before them, the finality of what had needed to be spoken. The reality of tomorrow.

"I need to get dressed." She tried to turn from him, but Alōs stopped her.

"Or you do not."

A flutter of nerves as she watched his eyes drop to her lips. "I don't?"

Alōs shook his head. "You're free now, remember? You can do whatever you want."

"You are also free," said Niya. "Free of the burden of me bound to you."

"No," said Alōs, his gaze consuming her, "even when you're gone, fire dancer, I will never be free of you." Alōs was her eclipse as he pulled her into his shadows and kissed her then. Niya fell into the darkness willingly, a whimper escaping her as his hands gathered her close, kneading along her back, over her hips.

Alōs claimed her mouth with a desperation Niya returned. She ran fingers through his hair as he lifted her and settled them atop her bed. His weight was delicious, rocking where she ached for him most. Her gown spread beneath them was forgotten as Alōs ran powerful hands up her thigh, over her waist, before parting her robe. He took one of her nipples into his mouth, and Niya groaned, arching her back.

Niya had been a fool to think she could have ever denied herself this man tonight. She couldn't, when she knew how perfectly they fit pressed against one another, their magic a swirling of opposite sensations, ones they each were ravenous to pull inside like their next breaths.

The hostile valley that had once existed between them had been blown apart and rebuilt. The foundation new, powerful. As powerful as each of them, which made it close to impenetrable.

"Niya," Alōs rumbled as he kissed his way up her neck, "I will never have enough of you."

"Tonight," said Niya, "we must each find our fills tonight."

"An impossible task," said Alōs. "My hunger for you is bottomless."

"Then you must do your best to fill me."

Alōs's grin was wicked. "With pleasure." He gathered her into his arms and took her mouth so no other words could be spoken.

They told each other what they needed with tugs and pulls, with fingers digging into skin and groans between thrusts.

Niya took Alōs into her world of movement, of vibrating sensations that racked each of their bodies with euphoria, only to be whipped back into another impossible hunger of desire. She rode him, staring deeply into the burning gaze of the pirate lord, once a prince and now a man she loved, and told him the words she could not speak out loud, could not share, for fear that her duty would then shift and she would find it impossible to leave him.

Yet even though she trapped the words inside, she could tell Alōs understood what she held back, for he pulled her down toward him and kissed her with a new sense of urgency. "Yes, fire dancer." His voice rumbled in a husky whisper against her lips. "Me too." He flipped her beneath him, spreading her wide before reentering her. "Me too," he repeated before he filled her again, completely, endlessly.

Niya's reality slipped away as Alōs moved to taste every curve of her body, lick his way over every hill. He poured out his magic to braid with her own, until Niya did not know which sensation was hers or his. There was only them, stretching and pulling everywhere.

That night, Niya knew Alōs would stay with her as long as he could. Because come morning, both would be leaving.

CHAPTER FORTY-NINE

Niya leaned along the banister at the bow of the *Crying Queen*, the sea air whipping her braid behind her as she watched the land draw nearer on the far horizon. They had slipped out of the Stream only a few sand falls ago, leaving Esrom far below the waves, before sailing the remaining short distance to Jabari.

Niya's resolve churned in a cascade of emotions, matching the waves cutting along the ship. Excitement, despair, relief, grief, triumph—but always mixed in with the lot was heartache.

She frowned against the constant painful throb in her chest as she took in the familiar harbor in the distance. White sails of other ships; the squawk of gulls soaring high above; the smell of fish in the air, netted and tugged onto decks. The city rose proudly from the sea, up a hill's crest, to peak at the very center with the gathering of proud marble dwellings. Her own home was somewhere up there, among the wealthy. Her father was most likely in his study or on the veranda with her sisters, all gathered, she hoped, to await her official return. A smile finally broke along her features. It would be a welcome distraction to run toward them, thought Niya. Her family was always the best poultice to any wound.

"Are you sure you don't want to remain a pirate?" asked Saffi, who had been leaning beside her on the railing with Bree. The master gunner's gray braids gleamed whiter in the morning light as she turned to regard Niya. "As much as it pains me to admit, Red, you are a competent artillery crew member. I will be sad to see you go."

"I only ever really cleaned the cannons," Niya pointed out.

"Yes, but they have never shone so bright," said Saffi with a smile.

"Death is better than goodbyes," said Bree, pouting on Niya's other side.

Niya turned to her with raised brows. "And how's that?"

"At least when the Fade takes you," explained Bree, "you have no choice but to go."

Niya's gaze softened, taking in the small girl. "My choice to go back to my home is not my way of abandoning you."

"Then what is it?" Bree folded her arms tightly.

Niya regarded her bunkmate, whom she had grown to cherish. "Would you consider Saffi a sister?"

"What?" Bree bounced her confused gaze to the master gunner beside Niya.

"You have sailed aboard this ship for a while now, yes?" asked Niya. Bree nodded.

"And though I know it probably goes against pirate code to call any of your shipmates friends," said Niya, "you certainly may think of them as family—am I correct?"

Bree frowned. "I suppose . . ."

"And though you may fight and disagree *a lot*, you still find you quite like them when all is said and done, right?"

"Well, yeah," said Bree. "So?"

"So that describes a lot of families. Which would make Saffi here like a sister to you."

"A much *wiser*, tougher, and more skilled older sister," Saffi added with a sly grin.

"Yes, of course, as only older sisters are," agreed Niya coyly before turning back to Bree. "Well, you see, I also have sisters that have missed me since I've been gone. It is unfair to keep them from my presence any longer, just as it would be unfair to rob any of your brothers and sisters aboard the *Crying Queen* of your charms if you left them for too long."

"I wouldn't exactly call it robbin' us if this mouse suddenly disappeared," said Saffi. "More like gifting us with quiet."

Niya bit back a laugh as she watched Bree glare toward the master gunner. "This must be the part of having a family member who you'd like to throw overboard."

"Mouse," chuckled Saffi, "if you could lift me overboard, I would give you my extra biscuits for a month."

"I see my lesson has taken on new meaning," mused Niya as she watched the young girl charge Saffi, grunting as she attempted to move the older woman's hulking form.

"What's going on here?" asked Therza, waddling toward them from the main deck.

"Mouse here is trying to throw me overboard," said Saffi, pushing Bree off from where she had climbed onto her shoulders.

She hit the deck with an *oof*.

Therza's dark brows rose. "She ain't doing much of a job of it, is she?"

"I don't think I like having sisters," Bree huffed from her spot by their feet.

"Sisters?" questioned Therza.

"Never mind." Niya rolled her eyes. "It was a failed explanation."

"We reach port!" called Boman from the wheel.

The four of them turned, taking in the scene.

It had been months since Niya had set eyes on her city of birth, and her magic rushed forward as she took in the familiar climbing white and sandstone buildings. Red-tiled roofs soared endlessly, with tightly built dwellings making up the outer ring of Jabari. The port was busy today, with many ships sliding in to anchor or unload crates filled with trade along the docks.

"Time to get workin', girls," said Saffi as they dispersed to prepare the *Crying Queen* to enter.

Niya helped, because how could she not? She did not know when she'd ever be back here to pull rope and line again. Plus, it distracted her from what would happen when the ship stilled and the gangplank lowered to connect with Jabari's harbor.

Which, as it was, happened much too quickly.

Soon Niya stood on the port side of the ship, the entire crew gathered around her.

Her heart pulled in two directions.

"Have you got your things?" asked Kintra from where she stood beside Saffi and Bree at the front.

"All I have to take is what's on me." Niya patted her blades at her hips.

Small arms jumped forward to wind around Niya's waist.

"Bree," admonished Kintra. "Best not be showing you've gone soft now."

"Sisters are allowed to hug goodbye," she said. "Right?" She peered up at Niya. "We are sisters?"

She smiled down at the girl and squeezed back, her heart aching. "Of course," she said. "And don't worry; it is the strongest of souls who are brave enough to bare emotions."

Kintra snorted. "Don't let the captain hear you say that."

At the mention of Alōs, Niya's pulse quickened, and she looked up to search the crew, but he was not among them.

A tightness twisted through Niya's chest.

She and Alōs had properly kept their distance after returning to the *Crying Queen*.

Niya knew it was for the best. Unlike Bree, the notorious pirate lord could not afford to show such emotions among his pirates. The *Crying Queen* had places to sail to next, wicked things to no doubt seize, and she had a Thief Kingdom to help keep in line, a duty to her family to return to.

"It's been an honor to sail with you." Kintra extended a hand. "Despite our differences."

Niya took the offered palm. "Differences only make us stronger."

The quartermaster laughed at that. "Aye, or fight each other."

"Which can make us stronger," she pushed.

Kintra smiled then, a genuine smile that showed her rows of checkered gold teeth. "Until we meet again, Red."

Stepping back, Kintra allowed the rest of the crew to approach and say their farewells. Mika slapped her on the back, as did Emanté, wishing her luck wherever she went next. Green Pea gave her a bit of tacking rope he had braided into a bracelet, causing Bree to push him in annoyance that she hadn't thought of that first. Felix merely smiled at her shyly before Therza pulled her into one of the longest hugs Niya had ever experienced.

"You be safe now, Red," she said, pulling back but holding on to her arms. "We'll miss you around these parts, so come and find us when yous can, or we might be inclined to kidnap you again." She cackled in delight as she let go.

Niya shook her head with a wistful smile and stepped onto the plank, which would take her to the dock below.

Regarding the pirates one last time, she gazed out at the sea of misfits who had started as her worst enemies and grown to be her closest friends.

If she had bet on how she would feel the day she was set free of this lot, she would have lost more than her purse, and most assuredly her mind, for how unexpected this journey had turned out to be. Taking a deep breath in, she made to descend the ship when a slip of cold magic touched along her shoulder.

Turning, her eyes collided with those of burning blue.

Alōs stood beside Boman up on the quarterdeck, looking down at her. He was a splotch of ink in the bright morning sun wrapped in his black coat, his broad shoulders leading to strong hands that grasped the banister before him.

Alōs's gaze consumed her from where he stood.

Everything in Niya's body told her to go to him.

To run up there and embrace him so she could feel his strength between her arms one last time.

But neither of them moved.

Because neither of them could.

They were a sun and a moon separated by an endless moving sky.

So Niya did the only thing she could: she smiled.

Alōs returned it with a nod.

It was not the final farewell Niya had hoped for, but that was perhaps for the best.

The curt gesture was the last severing of rope tying her to the ship. *You are free now,* his gaze said. *Go.*

And so, with determination burying deep her heavy heart, she did.

Niya turned and, without looking back, left the *Crying Queen* behind.

Months later,
when restless hearts
beat unchanged

CHAPTER FIFTY

The port was dark but not quiet. As were most sections of the city within the Thief Kingdom. Niya leaned against a post, gazing through her black eye mask into the dark and rowdy bar that was built along the harbor. It smelled of fish and fried food and patrons who cared more about their next drink than about their next bath.

Niya had found the Drowning Dog during one of her many strolls through this part of town.

The sea-weathered spirit den warmed her heart in a way she could not explain, except to say it reminded her of another place and time.

Arabessa and Larkyra, however, had not shared in her nostalgia as they'd followed her here tonight.

"We are meant to be at Macabris," Larkyra had exclaimed on their walk, "because it is midweek, and midweek means we are meant to be at Macabris!"

"What do you even find so appealing about this establishment that you must visit it so often?" Arabessa had asked. "I hear they sell watered-down ale and spoiled spirits."

Niya had quite plainly pointed out that neither of them had to tag along.

But that had only been met with more huffs and puffs and pointing out in return that this was meant to be a night out *together*.

So it was that the three Bassette sisters, dressed in the finest of disguises ever to grace such a dive as this, found themselves at the Drowning Dog.

And—despite rumors—learned quickly that their ale and spirits were certainly not watered down. In fact, they were quite liquored up.

"She may have unparalleled grace," said Arabessa beside Niya as they watched their youngest sister balance on a chair's back, her pearl disguise winking in the dim establishment. "But I fear all balance was lost after that fourth shot."

"I don't know," mused Niya. "If anything, it might have her concentrating more."

The bar erupted in cheers as Larkyra succeeded in jumping to her other foot, remaining poised on the edge of the chair's back. She waved in triumph to where Niya and Arabessa stood at the far end of the bar.

But this extra task appeared too much, for in the next moment Larkyra fell over, landing on the wood floor with an *oof.*

There was a collective gasp around the room before—

"I'm fine!" Larkyra bounced up.

Patrons pounded their glee on tables; a few others handed her another drink.

"We should probably trade that for water," said Arabessa.

"But then how will she ever learn to trade it herself?" countered Niya.

"And you both say I am the tougher sister," tsked Arabessa.

"No, we call you the most annoying one."

Arabessa shoved her with an elbow. "If anyone's been annoying lately, I'd say it's you and your gloomy moods."

Niya set her jaw, not meeting her sister's gaze. "I have not been moody."

"No? Then why have you been taking most of your meals in your rooms the past few weeks?"

"Perhaps because I find the company of others trying lately."

"*Or,*" suggested Arabessa, "you only wish for the company of the pirate variety?"

A new tension set along Niya's spine. "Don't be ridiculous, Ara."

Her elder sister fell quiet as Larkyra bounded toward them, three mugs of ale sloshing in her gloved hands. "Ladies," she called, handing them each a drink. "If we are to stand apart from the fun of this establishment, why are we here again?"

"Niya is moping," explained Arabessa.

"No I am not!" she said, irritation radiating.

"Is this about the *Crying Queen* docking at port yesterday?" asked Larkyra.

"What?" Niya's heart kicked over with a start.

"I thought you knew. Father said he was to have an audience with the pirate captain."

Niya frowned. She most certainly had *not* heard this.

"When did he tell you that?"

"At breakfast the other day," said Larkyra with a shrug.

"When you were most likely hiding in your rooms," explained Arabessa.

Niya's breathing grew quick, a new ache filling her chest. She was ashamed to admit it, but she had been secretly wishing to hear such news for weeks now, months even. A whisper that the notorious pirate ship was back at port. She'd even found herself searching the crowds during each of their Mousai performances, searching in the hopes of finding the captain's searing blue gaze, his wicked grin that sent shivers of desire through her.

But as the days had passed, filling her again and again with empty hope, she had grown distant from her surroundings. Numb to the merriment of the palace parties, which usually employed such enjoyable distractions.

And she hated it.

Niya needed to get over whatever it was she was clinging to.

"He's probably meeting with Alōs about their recent mission in the east," exclaimed Larkyra.

"I heard they were able to help all those villages," said Arabessa. "Give the lands back to the women who were meant to rule them."

Niya drank in her sisters' words, which set a deeper ache in her chest. One that was mixed with pride.

Over the months the pirates of the *Crying Queen* had become notorious for a different reason than thievery and sin.

Their ship had transformed into a mercenary's, sailing to distant places—towns and villages rumored to be run by tyrants or whose people had been forced into indentured servitude—to free them. It had started as a way to repay their debt to the Thief King and return to his good graces but appeared to have extended into a full-time position. The pirates of course were rewarded handsomely for their efforts, but Niya had her suspicions that after their experience helping Esrom, they quite liked the taste of being on the other side of bad. Not that their actions were any less lethal. It took just as much brutality to slay monsters as it did to be one.

Niya understood this, of course, because she and her sisters were such creatures themselves.

"Niya?" asked Larkyra. "Did you hear what I said?"

She blinked over to her sister, her thoughts coming back to the rowdy bar. "Sorry, I missed it."

"I asked if you wanted to play Split the Wood with us? We were invited by that group over there." Larkyra pointed to a gaggle of rough-edged men and women disguised in a variety of patchwork masks. They threw sharp axes at shards of wood nailed to the far wall, cheers erupting when one of them was able to split the thin material down the middle.

"Sure," said Niya. "I'll join you both in a moment. I need to get some fresh air first. That last mug of ale isn't sitting right."

"Fresh air on this side of the harbor?" asked Arabessa, brows rising above her mask. "I fear you won't find any."

"I'll attempt anyway," she said before waving off her sisters. Placing her mug on the table, she left to step outside.

The caved world greeted her with a refreshing, cool embrace. Far above, the glowworms pulsed on the ceiling, the stars of the kingdom, as the sounds of nightlife shuffled by. Niya stood on the muddy road, looking out at the boats tied to the thin docks that stretched along the harbor. Her gaze turned toward the masts peeking over the buildings on her right, where she knew the larger ships made anchor.

Her muscles ached to walk there, to see if one particular black beast floated in the dark water.

But she was frozen, knowing that path only led to disappointment.

If Alōs had wished to see her, he would have by now.

It wasn't as though *she* were the one traipsing about Aadilor these past months.

By the stars and sea, she thought, frowning, *have I become a bore?*

Since when did she sit still waiting for anyone?

Niya scratched the back of her neck, realizing Arabessa was right. She *was* moping.

Well, no longer!

Setting her shoulders, she readied herself to return to the bar but froze as a cool slip of energy caressed her back.

Her chest tightened.

No, she thought, closing her eyes, unsure if she could trust the sensation to be true or merely her body wishing it so.

But then it grew stronger, along with a wave of movement, and Niya heard him speak.

"I'd have lost good money," purred a familiar deep voice from behind her, "if I had bet where I'd find you this night."

An eruption of wings burst free in her chest as she smiled. Remaining still, she replied, "Then it is lucky for you I have given up gambling."

"Have you now?" Niya heard the amusement in his tone. "What a pity, for I so enjoyed finding you in my debt."

Niya turned then and drank in Alōs's presence.

His large form was swallowed by his dark coat, hair pulled back at the base of his neck to reveal his angular features and startling glowing eyes. Eyes that enveloped her with a burst of memories and desire.

"Hello, fire dancer," he rumbled.

"Hello, pirate."

For a moment they stood in silence, merely looking upon the other, studying what neither of them could forget: each other.

"I see your taste in establishments has changed since our last meeting." Alōs glanced to the crumbling bar beside them.

"And I hear your raids have turned honorable." She arched a brow.

A smile on his full lips. "Yes, it appears the actions of an old acquaintance have opened my eyes to my full capabilities in Aadilor."

"Have they? Well, I certainly hope to one day meet this person. They sound very wise."

"Mmm." He nodded. "And they're not so bad in bed either."

Niya kept herself from grinning at his crudeness, though a whip of heated pleasure ran through her. "So, Lord Ezra, what has you strolling through town at this time of night?"

He cocked his head to the side. "I'd have thought it was obvious," he said. "To find you."

"Me?" New anticipation swirled in her gut.

"Aye. The king said you could be found here these days."

Niya frowned at that. Not quite knowing how to feel about her father possibly understanding the emotions that had caused her to walk this part of town over and over. That they were connected to this man and his misfit crew. But then again, he was her father, the Thief King, and knew more than many.

"Why were you looking for me?" She peered up at Alōs through her mask.

"I'm always looking for you, fire dancer," he said. "In every port we dock, I search for hair that burns like yours." He lifted a hand to pull at a loose curl. "In every city we walk, I watch for curves that I have memorized with my fingers and mouth." His gaze drank in the length of her, sending warmth to pool deep in her core. "And when I sleep, that's when I search the hardest and where, most nights, I find you."

Niya's breathing quickened. "Well, you've found me again, but I assure you, I am not a dream."

"Aren't you?" he asked, sliding closer, his cool gifts flowing from him in a haze of green.

Her own magic responded with a sigh. *Ours,* it crooned, escaping her to mingle in the air with his.

They stood in a cloud of their power, their reunion.

"How long are you at port?" she dared ask.

"We leave tonight."

Her heart stuttered, disappointment gripping her. "So soon."

"Our next voyage is a long one. We most likely won't return to the kingdom for a month at least."

"I see." She tore her eyes from his, palm settling deep into the patch-work of her heart.

And this was why they could not have been together, always one of them leaving as soon as the other arrived.

"Yes, which is why I must know your answer quickly, I'm afraid. Though I hope it is an easy one for you to decide . . . considering."

"My answer?" She glanced back up at him in confusion.

"Would you care to be a pirate again? At least for this next voyage of ours?"

"What?"

"I appealed to the king that you could help with where he's asked us to sail next. He's agreed that it is a perfect mission for you and your gifts. It is far up north, at White Wall, a frozen tundra to be sure, but that's where you come in handy." He grinned. "With all your heat."

"You . . . wait, the Thief King . . ." Niya shook her head, trying to grasp what she was hearing. "He wants me to help you?"

Alōs's grin was sly. "Yes, it appears our duties no longer take us on as separate of journeys as they once did. You can serve your king and be with me."

A sizzle of hope ran through her. "Be with you?"

"Yes." He tipped her chin up so he could bend and brush his lips against hers. A tease of more to come. Niya's toes curled in her boots as his magic caressed down her front. "The *Crying Queen* and the Mousai have common interests now: containing chaos for our king." Alōs let his hand drop as he stood tall once more. Niya fought the urge to settle closer into his pulling power. "What do you think I've been busying myself about these past months?" he asked. "Did you think I was going to settle for a measly few sand falls with you every now and again?" Alōs shook his head. "As I have said once before, I can never have my fill of you, fire dancer."

Niya could only look up into his glowing gaze as the meaning of his words washed over her.

What do you think I've been busying myself about these past months? I can never have my fill of you, fire dancer.

"So?" asked Alōs in a husky rumble. "What shall be your answer? And let me remind you your king has given his blessing, so it would be a bit like undermining his authority to say no. In fact, he told me to give you this before we set sail. Though, I warn you, it appears like a rather useless trinket, given I can sense no magic within. It's also quite worn down for your expensive taste," he teased. "But who am I to question the Thief King and his reasons for doing anything."

Alōs pulled a pin from his pocket, the gold weavings flashing under the nearby streetlamp.

Niya's pulse thumped loudly in her head, nerves and anticipation building as she clasped the cool metal of her mother's compass brooch between her fingers.

She said when she touched it, it helped give her pause when she felt lost in her emotions. It allowed her to find her way.

Her father was giving this to her? Such a cherished item of both her parents?

So I can always find my way, she thought as she swallowed against the growing tightness in her throat, a well of emotion filling her chest.

Her father was trusting her to go, to burn as bright as she needed, as hot as he knew she could, because in the end, she would always find her way—home.

Niya blinked back the threat of tears as she pinned the compass brooch to her tunic, right over her heart.

Her heart, which was also standing in front of her.

"I suspect there's more to that accessory than meets the eye, given your reaction," said Alōs as he regarded her with an inquisitive stare.

"Isn't there always more than meets the eye?" she challenged. *Like you,* she thought.

Alōs, the ruthless, coldhearted pirate, had changed all this for her? Changed the purpose of his beloved *Crying Queen* so he could stand beside her again, with his crew, with her sisters, a common goal growing? They were now properly on the same side, guardians against the wicked. No longer enemies but indeed allies.

What shall be your answer?

Niya smiled wide, flames erupting inside for her to throw her arms around Alōs and give him her answer to his earlier question the best way she knew how—with action.

So she did just that. Niya tugged on his coat, pulling him close, and kissed him thoroughly. She kissed him as she had been aching to since the last time they'd been alone, drinking in his scent of sea air and midnight orchids.

Alōs rumbled his pleasure as he wound strong arms around her waist, lifting her off the ground.

She let out a laugh, holding him tight.

As he settled her back on the ground, his blue gaze was brighter than a clear day at sea.

"So can I take that as your willingness to help the *Crying Queen* on our next voyage?"

"Yes," she said, excitement soaring. "After all, I am in need of a little adventure."

"Oh, fire dancer"—Alōs smiled down at her—"don't you know by now? You are the adventure."

AUTHOR'S NOTE

J come from a lineage of artists. My grandparents were artists, and my parents are artists. I was taught from a young age the importance of opening the mind, of watching and listening for inspiration, as it often can come from the most unlikely places. The Mousai Series is no exception. It started from two things: the echoing of a cane clicking down a long hallway as I sat in an office working late, and a painting my father did titled *Muses*, which was inspired by my sisters and me as well as an interpretation of Botticelli's *Primavera*. Much like this tangling of inspiring seeds that would later grow into an epic world, many of the names and places in my books have been influenced by names and places in our world. Each was chosen for a reason: the feeling it evokes or its meaning or both. In the Mousai Series, every character's and place's name has been crafted or chosen with great care. This is the celebration of a diverse world. Below is an appendix of sorts, providing a background to my naming etymology.

The Mousai: A neologism inspired by the plural word *muses*.

Bassette: A surname. Inspired by the word *bassett* from Old French, which means "someone of humble origins."

Dolion Bassette (Count of Raveet of the second house of Jabari and also the Thief King): The father of Arabessa, Niya, and Larkyra. Husband of Johanna. Thief King and a member of the Jabari Council. Dolion is a neologism derived from the Greek verb *dolioo*, meaning "to lure, to deceive." I chose this for the many masks he must wear and roles he must play, from Jabari to the Thief Kingdom, as well as his most important role: father.

Raveet is influenced by the name Ravneet, which has a few known origins, but I was inspired by the Indian Sanskrit origin, which means "morality like the sun."

Johanna Bassette: The wife of Dolion and mother of the Mousai. Gifted with very ancient and powerful magic. The name Johanna is connected to many cultures: German, Swedish, Danish, and Hebrew, to name a few. The original meanings of its root names are said to be "gift of God" and "gracious," much like Johanna's character.

Mousai + Bassette daughters: I purposefully sought to create names that had tempo and lyricism to them, to connect to their magical gifts of song, dance, and music.

Arabessa Bassette: The eldest sister. Arabessa is a neologism created from the name Bessa, cited in some places to be of Albanian origin, meaning "loyalty."

Niya Bassette: The middle sister. Inspired by the name Nia (Celtic and Swahili origins), meaning "purpose," "radiance," "shine," and "beauty."

Larkyra Bassette: The youngest sister. Larkyra is a neologism created from the base word *lark*, which is a songbird. It is also inspired by the verb *lark*, which means "to behave mischievously" and "to have fun."

Zimri D'Enieu: Zimri is a Hebrew name meaning "my praise" or "my music." D'Enieu is a neologism I created after being inspired by French surnames.

Achak: A Native American (Algonquin) name meaning "spirit." When I learned of this name and meaning, I instantly fell in love and knew it embodied everything Achak was, from their history to how their spirit has lived on in many forms in many realms.

Charlotte: The Bassette sisters' lady's maid and loyal caregiver. I wanted to choose a *C* name for her, connecting her to my mother, Cynthia.

Alōs Ezra: Pronounced *Al-ohs*, this is a neologism, but without the macron accent of the *ō*, Alos is cited in some sources to mean "God's wealth" and is of Yoruba origin. It's also said to mean "charismatic." Ezra is a Hebrew name meaning "help" or "helper." I enjoyed this idea of a charismatic helper for Alōs combined with all his various roles.

Ariōn: Pronounced *Air-ee-ohn*, without the macron accent of the *ō*, this name is inspired by the Greek poet Arion, who was claimed by the islanders of Lesbos as their son. Arion also is mainly remembered for the fantastic myth of him being kidnapped by pirates.

Ixō: Pronounced *Icks-oh*, this is a neologism inspired by the Roman numeral IX, meaning "nine." The number nine is connected to spiritual enlightenment, service to humanity, and faith, all perfect for Ixō and his role as part of Esrom's holy order and his loyalty to Ariōn.

Kintra: A neologism inspired by the word *kin*, meaning "of one's family." Kintra very much acts as a surrogate family member to Alōs after he is banished from Esrom.

Saffi: Of Greek origin, meaning "wisdom."

Therza: A neologism inspired by the name Thirza, which is of Greek origin and means "delightful." Therza was very much a delight to write and, I can imagine, was a delightful crew member to have on board.

Aadilor: The realm where everything exists. Aadilor is a neologism inspired by the word "lore," which means "a body of traditions and knowledge passed from person to person by word of mouth."

Obasi Sea: The only sea in Aadilor. The language of origin for Obasi is Igbo and is said to mean "in honor of the supreme god" or "in honor of God." I loved this meaning and how Obasi flows off the tongue like water. I saw this sea being named this in honor of the lost gods gifting their people such beauty to sail upon.

Jabari: Aadilor's capital city. The Swahili name Jabari, meaning "brave [one]," is derived from the Arabic word *jabbār*, meaning "ruler."

Esrom: An underwater sanctuary kingdom that can only be located by those who were born there. The name can be traced back to biblical times and in some texts is said to mean "dart of joy."

ACKNOWLEDGMENTS

*G*etting down Niya's story was one of the toughest writing challenges I have yet faced. There is so much in Niya that burns to be free, to act on impulse and explore without thought or consequence. You can see how I, as the writer meant to stitch her adventures together, found such a temperamental character challenging to bring into focus. Adding in our dear brooding Alōs, a ship full of pirates, a heist, and a tumultuous burning attraction makes for a very tricky recipe to cook up indeed. Which is why this story would not have been completed without the helping minds and support of a few extraordinary crew members.

To my husband, Christopher, who has endlessly understood every weekend, early morning, or late night that I had to disappear into my writing cave for this story: I appreciate all you do to keep me fed, washed, and somewhat functional during these times I slip into another realm. I have been able to climb mountains knowing you have been beside me every step of the way. My love for you expands realms.

To my agent, Aimee Ashcraft at Brower Literary: You are more than an agent; you're a friend. Your dedication in helping me reach each milestone, along with your constant optimism, has truly been the biggest guiding light. Thank you for pushing me when I've wanted to stop and always being an understanding text and call away.

To Lauren Plude, my warrior-editor extraordinaire: With each book, you have taught me so much, have championed these sisters with a passion that matches my own, and have been one of my biggest advocates in ensuring my words get heard. I am thankful for more than what can be written in these acknowledgments, but know you are a goddess among the gods.

To everyone on the Montlake team who has helped this series shine so beautifully and brightly, especially Kris Beecroft, Lauren Grange, Jessica Preeg, and Elena Stokes: Thank you, thank you, thank you. Our dearest Bassette sisters would not have reached so many hands without your care and devotion.

To Micaela Alcaino, the genius artist behind the covers in the Mousai Series: Your vision and creativity know no bounds. I am continuously in awe that you are part of our team.

To my parents and sisters: It is the honest truth that this series would not exist if it weren't for each and every one of you. As I grew up, you inspired and advocated for wild imaginings, and every day since you have helped a young girl's fantasy to become a reality.

To my son, who will be born by the time this book releases: I wrote the majority of this story while you were kicking inside me. You were my constant companion through every round of rewrites and the tireless nights of edits, and you kept my head in the game while also helping me know when I needed to rest. You are my heart, and I cannot wait to one day write a story for you.

Staci Hart, a name synonymous with *powerhouse* and *devotion*, you were here before there was a "here" and have helped with every road I have dared to go down. Every person, every writer, should be so lucky as to have a friend like you by their side.

To my reader group, the Mellow Misfits, and every book blogger, reviewer, and reader who has supported, promoted, and shared their love for my books and this series: I humbly bow to you. I quite literally could not continue telling these stories without your support and devotion. You are the flame that moves my fingers across my keyboard and the pulse that keeps my heart beating to write.

ABOUT THE AUTHOR

Photo © 2020 Jacob Glazer

S. J. Mellow is an award-winning author of six novels. *Dance of a Burning Sea* is the second stand-alone romantic fantasy in her Mousai Series. She is also the cofounder of She Is Booked, a literary-themed fundraising organization that supports women's charities. With a bachelor's degree in fine arts, Mellow splits her time between her two loves—visual design and writing.